BIG PHA

A Novel

By
John Prieve

PublishAmerica
Baltimore

Second printing

This novel is a work of fiction. Names, characters, places, and incidents either are the product of the author's imagination or are used fictitiously, and any resemblance to actual persons, living or dead, businesses, companies, events, or locales is entirely coincidental.

PublishAmerica has allowed this work to remain exactly as the author intended, verbatim, without editorial input.

Softcover 1424133300
eBook 9781611023947
PUBLISHED BY PUBLISHAMERICA, LLLP
www.publishamerica.com
Baltimore

Printed in the United States of America

Dedication

Although Big Pharma is generally filled with well-intended people; greed, power, and the pursuit of personal wealth are simply a part of human nature. This book is dedicated to all the honest, hard-working people employed in the pharmaceutical industry.

Acknowledgements

I would like to acknowledge the people who surrounded me with support and friendship in order to make this book a reality. To my wife, Tracy, for all of her love, encouragement, and having to put up with the late night proof readings. To Connie Kuntz for her help with the final manuscript edits. Special thanks to Steve Edwards for the back cover photograph.

CHAPTER 1
COUNTY JAIL

Outside the San Diego County Jail it was a beautiful sunny day. Inside, curses, spit, and whistles were thrown at Jackson Ford as the guard shoved him down the corridor. Once inside his cell, he noticed the stains on his mattress, his toilet, his floor. Filth everywhere. The guard hissed, "Welcome to your new home, Princess," and shut the door.

YEAR 1

CHAPTER 2
RECRUITMENT

It was a cool rain that fell hard that night in late April, and he was in the hospital medical library searching through the Physicians' Desk Reference, which he would later learn that it was the second top-selling book in the United States behind the Bible. At six inches thick, the PDR contains a written description and photograph of all of the Food and Drug Administration approved drugs available in the U.S. pharmaceutical marketplace. The medicines are divided up by pharmaceutical company and then alphabetized. They are then sorted by category and again alphabetized for easy access.

Jackson Ford was in his early thirties, with compelling blue eyes, blond hair and classically handsome features. His six foot, 180-pound frame was tough, lean and sinewy from years of running. Jackson was as easygoing as he was driven to succeed. He was married to Lexi whose figure was curving and soft. She was a full six inches shorter than Jackson so she had to tilt her head up in order to see his face, which he loved. She was volatile when things didn't go her way, but Jackson could coax her into a smile with only a little effort. Lexi saw things clearly. Things were either right or wrong, good or bad.

They met while Lexi was in her senior year as a Communications major at the University of Wisconsin—Madison. Jackson was in Physical Therapy School at the time, but working nights as a bartender at the 4th Quarter bar on State Street in downtown Madison, just a few blocks from the State Capitol Building. Jackson was behind the bar on Halloween pouring quarter beers for all the maniacs that were out and about when he saw her. She wore a bunny costume complete with ears and whiskers. Lexi captured his heart from the moment he looked down into her brown eyes. He spent the rest of the night talking to her over the bar, and was immediately jealous when other guys would ask her to dance. They met for lunch the next day and afterwards, were inseparable until graduation the following May. While they finished the next seven months of school, they took long walks along Lake Mendota and in the Arboretum. Jackson helped Lexi with her term papers, and she let him practice his physical therapy rehabilitation exercises on her body.

They got married right after graduation. Lexi's father pulled Jackson aside during the wedding reception with some advice. "Jackson, she's a complicated girl who will demand all of your attention. But she will love you back all the way. That's the way her mother and I raised her, and you have to understand that completely. The girl is in love with you one hundred percent." He laughed heartily and slapped Jackson on the back, "Oh yeah, let me tell you something else. It'll be one helluva ride, but it'll be worth every minute of it."

After passing his national boards as a physical therapist, Jackson spent the next five years in a small hospital in Noblesville, Indiana, a northern suburb of Indianapolis. It was an okay job but he had maxed out on his upward mobility within the system. Even adding on additional responsibilities, providing sports medicine services for the local county high school teams didn't add much to his paycheck's bottom line. So he felt stuck in a dead end position. Respected in the medical community, but unable to live in the wealthy suburb because of the high housing costs, he and Lexi rented a two bedroom apartment in nearby Indianapolis.

Lexi worked in the city for a local radio station selling ads to area businesses. Although she loved the small company, her customers, and the sales process; the money wasn't the greatest. She was brought up much better than what she was living now. Her parents showered gifts, parties, clothes and trips all over their little angel when she lived under their roof. Jackson and Lexi found that saving for a down payment on a house was a drag when there were so many great nightclubs and restaurants to enjoy around Indianapolis. You could find Jackson and Lexi every Saturday at Sixty-Third Street and Broadway dining out alfresco on the warm summer nights.

Since cash was scarce, credit cards became the only way to finance their lifestyle. It seemed the credit card companies mailed out pre-approved applications to them each week. And how quickly the accounts reached their credit limits. With trips to Florida, the Bahamas, Las Vegas, and Vail, the monthly payments soon became tough to cover.

Lexi pressured Jackson to find a different career that would be more of a challenge for him and provide for all the finer things that they deserved, and to which she was accustomed. Deep in her heart, Lexi knew that he could be so much more. Given the right business opportunity, Jackson would shine. He was just simply bored out of his mind in his physical therapy job. He too, knew that he could do other things and get ahead in the business world, but he was stuck in a comfortable rut at the hospital. Heated discussions could frequently be heard through the walls of their apartment over money and the bills. The common theme surrounded how to make more of it given their respective science and communication educations. In fact, one night during a fiery finance discussion, a neighbor knocked on their door.

"Is everything OK?" he asked.

"Everything is fine," replied Jackson. He was barefoot and wore just running shorts and a T-shirt.

"Well, my wife and I heard voices and a loud crash from your apartment that woke up the baby, so I'm just checking out if everything is OK," he said without making eye contact.

"Yeah, I was just watching the TV, maybe a little too loud on the volume I'll admit, and stretching out, when I knocked over a lamp," he lied. Actually, in her fury, Lexi had thrown a hard covered book at his head but he ducked just in the nick of time.

"Maybe you can turn down the volume a little seeing how we have a three month old who we are now trying to get back to sleep," the neighbor said with one eyebrow raised.

"Yeah, OK. Sorry about the noise. I'll turn down the TV." Jackson closed and locked the door and thought, *I need a new job. I need to make more money!*

At the medical library, Jackson reviewed the PDR looking for the big pharmaceutical companies executing Phase One of his job search plan. He got interested in the pharmaceutical industry because he frequently saw the company sales representatives walking though the hospital discussing their products with the physicians, nurses and pharmacists. Intrigued by their nice suits, oxford shirts, and winged-tip shoes, he approached several drug reps and inquired about the industry and job opportunities. They were very helpful and encouraged him to look into applying since he seemed like a natural with his science background and pleasant personality.

A Pfizer sales representative advised Jackson, "Get a PDR to help you start your company research. It is literally a Who's Who of drug companies and their products. The more products that the company owns, the bigger they are, the more profits they have, and the more products that are likely to be in their R & D pipeline as well."

"How many drug companies are there?" Jackson asked the rep.

"There are hundreds around the world, but Fortune Magazine reports that Pfizer, GlaxoSmithKline, Merck, Johnson & Johnson, Aventis, Alsace, and AstraZeneca are all bell-weather companies. They have solid financial performance with lots of approved drugs and robust pipelines. They'd be good companies to start your job search," the Pfizer rep replied.

After two hours of research and note taking, Jackson rubbed the fatigue from his eyes. *What the hell do some of these terms mean? Cytochrome P450 system, renal necrosis, renal aldosterone system, glomerular filtration rates. This stuff looks pretty technical. My science courses at Madison barely scratched the surface of this stuff. I can barely pronounce some of these terms, let alone figure out what it means. Am I doing the right thing?* His confidence was wobbly at best.

It was late when Jackson left the medical library and returned to the apartment, where Lexi was already asleep. Jackson kissed her forehead and pulled the blankets up over her shoulders. He decided to stay up a little while longer to start Phase Two of the job search process. His plan was to go online and submit his cover letter and resume.

The process was relatively easy. After logging on and establishing an account and password, he searched each of the job boards for entry-level pharmaceutical sales positions in the Indianapolis and Chicago areas. Finding several, he electronically submitted his cover letter and resume for each of the openings. After several hours, Jackson fell into bed exhausted, but feeling good about what he had accomplished.

Several weeks later as Jackson and Lexi were hustling to get out of the apartment for the morning commute, his cellphone rang.

Jackson answered, "This is Jackson Ford."

"Good morning. My name is Larry Hooper. Is this a good time to talk?"

"Yes it is."

"Great. I'm with Hooper Staffing in Columbus, Ohio. I received your resume off one of the Internet job boards. I have been retained by Alsace Pharmaceuticals to source candidates for a primary care sales force expansion. They have approved openings throughout the country to support the launch of a new product. According to your cover letter and resume, you've indicated that you have an interest in gaining an entry level sales position in the pharmaceutical industry located in the Midwest. Is this still your intent?"

"Yes, it is my intent, Larry," replied Jackson.

"Great! Let me give you a little information about the company. Alsace Pharmaceuticals is a French company but they have a U.S. headquarters in the Balboa Park area of San Diego. They are a Fortune 500 company publicly traded on the Dow. Their current product line involves medicines for hypertension, cholesterol, cancer, arthritis, and depression. The new near-term product will be an anti-ulcer drug that is expected to be first in class in a new therapeutic area. The company currently has over 2,500 sales representatives and is looking to add another 500 reps to support the new product once the FDA approves it. We are looking to source a pool of candidates for interviews in two weeks in Chicago. Is your schedule flexible to be available on the first Monday of June?"

Without hesitation Jackson responded, "Absolutely. Will I need to be available all day?"

"Yes. The Alsace Pharmaceuticals travel department will make your flight arrangements from Indianapolis to O'Hare. You simply need to make the flights. If you have a few minutes, I would like to go over your background information, and then prep you for the interview process."

"I'm available this morning as long as you need me," said as his face split into a wide grin.

Lexi's heart soared as she read the notes Jackson was scrawling on the notepad on the kitchen counter. An actual interview in two weeks! It had been several weeks of recruiters calling and conducting telephone interviews with Jackson, but so far, no actual face-to-face interviews with pharmaceutical companies. She kissed him on the cheek and left for work and the morning commute. She was so excited.

Jackson in the pharmaceutical industry! Just imagine how handsome he'll look wearing suits.

Within the week, Lexi was helping Jackson pick out a new suit, blue shirt, and tie. After much debate, they settled on an Italian designed Krizia suit. The shirt was Italian as well, Pronto-Uomo. The new tie was by Joseph & Fleiss. After the fitting, she selected a new pair of Johnston & murphy winged tip shoes. Finally, they ended up at a fine leather goods store to select a new black portfolio. The ended the day with dinner at Peterson's restaurant. Another new Visa card practically at its limit.

"I'm starting to worry about our finances," Jackson said.

"Please honey. Not now. Can't we just enjoy ourselves tonight? How do you feel? Are you prepared for your interviews?"

"Well, Larry Hooper has me feeling pretty confident. He says that with my science background, physical therapy and sports medicine experience, plus my knowledge of hospital systems, I should do well. As long as I demonstrate good communication skills and eye contact, my science background and work experience should make up for my lack of direct sales experience. He also said that if I don't throw up on them, then I should advance along just fine in the interviewing process."

Lexi reassured him, "I know you are going to do just fine."

He leaned in. "The salary is substantially more than I make now, and that's what excites me!"

"Jackson, I don't think you should be going into the pharmaceutical industry just for the money, but rather for the long-term opportunities. Didn't you tell me that these Big Pharma companies have a ton of different career paths?"

"Yeah, all the different company websites said about the same things on career pathing." He paused for a moment and then continued, "Hey, Alsace Pharmaceuticals has their world headquarters in France. Wouldn't it be great to live in France?"

A slow smile came to Lexi's face. It would indeed be great to live in France. She touched Jackson's hand and said *"Oui."*

On the first Monday in June, Jackson sat in the Indianapolis International Airport waiting for the United Airlines commuter flight to arrive from Ft. Wayne so that it could continue on to Chicago O'Hare. The gate area was filled with about two dozen men and women in their mid-to-late twenties all wearing dark gray or blue suits and white shirts or blouses. They all appeared to be reading the Wall Street Journal and carrying black portfolios. When the flight to O'Hare was announced, everyone put their magazines and newspapers away, took out their tickets, and headed to the departure gate door. Jackson heard several of them talking while in route to

Chicago exchanging information about their backgrounds and about Alsace Pharmaceuticals.

Could we all be going to the same interview session? Jackson wondered.

After they landed, the bell chimed, and the passengers all stood up, gathered their portfolios and magazines, and marched in a file along the yellow line to the terminal. In their gray and blue suits it looked like a parade of penguins.

Waiting to greet the arriving plane was a plump, middle-aged woman holding a sign that read, Alsace Pharmaceuticals. After announcing that the group should follow her, she led them downstairs out of baggage claim to the shuttle bus. After everyone had boarded, it proceeded directly to the Embassy Suites Hotel located near the airport.

The hotel lobby looked like a convention center event. The hotel was filled with men and women wearing gray and blue suits. A registration area had signs asking for candidates to identify themselves by last name. Jackson got in line for the D-G candidates.

When it was his turn at the front of the line, a smartly dressed woman looked up and smiled at him. "Good morning. What is your name, please?" she asked.

"Jackson Ford."

After flipping through a few manila envelopes she looked up and said, "OK, Mr. Ford, here is your packet of information. After you complete the application please proceed to the second floor of the hotel for your first interview which is scheduled for ten o'clock."

"Thank you. May I ask how many interviews I'll have today?"

"That all depends on how well you do," she replied.

Jackson walked over to the conference area of the hotel, found a table, and began completing the application. Promptly at ten o'clock he was found waiting outside of suite 2106 for his first interview.

Four interviews later, and each on different floors of the hotel, he was sitting across from a Human Resources Manager for Alsace

Pharmaceuticals, Dee Dee Wallace. She had plain features, brown eyes, brown hair, and wore a pair of chic glasses.

"Well, Mr. Ford, it would appear that you've done very well today in our interviewing process. I'm available for the next few minutes to answer any questions you might have about the company or our benefits package."

"The Alsace corporate website was very complete as well as Mr. Hooper, my recruiter, but could you please give me a general overview of the benefits package?" Jackson asked.

"Certainly. If you're offered a sales representative position with Alsace Pharmaceuticals, you'll find that we have a competitive compensation package that compares favorably to other companies our size and with whom we compete. We offer starting salaries that are eighty percent of the industry average or a range between fifty thousand to seventy thousand dollars a year, an incentive compensation or bonus program that is paid quarterly for achieving sales objectives, full medical, dental and life insurance, a 401K program where we contribute a hundred percent match up to five percent of the employee's contribution, and a stock option grant program as well as an employee stock purchase plan that is discounted fifteen percent. All field sales representatives receive a company car, a Ford Taurus, where we pay for all the expenses like gas, oil, insurance, and any repair service. The Company also issues you a home office computer package, cell phone, and pager for your communication needs. Lastly, so that you can conduct business entertainment on behalf of the Company, we order an American Express card with no limit and allow you to designate the rewards points earned to any hotel or airline points program you wish."

Jackson's head was spinning. *Am I hearing all this? This is unbelievable. If I'm offered a job with Alsace, I'll make more money in one year than Dad made in two!*

"When will Alsace make their final decisions on candidate selection?" he asked.

Dee Dee replied, "The District Managers will make their final selections by this Friday and contact the candidates with job offers and territory assignments. We are under a very tight timeline to fill all five hundred territories for a training class that begins on the first of July."

Jackson had no other questions, so he thanked Dee Dee and left the room for the hotel lobby where he found the shuttle bus back to the airport. He wanted to go for a run, but it was already time for him to board the plane.

The flight back to Indianapolis was uneventful. There were candidates who obviously did not have the banner day that Jackson had. Some of the candidates hung their heads because they never made it past the second floor. This would be Jackson's first lesson in understanding how extremely competitive the industry is.

That night at the Embassy Suites Hotel, the District Managers assembled in a conference room that they called the War Room. Candidate names, territories, districts, and resumes were all posted on a large white board to organize the interview and hiring process. A certain Asian male candidate by the name of Dong Chu had actually done very well in the interview rotation, but during the review session the District Managers just couldn't get past poking fun of his first name. Finally, after about ten minutes of discussion laced with crude remarks involving the name Dong or Donger, Dee Dee Wallace cut off the conversation by removing Mr. Chu from the list of viable candidates. He would be sent a rejection letter the next day stating,

Although impressed with your credentials Alsace Pharmaceuticals will be moving forward in the selection process with better qualified candidates.

On Friday Jackson was offered an entry-level sales position with Alsace Pharmaceuticals. Associate Professional Sales Representative was to be his new title for six months. This period would serve as a probation period before he would be promoted to Professional Sales Representative. He would make fifteen thousand dollars a year more than his old hospital salary, plus he would have the opportunity to earn significant bonus dollars through the incentive compensation program.

Before he could officially be on the Alsace payroll, he first had to submit to a urine test and physical examination at a local clinic.

"We're basically screening for illicit drugs," the District Manager told him.

"Oh, OK. I should be fine there," Jackson said with a smile.

Background checks were then conducted over the next several days to confirm his college education, criminal history, credit history, and traffic violations by a third-party vendor contracted by Alsace. This would be a thorough screening whose sole purpose was to knock out any potential bad apples from the candidate pool.

Jackson passed the background checks and drug tests with flying colors, and to celebrate the new job, Jackson and Lexi went back to the mall to buy more suits, shirts and ties.

Jackson was hesitant with every new suit the salesman brought out to them. He said, "Lexi, I'm worried about the additional costs of more clothes. Can't I just keep wearing the same ones I've got and just rotate them to the dry cleaners periodically?"

Lexi wrinkled up her nose and said, "Jackson, you have to dress for the next level if you want to get promoted."

Another fifteen hundred dollars was charged to their Visa account before they returned to their apartment. Lexi spent the next hour showing Jackson which suits, shirts and ties went together, while he actually took notes on a three by five card and placed it in his shaving kit for future reference.

Later that night, Jackson and Lexi went to dinner at The Eagle's Nest. It was a five-star restaurant located on the top floor of the Hyatt Regency hotel in downtown Indianapolis. The restaurant did a complete 360-degree revolution every hour, so the diners got a fantastic view of the city's lights during the course of the evening. After a hundred dollar bottle of merlot, they dined on the house specialty, duck, and grazed through the chocolate bar for dessert. They were just beginning to get a glimpse of the good life that the pharmaceutical industry would offer.

CHAPTER 3
TRAINING

Phase One of Alsace Pharmaceuticals training for the five hundred new sales representatives was scheduled for six weeks in various regional sites around the United States. Jackson reported to the Chicago Region so his home for the next six weeks was the Marriott Residence Inn in Lombard, Illinois. The company had thirty new hires at the hotel providing them with all their meals, laundry and dry cleaning service, and transportation to and from the Regional office in nearby Oak Brook. The Region Training Manager and several District Sales Managers were tasked with conducting the training process that included lectures on basic anatomy and physiology, disease state knowledge, product knowledge, and the selling model used during interactions with physicians.

Kurt Braden was the Regional Training Manager for the Chicago Region. He was from Woodbury, Minnesota and loved to fish walleyes during the summer in northwest Ontario where his father had a cabin. Promoted at the age of twenty-eight, he had been a successful territory and hospital sales representative hired straight out of Carleton College. The training position was a developmental job in what was known as the developmental loop. The developmental loop was a short series of two to three jobs that could last anywhere between six to eighteen months each. Positions in departments such as Training, Professional Education, Recruiting, Marketing, or Meeting Planning were all part of the developmental loop. It is where the newly promoted go to not only learn more about the Company, but also about themselves as potential sales managers and future leaders. It is also where the field sales and headquarters Directors assess their skills for management positions.

More than anything, Kurt wanted to be promoted to a District Manager. He saw a DM position as a stepping-stone to a rotation into product marketing position and then on to a Regional Sales Director position, and eventually to a Vice President position. "Getting promoted matters above all else," he would say to the new hires in his training class. With every promotion came more money, more power, and, of course, more Alsace stock options. Kurt laid the rules down on Day One with the new hires.

"Good morning. My name is Kurt Braden, and I am responsible for leading and managing this training class for the next six weeks."

"Good morning," the class responded in unison.

"Let me start out by saying that each of you costs Alsace about two hundred thousand dollars in your first year."

The class raised their eyebrows and began to look around at one another. Braden continued, "The first year costs of a new sales representative in the pharmaceutical industry are approximately two hundred thousand dollars. By the time we pay for your salary, bonus, benefits, car, auto insurance, gasoline, expenses, training, plane tickets, and the like; the cost is almost two hundred grand. Knowing that cost, it is extremely important that you stay completely focused on the training materials for the next six weeks.

"To ensure a maximum success rate, I need you to understand a few simple things. First, you are considered late if you are not seated and ready to participate five minutes before the scheduled starting time. Alsace Pharmaceuticals time is being five minutes early for all scheduled events. Second, if you fail more than two tests during Phase One training, you will be terminated immediately. You will be allowed one make-up opportunity for each failure. Any score below ninety percent is considered a failing grade. Third, I expect a high degree of professionalism at all times for which you will be evaluated weekly. Since there are thirty new hires in this class, I cannot monitor the group constantly so I ask that you police each other. That includes time away from the Regional Office such as back at the Marriott, at restaurants or at evening social functions. This particularly includes times when the Regional Sales Director is present, during Doctor Detailing, or when any home office personnel are here. Lastly, the dress for training is business. That means wearing suits every day. Any questions?"

Lexi was right about the suits, Jackson thought.

Since there were no questions, Braden continued, "The agenda, which is included in your binder, is packed for the next six weeks. We will be covering every aspect of human anatomy, disease states, product knowledge, competitive products, clinical studies, territory management, and the Alsace selling model. The morning sessions start at eight o'clock and continue until five-thirty in the afternoon, at which point you will be excused to go back to the hotel and prepare for the next day's test. We will have organized study groups back at the hotel in the evenings to ensure your preparation for the material. The assigned study groups are also in your binder. OK, let's get started with the first lecture on the anatomy of the heart and circulatory system."

Since the new hires were assigned to a sales division that had responsibility for the promotion of four different products, it went without saying that the training was intense. Although Jackson successfully passed all the written tests, there were two individuals that were not so fortunate, even on the retakes. They, of course, were asked to leave the company immediately. All the appropriate travel arrangements were provided and paid for by Alsace to accommodate getting the two individuals back home. The message to the others, however, was clear. Do not screw up in training or you'll be promptly let go.

Enric Delgado was one such unfortunate dismissal. He was from a large Hispanic family located on the south side of Chicago. He was hired for a territory that was largely Hispanic and bilingual language skills were essential for the job. The potential pool of candidates that could have filled this position was limited.

Braden had Enric's number right from the start. Enric didn't come from a wealthy background, and subsequently, he didn't have the finest clothing in his wardrobe. On some days he would arrive at the Regional Office with the end of his tie around the fifth button on a seven-button-hole shirt.

Henry Perez joked, "Enric, you could build a Super K-Mart between your belt and the end of your tie, amigo!"

Braden called Delgado into the bathroom one morning to help him tie his necktie with a nice Windsor half-knot at the appropriate professional length. Sadly, however, he failed two make-up tests over the next three weeks and was asked to leave the Company.

However, because of Enric's dressing violation, Braden arranged for the group to attend Macy's Oakbrook to participate in a two-hour dress-for-success seminar. Jackson was complimented twice during the presentation for his distinctive look.

He sheepishly admitted to the group, "Hey, it's my wife who has the good taste, not me."

Afterwards, the group stayed behind to shop. Jackson selected three new Italian button-down collar shirts. Braden refused to consider giving the group a hall pass on the next day's test even though the field trip ate up several hours of precious study time.

As is common in the military, the Alsace trainees developed close friendships with one another during their corporate boot camp. Jackson's new buddy was Henry Perez, an Hispanic male who was about the same age as Jackson. They were both married, Catholic, and runners. The main difference was that Henry had three young children. Since Jackson and Henry were also the two oldest members of the training class, they stepped up into leadership roles. Each would take charge of study hours and clinical study assignments. They both caught Braden's eye early on as having strong work ethics. These two guys took the training seriously and didn't go out clubbing like some of the younger reps did. They often spoke about the squeaky clean image of the pharmaceutical industry and how the values of Alsace were in alignment with their own personal beliefs.

About mid-way through Phase One training, the class was allowed a trip home for the weekend. On the way out the door they received a home study packet of clinical studies.

Braden commanded the trainees, "I want everyone to review the information over the weekend and be prepared to take a test next Monday morning."

Jackson set a personal record during his drive back to Indianapolis. It took him less than three hours. He missed Lexi madly. They ordered in Chinese food and talked.

Lexi asked, "Who's the best trainee so far? Is it you, Jackson?"

"You know, I don't pay attention to those things."

"Come on, Jackson, this company represents a great opportunity for us, and it starts with the initial training program where you can impress others. You know, you never get a second chance to make a first impression."

Feeling uncomfortable with the new pressure she was applying, Jackson responded, "Lexi, I want you to know that I'm working hard and trying to figure out the politics in this organization. It was a whole lot easier at the hospital where the numbers of suits were so few. But I do think Braden has taken a liking to me, so that's good."

In a throaty voice Lexi said, "What's not to like?" She took his hand and pulled him off the couch. They spent the rest of the night reacquainting themselves with what they liked about each other.

The following Monday a home office manager arrived in Chicago to visit with the training class and give a lecture on the company's ethics and values. The class was seated promptly at five minutes to one o'clock eager to listen with their Mont Blanc pens poised over their black portfolios. Braden introduced Susan Bowers as a member of the Alsace Pharmaceuticals Office of Ethics. Bowers proceeded to use a number of PowerPoint slides to present the ethical standards and guidelines that were widely publicized throughout the company. The new hires were handed a spiral-bound, blue and white laminated brochure that had each of the Alsace Core Values printed on them.

The intent was to have the notepad sit on one's desk for easy viewing by all employees.

Bowers began, "The Alsace Values are the centerpiece of our business ethics model. Ethics are part of our core values that we live every day. They are a competitive advantage for Alsace. In fact, recently Alsace was evaluated by a prestigious research survey organization and honored with a AAA rating. Only two pharmaceutical companies received this award. The other was Merck. We believe that having a strong ethics reputation will help us outperform companies with a weaker reputation. We can also use this award as a way to recruit, develop, and retain high potential individuals to work for Alsace.

"We want to raise the bar for the rest of the pharmaceutical industry, and always do the right thing. The four Alsace Values that you should know for the test tomorrow are:

1. Respect and Trust One Another
2. Adhere to Ethical Business Practices
3. Leadership by Example at All Levels
4. Deliver Superior Shareholder Returns"

After the lecture, Bowers answered a few questions about product promotion and patient privacy. The topics clearly fell under the value of Ethical Business Practices. It seemed that Bowers wanted to underscore this value specifically with the class.

Braden took the opportunity to provide an example of a recent sales representative dismissal from the Company. "A representative in his mid-twenties was assigned a territory in downstate Illinois where he also trained and competed in a number of triathlons each year. With the intense workout schedule, he aggravated an old knee injury from college and needed some painkillers to help him through his workouts. He permanently borrowed a physician's prescription pad from a local clinic and began writing himself prescriptions for Vicodin. Apparently, his left-handed scribble did not match the physician's signature on file and the pharmacist noticed. He called the doctor, the local sheriff, and the FDA which resulted in the sales rep being taken into custody during the middle of a five mile workout. Alsace quickly distanced itself from the rep and publicly stated that this abhorrent behavior was not an acceptable business practice and in clear violation of Company policy. We cited in a press release our commitment to the Adhere to Ethical Business Practices value."

After Bowers left the training room, Braden and the other District Managers looked at each other and nodded their heads in agreement. Braden started speaking first. "Susan did a great job with the presentation of ethics and values, but let's not forget the last value, Deliver Superior Shareholder Returns. After all, we're all stockholders in Alsace with the stock options you received in your offer letters upon employment. We have an aggressive stock option grant and stock purchase program here at Alsace, and let me remind you that it is a viable path to personal wealth. Our CEO, Kevin Steer, has said many times at national sales meetings, 'Don't let the science get in the way of the selling.'"

He continued, "Alsace has very experienced lawyers who assess the risks of certain promotional activities, and we have a reputation for pushing the envelope in order to hit our quarterly earnings number for Wall Street and, subsequently, deliver superior shareholder returns. We are proud of the fact that we have received several speeding tickets from the FDA in response to our aggressive marketing and promotional campaigns. Let's keep Value #4 in the fore-front of our minds at all times." He then dismissed them for a fifteen-minute break.

Over the next two weeks, the new hires were content with working hard to get through the lectures and tests and not end up like that weakling Enric.

The final week was reserved for the Alsace Selling Model and "Doc Detailing." Braden started his lecture on the sales model by showing a slide entitled, *Customer-Focused Selling*.

"Customer-Focused Selling is the core sales program that we use here at Alsace," he began, "It is a multi-layered program consisting of the following elements: Pre-Call Planning, Approach, Engagement, Need Development, Demonstration, Validation, Handling Feedback, Overcoming Resistance, Closing, and Post-Call Analysis.

"The Need Development portion will include the SPIN Model which consists of a series of Situation, Problem, Implication, and Need-Payoff questions. This is an important part of the overall model as it will train you to fully understand the physician's business and therapeutic practices as you position Alsace products in appropriate patients. You will be evaluated on your use of both models during the Doc Detailing sessions."

Jackson raised his hand, "Kurt, could you explain what exactly is Doc Detailing?"

Braden replied, "Doc Detailing is a three-day session where forty physicians and nurses are brought into a hotel ballroom for you to practice your role playing and selling skills with actual customers. We will have the ballroom divided up into the forty 'offices' separated by curtains where you will be assigned to appointments with the various physicians. We will provide background information on the fictitious doctors such as their specialty, practice size, and medicine preferences so that you can plan your call objectives for each of the successive calls over the three days. Your role-plays will be anywhere from thirty seconds in a hallway to fifteen minutes in an office setting. You will filmed for all of your presentations."

The class let out a collective groan upon hearing the last statement.

Jackson actually enjoyed himself in what was later dubbed, *Territory Oak Brook*. It was exciting to manage an imaginary territory and detail physicians and nurses about Alsace products. He couldn't wait to get out in the field and manage his own territory. He also couldn't wait to get out of the Residence Inn where he had been holed up for the last six weeks. He hated to be away from Lexi.

At the end of the six-week training program, Alsace sponsored an extravagant celebration dinner for the new hires. It was held at a Smith and Wollensky's in downtown Chicago. After dessert, Braden moderated an informal awards recognition program. It was a combination of serious and funny awards. Henry Perez won the award for the highest test score average of the group. Theresa Barnhardt won the award for highest evaluation scores for Doc Detailing. Jackson won the award for being voted by his peers as *Most Likely To Be Promoted*. Braden also awarded Jackson the *Most Consistently Late in Submitting Expense Reports*.

"But hey, it's only money, right Jackson? Sales are what counts!" Braden laughed.

Finally, Dana Moorehouse was honored with the *Twin Peaks* award. Dana was a former Miss Illinois finalist, who secretly admitted to her girlfriends during training that she had breast augmentation surgery prior to the pageant, and it probably contributed to the reason she won the swimsuit competition and overall crown. But secrets like that don't stay secrets forever at Alsace. Overwhelmingly embarrassed, Dana walked to the front of the private dining room to accept the award certificate from Braden who created it that morning using Microsoft PowerPoint and some clip art downloaded off the Internet. The other District Managers and the Region Director slapped each other on their backs and had a good laugh.

Well, so much for Value #1: Respect and Trust One Another, Jackson thought.

CHAPTER 4
NEW TERRITORY

Jackson's territory assignment took him and Lexi away from Indianapolis to just outside Chicago to a small town in northwest Indiana called Merrillville. Although sad to leave their friends in Indy, they were glad to be closer to their parents. Merrillville was less than three hours away from Wisconsin, instead of six like Indianapolis. Lexi was thrilled to be closer to Chicago's Michigan Avenue for the shopping. The northwest Indiana apartment complexes, however, left something to be desired. They reflected an area that was more steel mill and industry-oriented rather than the upscale Yuppie culture from which they came. After touring a number of apartment complexes in the area, they moved, reluctantly, into a small two-bedroom apartment on the Broadmoor Golf Course.

"You are going to need to make a lot more money so we can afford to move out of this dump," remarked Lexi.

Jackson had a lot to learn, but was determined to succeed. Kurt Braden mentored Jackson and gave him advice on gaining access to physician offices and growing new prescription market shares.

"This is a promotion and sample sensitive market. Make more calls each day than the Company expects," Braden said repeatedly.

Jackson had a lot of up-front organization to do for his territory. He had received a Practitioner Call List, physician level Prescription Data, and a computer loaded with an Electronic Territory Management software system. The ETM system had to be replicated each night with the home office server after Jackson entered his daily physician calls. The company database maintained records of the physician calls, products promoted, and the number of samples distributed. Other pertinent information was also maintained in the database such as best call day and time, staff names, managed care providers, hospital affiliations, and Pharmacy and Therapeutics Committee membership. The last item was extremely important since hospitals follow a strict formulary protocol of what drugs they allow to be used in the hospital. The P & T Committee members represented the actual voting members of the hospital, and the identification and promotion of new products to them was key to getting a new drug used in a hospital system.

The call cycle system that Jackson followed allowed him to organize his highest volume doctors by best call day and time into a monthly routing, and this routing enabled him to work in certain geographic locations for efficiency in selling and time management. For example, Mondays and Fridays were good days to work Merrillville, Tuesdays were good for Gary and La Porte, Wednesdays were good for Michigan City and Chesterton, and finally, Thursdays were good for Valparaiso. He then had to organize his 300 physicians into a certain day and week each month so that he would see them at least once a month. There were other Alsace Pharmaceutical representatives in the same territory that would call on the same physicians in between his visits to reinforce the product promotional messages, but they were assigned a different product sequencing and promotional theme. For example, one representative would promote the message of Alsace's blood pressure drug as a fast acting agent while another would promote the fact the medicine worked for twenty-four hours a day. At the end of the day, they both said the name of the drug and asked the physician to use it. The doctors promised to prescribe it for every patient in their practice. Jackson learned quickly that all of the doctors made that promise to every drug rep.

Jackson settled into his territory and quickly established a rapport with key physicians who could grow his new prescription market share. The nurses looked forward to his visits in the office because he seemed to care about them and their families. His good looks didn't hurt, either. His hospital and physical therapy experience added to his credibility and he was able to gain additional time with the doctors and promote his Alsace product line.

Territory management was time consuming. Jackson would get up at 5AM to work on his database and analyze his market share data. Lexi would still be asleep when Jackson would wake her with a cup of coffee each morning. She had landed a sales position at one of the Chicago television stations so she commuted into the city each day for her nine to five routine. When she returned home, she typically found Jackson working on his computer again. He would be entering his daily calls, notes, and sample inventory levels and then would replicate his computer with the database at the Alsace home office. Then there were the daily emails which added another two to three hours to the work day.

Lexi accepted the challenges of the new job at first, but after a few months she became resentful of all the time Jackson put in for Alsace.

"How about taking a break tonight?" Lexi suggested in a soft, low voice.

"Honey, my District Manager expects an analysis by tomorrow morning. Plus, I'm behind on my expense reports again."

"We could snuggle." She opened her robe to give him a peek of her lace-trimmed silk teddy.He didn't even look up.

"Just a half-hour more, babe."

Two hours later, Lexi got up off the couch and turned off the TV set. Jackson was still working on his computer in the other room. "You're still working?"

"I know, I know. My computer crashed on me while I was replicating my emails with the server in San Diego."

"Any reason why couldn't you step out of your office and tell me what was going on? How about communicating with me, instead of the home office?" Lexi stormed out and slammed the office door shut.

Jackson knew that he should apologize to Lexi, but he still had to finish his assignment and he wasn't up for more of her late night drama. He would rather work.

There were certain safety rules about his territory, particularly the inner city Gary, which Jackson learned right away. For example, as a white male wearing an expensive suit and driving a nice car, he learned that when four o'clock in the afternoon hit, he needed to be driving south toward Merrillville and away from Gary. He also knew that if he saw gang bangers hanging out in front of the liquor stores across from certain physician offices along Broadway Avenue, then he should just keep on driving. He heard the story of one Big Pharma sales rep who climbed the stairs to a second floor physician office and was nearly stabbed in the chest. Luckily for that rep, the guy was able to bring his sample bag up in time to block the knife from slicing into his chest. A quick kick in the groin sent the slasher tumbling down the steps with the drug rep sprinting right behind him and out the door and to the safety of his company car.

There was a tactical item that Jackson learned quickly as well as he worked his new territory. Big Pharma companies all provided fleet or leased vehicles to their sales representatives. By far, the Ford Taurus was the automobile of choice for the pharmaceutical company fleets, but Dodge Intrepid, Chevy Lumina, and Pontiac Grand Prix were also on the selection list for most of the companies. The only good thing about any of the cars was that the price was right. *It's a free car,* Jackson would say to himself.

Since his territory was in the state of Indiana, Jackson could tell as soon as he drove into a physician's parking lot how many other drug reps were in the building. Each pharmaceutical fleet car had a red sticker in the upper right hand corner of the license plate denoting the month of the year that the license and registration were to be renewed by the company's fleet operations department. All leased cars in Indiana were renewed in the month of December. Though he couldn't tell which pharmaceutical company was inside the building, he could glean an approximate number of the sales reps who were inside. That number gave him an indication about how long his waiting time would be.

Once inside, there were always policies or rules set down by the office manager for pharmaceutical representatives specific to promotion of products, or sampling, or even getting signatures for the samples left. In one particularly busy office, Jackson had a terrible time accessing the doctor. The nurse just wouldn't let him back, but they always wanted samples of Alsace products.

"I'm sorry. The doctor is very busy today and won't have time to see you," the nurse would say. No doubt the standard line for every sales rep.

Remembering his Alsace selling model Jackson replied, "I just have two quick questions for the doctor today."

"Sorry, no," she responded coolly. "But we will take some samples. If you wait in the lobby I will get you a signature."

"But I need to witness the doctor's signature," he said urgently.

"Jackson, if you ever want a chance at seeing him in the future, you will go and wait in the lobby while I get you a signature." It was an order, not a request.

Jackson nodded in agreement, turned and walked back to the lobby knowing that he was about to break company policy on witnessing a physician's signature.

The nurse returned a few minutes later to the lobby waving the Sample Request Form at Jackson. She took the opportunity to continue her lecture. "Jackson, this is the way this office works when it comes to physician signatures. If you want us to use your products, then you better follow our rules. Please leave your samples at the front desk."

Well, so much for Alsace Value Number Two: Adhere to Ethical Business Practices, he thought.

About two months after Jackson was assigned to the Merrillville territory, a broadcast voicemail message was delivered to his mailbox from the Senior Region Director for Chicago. He started off explaining that Jackson's current District Manager had accepted an early retirement package from Alsace, and that Kurt Braden had been promoted to replace him. The change was effective immediately.

"Kurt has been appointed to this new position of responsibility for an important district after successfully leading and managing the recent training class where a ninety percent retention and graduation rate were achieved. This was the highest rate in the country of the sixteen regional training programs. Please help me congratulate and welcome Kurt as the new District Sales Manager in Chicago" the Region Director stated.

Jackson nearly leapt for joy after listening to the message. He respected Braden and was excited to have him for a new boss.

Braden's first order of business was to hold a teleconference call at the end of the week with his new district sales team members. After the perfunctory introductions and a brief review of the business plans and sales objectives, Braden announced a new sales contest.

"Alsace has approved the implementation of an additional sales contest that is separate from the regular bonus plan. Over the next twelve months, the two representatives in the region who have the highest market share percentage gains compared to the base period will win a Spot Stock grant. A Spot Stock award is a one-time grant of five hundred stock options that are purchased by the Company on behalf of the individual and are immediately vested. You can hold the options for as long as you like until you decide to cash them out. The stock grant and a small statue of a Dalmatian Dog, that we commonly call *Spot*, will be awarded by our CEO at the annual awards trip to the lucky winners." Braden then went on to describe the criteria for the top two district members to earn the awards trip.

The desire to be successful and get promoted to the next level was planted early in Jackson's thinking by Braden. He just had to figure out how to work efficiently and grow his business with all the quirky FDA policies and physician office rules. He also needed to figure out how to spend more time with Lexi.

The telephone on the bedside table shrilled. Jackson sat straight up in bed. Locating the clock radio he saw that it was 5:45 AM. His head felt like a sledgehammer was banging on it. He had too much tequila last night at Mother's on Rush Street with the rest of the team, but the karaoke was fun. Leading the songs *Shake It Up Baby* by The Beatles and *Surrender* by Cheap Trick brought him instant fame at the bar, at least with his teammates. He would have to remember to expense the twenty dollar tip to the DJ for letting him do two songs in a row, as well as expensing the several rounds of drinks that he bought. *That reminds me, I better get my expenses caught up this weekend since they are already two weeks overdue,* he thought.

Another shrill from the telephone helped him remember that he was at the Drake Hotel for a team Plan of Action or POA meeting.

Fumbling for the receiver he cleared his throat in case it was Lexi, "Hello?"

"Jackson, I am canceling the rest of the District Meeting. You can go home whenever you want this morning. Henry died last night in a car accident," explained Kurt Braden in a sober voice.

"What?"

"You know how we were waiting on Henry to show up for our dinner reservation at Joe's Seafood, and he never showed up?"

"Yeah, I mean, Yes," Jackson corrected himself.

"Henry was involved in a terrible traffic accident last night on Lake Shore Drive, and it was fatal. I just found out a half-hour ago. I've made the decision to cancel our POA meeting and reschedule it for next month. You can make your big presentation then, which is a good thing because the Region Sales Director should be able to attend. It'll be better positioning for you for a possible promotion if we move this whole thing back a few weeks. Listen, I'll talk to you later. I need to call Henry's wife, Rosalita, and ask about funeral arrangements so I can attend." Then he hung up.

"OK, good-bye," Jackson said to a dead phone line.

If Jackson's head ached before, then it was a full-fledged migraine now. Since they had met in Phase One training, they had become close friends. with similar ethics and values. The only big difference between the two of them was that Henry and his wife, Rosalita, had three kids already. A five-year-old girl and twin boys.

Henry was a devoted husband and father with a lot of relatives all located on the south side of Chicago within his territory. His family had been in Chicago for three generations and owned several Laundromats and a cleaning service. He was an awesome sales rep and perfect for the demographics of his territory because it had a high number of Hispanic physicians and office staff. His customers nicknamed him "The Churros Guy" because he frequently brought fresh, hot Churros that Rosalita would fry and coat with cinnamon sugar in the morning before he left for his territory. Sometimes he would bring his guy doctors boxes of Partagas cigars complete with cutters and Zippo lighters. They all loved Henry. No doubt they were all going to miss him.

By the end of the week, the police pieced together the fate of Henry, and informed Alsace management. After he worked a full day in his territory, Henry stopped by the house to pick up his garment bag and kiss his family good-bye. He was tired, not feeling well, and thinking that he probably picked up a touch of the flu in one of his many doctor's offices. He had a headache, the chills, and a slight fever. He wished he could just get a good night's sleep in his own bed and then drive the ten miles to the Drake Hotel in the morning, but his District Manager was quite clear in his voice mail message about expecting everyone at the team dinner at Joe's Seafood. In addition, company policy stated that all employees had to stay at the designated hotel for the duration of all meetings. What the policy did not state was that Alsace did not want employees to be driving cars after they had been drinking company bought liquor because a liability settlement would be significant if someone got hurt. Therefore, Alsace figured, better safe than paying out of our profits. It did not matter to the company if a few hotel room rentals could be saved. They had trunk-loads of cash hidden away.

Henry drove north on Lake Shore Drive. The weather was terrible and not a good match for his throbbing temples. A cold front had moved in from the northeast off Lake Michigan. It brought winds of thirty miles-per-hour with gusts that reached up to fifty miles-per-hour, and a temperature of about twenty-five degrees. The rain that accompanied the cold front was actually driving sideways off the lake, and, in a manner of minutes, LSD was icy. The drivers couldn't tell yet. It was too early and the salt trucks weren't out.

Henry did not want to be late so he maintained his speed. He hit a slick spot and began to swerve. The car behind him caught Henry's front end at just the right angle. The impact flipped Henry's car up and over the three-foot divider wall and into the southbound lane. No one heard Henry scream as he hung suspended by his seat belt when a delivery truck smashed into the driver's side of the car.

From a financial perspective, it was lucky for Rosalita and the kids that Henry was wearing a suit. That meant he was on Alsace company time when he died. A loss of life while on company time meant a substantial death benefit payout. Rosalita would receive his term life insurance benefit, which was valued at five times Henry's base salary or $275,000; she would also receive an Accidental Death and Dismemberment benefit worth $250,000; and finally she would receive a special insurance policy rider for $500,000 designated as catastrophic loss since he was the sole breadwinner for the family. Alsace would authorize the insurance payment of over $1.2 million to Rosalita. If invested wisely, she and the kids could live quite comfortably and easily pay for private school and college educations.

All because of the damn inflexible company policy requiring all employees to stay at the hotel for meetings, thought Jackson as he stood at the grave and watched Henry's casket being lowered into the ground.

CHAPTER 5
DINE AND DASH

Money is the biggest resource to pharmaceutical companies. With some of the highest profit margins of any industry, Big Pharma invests a tremendous amount of money into helping its field sales force develop access and relationships with key offices with high patient or disease state volume that represent opportunity for increasing sales and growing market share. Catering meals, called Lunch and Learns, for clinics and hospital departments is one method used by drug reps to gain precious time in front of important decision makers. Based on the premise that if a sales representative brings in a lunch, or some other type of meal, then the physician and staff will stop to eat for about fifteen minutes and listen to a presentation about a company's product or clinical study. It is not uncommon for each Big Pharma sales representative to be allocated an annual budget of over $50,000 to use for Lunch and Learn programs. With an army of sales reps, it was a huge expense line.

Alsace Pharmaceuticals was no different from other Big Pharma companies when it came to resources and programs. In highly competitive therapeutic markets such as oncology, hypertension, cholesterol, ulcers, diabetes, depression, allergies, and arthritis; Alsace Pharmaceuticals was up against significant competition from Merck, Pfizer, Glaxo, Aventis, AstraZeneca, Johnson & Johnson, Amgen, and Lilly. These companies were also staffed with legions of sales representatives who, if directed to and appropriately armed with military weapons, could potentially overthrow the governments of many third-world countries just by the mere show of force. But alas, they were simply armed with millions of dollars in their respective promotional budgets for breakfasts, lunches, and dinners. Then, there were the endless streams of donuts, cookies, candy, nuts, fancy coffee drinks, sodas, teas, and liquor that were constantly dropped off at frequent intervals to the important offices. The huge budgets were no secret among physician offices and hospital staffs. In fact, it was often advertised in local classifieds that when a big, busy clinic sought a new nursing staff member or medical technician, that *lunch provided daily* was part of the benefit plan. Drug reps would often chuckle when they saw those classified ads announcing the perk because they knew who was really providing the lunch.

Jackson worked his calendar diligently to utilize his promotional budgets to the fullest. Being new on territory, he needed access to the busiest offices and doctors to help him grow his sales. He also worked the bonus calculator.

"Lexi, the quarterly bonus payouts can be awesome if I hit my numbers. The annual awards trips are fantastic! I heard that a cruise is in the works," Jackson would explain. He hoped to keep her focused on the perks of the job as opposed to the hours of the job.

"Just don't let this job take over our life."

"I'm not. Besides, I've got a good chance to be fast-tracked for promotion in addition to the Spot Stock awards.

"If it happens, it happens. We're doing fine with both our salaries. If you start going too fast up the ladder, I won't ever see you."

"Lexi. That will never happen."

Even though some of the offices had lunches booked up for the next six months, Jackson took the advice of his District Manager, Kurt Braden, and implemented other "acceptable activities" that would still get him access to key decision makers. Where Henry Perez had been known as *The Churros Guy*, Jackson got to be known as *The Dine and Dash Guy*. Not that he wanted the reputation, but it was the only way to get in front of his key doctors and nurses in order to promote his products. He didn't intend for it to happen, but the desire to grow sales, make good bonus dollars, and get promoted to the next level consumed him.

The process he used was quite simple. Jackson made arrangements with some restaurants that accepted his Corporate American Express card and would hold his signature on file in order to set up his programs. Physicians and staff would then be encouraged to go to their neighborhood Chili's or Outback Steakhouse or some other restaurant that Jackson suggested, and place a dinner order for carryout on their way home. The restaurant would simply bill Jackson's credit card for the meals and add the customary twenty percent tip to the bill. Whether Jackson made it to the restaurant at exactly the precise time the physician showed up was anybody's guess. Some doctors and staff got to hear a product presentation, but most did not. In the end, the doctors and nurses appreciated that their families got dinner that particular night courtesy of Jackson and Alsace. The restaurant managers were happy to accommodate Jackson's requests because their dinner orders and subsequent sales numbers went up accordingly.

Everybody won. Jackson got to spend his full promotional budget, the doctors and nurses and their families were fed, some customers got to hear about an Alsace product or new clinical study, and the restaurants got to sell more carryout dinners. *The Dine and Dash Guy* was born, and his sales numbers skyrocketed. The Region and District Sales Managers were ecstatic with Jackson Ford. He was an amazing sales rep. Not only did he just hit his numbers, he blew them away!

In his mind, Jackson justified the whole concept through the support of his manager, *Alsace Value #4 says Deliver Superior Shareholder Returns. That's exactly what I'm doing!*

Jackson was out early one Tuesday morning working Gary. It was a crisp autumn day with the sun shining and the wind coming off Lake Michigan. He knew that later in the afternoon when the steel factories blew off the steam from the mills, that Merrillville would be in direct line of the air pollution that would drift due south from Gary. The smell was like sulfur. *Well, for now let me just enjoy this wonderful day,* he thought.

As he prepared to turn the Ford Taurus into a large clinic parking lot, he first checked the liquor store parking lot across the street for any gang bangers. *Nope. Must still be sleeping it off.*

Jackson scanned the parking lot for other rep cars. Since this clinic had several high prescribing physicians, reps were there all the time. Out of the corner of his eye, he spied two cars at the far end of the lot with their trunks open. Two guys dressed in suits stood nearby. One was taller than the other, and Jackson couldn't place them since he was still fairly new to the territory. There were hundreds of drug reps. It was clear that they knew each other by the way they were talking, particularly with the handshakes and other manly gestures. Jackson watched for a minute from the opposite end of the lot trying to decide if he should come back to the clinic later in the morning.

Maybe I should go over to the infamous second floor office and call on them before the slasher wakes up to start his day, Jackson chuckled to himself.

Suddenly, something odd happened. The two men exchanged a case of samples. *Well, no big deal, they probably work for the same company and are doing a sample transfer,* thought Jackson. Then his jaw nearly dropped in his lap. The taller guy handed over a wad of bills to the short guy.

They both got back in their cars and headed off on Broadway Avenue in opposite directions. Jackson spotted their license plates, and sure enough, saw the little red fleet car sticker in the upper right hand corner.

They're pharmaceutical reps!

His curiosity heightened, Jackson put his car in gear and followed the taller guy's car. Staying back a safe distance and keeping several cars between them, Jackson tailed the car for about ten minutes. Finally, the car pulled over to the curb in front of a boarded-up storefront. The big guy popped the trunk, opened the door, and walked to the rear of the car. Before he lifted the trunk, he looked around nervously. He then lifted the trunk, reached in, and pulled out the sample box that the short guy had given him.

That sure looks like the same box. Yep. There's the white packing slip label on the side above the company name.

While the big guy went into the storefront door, Jackson decided to park his car so that he could get an unobstructed view. He checked his Practitioner Call List documents for any doctors located at this address. A minute later he remarked to himself, *Nope. No doctors at this address. What is this guy doing?*

Ten minutes went by. The big guy walked out of the storefront empty-handed and quickly got into his car. Instead of driving off right away, the car remained parked with the big guy behind the steering wheel.

What's he got in his hands? Jackson squinted for a closer look. *Money! He's counting bills. He's selling his samples!*

Jackson was thoroughly disgusted, and he struggled with his indecision as to what to do next, if anything. *This is not right.*

He called his District Manager and described what he had witnessed. Braden responded cautiously, "Leave it alone, Jackson. You don't want the FDA snooping around your physician offices."

In disbelief Jackson responded, "But there isn't a physician office there! And more importantly, it's not ethical, Kurt!"

"Again, you don't want to involve the FDA if you can help it," Braden said firmly.

"I feel like I should do something, though. It just doesn't seem right to look the other way." Jackson had a bad feeling welling up inside him.

"Well, let me fill you in on a little secret, Jackson. Those Dine & Dash dinners that you put on aren't a hundred percent ethical either, but they work. I've just reviewed your latest sales numbers, and they're going through the roof! The Region Sales Director left me a voicemail this morning saying that we need to look for ways to get you promoted. You're getting noticed for the most important thing that Alsace cares about, Jackson. Sales. Now listen, I can help you move ahead in this company. Stay focused. Don't get distracted by some of the things that you may see out there. Remember Value #4: *Deliver Superior Shareholder Results!*"

The sick feeling passed immediately and was replaced by a sense of pride and accomplishment. He was delivering results and upper management noticed. "OK Kurt. I'm glad I called to talk to you. I'm focused. Don't worry about me."

"Remember the ABC rule, Jackson. ABC, Always Be Closing. I'll talk to you later."

After they hung up, Jackson drove down Broadway toward Mercy Hospital. There were several clinics located around the hospital that had high volume physician targets for him to call on. The patient population that they served was Medicaid and cash patients. Medicaid is a state program for patients who fall below a certain income level, and since his products were covered on the Indiana State Medicaid Formulary, these physician offices became very important for him to visit. Alsace Pharmaceuticals, like other Big Pharma companies had approved direct accounts with these offices, meaning, the physicians were able to buy medicines direct from the company after a credit review and approval process. These same physicians could then sell the medicines directly to patients, and this was confirmed by the large number of yellow prescription containers generally found in the back sample room with customized labels. Patients would generally leave the office with several vials in a brown paper bag. Funny thing was, that these same offices would often accept large numbers of samples on each of his visits. Other reps also made comments about the strange requests for large sample quantities.

Trying to shake off the weird scene from earlier in the day, Jackson greeted the receptionist with a big smile, "Morning, Preeta!"

"Good morning, Jackson," Preeta replied.

"Is the doctor available today? I have some important new information that I would like to share with him from a new clinical study that Alsace just completed."

"Why don't you go back and ask one of the nurses? We're pretty busy this morning," Preeta replied as she nodded behind Jackson at the over-flowing waiting room.

As Jackson walked back toward the sample room, he pulled out a copy of the new clinical trial paper. It was printed on glossy paper and was called a reprint by the sales reps. Reprints were actual copies of a specific clinical study that was conducted and approved for publication in one of the peer-reviewed medical journals. This particular study was recognized by national medical thought-leaders as top-notch since it had been accepted for publication by a leading cardiology journal. Jackson had gotten his confidence back after the telephone call with Braden and looked forward to what he hoped would be a fruitful interaction with this doctor.

A door was open about halfway down the hall. Jackson slowed his pace as he passed it to quickly glance in. What he saw made him stop in his tracks just after he slid by the room. He backed up half a step and peered into the room. At a table in the middle of the room was a cutting board much like one would find in a kitchen. Scattered on top of the cutting board were tablets, razor blades, and yellow prescription vials with customized office labels.

That's odd, he thought as he tilted his head to the side.

Suddenly, a staff member inside the room walked out from behind a closet door and went to the table. Her side was to the door where Jackson continued to peer in with great interest. She picked up one of the razors and began to scrape a tablet. Very slowly and carefully. When she finished the scraping, she placed the tablet into the vial and started to scrape another tablet. The containers looked like the same yellow prescription vials and labels that Jackson had seen several times before at this office. Preeta would usually placed them into brown lunch bags and hand them across the counter to patients as they settled their account. In fact, he could recall bits and pieces of conversations where patients paying for the medicines in the vials.

Why is she scraping those tablets? If the office has a direct purchase agreement that enables them to buy products directly from pharmaceutical companies at discounted prices, then why were they seemingly altering the drug by scraping it with a razor blade? He raised his eyebrows as a connection was made. *Maybe the tablets aren't purchased medicines from a manufacturer. Maybe they're samples!*

Jackson's head jerked back as a voice boomed from down the hallway, "Jackson, come down here to the sample room!" It was Tuwana, the head nurse in the office. "What are you doing?" she demanded. Her arms were crossed as she peered over the top of her reading glasses.

"I, ah, I guess I, ah, got confused about where the sample room was," he lied. He quickly recovered his composure and said, "I have a new clinical study that I would like to share with you and the doctor. Do you have a few minutes?" He held the reprint up high as he strode toward her.

"Jackson, you know that with the reductions in state Medicaid reimbursements and all these indigent and cash patients that we care for, most days it's like a damn factory around here. We just rotate the patients through as fast as we can. We barely cover our overhead expenses. So we have very little time for lengthy discussions with you fancy drug reps. And today is just another one of those days. You see the lobby filled up when you came in?"

"Yes. Every chair was full."

"Well, there you go. Just leave your literature and the study, and I'll make sure the doctor sees it." She paused for a moment. "Oh, and we need plenty of samples today. We seem to be going through them lately. You have that tablet form of your anti-hypertensive right?" Tuwana asked.

"Yes, I do but it's out in the car. But I'll bring some in if you tell me how many boxes that you need." It was Jackson's turn to pause. "Tuwana, I noticed that your direct orders for the product aren't as high as they have been previously…"

Before he could go on Tuwana cut him off, "We're ordering more than ever direct from Alsace because the doctor is switching all his patients to your blood pressure medicine. Seems like everyone coming in these days with high blood pressure is walking out on your product."

Jackson felt good about that comment thinking that he was making a difference with this office promoting the features and benefits of his product compared to the competition. The contract price was attractive too, especially to direct purchasers. "That's great, Tuwana," responded Jackson completing forgetting about the decreased volume of direct order sales. *The doctor must be using all my samples to convert over his existing patients. I know that he's got a lot of low income and uninsured patients that probably can't afford to pay retail pharmacy prices. I'll bet that he probably gives them a good deal.*

As Jackson walked back down the hallway to go outside and get some samples of the tablet formulation of the blood pressure drug, he snuck another peek into the little repackaging room. The staff member was still at the table with the razor blade and the prescription vials. As he passed by the front counter, he overheard a conversation between Preeta and an elderly guy.

"Mr. Jones, your office visit today is twenty dollars, and your blood pressure prescription is thirty-five dollars."

"Tell the doctor that I said thank you for helping me with the blood pressure medicine. That damn Walgreens charges me twice that price every month," the man seethed through clenched teeth. He held one of the brown lunch bags in his hand.

"We're glad that we can help you out, Mr. Jones," Preeta said warmly.

Back at his car, Jackson opened the trunk and tore open one of the sample boxes that contained the blood pressure medication tablets. His curiosity was peaked now. After removing the foil seal and cotton, he poured out the seven tablets into his palm. On one side of the tablet was etched *ALSACE 750.* On the other side was etched *SAMPLE.*

I'll bet that the staff is scraping off the word SAMPLE and repackaging them in the yellow vials for sale to their patients, he thought. *Jesus! Now what am I supposed to do? This office is one of my top market share clinics, and we have a new product launch coming up! With a new product launch there's sure to be promotional opportunities like an additional sales force and new management positions. Lexi is counting on me doing well here at Alsace, getting promoted, and getting the hell out of northwest Indiana. This company can be our ticket to the good life. Shit!*

He slammed the trunk and carried the samples back inside. Jackson felt like he just got kicked in the gut. *This isn't right,* he thought.

"Here are your tablet formulations," he said to Tuwana who stood at the front counter talking with Mr. Jones.

"Thanks, Jackson. I have your signed Sample Form here for you. The doctor signed just before he went in with a patient," Tuwana said as she waved the document in the air. "I already tore off the office copy and filed it." She leaned into Jackson and added with a low voice, "Just remember, Jackson, we know full well the size of our practice and how significant our business is to the local drug reps. Just play along with us, and you'll do just fine. Your District Manager will see good things happening with your market shares. We've been around awhile. We know how the game is played."

Jackson was unsure what to say. "Thanks, I'll see you again in two weeks," Jackson promised. He turned and walked out of the office.

What the hell am I going to do now? I can't call Kurt back because all I'll get from him is the company line. "You don't want the FDA snooping around your physician offices. You don't want to involve the FDA if you can help it." Dammit! What am I going to do? It's clear that this office is selling my samples. But like Tuwana said, they write a lot of prescriptions and I need to play along if I'm going to grow my market shares. A minute passed as he thought about the situation. *Ah, what's it gonna hurt? That old guy paid less than if he went to Walgreens, the office is making less from their Medicaid reimbursements so they need to make it up somewhere, and the economy basically sucks here in Gary. I just gotta let it go.*

Back in his car he realized that he once again didn't witness the physician signing the sample request card. The way his morning had been going so far, it felt like he just got kicked in the nuts.

CHAPTER 6
CONSULTANT MEETINGS

Big Pharma companies use advisors or consultants to help provide direction for new and existing medicines. The companies routinely retain groups of nationally known physicians to render advice on general medical and business issues as well as specific product development and marketing programs. Significant fees for each interaction that range from $5,000 to $10,000 are paid to those lucky physicians that are hand-picked as a national consultant to a drug company. The consultants are typically sequestered to an all-expenses-paid resort location with their spouse or significant other. The typical golf resort location usually provides incentive enough to attract the consultants because of the variety of recreational activities available either on-site or nearby. A rigorous agenda is typically scheduled to discuss product data, research and development progress, and promotional plans. In addition, hundreds of trained speakers are often needed to help support the promotion of a new product after it is launched into the market. The companies typically estimate how many speakers they will actually need to conduct local speaker programs, then ask the District Managers to recruit an appropriate number of potential speakers to invite to a national training program. The two to three day national training programs generally serve the purpose of providing the new consultant with education on the full range of disease state data, the company's new drug, the competitor's products, and on their presentation skills. After they receive a complimentary slide kit and a hefty honoraria or fee for attending, the physicians are then able to play golf for a day or two before flying back home to conduct some programs on behalf of the drug company.

Dr. Sanjeet Chabra was one of the lucky physicians selected from the Chicago area and trained by Alsace to conduct speaker programs. He was a well-known cardiologist who was respected in the medical community due to his affiliation with Northwestern University Medical Center. Dr. Chabra loved the good life. And he paid for it by billing high fees for the cardiac procedures that he performed on very sick patients. He and his family lived in a high-rise condominium tower in the Gold Coast section off Lake Shore Drive where the higher the floor and better the view of Lake Michigan, then the higher the price of the condo. Dr. Chabra lived on the penthouse floor facing the lake, which he could afford because his cardiology practice had historically done very, very well. He also supplemented his physician income with Big Pharma consultant fees.

However, times were changing in the medical community. Especially if you were a high-priced heart specialist like a Dr. Chabra. Health Maintenance Organizations were implementing procedural changes faster than the hospitals and physicians could keep up with them. By representing hundreds of thousands, sometimes millions, of patients through a variety of employer groups, the HMOs had clout like never before. They literally came in overnight and changed billing fee structures and referral procedures. They turned the whole thing upside down, in fact. Instead of Dr. Chabra being able to tell the insurance company what his fees were for a cardiac catheter procedure, the HMO told him and the hospital what payment they were going to make for the procedure. His fees and that of the hospital were nearly cut in half in most cases! The nerve!

"This is absurd! I am a doctor. Nobody tells me what amount I can bill!" Dr. Chabra was often heard yelling these statements at the HMO Finance Department Directors.

But the HMOs had the ultimate power because if he didn't play ball, then they threatened to take the hundreds of thousands of patients that they represented and refer them for cardiac visits and procedures to other cardiology practices and hospitals in the Chicago area who were willing to accept the HMO's terms and payments. He would not get a single referral. In the end, a defeated Dr. Chabra figured it was better to have the referrals than not even if it meant that his personal income would be drastically reduced.

The Alsace sales representative who called on Dr. Chabra was Scott Evans, the son of a former thirty-year pharmaceutical representative who was never promoted out of the field sales ranks. Evans loathed his father for never even trying to move up within his company, and he vowed to do whatever it took to get promoted at Alsace. Evans was a Chicago native who got his undergraduate degree in marketing at the University of Illinois in Champaign. The company reimbursed his tuition to the tune of $6,000 a year for night school so he could earn his MBA degree. With it, Evans was a sure bet to get promoted into headquarters as an entry-level marketing manager for one of the many Alsace product teams. He found, however, that between work and graduate school, good grades were often difficult to attain without help. Evans would single out the graduate assistants for his classes and treat them to dinner and drinks prior to the exams in order to get the professor's main review points for the upcoming tests. Single, with dark hair and an athletic build, he loved to play sixteen-inch softball with his buddies in the Chicago Park District leagues.

Evans considered Jackson as his arch nemesis because before Kurt Braden got his DM promotion. Evans was the golden boy in the Chicago Region. With Jackson as Braden's pet and doing so well, Evans had to start all over to get the same level of recognition he had before the old manager retired. They were neck and neck on the district market share growth charts, and each of them wanted desperately to get promoted over the other. Scott had been with Alsace for three years, and his ego felt threatened by Jackson. When Braden announced the Spot Stock award along with the awards trip, Evans decided then and there that Jackson would be in his gun sights for both of the honors.

Jackson Ford is off to a fast start, thought Evans. *It would help if I could win that awards trip. That would get me back to where I was before he came along. This grad school schedule is killing me, though. There's got to be an easier and faster way to make sales happen.*

Evans was well versed in the billing reforms being implemented by the HMOs as he heard about it from of all his cardiology specialists, and they all whined about making less money with the new reimbursement changes. Dr. Chabra was a key physician that Evans had identified to help promote his blood pressure and cholesterol drugs. Since Dr. Chabra had been trained by Alsace as a speaker for both products, Evans was going to put him to good use in his territory and throughout the Chicagoland area if need be. After all, he had a promotional budget for speaker programs of $50,000. Of course, out of that budget he had to pay Dr. Chabra's honoraria fee and the meals for the participants, so Evans worked out a plan with Dr. Chabra.

"I want to make thirty thousand dollars in speaker fees this year from Alsace. Since my honoraria per program is fifteen hundred dollars, I need to do twenty programs," demanded Dr. Chabra.

Evans realized that Dr. Chabra was more than a little stressed about his financial situation from their discussion the previous week over the new HMO reimbursement schedules, "Not a problem, Dr. Chabra. I can make arrangements for at least fifteen speaker programs myself in this territory, and we can also use you in other territories around the Chicago area. I'll personally see to it."

"Good," came the reply. "Just set up the schedule with my secretary. Are there any other forms that I need to fill out so that I get my honoraria paid promptly?"

"No, I'll handle sending in all the paperwork for your speaker fees. Shall I have the checks sent here to your office?" asked Evans.

"Absolutely not. Have them sent to my home address," said Dr. Chabra.

"OK, I will," replied Evans confidently.

The first eight programs went super. Dr. Chabra conducted five dinner programs and three lunch programs for Scott on behalf of Alsace. The best thing was that the new prescriptions from the attending physicians were starting to show up in the most recent sales data. But Dr. Chabra quickly began to tire of the extra hours he was putting in for Alsace for only fifteen hundred dollars a talk, and he complained bitterly to Evans every chance he could.

"Scott, you know, Merck and AstraZeneca pay me twenty-five hundred dollars each time I speak for them," said Dr. Chabra. "Alsace is paying too low for someone like me."

"I realize that Dr. Chabra, but our speaker agreement only allows us to pay you fifteen hundred dollars for each program. That's what you agreed to!"

Not backing down, Dr. Chabra continued, "Scott, you talk to your District Manager and ask him for more money or I will cancel the rest of the schedule. I am losing money to the HMOs and now I lose money to Alsace every time I do a speaker program. Alsace makes up the fee many times over with just the start of one new patient on their drug. They're usually on it for the rest of their life, you know."

Evans thought about the ultimatum for a moment and cringed at the thought of losing Dr. Chabra's business and the momentum he now had for his products, "How about if I work out something with the other offices where you are scheduled to speak? How about if I reduce the number of programs you actually conduct but still get you the entire thirty thousand dollars in total honoraria payments?"

"That would be acceptable. You work out the new schedule with my secretary, but the agreement on the total honoraria amount remains the same, agreed?" asked Dr. Chabra.

"Yes. Let me work something out to both our satisfaction," he replied.

Crap, thought Evans as he left Dr. Chabra's office. *This is going to be more work now. What I'll have to do is combine several offices into one program, but record the paperwork as if it were two separate programs. I'll need two dinner receipts for two separate restaurants on different nights. Shouldn't be a problem, I have lots of friends in Chicago that would love a good night out at a fancy restaurant pretending to be one of my doctors!* he laughed to himself all the way to the elevator.

As the elevator began to descend Evans thought, *Bite me, Jackson Ford. I'm going to beat you out for the awards trip, win the Spot Stock award, and still get promoted before you!* The other people in the elevator thought Evans had an odd grin on his face.

As the year progressed, Jackson and Evans continued their tight race for the market share growth awards. Dr. Chabra turned out to be Evans's number one physician fueling his product sales growth as he exceeded his territory goals. As the year neared the end, Evans offered to host Dr. Chabra's office holiday party on the Saturday night before the Christmas weekend. He made the arrangements at Giovanni's Restaurant in downtown Chicago. True to his method of cutting corners, Evans intended to not only write off the dinner expenses as a Customer Entertainment meal, but also to submit Dr. Chabra for another fifteen hundred dollar honoraria reimbursement that would actually push him over the thirty thousand dollar level. Dr. Chabra wasn't actually scheduled to speak that night. It was just the office holiday party.

It's just my way of saying thanks to Dr. Chabra, Evans said to himself.

The entire office staff including spouses and significant others showed up for the dinner party that night. Evans ordered the finest hors d'oeurves, wine, entrees, and desserts that the restaurant offered. What turned a wonderful holiday party into a nightmare was that Dr. Chabra got very drunk. He complained bitterly to Evans about Alsace and the fifteen hundred dollar honoraria level all night. His wife was completely shocked and embarrassed by his behavior. When it came time to leave, Dr. Chabra tripped and fell over a chair. Obviously, he was in no condition to drive but he held the car keys tightly in his hands and would not give them up. The foul language used by Dr. Chabra upset several members of his staff who decided to leave early themselves. Evans and Mrs. Chabra tried in vain to wrestle away the car keys from the very inebriated doctor who cursed them both and actually tried to take a swing at Evans. Mrs. Chabra finally stormed out of the restaurant and took a taxi back home. Evans continued to hound Dr. Chabra all the way out into the parking lot begging him not to drive. Dr. Chabra would not listen, however. He got behind the wheel and drove away with tires squealing. It was the last time Evans would see Dr. Chabra alive because three blocks later he ran a red light and was broadsided by a city bus. Without a seatbelt, the impact threw Dr. Chabra head first over the air bag and through the windshield. He was killed instantly.

Evans learned of the tragic news the next morning as he watched the Channel 2 news. With a cold heart Evans thought, *At least he helped me exceed my sales quota for this year. Now I need to find a replacement to do my programs next year.*

YEAR 2

CHAPTER 7
AWARDS TRIP

Alsace Pharmaceuticals offered exciting awards programs for its top field sales representatives, District Managers, Regional and National Account Managers, and Directors. It was the envy of the industry according to reps that came to work for Alsace from other companies. The year that Jackson and Scott Evans both qualified, the awards trip was outstanding. Kurt Braden's Chicago District had done exceptionally well by growing their overall product sales one hundred and twenty-seven percent over the prior year. Jackson and Evans ran a close one-two, but Jackson ended up on top in the category that examined the growth of territory business over the assigned planned sales objective. Evans was excited to have earned the trip, but a rookie beat him out from within his own district by one percentage point. Evans was furious.

Alsace continued to raise its own standard for awards trips through the use of a Caribbean cruise during April as the reward for the top performers. A four-day, three night cruise of several Caribbean islands departing from San Juan, Puerto Rico was scheduled in the spring with Wind Surfer Cruise Lines. After sailing past the east end of the island, the ship would head due south for the ports of Philipsburg in St. Maarten and Gustavia in St. Barts. The vessel reserved for the trip was the *Wind Rider,* which looked more like a large yacht than a cruise ship. With five masts and seven decks, the *Wind Rider* measured 650 feet in length with a seventy-five foot beam. With a capacity for

325 passengers and a service crew of 175, it was the perfect ship for the awards trip because only the top 150 performers were invited to attend with their spouses or significant others.

The high ratio of service crew to Alsace employees ensured exceptional customer service during the cruise. The sales reps and Account Managers were assigned an ocean-view cabin while the Directors would be enjoying the luxury of one of the forty suites on board the *Wind Rider*. An open-air water sports platform, two pools, two hot tubs, a fitness center, a salon, and a day spa, would ensure plenty of pampering over the next four days. Evening entertainment would include two bands hired specifically by Alsace for the cruise to perform in the ship's lounge. It was common practice for most cruise ships to charge for alcoholic drinks, but since Alsace had reserved the entire ship for the awards trip, the company was picking up the tab for all food and beverage. Alsace ordered the casino to change out the monetary system to Monopoly bills so that everyone could enjoy some gambling for a few hours without the risk of losing their own hard earned cash. Upon boarding the ship, each couple received five one-hundred dollar bills in an unmarked envelope. They could spend it however they wanted either on board or at the two ports of call. After all, why should they have to spend they own money when they were the superstars? It would be an awesome cruise.

After their arrival in San Juan, Jackson and Lexi checked into the Marriott Hotel where the week would start with a one-day business meeting just for the Alsace employees to kick off the trip. Essentially, it amounted to nothing more than a sales performance overview and product pipeline presentation over a morning session. It allowed the company could pass the red face test by stating that the entire trip was business oriented. Jackson observed that the same exact slide presentations were shown that were used during the national sales meeting held in Orlando back in early February. In addition, the 150 market share growth award winner's performances were put up on the screen along with their pictures to serve as a reminder to everyone why they were in San Juan.

"You are the best of the best at Alsace," said CEO, Kevin Steer, as each individual was called up on stage. Steer shook their hands and thanked each award winner for their hard work just before posing for a picture that arrived in their rooms that evening placed inside a gold-plated frame along with a signed thank-you card from the CEO. He instilled enormous pride in the group.

Afterwards, the group was loaded onto buses for a tour of the Alsace manufacturing plant located just ten miles away.

Being a territory of the United States, Puerto Rico offered U.S. drug companies tremendous savings on manufacturing costs with cheap labor in addition to the federal government tax breaks for providing employment to the citizens of Puerto Rico. All the Big Pharma companies built sprawling manufacturing facilities on the island in order to take advantage of the minimum wages and federal tax incentives. Roughly 25,000 Puerto Ricans are employed by Big Pharma companies who operate manufacturing facilities for medicine production making the industry a huge employer for the country followed by the textile industry. Since Alsace's U.S. operations were headquartered in the earthquake haven of San Diego, it made sense for the company to have a back-up manufacturing plant outside the U.S. while keeping production costs low in order to ship their products throughout the world.

After the plant tour, Jackson and Lexi used the next several hours to explore historic Old San Juan, tour the fort, and shop. Although an island paradise, Puerto Rico is geographically small, only a hundred miles long by thirty-five miles wide or roughly three times the size of Rhode Island. A high percentage of its four million citizens are cramped into a few urban areas.

Except rum production, Puerto Rico had few natural resources of economic value. Their economy relied extensively on federal aid from the U.S. government, which in turn, relied on tax revenues from the U.S. manufacturing facilities. Because of these factors and limited employment opportunities, nearly twelve percent of the population could be found without jobs at any given point in time. As with any big city, San Juan had its share of crime. With a murder rate of twenty-five deaths for every 100,000 persons, bicycle-riding police wearing bulletproof vests could be seen patrolling the tourist areas.

"Jackson, isn't it reassuring that so many police officers patrol the Old Town area?" asked Lexi.

"Yes, it is. Even though we're in another country, it seems just like downtown Chicago," Jackson replied.

After a relaxing afternoon of enjoying the ocean breezes and warm tropical weather, Jackson and Lexi ended the day with a wonderful dinner of island food followed *Tres Leche.* On the way back to the hotel they shopped. They stopped in a cigar shop so Jackson could buy some Cohibas. Since the famous Cuban cigars are forbidden from importation and sale in the U.S., Jackson stocked up with a box to put in his humidor back home. Then they stopped in a boutique and Lexi purchased a half-dozen swimsuits, matching sarongs, and sandals. A new beach bag had to be bought as well.

"Jackson, you want me to look good walking from our cabin to the pool deck, don't you?" she asked.

"You know I do, honey," he replied. *She looks terrific!*

Later that night, they held hands while they sat on a dock at a hotel property just west of the Marriott and drank glasses of rum punch. They faced the beach where a steel drum band played on a stage and tourists danced in the sand. It was a festive atmosphere where Jackson and Lexi couldn't tell if it was tropical weather or the rum punch or the excitement of the trip gave them the warm glow that enveloped them. Lexi noticed that he watched her intently, and she broke into a wide, open smile.

"What are you looking at?" she asked.

"You. I love you."

After a romantic night, they awoke the next day to ready themselves for the cruise to St. Maarten. The awards ceremony for the employees and spouses was held the first day in a small theatre on board the ship. Kevin Steer served as the Master of Ceremonies, and as he announced the names of the Spot Stock winners, he also gave a short description of their sales and market share growth accomplishments that had earned them the trip. Pretty dry stuff except to the Type A personalities that filled the room. Winners, along with their guests, were invited onto the stage to receive their awards and to have a photo taken with the CEO. Lexi beamed with pride as Jackson accepted the six-inch statue of the spotty Dalmatian dog and stock grant paperwork.

"I'm so proud of you!" she exclaimed as they took their seats. "You have come so far in such a short time."

"I did have a good year. My doctors came through for me on every product." Jackson pointed at a row of seats, "Do you see that group of guys sitting in the middle section there? They're District Managers, and that's the next step up in the company. After that, it's the group over by the far wall, the Account Managers. They call on managed care plans and pharmacy benefits management organizations."

"Really? What kind of money do they make, and how many stock option grants do they get?" Lexi asked suddenly caught up in the opportunity for promotion.

"Those jobs all pay much more than I make now and have more chunks of stock options that go along with them. That's where I'm setting my goal. You know, Braden always says, 'Getting promoted matters above all else.'"

She lowered her voice and leaned over to him, "I guess I should be more patient with you on those nights when you're working late. I mean, if this is the kind of awards program and promotions that they offer, I guess that it's worth it. You understand that I miss spending time with you. Last night you were so attentive. You're not like that back home. You seem so distracted all the time."

"I know, Lexi. It's hard for me to turn off the work. I'll do better if last night is any indication of the Lexi Ford rewards program!" he promised.

After the program, the group filed out of the theatre and gathered for a cocktail reception in a large conference room where Evans and his guest approached Jackson and Lexi.

"Hey, Double D!" Evans said to Jackson. It was evident that he was quite drunk.

"Hi, Scott," Jackson replied. Turning he said, "This is my wife, Lexi."

Evans introduced his date whose name was Tori. Her hair tumbled down her back, and she moved like a dancer. As Lexi and Tori greeted each other, Evans leaned into Jackson and said, "She's twenty-two years old. She's basically the flavor of the month for me."

Evans then proposed a toast just for the four of them, "Here's to Double D and his Spot Stock award!"

"Hey, come on Scott. Don't call me that," Jackson retorted. He and Lexi didn't raise their glasses.

"Well, how about a toast to my Dr. Chabra! Without him I couldn't have brought in the big numbers to qualify for the trip!"

"Isn't he that physician who died in the car wreck?" asked Lexi.

"Yeah, he got all liquored up at a dinner meeting I had before Christmas, and then he smashed his car into a bus. His death is costing me market share growth this year," said Evans sarcastically.

Jackson and Lexi couldn't wait to get away from Evans and Tori.

Later that night in the ship's casino, Lexi was troubled. "Jackson, I don't like that Scott Evans. His little date looks like a stripper." She paused before continuing, "I want to know something. Why did he keep calling you Double D?"

"Don't pay any attention to him," Jackson replied trying to brush off the question.

"Answer me. I want to know why he called you Double D!"

"There's this type of program called a Dine and Dash that I used a lot to help me get access to physicians and grow my market share," he started.

"What's a Dine and Dash? Is that what Double D stands for?" she asked.

"Yes. I would arrange with certain restaurants so doctors and their staff stop by after office hours and pick up some dinner for their families on their way home courtesy of Alsace. Sometimes I'd be there to greet them and give them a short promotional spiel on one of our products, but oftentimes, not," he explained.

"How many of these Dine and Dashes did you do?"

"I spent over $30,000 of my Promotional Budget."

"Are you kidding me? Is that even ethical?"

He hesitated, "Braden approved them."

"I didn't ask if Braden approved them, I asked if they were ethical!" she exclaimed.

"They may not be totally ethical, Lexi. But they sure were effective in driving sales! Look where we are! I made the cruise trip after my first full year on territory! That doesn't happen every day. Remember how Braden told me that the Region Sales Director wanted to look for ways to promote me? I'm getting noticed, Lexi! The Dine and Dashes helped get me noticed!"

"I appreciate the trip, but you've got to do it ethically."

"Hey, if it was totally out of bounds I'm sure Braden would have said something."

Lexi thought for a moment, "Well, I guess you're right."

At that moment Steer happened to stop by. "Jackson, congratulations again! He's quite a performer, Lexi. You're a lucky woman."

Jackson beamed with pride, as he stood tall by Lexi's side.

It turned out to be a wonderful trip with perfect Caribbean weather each day. Jackson and Lexi were convinced that Alsace Pharmaceuticals was the greatest company in the world.

Within six months of returning from San Juan, both Jackson and Evans received their first promotions. The golden boys were on their way. One fact that would not be forgotten by Evans was that Jackson was notified of his promotion exactly one week before he was.

That weekend, Jackson bought Lexi a bracelet designed by Patricia Locke, and then they went out to dinner to celebrate his promotion at the Rosebud Café, a great little Italian restaurant in the Little Italy section of Chicago. They talked about how they could not wait to move out of the tiny apartment and away from the steel mills of northwest Indiana.

YEARS 3-8

CHAPTER 8
BUSINESS MANAGER

Jackson received his first promotion with Alsace Pharmaceuticals to a newly created position of Business Manager, which was to be located within a brand new division of the company. With the launch of a new Proton Pump Inhibitor medicine, LOMEC, for gastric ulcers and erosive esophagitis, Alsace needed an entirely new sales force called the LOMEC division that was to be deployed to promote to the gastro-intestinal therapeutic market. The company intended to roll out a new vertically integrated business model where much of the marketing and promotional strategy, training, budgets, programs, and personnel decision-making would take place within the sixteen regional business unit centers located in large metropolitan statistical areas or MSAs around the country. This would be completely opposite of the normal corporate decision-making process at Alsace that typically followed a strictly regimented central command structure that flowed from headquarters in San Diego to the field sales force.

The regional business unit centers, or BUs, were designed to have a large number of mid-level managers reporting to a BU Director as well as the supporting field sales representatives. The middle manager positions included a Training Manager, Customer Service Manager, Marketing Manager, Business Analyst, Regional Accounts Manager, and a Business Manager. Jackson's job as a Business Manager was essentially a combination of responsibilities between a District Sales Manager and a Business Planner so Jackson not only managed eight pharmaceutical sales representatives, but also did the strategic planning for the BU. Ultimately, the Director had final authority and responsibility for all aspects of the Business Unit, but there was tremendous autonomy with his position, and Jackson loved it. This was truly going to help fast track him within the Alsace organization as Jackson was the only one of his peers at the BU that came directly from a field sales position. He did not have to go through one or two different developmental loop positions before landing a sales management position that allowed him to directly manage field sales representatives. This made his promotion all the more special, but it drew the envy of his peers.

The promotion meant a move from Chicago to Kansas City, however, which was a downside of the new job in Lexi's mind since the relocation would obviously take them further away from their parents and Chicago. She and Jackson had never been to Kansas City before.

"The only city I know of between Chicago and LA is Las Vegas! You want me to move to a Cow Town with no shopping, no museums, and no culture? Isn't there a similar position here in Chicago or maybe back in Indianapolis?"

"No. There isn't," he started. "It will be OK, honey. With the relocation package that Alsace is offering we'll be able to buy our first house! They're paying for all the moving expenses, five thousand dollars toward a down payment, up to three points at closing, all the other closing costs, and two months extra salary to help with getting started with new home furnishings," Jackson said assuredly as he wrapped his arms around her.

Lexi did want a house badly and to move out of the Gary area. With the promotion and house, as well as the increase in Jackson's salary, she could finally stop working and start a family.

"Jackson, in this new job do you think that we'll be available to spend more time together? You know once we have a baby, you've got to be a good dad, and that means time."

Jackson promised her that he would be around more.

The three-day house-hunting trip to Kansas City was scheduled for the end of November. The temperatures in KC were mild compared to Chicago where an arctic blast was blowing out of the northeast off Lake Michigan when they flew out of the O'Hare airport to the Kansas City International airport. Since Jackson had just recently visited Kansas City a couple of times for business meetings with his Director and management team, he developed a plan to win over Lexi. He rented a premium car from Hertz and booked a room at the InterContinental hotel. The InterContinental was located on Brush Creek in the renowned Country Club Plaza district of Kansas City, which was the premier shopping area of the city of fountains.

At check-in, the concierge explained to Jackson and Lexi, "Seville, Spain is the sister city of Kansas City. You can see evidence of this by all the fountains and Spanish architecture that are found in the Plaza area."

The Nelson Art Gallery was located just a few blocks from the Ritz, and it was their first stop. Although not as grand as the Art Institute in Chicago, Lexi thought, *The art collection is certainly impressive.*

Jackson and Lexi walked and window-shopped through the Plaza in the afternoon. Lexi was entranced.

At precisely 4:00 PM, they were back at the InterContinental for high tea. Lexi noticed that the other ladies were dressed to the nines for the event. Many even wore hats. *Pretty classy,* she thought. Slowly the apprehension of the pending relocation faded.

After tea, they stopped in the lobby to admire the craftsmanship of the pastry chef who was putting the final touches on a life-sized gingerbread house baked and assembled right in the hotel kitchen. He broke off a couple of pieces of candy and handed them to Jackson. There were a number of children in the lobby as well visiting with Santa and lining up to get a piece of the gingerbread house.

After a steak dinner that night at the five-star restaurant called Plaza III, Jackson and Lexi returned to their hotel room and stood out on the balcony that overlooked the Plaza. A huge crowd had gathered all through the streets to attend the annual Christmas lighting ceremony. At exactly nine o'clock, when the lights were switched on, they were amazed to see that all the buildings in the Plaza area were outlined in white lights.

"It is so beautiful. OK, I can live here now," Lexi announced.

Jackson had turned her around. *I love it when a plan comes together,* he thought. They went back inside their room and switched off all the lights leaving the curtains open. They stayed up until the Plaza lights went off just before the sunrise.

They built a home in Overland Park, Kansas just five minutes from the BU office. While their home was being constructed, Alsace put Jackson and Lexi up at the Marriott Residence Inn for three months with all expenses paid. They banked his salary and picked out new furniture and accessories at a local Ethan Allen store. Lexi ordered hardwood kitchen floors, marble countertops, tiled bathrooms, upgraded carpeting, faux painting, and wallpaper directly from the builder.

At lunch after the house closing, Lexi remarked in a dead serious voice, "I've got a secret, Jackson, and I wanted to wait until we closed on the new house to share it."

"What is it, honey?" Jackson asked with a curious look on his face.

"We're going to have a baby!" she exclaimed. Some of the other customers looked over at the couple and began to applaud.

"What?" Jackson's eyes were wide with amazement.

"I bought an Early Pregnancy Test kit yesterday while you were at the office and took it this morning while you were in the lobby buying a newspaper and coffee. The test was pink, Jackson! We're going to have a baby!"

"I'm thrilled!" he said excitedly.

"I've been dying to tell you all morning, but I wanted to wait until after the closing to tell you. Isn't this exciting? I can't wait to call our parents!"

Jackson stood up and walked around to Lexi. He bent down on one knee and hugged her. "I love you so much, Lexi. You're going to be a good mom."

Lexi cried when she heard his last remark.

The Vice President of Sales for the new LOMEC division was Matt York. York was a long time Alsace employee who previously had been a Region Sales Director in Dallas for the hospital sales division and had held a number of marketing positions in headquarters prior to his promotion to VP. He was tasked by the CEO, Kevin Steer, to implement the new company business model within the LOMEC division. It would be a pilot program to test a vertically integrated business structure to determine if it would be appropriate within other divisions, and Steer arranged for an open checkbook to be made available to York from the Finance department in order to fund the new division.

York was a touchy, feely manager. He was interested in how people felt and what they thought as they went about the process of selling Alsace products. Because of his style, the sales reps and managers that reported to York loved him. They would take a bullet for the guy, and because of the love-fest factor, they responded and put up big sales numbers, which made York a god-like figure in the Company. The Executive Oversight Committee loved the sales performance as well. The EOC knew as well that the kind of loyalty that York generated was generally unheard of in the competitive business of Big Pharma, but he was truly a master of fielding the feelings and nailing the numbers.

York was also big on teams and teamwork. His first order of business was to fly all sixteen BUs, four at a time, to Flagstaff, Arizona for a four-day team-building seminar. He believed that if everyone liked each other and understood each other's backgrounds and motivations, they would then learn to rely on each other, and sales would skyrocket.

"When they leave the seminar, this cohesive group of sales reps and managers will drive LOMEC sales to the coveted one billion dollar blockbuster status," York promised the EOC and Steer.

In the mountains just south of Flagstaff, a huge, sprawling ranch was nestled in the Prescott Valley. The core business of Prescott

Valley, Ltd. centered on helping organizations develop a business culture of innovation and excitement. Employees were empowered to leverage their strengths, improve communication skills, and take initiative. Their business model was to bring in a variety of companies from several industries for a weeklong seminar. Never before in the long history of the Prescott Valley Company were the participants from just a single industry, let alone a single company like Alsace. With York's influence and a grant check for five million dollars, the Prescott Valley Company agreed to take on the task of teaching their team-centered business culture solely to his new LOMEC sales division. The Prescott group was charged with leading the Alsace teams through a series of modules that focused on the Company's business objectives and customer service as well as the implementation of certain business initiatives. The modules were designed to help the Alsace teams better understand each other. Personal fears, motivations, aspirations, communication styles, and personal challenges were all to be explored during the weeklong experience. Mostly, the Prescott Valley instructors were to focus the Alsace teams on working together toward a common goal of winning in the upcoming LOMEC product launch process.

The ranch had a southwestern mining camp look and feel to it with cabins that slept four persons to a room, but that also included all the amenities that you would find at a condo in Aspen. There was little roughing it here. Hot tubs, mini bars, cable TV, high speed internet, expensive hand soaps and lotions, and fruit baskets that made the Alsace employees feel very comfortable and pampered even though they had roommates for the first time ever in their careers with the Company. Of course, this was an integral part of the Prescott Valley program design that would help with the LOMEC sales division team building and communication process. A separate lodge building where all the meals were served was reminiscent of a five-star restaurant. Four large buildings located near the lodge were designed like classrooms for purposes of teaching the all-important modules to the participants.

The centerpiece of Prescott Valley experience was the Ropes Course area. Spread out over twenty acres, the Ropes Course was a series of physically challenging stations that would most likely be found at an Army boot camp. Each station was designed to teach teamwork, overcome fear, discover inner strengths, and instill confidence. The first station was a five-foot tall wooden wall that had steps leading to the top. A participant was asked to climb to the top of the wall, walk to the center, and turn their back to their teammates who were all gathered below. The group then formed two lines facing each other and interlocked their arms in order to form a human net. A safety check was mandatory for this station and consisted of the participant calling out, "Spotters ready?" When an affirmative response was returned, the participant then fell backwards off the wall and into his or her teammates' arms for a safe, gentle landing. A mighty cheer usually went up by the teammates after setting the daredevil back on his or her feet.

The stations gradually became increasingly more difficult over time, challenging both the fear, skill, and courage of the participants. The fifty-foot team rock-climbing wall was especially challenging when three participants were tethered together and asked to ring the bell at the top of the cliff. The forty-foot telephone pole climb was also interesting particularly when the two teammates had to climb up together where they were then asked to stand together atop the pole and jump off into mid-air in order to ring a bell that was suspended five feet away. The belay lines and carabineers assured the ultimate safety of the jumpers.

The final team building challenge came at the station known as the zip line. After climbing a trail up a narrow three hundred foot cliff, the participants peered over the side to see a spectacular view of the Prescott Valley creek and a zip line or cable that hung suspended from the top of the cliff, extended over the creek, and came to an end over five hundred feet away on the other side. A huge football-tackling dummy provided padding at the stopping zone of the zip line on the other side of the creek as well as a team of spotters. The purpose of this station was to help the participants overcome the fear of heights.

After the two teammates were strapped in with double redundancy safety harnesses, they were whisked away down the zip line, over the creek, to their waiting teammates who again formed a huge human safety net designed to catch the flying daredevils. Most of the zip line participants screamed at the tops of their lungs but also exclaimed, "I want to do that one again!" just after they landed.

After the evening classroom sessions concluded, the lodge was transformed into a huge bar where cocktails and snacks were served and a high-tech stereo system blasted out the latest pop music for those who wanted to shake it up on the dance floor. With their newfound courage and improved communication skills, many teammates did just that. In fact, the brave ones grabbed several bottles of their favorite libation and headed off for the hot tubs where they got to thank their teammates in a more intimate setting.

With newfound courage, communication, and leadership skills, the new LOMEC sales force was ready for the ultimate battle of launching the new therapeutic agent and bringing ulcer relief to millions of patients not to mention billions of dollars in profit to Alsace. The Prescott Valley experience would pay dividends to the Alsace stockholders like never before. York beamed with pride as he shook hands and presented each participant with a piece of rock taken from zip line cliff. It would become a symbol of unity among the LOMEC sales force for years to come.

The launch of LOMEC as a new therapeutic medicine for the treatment of ulcers was going to be significant milestone event for Alsace Pharmaceuticals. The medicine promised to bring new revenues sorely needed by the organization to ensure continued profitability growth for the Company and the funding of key research projects currently under development. If blockbuster status could be achieved early in the product life cycle, then many financial sins could be covered up before outside auditors uncovered them. The Prescott Valley experience was crucial to set the tone for the new sales force working within an untested business model of teamwork, communication, integration, and collaboration. Product launch meetings were always an essential component of the sales motivation process at Alsace. They served to introduce the product and instill confidence in the clinical data. The launch meetings also served to introduce the brand strategy and promotional tactics that would help the reps sell the new medicine to the high-ranking physicians within each territory. Matt York and the LOMEC marketing team were not going to let the new sales force down when it came to getting the reps prepared and excited about the launching the new drug. The open checkbook promise from Finance was still available to York as he and the management team hosted the launch meeting.

The Hilton Hawaiian Village Resort in Honolulu was selected as the launch site, and Alsace rented out the entire resort. The four-day meeting was timed so that persons traveling from the Midwest and east coast regions could either tag on an additional few days before or after the meeting for vacation time. Spouses or significant others could attend and stay in the hotel room as long as they paid for their own airfare and meals. Of the 625 reps, managers, and directors who worked in some capacity for the LOMEC sales force, over half of the personnel brought a guest, and some even brought kids that stayed in the hotel room as well. Jackson came alone to Honolulu. Lexi was experiencing a difficult pregnancy so her doctor advised her not to travel, especially not with an eight-hour flight one way to Hawaii. She was sorely disappointed about not being able to go with Jackson.

I'm going to have to bring Lexi back a nice present to show her that I was thinking of her, Jackson thought. He called every night and during all the bathroom breaks to check on her. He missed her, and wished she could have made the trip.

The excitement level was high right from the minute the reps departed the airport transfer buses dropping them at the Hilton all the way through to the last presentation.

Camera crews pulled employees from the check-in lines at registration or stopped them in the hallways to interview them, and later in the week, the same tapes were edited and shown at the wrap-up ceremony. Who wouldn't get excited about seeing oneself on the big screen?

No expense was spared for the giveaways for the LOMEC sales force. Tommy Bahama sports shirts, Swiss Army watches, Ray Ban sunglasses, and Mont Blanc pens were just some examples of the gifts left each night in each team member's room with a little note from either some member of the marketing team or Matt York. The events each evening featured a reception or formal dinner where special acts were brought in: Bill Cosby, Jay Leno, Sheryl Crow, and Huey Lewis all entertained the Alsace sales force. The final night included a huge beach party that featured the Million Dollar Quartet as the entertainment. Booths were set up along the beach for the employees to play arcade games, get henna tattoos, learn magic tricks, or have a character drawing.

The buffet lines were outstanding. Each night a different theme was set up for food and beverages: Mardi Gras, Seafood, Western B-B-Q, and, of course, a luau on the last night. Everybody wore leis on the final night. Some of the single reps exchanged leis with newfound partners in their single-occupancy rooms later in the evening. It must have all been in the spirit of teamwork and cooperation that was instilled during the Prescott Valley trips. It certainly could not have been all the rum Mai Tais.

The three days of marketing presentations were the same boring run-of-the-mill grind. From 8:00 AM to 5:30 PM everyday it was the same boring agenda of presentation after presentation. Fifteen-minute breaks were taken at precisely 10:00 AM and 3:00 PM with an hour for lunch at noon sharp. You could set your new Swiss Army watch by it. Brand strategy, clinical overview, prescribing information, promotional strategy, product features and benefits, promotional sequencing, patient types, managed care strategy, contracting strategy, and market development were all mind-numbing components of the presentations made by the marketing managers. If razor blades had been included in the training binders or as a nightly giveaway, there probably would have been several 911 calls made. The ultimate torture was the dreaded Doc Detailing on the last day, which was used to ensure appropriate learning of the new promotional messages in a role-play setting. The reps hated it with a passion.

Thank God for the free liquor every night, Jackson thought.

Jackson met a new friend at the LOMEC launch meeting. Tam Martin was a Regional Account Manager assigned to the Tampa Business Unit. Tam had a slim, wild beauty and was tall. She turned heads whenever she walked into a room.

Although she would run most mornings, her true love was roller blading. As she traveled throughout the southeast calling on the local managed care plans, her roller blades were a part of her luggage so that she could get in a workout in the late afternoons. Wearing just a sports bra workout top and short shorts, Tam could be found roller blading for up to an hour on most days. Of course, Honolulu offered the perfect setting for her sport with the wide sidewalks along Waikiki Beach.

Jackson and Tam met at the opening reception while standing in line at one of the many bars set up around the pool. They discovered that they were both married, had the same tenure with Alsace, and were each newly promoted to their respective jobs. Since neither had brought their spouse to the meeting, they hit it off from the start and got to know each other better over the four days by sitting together during the marketing sessions and meals. They even went running on a couple of mornings.

Although others in the company didn't seem to play by the same rule, Jackson would often think to himself, *Don't dip the company pen in the company inkwell.* Jackson and Tam would become very close friends over the next several years because they were selected to be representatives on two important headquarters-based task forces for Alsace. One was the managed care task force, and the other was the hospital integration task force. They saw each other nearly every month in San Diego as participants on the task forces.

Just when the motivation barometer was nearly at zero because of the marketing presentations and Doc Detailing, York surprised the sales force with an afternoon of fun on the last day. Of course, he had it planned all along, but he wanted the crowd to know that he knew the meaning of "I feel your pain!" The sales force were given their choice of golf, surfing, boogie boarding, hiking up Diamond Head crater, spa activities, a jeep tour of Oahu, or a visit to Pearl Harbor complete with a tour of the USS Arizona Memorial. Cheers erupted at the announcement. One row down in the front even did the wave. York had the gift for getting loyalty and high performance from his teams. The LOMEC sales force loved him and probably would have followed him off the lookout bunker at the top of Diamond Head crater if he had asked them. Of course, York wasn't going to demand that, he simply asked for a 150% effort from the sales force when they sold LOMEC in order to push it to blockbuster status. He closed the meeting by thanking them in advance for what he knew would be a Herculean effort on their part.

When Jackson returned from Honolulu he stopped and bought flowers and a card for Lexi on his drive home from the KCI airport to go with the fourteen-karat gold bracelet that he bought in Hawaii. He missed her terribly.

CHAPTER 9
KANSAS CITY

Their house was built in a gated subdivision in southern Overland Park. It was a tight-knit community. There were over 100,000 people in Johnson County and they took great pride in having affordable housing, a low crime rate, and the best public schools in Kansas. The home was a 2,800 square foot, four-bedroom home with a finished basement and fenced yard. Lexi selected every finish that was installed in the home. They poured every dollar of Jackson's bonus checks into furnishing the house with art, window treatments, extensive landscaping, and a small lap pool.

After the promotion to Business Manager, Jackson and Lexi's life seemed to be going exactly in the direction that one would expect when working in Big Pharma. With the move to Kansas City, Lexi had quit working in the communications industry and began working on their family and home life. The pregnancy did not come easy for Lexi. Because of complications, she was forced to spend the last four months in bed to ensure a viable delivery of their son, Jake. Upon his arrival, they were both thrilled. Lexi became very serious about her role as a homemaker and parent. Over the years she planned and hosted elaborate birthday, Halloween, and Christmas parties for little Jake. And she did it all alone.

Jackson worked long hours at the office, and he also traveled extensively. He was responsible for managing eight sales representatives, but the two assignments to the headquarters-based task forces took him out to San Diego at least once a month. He loved the exposure and experience, but on top of his regular long hours this additional time away from home didn't make Lexi happy. She missed

Jackson and wanted to spend more time with him away from Alsace and his sales representatives. She felt as if their home was constantly being invaded by the company, especially when the reps would call and interrupt their dinner with their mundane questions about some stupid promotional giveaway item or program.

It's bad enough that Jackson just sits in his chair reading his emails while we're watching TV every night. But to have these reps calling at all hours is ludicrous! she thought. She soon felt super-neglected by Jackson. *Shopping with Little Jake at Town Center Mall just doesn't cut it anymore.*

"Jackson, we need to talk. Can you take a break?" Lexi asked.

"Yeah OK, just let me just close out my email program," Jackson responded with an irritated tone.

Knowing that the following conversation was not going to be any fun, Jack finally finished shutting down his laptop and said, "OK. What's up?"

"I'm angry about all the time you spend away from Jake and me. You travel with your reps, you travel to San Diego, you spend long hours in that office, and you bring work home on weekends!" She paused to catch her breath before she asked the obvious question, "When are you ever going to spend time with us?"

"Lexi, why do you think I'm doing this? It's all about doing a good job, getting promoted, and making more bonus money. I'm doing this for us, honey," Jackson explained. *Why doesn't she understand? Why doesn't she get it?* "I'm doing so well at work. My Director loves me, my reps love him, and I get along well with my peers."

"I know you think that you are doing this for us, Jackson, but where does the 'us' fit in with your work schedule? Look at you right now! You sit there in your chair during 'our time' and check your email! You pay hardly any attention to Jake or me, and just because you clean the bathrooms and wash the dishes, you think you're a real part of this family." She was exasperated.

"These long hours are temporary. Once I get my systems and processes down, I promise my schedule will ease up," said Jackson. He secretly hoped that what he said was true. The reality was that he had no control whatsoever over his own schedule. He had his reps, his Director, and home office managers all pulling at him for his time.

"That's what you said as a sales rep, and you never stopped working at night or on weekends. This company will take from you what you allow them to take. They don't care. It's like any other company where you are their property to use as they want, and when they tire of you, they throw you out."

"That's not true, Lexi, Alsace is different. Matt York is a family-oriented guy. At meetings, he is always telling stories about his wife and kids and reminding us that family is number one at Alsace. Remember last year's Fortune Magazine where Alsace rated very highly for the 'ability to attract, recruit, and retain employees?' Well, you just don't get that kind of recognition by throwing away your most valuable asset, your employees."

"Jackson, you're so full of the company line it makes me sick."

Jackson tried for a compromise, "OK, how about if I tell my team not to call me here at the house after dinner anymore?"

Realizing that there was no real good solution, Lexi gave in a bit initially, "Well, that would be a start. But you have got to do more than just show up around here like a Disney Dad where you just entertain Jake and do what I tell you to do. You've got to think on your own and be a team player! Didn't you learn anything during that Prescott Valley trip? Or does that only work with other Alsace employees and not with your own wife?"

"OK, I will. I promise," he said. And he meant it at the time.

One day it happened. A story broke in the news that described marijuana use in the middle school located right in their subdivision. Lexi was shocked, and she vowed that day to send Jake to Catholic school. As it happened, their parish, St. Peter's, was building a new church and school located just two miles away from their home. Knowing that it was very competitive to get into Catholic schools, and with Jackson traveling all the time, Lexi assumed the responsibility of making sure that Jake got into St. Peter's. Since the Catholic schools in the area essentially looked at either a family's financial contributions to the parish or time spent involved with committees, Lexi quickly became a member of the school advisory board and PTO before the school opened. With the help of two other moms, she volunteered to start the library because it wasn't in the school budget initially to hire a librarian or fund a media center. She also worked as a room mom in all of Jake's classes and built a close circle of friends for their social life. St. Peter's and the school became the focal point of her life with little Jake in the center. Because of Jackson's demanding schedule, Lexi created her own life with her volunteer work at Jake's school and with a close group of girlfriends, but she still felt alone.

As the years went by and as Jake got older, Lexi was determined to get Jackson connected with his family. She demanded that Jackson get involved with church committees and school activities. With the little time he had away from Alsace and to get her off his back, Jackson became a member of the school fund raising committee. He also helped as an assistant soccer and basketball coach, and was the Pack Leader for the Cub Scouts. He figured as long as he showed up, Lexi would leave him alone. However, he joined the Knights of Columbus on his own because so many of his buddies were active members. After progressing through the ranks to become a Third Degree Knight, Jackson was officially given the combination to the lock that secured the beer in the refrigerator located in the Parish Center. He was favored for this honor because he would frequently bring left over beverages like beer and wine from his sales representative's dinner programs. So his donations made him the unofficial Sergeant-At-Arms of the Knights of Columbus beer fridge. Because of his K of C membership and important title, he earned the right to have one night out with the boys each month, even though it was only to the church basement for a business meeting and some major beer drinking.

Throughout young Jake's elementary school years, there was one annual fund raising event for the St. Peter's Cub Scout Pack that was highly anticipated throughout the year. It was known as Chili Bingo. Chili Bingo was a dinner function that helped the Cub Scout Pack raise money to pay for their camping trips, uniforms, books, and awards. It typically raised over ten thousand dollars in profits for the Pack. The fathers would get nearly all the food, beverages, and prizes donated from local businesses so they could maximize the profits from the sale of the items. Using the Parish Center's kitchen facilities, the men put on a feast that included hot dogs, chili, hamburgers, chips, beans, and desserts that would make any Kansas City Chiefs tailgate party aficionado proud.

Of course, being good Catholics they had the bingo component down to a science to maximize the income on the fundraising side of the event. Games like 50-50, four corners, diagonals, and worst bingo card were just of few of the popular games that everyone tried like crazy to win. It was basically a legalized gambling opportunity that brought out the hard-core Catholics who played with a vengeance. With a parish size of over 2,000 families and the event always the weekend before the Super Bowl when there was basically nothing else going on, the Pack leaders found that they always sold out the event at least two weeks ahead of time. The St. Peter's Church Finance Committee was interested as well in the final money count after Chili Bingo ended because they had their fingers in the Scout's pot for a mandatory twenty percent donation back to the Church for the free use of the Parish Center. With the obligatory Catholic guilt component, the Pack Leaders were only too happy to comply with the unwritten policy.

The only thing that would have made Chili Bingo an even greater success would have been the permission to sell beer. But because it was a Cub Scout sanctioned program, the sale of beer was not permitted. There was to be no alcohol served at Scout programs. The program would typically conclude around 10:00 PM whereupon the moms would all take their little Scouts home and put them to bed. A group of dads were responsible for the cleanup duties, and that's when the beer came out. Cleanup didn't take very long since the Tiger Cubs, Bears, Wolves, and Webelos dens always had done a great job earlier in the evening. So, after the floor was mopped, the rest of the night became a beer drinking session in the Parish Center. Jackson loved this part. He worked his butt off leading up to and including the night of Chili Bingo. The way he figured was that he and his buddies had earned the right to unwind and kick back. He typically rolled in around three o'clock in the morning and slept in until it was time to go to the eleven o'clock Mass.

After one particular Mass service, Lexi lit into Jackson while Jake was in the backyard playing in the snow.

"Three o'clock in the morning! Did it actually take five hours to clean up?"

"Look, I'm hung over and not in the mood for this conversation," Jackson replied calmly.

"Well, you better get in the mood because I'm not taking this from you anymore. You either change your ways or you can move out!" Lexi screamed.

"Ah, come on Lexi. I'm doing what you want me to do. I'm involved at school and at church. I practically managed that whole Chili Bingo function!"

"Jackson, what you do is nothing more than a show for our friends. You go to these things because you think it makes you think it makes you look like a good corporate citizen. You bring Jake and me along because we make you look good. So that people will think, 'Man, that Jackson Ford has the perfect little family, and the perfect job, and he's just got it all!' You don't want to be at church or with us for that matter. I truly believe that you'd be content to go to work every day and not have to worry about all the messy stuff that makes up what life is all about!"

"Now that is not true, Lexi," Jackson lied. *She actually hit the nail on the head. I'd be happy as hell to just go do my job. It's challenging, it's interesting, and I get all kinds of positive reinforcement. I don't get anything but grief here at home.*

"We're going to go to see a marriage counselor this week. This relationship is going to get fixed, and you're going to start keeping your promises."

"OK, honey," Jackson agreed. Maybe this would calm her down somewhat. "May I just suggest that we try for a Saturday appointment because my schedule this week is pretty full, and I have to go to San Diego for two days."

Lexi hit the roof.

The following Saturday morning, Jackson and Lexi sat in the office of Brian Thomas, Ph. D, whose specialty was family and marriage counseling. Jackson found him on the Alsace Human Resources Benefits website. Dr. Thomas was in the network of approved providers, which meant that the company health insurance plan would pick up eighty percent of his usual and customary fees. Since his professional hourly rate of forty-five minutes was $100, Jackson and Lexi were only responsible for a twenty dollar out-of-pocket charge for each counseling session with a maximum of thirty sessions annually. Jackson was so proud of himself for staying in the provider network, but more importantly, for finding a guy counselor instead some uptight woman who would probably side with Lexi no matter what he said or did. Over a series of counseling sessions, Jackson said all the right things and made all the right promises to smooth things over with Lexi. But back at home things were pretty much as they always were. Jackson would work long hours at the office, bring work home, take calls from reps during dinner, and check his emails while he watched TV with Lexi.

One night after Lexi had spent the better part of the afternoon making lasagna for dinner, which was Jackson's favorite meal, he suddenly announced, "I'm going to have to eat quick because I need to get over to the driving range to practice my swing. I've got a golf tournament tomorrow morning, a scramble actually, with two key doctors and my rep. I'll wash the dishes when I get home."

"It would be nice, Jackson, if you would let me know farther ahead of time if we need a fast meal because of your schedule or if I can make a full course meal like I did tonight. I worked hard on this today, and I was looking forward to a nice relaxing dinner with you!" Lexi said tersely.

"Honey, the lasagna looks great, and I can hardly wait to eat it, but I don't want to look like an idiot tomorrow in front of these customers. I've got a slight hook in my swing path that I want to work out."

"That's just great, Jackson. Don't put your family ahead of your golf game."

After he rushed through his meal, Jackson left the house and spent the next two hours hitting golf balls at the range, at the bunker practice area, and at the putting green before he returned home.

"Nothing ever changes!" Lexi would complain to her girlfriends.

"Why don't you leave him?" they would ask.

"Because I feel so trapped. Jackson has a good job, he makes good money, we've got life and health insurance, my son is in private school, we've got like a zillion stock options, and I've been out of the work force for almost seven years! Who's going to hire me? How can I make it on my own? He's not a drunk, he doesn't do drugs, he doesn't fool around that I can tell, and he doesn't beat me. I don't have to work, and I get to spend my day with my son. Compared to what could be, I've got it pretty good. But I feel stuck with a husband who pays so much more attention to his work and his sales reps than his family." Over time, Lexi sank into a funk.

Over the next few years, Jackson continued to remain busy on many fronts. Of course, his responsibilities at Alsace kept him very occupied, but he continued to serve in the church and volunteer at Jake's school. In reality, however, he was just going through the motions while at the church and school activities. His whole self-image became wrapped up in Alsace, and his desire to move up in the Company was his primary motivation. His marriage and passion for Lexi were not what they once were. Alsace was the sole focus in his life.

He did, however, find a new focal point from a personal relationship standpoint. Since Tam Martin and Jackson were appointed to the same two task forces, they saw each other at meetings in San Diego at least once a month. There they would sit together in the group meetings and plan strategies and tactics that were adopted by the various marketing teams and implemented by the field sales force. It was a platonic relationship, but it did involve a number of dinners, runs, and long telephone conversations about business events and the sharing of secrets from their personal lives. Over time, Jackson and Tam discovered that they were attracted to each other for completely opposite reasons.

She's just a great person to be able to talk about Alsace and business events within the Company. She also understands my career motivations, unlike Lexi, he thought.

Tam's attraction to Jackson, however, was motivated by his potential upward mobility in the Company and his handsome features. *Here is a guy that will be moving up quickly within Alsace. He also has unlimited career potential, unlike my husband who works in the family paving business. It's too bad that he's married because he is so good looking, and I have a hard time controlling myself when he's near me,* she admitted to herself.

YEARS 9-12

CHAPTER 10
NATIONAL ACCOUNTS

The National Accounts department announced an opening in early May for a National Account Manager position. This individual would be responsible for the federal market that included the Department of Veterans Affairs health system and the Department of Defense Medical Centers. All of the NAMs reported to Rick Thompson, Director, whose office was located in the Alsace headquarters in San Diego. As a Business Manager, Jackson had developed an impeccable record of sales performance and people management skills. His sales representatives consistently exceeded their planned sales objectives, and along the way, Jackson developed two representatives for promotions into developmental loop positions based in other Alsace sales divisions. In addition, he showed superior leadership skills working successfully with his reps to get LOMEC on formulary at all of the VA Medical Centers and Military Treatment Centers within his district. Specifically, the big formulary wins at Fort Leonard Wood Army base, Fort Riley Army base, and the three Air Force bases: McConnell, Offutt, and Whiteman, helped put his LOMEC sales over the top each year. The significant number of retired military personnel who stayed within the catchment areas surrounding the bases in order to use the military hospitals as their primary care centers became a great feeder pool of potential patients with gastrointestinal diseases. This made them perfect candidates for LOMEC therapy. Jackson recognized this early in the launch process for the drug, and took advantage of the sales opportunity. Other districts were either slow to respond or had poor working knowledge of the Federal market opportunity. Unlike Jackson, they didn't know how to work within the unique formulary system for each hospital.

Because of his sales success within his own District's Federal segment, Jackson was uniquely qualified to interview for the NAM opening. It also did not hurt in the decision-making process that Kevin Steer was once stationed at Offutt Air Force base, the former home to the Strategic Air Command or SAC. Steer had a soft spot for Offutt AFB, and he watched the sales numbers each month for the hospital and was pleased with the results. Jackson prepped for two days and spent several hours with his Business Unit Director conducting mock interviews. He was overly prepared for any question; he even had extra copies of his brag book at the ready. The brag book was a three ring binder that employees prepared prior to important interviews. It included copies of their current resume, sales performance records, annual evaluations forms, and specific accomplishments that would most likely be discussed during the interview process. Jackson had his charts and graphs all organized and printed in color for high visual impact. His Director called Thompson three days prior to his interview and he gave Jackson a glowing recommendation.

The discussion that Jackson was not fully prepped for was the one he had at home with Lexi a week before he was scheduled to fly out to San Diego for his interviews with Thompson.

"Jackson, you need to explain to me why you want this job"

"Honey, I've been *asked* to interview for this NAM position. The company and Rick Thompson have been impressed with my performance over the last several years as a Business Manager. Specifically, they like the skills and knowledge I've developed in the federal market. Plus, my participation on the managed care task force and the hospital marketing task force over the last several years has broadened out my strategic planning skills and contacts within headquarters. These are two key areas that they look at when they look at skill sets. The interview for a National Accounts position is a major step in my career!" Jackson was excited now. "The current NAMs have had to get experience as Regional Accounts Managers and District Managers first before they were even considered for interviews for a NAM position. It's like the company has a high confidence level in me to be able to skip over the RAM job and go straight to National Accounts, just like I was able to skip over jobs in the developmental loop and go straight to a Business Manager position and manage sales representatives. This kind of stuff doesn't happen every day at a big company like Alsace."

"Jackson, you know I'm proud of you. You're good at what you do. But you're gone so much now and so busy with work. When are you ever going to have time for your family? How much travel is there with this job?" she asked.

"The job is about eighty percent travel because I'll be responsible for the entire country, but I'll be working out of the house and not out of the region office like now, so at least on my office days I'll be here at home. Plus, I determine my schedule of when and where I travel. So we can go to lunch, do some shopping, and go to Jake's classroom parties and activities together," Jackson explained trying to pacify her. Then he suddenly remembered, "Oh, I forgot to do my expenses again for last week. I need to go do them."

"Jackson, stay focused! We're trying to talk here about our future! Quit thinking about your Alsace To-Do list," her voice rose as she tried to get his attention. "Now, this job is still a lot of travel. And it's not travel where you're simply driving to Des Moines or St. Louis or Omaha like now, you're going to be flying to either coast and that means longer trips, airport delays, and stuff that you can't control. When are you ever going to see Jake?"

Jackson tried again in a determined voice. "Like I just said, I'll be here for class parties and to help with class activities on my home office days. Come on, Lexi, we'll make it work."

"Don't you mean that I'll make it work? Like I've always made it work anytime it involves our family? Jackson, your career and Alsace have become your family. You basically just continue to show up around here!"

Lexi felt that Jackson was continuing to put himself ahead of them. She didn't care so much about herself since she had already built a life separate from Jackson's, but she was concerned for about Jake.

"Lexi, you need to remember that I get to manage the travel part. I can be in my office on Monday mornings and then fly out in the afternoon, be home on Thursday nights, and then in my office on Friday. When you count the weekends, I'm home more than I am away. Jake's basketball and football games and Cub Scout activities are usually on the weekends so I'll be around for him. It'll be OK, honey, if I do well in this job, then the next step will be to a headquarters or regional Director position. There will be very limited travel then. It'll all work out just fine."

"The next promotion after National Accounts means moving to San Diego or another city, Jackson. I like it here in Kansas City. Jake's in a great school, he's got wonderful friends. We have a life here!"

"When we first moved here, we agreed that my career would be the one to provide for us. That's why you quit working. The big payoff from salary, bonus, and stock options is at a Director level position. Yes, that means we'll probably have to move. You knew that, and I'm trying to get us to that level. I'm doing this for us. And if we have to move, it's better if we do it before Jake hits high school. So I need this National Accounts job to get to a Director's position. That's how it works!"

"I know how it works, Jackson. I'm not some stupid housewife. I have a college degree just like you do. And don't forget, you wouldn't be where you are today if it wasn't for me. I'm the one that pushed you to get into Big Pharma in the first place. Hell, you'd probably still be working as a measly physical therapist in that puny hospital. I'm the one that dressed you right and taught you which fork to use to eat your salad!"

"I know you did, honey."

"So then don't talk down to me." Lexi had moved beyond tears to steaming mad.

"I'm not trying to talk down to you. I'm just trying to have a conversation about our future. How about if we have this discussion with the counselor?" Jackson offered.

"No, because all that means is that you get to slide for another week and not have to talk to me. Then you have your precious interviews, which you can't cancel. I mean, how would that look? What? Superstar Jackson Ford can't make a decision about a career move? Just go to your interviews. I'm sure they'll give you the job. Jake and I will keep living our own lives without you."

"Look, Lexi, I'm trying to do this for us," but she had already left the room.

She had heard the conversation that was going to come out of his mouth next a dozen times before, and she didn't want to hear it again. It was just so frustrating feeling trapped in a life that they both had wanted at first, and then once they actually you got it, it was not at all what it seemed.

I always knew deep down that Jackson would be successful, but I didn't expect him to be so consumed by his damn job and want to be gone so much. And it sure feels to me like he wants to be gone, that we're just an afterthought, she thought.

As she pulled out the clothes to hang them up to dry she continued her thought, *Jackson is just in this for himself. He feels good every day because everybody strokes him and praises him and promotes him. But he doesn't really care about anyone or anything except Alsace!* She slammed the washer lid shut in frustration of years of her own needs never being met.

A week later in San Diego at the Alsace headquarters, Jackson impressed Rick Thompson during their interview. The other interviews with Jim Larson, the VP, and Dee Dee Wallace from Human Resources went just as well. Two days later on Friday afternoon he was offered the job as the National Account Manager for the federal market reporting directly to Rick Thompson. Just a few years ago, Jackson took Lexi out to dinner and bought her a present to celebrate his Business Manager promotion, this time he didn't even so much rent a movie for them to watch after Jake went to bed.

The following Monday morning Jackson called Tam to tell her about his new promotion.

"Oh Jackson, that's wonderful news. I'll bet your wife is happy," Tam said. *God, this guy is moving up quickly!*

"Not really, Tam. Lexi is less than thrilled about the job and the travel. I tried to explain that it helps me move up quickly within the company, but she wasn't buying it," Jackson said with disappointment.

"That's too bad, Jackson. She ought to be proud of you and support you. You work so hard, and you're so good at what you do. From what you've told me, your wife has had it easy all her life. It's not like she's ever had to work for anything. I'm sure that she'll come around once she sees the increased salary, bonus and stock options. Hey, you know what is great about your new job?" asked Tam.

"What?"

"We'll be able to see even more of each other aside from the task force meetings since we'll both be working in the managed care division. There's always several company meetings a year just for RAMs and NAMs on strategic planning, contract and negotiations training, and team building activities. This will be great!" she laughed. *I can't wait to see more of him.*

Jackson perked up. "Hey, that's right. Rick did mention that he was planning on a meeting in Santa Monica and in Park City, Utah for next year with the entire department. Skiing and the beach! I can't wait!"

"Look Jackson, I think this is a good move for you professionally. I mean, look at some of the positions that you've been able to pass right by. You'll be a Director in no time! Hey, you won't forget about me when you become President of Alsace will you?"

"I wouldn't do that, Tam. OK, I've got to go. I'll call you later this week. Bye now."

"Bye Jackson, and congratulations. I'm happy for you."

Later that week Tam sent Jackson a congratulations card to the Region Office. She wrote on the left inside panel,

To my best friend at Alsace. I'm proud of you. Love, Tam.

Jackson attended his first official team meeting with the nine other National Account Managers at a ski resort in Winter Park, Colorado. Thompson hosted the team-building meeting in late June. The mountain snows had melted creating swollen creeks and rivers that were perfect for whitewater rafting. A local rafting company was contracted to guide the group on a half-day trip down Clear Creek near Winter Park. The team met in the morning for a business strategy meeting to review the major managed care plans and pharmacy benefits management companies, Alsace product formulary status and contract terms. Then it was off to meet the rafting company at one o'clock for some wet fun in class three and four rapids. The group showed up for the business meeting dressed in shorts or swimsuits and T-shirts. Dry bags were packed to hold cameras, sweatshirts and Jackets. Because of Winter Park's elevation, waterproofed sunscreen was liberally applied to exposed skin, and sunglasses were secured around necks with elastic bands. Over the course of the four-hour adventure, the NAMs shot through rapids and slammed into boulders yelling and screaming at the tops of their lungs. When five o'clock hit, they were wet and exhausted, but thrilled to their bones. A valuable lesson about teamwork was learned along the way. Flawless execution of the guide's commands, paddling together in unison, and leaning certain directions at key times got them safely through the rough and dangerous currents of Clear Creek.

If I can get the team to work together maximizing sales from the nation's biggest health plans, then the $2,000 cost was worth every penny of this little rafting trip, thought Thompson.

The next morning found the NAM group tired and sore. Brent Curran had brought along a tube of Ben-Gay, and it was being passed around during breakfast in the meeting room.

Smells like a locker room in here, Jackson thought.

Curran was one of the NAMs assigned to the large Group Purchasing Organizations or GPOs. These were customers who negotiated pharmaceutical and medical supply contracts for huge hospital systems located throughout the country. Only forty-six years old, Curran was a legend in the National Accounts department for his voracious appetite for both food and golf. He was a five-foot eight-inch, 225 pound five handicapper whose aspiration in life was to play all of Golf Magazine's Top 100 Public Courses. This goal was extremely realistic given the fact that his customers were not only the GPOs, but also their affiliated networks of hospital systems that they serviced. His access to golf courses just by virtue of his job responsibilities and customer base was guaranteed; he just needed to have enough time and budget dollars in his NAM job to get to the Top 100 list. Not that budget dollars were a limitation because the NAMs typically had access to over $20,000 a year for walking around money earmarked for customer entertainment. Curran was also equally renowned for his frequenting of strip clubs with his customers.

"There's nothing better than playing golf with customers in the morning and then taking them to a strip club in the evening," he would say. "As long as the Finance Department only checks one out of every twenty expense reports for the entire company every week, I'm safe. I always turn in receipts, and I can explain any expense to one of our bean counters that Cheetahs, the Sugar Shack, and Scores all offer a full-service dinner menus. They don't have to know that the meals are served by half-naked women!"

Thompson called the meeting to order and, to Curran's delight, immediately launched into preliminary budget forecasts for next year. "We've got a number of customer entertainment venues available for next year," he started. "The U.S. Open Golf Championship is at Pebble Beach, and I've got about significant budget dollars earmarked as a separate line item for one NAM and three customers. Any takers?"

Curran's hand immediately shot up. "I'm in, boss."

"I would have never guessed you'd be interested, Brent," said Thompson sarcastically. "OK, here's the deal. With three customers, you get two rounds of golf each, one at Spyglass and the other at Pebble Beach; tips for the caddies; four nights at the Inn at Spanish Bay in Monterey; tickets to all four rounds of the Open; airline tickets and honoraria for your customers; and food and beverage. After about a thousand dollars for souvenirs, I figure the entire weekend should cost about twenty thousand dollars."

Curran had a calculator on his iPhone and was putting it to good use as Thompson described the activities. He finally quipped, "Yup, that's about what I get as well, boss."

"Choose your customers wisely for this event, Brent. Ask yourself, 'Who can drive the most business for us this year?' This one's the most expensive venue by far, and I don't want to waste it on some lower level pharmacy manager," Thompson said.

"What other customer entertainment opportunities do we have arranged for the year?" asked Jackson. "Being relatively new to National Accounts, I'm looking for ways to work with some of my regional sales teams and hospital representatives to partner on certain events."

Thompson replied, "Well Jackson, as you recall from your days as a Business Manager, there are entertainment budgets set up for local sporting events. The divisions in Kansas City probably all chipped in from their budgets and split the costs of box seats to Royals and Chiefs games, right?"

"That's correct," Jackson replied.

"Well, in National Accounts we can get access to those season tickets if we've got customers locally that you want to entertain, like in KC for example. But really, at our level, the stakes are much higher. We have access to ticket buyers for national sporting events like the Super Bowl, World Series, Final Four, NBA Playoffs, The Masters, Indy 500, and the like. You just need to let me know where you want to go and with how many customers, and I'll make the arrangements."

"Rick, how do some of those events affect my overall budget? Like Brent here, it's twenty grand for the U.S. Open. That's his *annual* budget for entertainment."

Thompson chuckled at the new guy, "Well, that's the beauty of it. The special events are all paid for out of a separate marketing budget. You still have twenty thousand bucks for regular customer entertainment out of the National Accounts budgets."

Jackson's head was spinning. *How am I going to spend all this cash? What the hell happened to just doing business and getting formulary access and contracts? I guess I'd better go with the flow here. Hey, it doesn't sound too rough so far! Welcome to the big leagues, Jackson!*

CHAPTER 11
FEDERAL NAM

The Department of Veterans Affairs was recognized as the largest vertically integrated health care system in the United States. With over 165 VA Medical Centers and dozens of outpatient satellite clinics throughout the U.S., the VA easily handled the medical needs of the three million eligible beneficiaries that used the VA health care system as their primary medical care. A typical VA hospital was equipped to treat ailments as simple as the common cold to complicated procedures like spinal cord injuries or bone marrow transplants. Generally located on or near major university teaching hospitals, the VA was also a medical training ground for medical residents and fellows, nurses, dentists, and pharmacists. Oftentimes, the department chair of a VA hospital would have the same title and role at the adjacent university teaching hospital. This amazing and important health care system received funding solely from taxpayer's dollars through the federal budget as approved by Congress.

Historically, the VA Medical Centers operated as stand-alone facilities or mini-HMO plans under an emergency medicine model of care. Medical service redundancies and annual cost overruns were the accepted norm. However, with the appointment of a new Undersecretary of the VA, startling changes would be made to the health care system that was layered in red tape and inefficiencies. The Undersecretary was charged to dissect the system and make recommendations for change so that overall, it would survive in the twenty-first century as a health care provider for our nations' veterans.

The analysis was extensive and the recommendations would, upon implementation, turn the VA system upside down, but for the better.

The Undersecretary of the VA recommended that the system adopt a primary care model and reorganize into twenty-two regions in order to reduce the duplication of services and to take advantage of economies of scale by using its new-found purchasing clout with suppliers. The twenty-two regions were named Veterans Integrated Service Networks or VISNs, and each VISN had a lead medical center and board of directors that were charged with managing the five to eight hospitals that comprised each VISN. Upon implementation of this change, the political infighting proved tremendous. The egos of medical directors, administrators, physicians and pharmacists were battered and bruised along the path of implementation. However, after initial in-fighting, the VISN board of directors charged each department chair with evaluating its spending, purchasing, practice patterns, and cost overruns in order to put new systems and processes in place to become a cost efficient model of health care delivery.

One such area in need of a major overhaul was the pharmacy service line. Wholesale changes were needed from the way the VA selected which drugs were going to be available to patients to the way it purchased drugs to the way the physicians actually used the medicines when treating diseases. The pharmacy division was a significant cost center to the overall VA health care system, meaning that the division routinely spent over two billion dollars annually with virtually no operational or cost efficiencies built in.

It was time for a major change. The VA created a Pharmacy Benefits Management department within the pharmacy division, and it was located at the Hines VA Medical Center campus in the western suburbs of Chicago. Bob Johnson was the Chief of Pharmacy at the Hines VAMC, and he was selected by the Undersecretary to design and manage the new VA pharmacy model. Within the VA pharmacy community Bob was known as Steelballs Johnson. He earned the nickname Steelballs for not only his reputation as a hard nose Pharmacy Director who hated the federal bureaucracy, but because he was a member of the Lake Michigan Polar Bear Club, a group famous for taking annual dips in the frigid lake waters every New Year's Day.

Johnson approached his new job with a voracious work ethic that included long hours. Being centrally located in Chicago, he would arrive at the office promptly at 7:00 AM central time every morning because the Undersecretary was in his office in Washington DC at 8:00 AM eastern time. Johnson would then stay until 7:00 PM central time in order to be available and have access to the west coast Pharmacy Directors who typically were in their own offices until 5:00 PM pacific time. The long hours certainly did not do much to improve Johnson's thorough disdain for the operational inefficiencies embedded in the VA pharmacy division.

Steelballs's first order of business in his new role of change management was to reform the pharmaceutical procurement process; the way the VA purchased drugs. A gigantic warehouse that was used to stockpile medicine was located on the Hines VA campus. It was the central location for all two billion dollars of pharmaceuticals that the 165 VAMCs used each year. With lightning speed of sometimes up to four weeks, the product would eventually be received by the local pharmacy with a bill that included an eighteen percent surcharge for filling the order. The inane process drove VA pharmacists crazy.

The depot system was loathed by all VA pharmacists, especially Johnson. *Hell, it takes my pharmacy at Hines nearly two weeks to receive product from the depot, and we're only one block away!*

He blew up the depot overnight, which translated from government-speak, meant he did away with the depot system in about twelve months. Working with a nationally known drug wholesaler company, Johnson designed a prime vendor inventory management system that allowed the local VA hospital pharmacy to order medicine electronically and receive the products within twenty-four hours at federal government contract prices thus eliminating the eighteen percent surcharge automatically. The direct savings alone were valued at over $200 million year! The extra money was sorely needed to provide for the increases anticipated in medicines to be dispensed to patients with the Undersecretaries' plan to turn the VA into a primary care health care model, and it all had to be done with no budget increases from Congress.

With a MBA degree and extensive contacts within the commercial managed health care industry, which included National Healthcare, which was the largest managed care plan in the United States, Johnson became a visionary within the VA system. After the rousing success of the prime vendor inventory management system, Johnson soon presented three additional proposals to the Undersecretary where they met with his immediate approval.

The first proposal was to implement a centrally controlled national formulary where only a specific number of drugs in each major therapeutic class were to be available in all VA pharmacies. The second proposal was the development of disease-specific drug treatment guidelines that essentially would dictate to physicians how they were to treat various diseases and with what medications. It was a "cook book" approach to the practice of medicine. The last proposal was for the development of a mail order pharmacy program that would establish eight warehouses around the country each capable of mailing out over 25,000 prescriptions each day to veterans' homes. This was intended to relieve the patient of having to drive to the VA hospital each month to receive a thirty-day supply of medicine. This last proposal was estimated to free-up five hundred pharmacy personnel across the country to be deployed in other units of the hospital charged with patient consulting and overseeing the drug treatment guidelines that was proposal number two.

"There's no way that we're letting the VA physicians off the hook from following our drug treatment guidelines. If fact, we're going to create report cards on their adherence to them!" old Steelballs would exclaim to his staff.

It was clear from the start that the Undersecretary picked the right guy to head up the VA Pharmacy Benefits Management division in order to support his vision of the VA health care reform initiatives.

Being the National Account Manager for the Federal market, the first appointment Jackson scheduled was with Steelballs. Although more than just a tad bit intimidated at first, he quickly learned a few important personal facts about him that helped ease him into a great relationship over time. First, Johnson was a die-hard Chicago Bears fan, *OK, I'll have to get past Johnson's character flaw,* thought Jackson. Second, Johnson owned a summer home on Lake Geneva located in southeastern Wisconsin. The home was actually situated just five lots down from Lexi's parents' summer home. *Well alright, I'll have to have him over to the in-laws' house to grill brats and drink beer over the Fourth of July.* Third, Johnson's oldest son was currently a member of the ski show at Sea World in San Diego but looking to get into pharmaceutical sales. *Perfect!* thought Jackson again. *The Alsace headquarters is in San Diego. I might be able to help him get a sales rep job. I'll get his resume to Dee Dee Wallace in HR.* Lastly, Johnson was a golf nut who had learned to make custom golf clubs. In fact, about half of the VA Pharmacy Chiefs all owned a set of clubs custom-made by Johnson. *I'll have to check out his clubs and see about having him make me a set,* Jackson said to himself.

Over the next six months Jackson worked directly with Johnson to negotiate various tiered market share contracts using what were known as Blanket Purchase Agreements for the majority of Alsace products to be included on the VA national formulary. He was quite proud of himself for putting together the deal on LOMEC. The contract terms were so good that the VA designated the drug as the exclusive proton pump inhibitor on the national formulary subsequently removing the competitor products from TAP, Wyeth, and AstraZeneca. Within one year, sales of LOMEC were over $100 million in the VA market. For that accomplishment, Jackson received a stock option grant of 3,000 shares of Alsace stock. His portfolio continued to grow with each year as Alsace stock screamed off the charts.

This is why I got into this industry! he thought.

The Department of Defense health care system was very similar to that of the VA relative to size, structure, and bureaucracy. The DoD was comprised of 150 Military Treatment Facilities or hospitals spread across the United States with another two dozen hospitals in Europe and Asia all of which were located on U.S. military bases.

The big three centers of influence, however, were located in the Washington DC area: Bethesda Naval Medical Center, Andrews Air Force Base Medical Center, and Walter Reed Army Medical Center. Access to any of the military bases, and subsequently their medical centers, depended on the threat condition level posted for the day. At Threat Con Alpha or Bravo, the access followed a routine procedure whereby a vendor would simply sign in at the outpost and then enter the base. However, at Threat Con Charlie or Delta, access procedures were much stricter and an appointment and personal escort was generally needed for the vendor to gain permission to access to the base hospital.

The DoD health care system was comprised of over eight million beneficiaries of whom two million were designated as active duty. The age range for the beneficiaries was from one day old up to and including death, so the medical care was cradle-to-grave for anyone who was either active duty in the military, an active duty dependent, or a retiree and their spouse. The DoD called their health care system TRICARE representing the three branches of the service in the name: Army, Air Force, and Navy. The eight million beneficiaries had to elect the type of medical service in which they would participate each year. The base hospital physicians served as the primary healthcare providers for most of the beneficiaries, but a preferred provider network of physicians was also established to provide care for beneficiaries who did not live on or near the military bases but still lived within the catchment area or who did not want to utilize a military physician. Retirees mainly utilized the preferred provider network of physicians for their health care needs that was managed under contract with the military by a large commercial managed care organization like Humana or Foundation Healthcare.

The military beneficiaries had three different methods for obtaining prescriptions: at the military hospital pharmacy, at a network retail pharmacy, or through the mail order system managed by Medco Prescription Services. Patients generally had prescription co-pay levels ranging from free to eight bucks for each prescription depending on which pharmacy service was utilized. The best deal was to fill one's prescriptions through the base hospital pharmacy since the zero dollar co-pay applied, and that's generally what most of the beneficiaries would do even though the wait times were significantly longer than Space Mountain at Disneyland on a warm summer day. The retirees that lived far away from the hospitals would simply make a day of the trip each month by starting out early in the morning driving to the base hospital, order their prescriptions at the pharmacy, do some shopping at the commissary for a few hours to take advantage of low government prices, and then pick up their prescriptions later in the day before they made the return trip home. Usually, many of the retirees had friends who would make the same pilgrimage at the end of each month so they would hook up in the Mess Hall for lunch and catch up with each other by exchanging the same old war stories and sharing updates on their children's lives.

The TRICARE health care system had already organized itself into twelve TRICARE Regions long before the VA had organized into twenty-two VISNs, but in a never-ending attempt to reduce costs and improve operational efficiencies (an oxymoron for the military), the General and Admirals in the Pentagon insisted on a national formulary aligned with the VA so that even greater economies of scale and purchasing power could be realized to reduce pharmacy acquisition costs from Big Pharma. Over time, the two entities did, in fact, merge many therapeutic classes but ultimately the DoD needed additional specialized classes such as OB/GYN and pediatrics to provide for coverage for their beneficiaries. The VA, of course, did not need those therapeutic classes since their average patient was a sixty-two year-old male.

Colonel Frank Buck, Army, was the Director of the TRICARE Pharmacoeconomic Center located at Fort Sam Houston just outside San Antonio, Texas. His staff of twenty pharmacists that was comprised of Army, Air Force, Navy, and civilian contractors did much of the same type of work as was being provided by Bob Johnson's staff at the VA PBM. They managed the national formulary, the mail order prescription program, the medical treatment guidelines, contracting initiatives, and the retail pharmacy network. The VA prime vendor inventory management program created by Johnson for the VA was also extended to and adopted by TRICARE allowing for closure of the military depot system for pharmaceuticals. Hundreds of millions of dollars in savings were realized by TRICARE. In an era of budget reductions from Congress, this and other measures also helped TRICARE sustain itself financially in order to provide high quality medical care and medicines to its beneficiaries.

Jackson's first appointment with Colonel Buck was extremely worthwhile as he gained insightful information on TRICARE such as its mission, structure, organizational design, formulary processes, and opportunities for collaboration with industry. Buck, like Johnson, was an avid golfer. After fifteen years of active duty and assignments to a number of Army bases that all had golf courses located upon them, Buck was an eight handicap and played whenever he got the chance. Jackson found out that even Colonel Buck bought a set of golf clubs from Bob Johnson, and that the two of them liked to play together during free time at several of the national pharmacy conferences.

I'm going to have to improve my game just to hang with these guys. One more thing that is sure to enrage Lexi, thought Jackson.

As TRICARE aligned its national formulary with the VA, Jackson was able to successfully negotiate an extension of the VA market share contract to include the requirements of the military. Although one-half the prescription sales potential of the VA market for ulcers and erosive esophagitis, the DoD added an additional fifty million dollars a year to Jackson's sales performance for the Federal market earning him another 2,000 Alsace stock options and special recognition at the national sales meeting the following year.

Scott Evans, who was a Marketing Director for LOMEC, sat fuming in the audience as Jackson received his award on the stage. Evans was the lone marketing manager who did not support the idea of offering aggressive discounts to the VA and Military markets since the products were already steeply discounted as mandated by federal law on the Alsace Federal Supply Schedule contracts. Evans was paid bonus based on net sales after discounts and rebates for LOMEC and not gross sales like the field sales organization was paid. In the end, the Pricing Committee chaired by the Director of National Accounts, Rick Thompson, out voted Evans and approved the additional discounts in order to get the increased sales.

These National Accounts Managers have these cushy jobs where they fly around the country racking up frequent flyer miles, have lunch or dinner with customers, get a shoe shine at the airport, and then fly home to have two office days a week. Arranging tee times for their customers so they can play golf together is the most difficult thing they do all day, thought Evans as he watched Jackson shake hands with Kevin Steer and accept his 2,000 share of Alsace stock options. *They are giving away the profit margins without any thought as to how to do it differently. If I can help it, this will stop!*

Jackson did ask Steelballs to make a set of golf clubs for Lexi. She took lessons from a local golf pro and was quite good on Par Three courses, which was more than enough golf for her. Jackson, however, was a serious golfer. He wanted to play the regular eighteen holes with Lexi. He even offered to rent a cart, but the four to five hour commitment that was required to play an entire round was too boring for Lexi. She was a social golfer, not someone who was disciplined and committed to playing the game. What started off with good intentions became a point of contention between the two. Lexi's golf clubs stood in a corner of the garage and gathered dust.

CHAPTER 12
MANAGED CARE

With Jackson's promotion to a National Account Manager position he learned very quickly that the health care insurance companies played serious hardball. The Goliath in the industry was National Healthcare. With over nine million covered lives, over 100,000 physicians and nurses on staff, and a network of hospitals in fifteen major metropolitan areas, National was the single largest for-profit commercial health insurance company in the United States. National used what is called a staff model principle in its organizational design; meaning, all the physicians, nurses, and support staff members were paid employees of National as compared to a network of physicians, nurses and hospitals contracted for their services like one would typically find in most Blue Cross health plans. Human Resource departments from big employer groups like Philip Morris loved National Healthcare because the plan offered good access to health care providers and hospitals. More importantly, it offered low premiums to the employers and, ultimately, the employees.

National Healthcare was headquartered in Detroit. The company was started in the 1920's when the Big Three auto companies were looking to offer health care benefits (with the overriding goal of cost containment) to their union employees. The managed health care concept grew by leaps and bounds across the country in mainly unionized regions such as the Rust Belt and California, homes to huge manufacturing and agriculture industries.

Because the medical groups were totally at risk for pharmaceuticals, including injectables, National used a centrally controlled formulary or list of drugs to which their physicians and patients could access. The high control over the pharmaceuticals utilized within the healthcare system allowed National to negotiate the lowest acquisition prices from Big Pharma of any commercial managed care provider. In fact, National utilized information technology and central purchasing to enforce the high control formulary model. Computer systems were installed in the medical clinics, hospitals, and staff pharmacies for National physicians and pharmacists to access the formulary list. If a drug was not on the preferred drug list, then the physician either could not prescribe it or had to fill out a prior authorization or permission form in order to gain approval from the pharmacy to use it with a patient. Physicians received report cards every quarter that showed their compliance to the formulary list. They were penalized through a bonus incentive program if their use of non-formulary drugs was more than ten percent of the overall number of prescriptions written.

Lastly, National had a complex procurement or purchasing system through which they acquired drugs directly from Big Pharma companies instead of through wholesalers. Several gigantic warehouses served as holding areas for all pharmaceuticals entering into the National Healthcare system. From the warehouses, the medicines were then shipped to the network of National staff pharmacies located within the medical clinics and hospitals. In addition, National had the country's first mail order prescription service system for its beneficiaries. This allowed patients to receive ninety days of medicine through the mail rather than refilling at the pharmacy once a month. These measures allowed National to demonstrate to potential employer groups that it was able to contain costs and justify the low premiums it charged while negotiating favorable contract terms with Big Pharma companies.

Jerry Kramer was the Pharmacy Director for all of National Healthcare. He ruled the Pharmacy and Therapeutics Committee with an iron hand. Because the Pharmacy department was considered a profit center for National, he had the total support of the Board of Directors to do whatever it took to maintain acceptable profit margins on the products added to the preferred drug list. With all the cost containment measures and operational efficiencies built into the National pharmacy system, the dispensing of medicines, and more importantly, the managing of the pharmaceutical rebate contracts, were both important sources of revenue for the National Healthcare organization. This was especially important since National was a for profit health plan.

Kramer was a short, slightly built, balding man who wore thick glasses, and he displayed a foul temper and little time for inexperienced people from the drug industry. He watched every penny of the finance sheets pertaining to pharmaceuticals and had high expectations of anyone who made an appointment with him. They had better know their stuff and his business model, or he would personally berate them during meetings. Big Pharma knew this and only assigned the best, brightest, and most capable National Account Managers to National.

All National Account Managers had to come through Kramer to present contract proposals, Quality of Life data, and pharmacoeconomics outcomes data that would support the addition of their products to the almighty National formulary. Deep down all NAMs feared Kramer's temper. They also tried to keep senior managers from their respective companies away from Kramer because they knew that he would shame them by exposing their lack of managed care knowledge and inexperience.

NAMs mistakenly believed that since National was the largest commercial health plan with a high control formulary model, that other large health plans would look to National for guidance on such issues as medicines on the preferred drug list or formulary benefit design related specifically to co-pay levels. This was not the case because National was an enigma unto itself. NAMs were also mistaken in their belief that they just had to give National the best contract deals in order to get on formulary and then be used within the National healthcare system. Big Pharma companies would routinely break Medicaid best price levels during two quarters of each fiscal year just to sell and ship their product into National's warehouses. Of course, Disproportionate Share Hospitals or high Medicaid patient hospitals and clinics, like

Cook County Hospital in Jackson's old Chicago District, would take advantage of Big Pharma selling practices to National on certain high volume drugs. Cook County Hospital, along with the other high Medicaid patient hospitals across the U.S., would simply wait until the right two quarters for the Public Health Service 340b contract prices to fall significantly, and then buy huge volumes of medicines at super-reduced prices. All thanks to the low drug prices that Jerry Kramer was able to negotiate for his precious National.

The twenty member Pharmacy and Therapeutics Committee was made up of the Medical Directors from the major therapeutic divisions at National Healthcare and several members of the Pharmacy staff, including, of course, Jerry Kramer. The term therapeutics in the title of the committee name did not mean much or have much influence in the preferred drug list decisions for National. Since all drugs on the U.S. market had to go through an FDA approval process, National's P & T Committee naturally assumed that the majority of products on the market were me-too drugs or therapeutically equivalent. Meaning that a physician could swap one ulcer drug for another and still get the desired effect of controlling acid reflux disease or erosive esophagitis. And they were basically right about that. This created a situation whereby about ninety percent of the decisions that were made by the National P & T Committee about medicines listed on the preferred drug list boiled down to pharmacoeconomics or best value.

"Which Big Pharma company is bringing the best deal to National and what does the deal look like?" were the two most common questions asked by the P & T Committee members.

Factors that were reviewed by the committee when considering a new drug or class of drugs were as follows: up front discounts, back end rebates, market share tiers, volume tier incentives, VIP monies, research grants, estimates on product failures, non-compliance with products, estimates on hospital admissions or emergency room visits, additional physician office visits, loss of existing rebates or discounts on current products, and substitution with new drugs through the pharmacy mail order service. A somewhat complicated pharmacoeconomic model was constructed using a super-computer software model in order to determine what products were to make up the preferred drug list. Making the list was not always a big win for Big Pharma as the profit margins on drugs sold to National were significantly reduced. But it put big sales on the board to show Wall Street that a successful product launch was underway for a new product or that sales were continuing with a mature product. Either way, Wall Street's impression of the formulary status of Big Pharma medicines on the major health plans was an important contributing factor to company evaluations and the buy or hold status that was placed on a company's stock.

Robert Borman was the Alsace National Account Manager responsible for National Healthcare. National was his only assigned account. He preferred to be called Bo Bo by his friends and family.

Bo Bo was known as the six million dollar NAM within the Alsace National Accounts division because of an initial deal for LOMEC that he successfully negotiated with Jerry Kramer. It was valued at six million dollars a year in direct purchase sales. Of course, this was the net sales amount after all the discounts and rebates were applied which, if the truth be told, amounted to about one-half of the gross sales price or list price for LOMEC. Over time, the direct sales of LOMEC to National Healthcare grew to over $100 million a year. Each year a special repackaging run of LOMEC was performed on a precise schedule by the manufacturing facility in Puerto Rico that Jackson and Lexi had toured while they attended their first awards trip. The plant would shrink wrap hundreds of cases of LOMEC on pallets to ship out to the three National warehouses. Upon receipt of the product, the National warehouse workers would place the cases into their inventory for either direct shipment to the National-owned pharmacies or mail out individual stock bottles to patients enrolled in the mail order prescription drug program. National was efficient as hell.

When asked to tell the story how he got the LOMEC deal done with National, Borman would reply, "Well, Jerry and I went out to lunch one day, and we had a few drinks, and then boom, I pitched him on my proposal, which I wrote out on a few bar napkins. Then we went back to his office, did some calculations to check my numbers, and boom, they checked out. Jerry then pulls into his office the head of Contracting who looked at the deal from Merck and then mine, and boom, he liked ours better! After a couple hours we went out to dinner, had a few more cocktails, and boom, he signs the contract over coffee and dessert." Bo Bo was known by the name Boomer within the halls of Alsace ever since the deal was struck.

Boomer stood 6'4" tall and weighed three bills or just over three hundred pounds. He was a former defensive nose tackle in college for Texas Christian University, and he looked exactly like Jackie Gleason with his facial expressions and mannerisms. He probably could have floated a battleship with all the single malt scotch that he consumed over his life span, and as well, Boomer quite possibly was the single number one consumer of Swisher Sweet cigars in the United States. *No plastic tips, thank you.* Even though only forty-five years old, Boomer was already on medication for high blood pressure, high blood cholesterol, hypothyroidism, and gout. He was a very friendly and talkative drunk, but the ever-present cigar ashes and food crumbs that set up camp on all his shirts and ties gave everyone who ever met him reason to chuckle to themselves at his expense.

Boomer was a good dad to his three daughters and had a typical 1950s marriage. His wife, Jeannie, was a stay at home mom who cooked, cleaned, and kept the house and girls all on schedule. She also packed Boomer's suitcase before every business trip. One time, however, there was a mishap in the packing process.

Boomer was scheduled to meet with several Clinical Research Directors at National's headquarters in Detroit with his boss, Rick Thompson and two Clinical Development Managers from Alsace. The purpose of the meeting was to present some Phase III study protocols for two Alsace products that were still in the Research and Development pipeline for possible implementation in the clinical research program at several National Healthcare medical clinics. These were crucial protocols because they would greatly influence the overall product submission process from Alsace to the FDA. The projection of a sharp professional image was an important quality that the National team expected.

At 7:30 AM on the morning of the meeting, Thompson pounded on Boomer's hotel room door, "Come on, Boomer, we have to go. We're late!"

"Ah, I'll be there in a minute," came the response from inside the door as well as a few curses.

Three minutes passed, "Boomer, let's go!"

"OK, OK! I'm coming!" The door swung open and Boomer stood towering over Thompson and appeared ready to go.

"Boomer, what happened to your face?" demanded Thompson.

His cheeks, upper lip, and neck were dotted with at least a dozen pieces of light blue toilet paper each with a red dot in the center. "Ah, that damn Jeannie forgot to pack my electric razor so I had to go down to the gift shop this morning and buy a disposable razor. It cut the hell outta me! I was bleeding like a stuck pig!" Boomer was enraged.

"Look Boomer, we can't go to this meeting with you wearing blue toilet paper with red dots all over your face! Come on, let's go into your bathroom and clean you up."

For the next ten minutes Thompson dabbed Boomer's face with a cold washcloth to stop the cuts from bleeding.

Of course, they arrived late for the meeting with National. But in the end, the protocols were accepted and the clinical studies were conducted on behalf of Alsace so that the Company could submit its information to the FDA. There was never any doubt in Boomer's mind that the protocols would not be accepted by National since Boomer and Thompson had sweetened the LOMEC deal by striking an agreement with Jerry Kramer several weeks before. Alsace had agreed to provide a grant for $2,000 for each of the 1,000 National patients enrolled in the studies. That was a cool two million dollar grant check that went straight to National.

National simply cashed the check and put the money into their general ledger account.

Boomer had known from a number of private conversations with Kramer that National had an extensive profit sharing program for its upper management staff of which Kramer was a member. Boomer also learned that the profit sharing program over the last several years was nearly as lucrative as the Alsace stock option program. Through savvy negotiations with Big Pharma companies, Kramer and his peers at National were very wealthy individuals.

CHAPTER 13
ghostbar

Long before movie stars, rock bands, or professional athletes made Las Vegas a highly sought after and cool travel destination, convention organizers recognized that the ample supply of hotel sleeping rooms, restaurants, and meeting rooms made Sin City the perfect location to host conventions that could accommodate memberships sometimes equaling the populations of some small towns. One such organization was the American Society of Health-System Pharmacists or ASHP. ASHP is a national professional association that represents over 30,000 pharmacists who practice in hospitals, HMOs, long-term care facilities, and other components of health care systems.

For Jackson's first ASHP convention, over one-half of the membership descended upon Las Vegas for the annual week-long meeting held during the first week of December, and Jackson's federal hospital Pharmacy Directors were there in full force. In fact, the ASHP agenda called for a specific day whereby the VA and DoD pharmacists had separate reserved meeting rooms just to conduct the business of improving the educational quality of their pharmacy staff. Of course, Jackson was glued to these rooms throughout the week in order to continue to learn as much as he could about the federal market and make specific contacts with key individuals within the VISNs and TRICARE Regions. He even scheduled a number of separate lunches and dinners with select individuals like Bob Johnson and Colonel Frank Buck and their staff to further his personal and business relationships. He selected Charlie Palmer's Steakhouse, located high atop the Four Seasons Hotel providing a spectacular view of the city, for his entertainment venue. Although a fairly expensive choice of restaurants, Jackson's ultimate goal was to impress his customers by dining on the best steaks and chops in Las Vegas. When the fifteen VA pharmacists joined him, he let the little short guy from the San Diego VAMC pick out the $150 a bottle wine for the evening. After a delicious meal, his customers thanked him and said their goodbyes while the headwaiter presented Jackson with a $2,500 bill for his review and, of course, to add on the tip. As he looked over the bill, Jackson thought that maybe next time he better take more control of the menu items, or at least wrestle the wine list away from the San Diego Pharmacy Director.

The wine alone cost almost $1,000, he said to himself. More than a little tipsy, he added on a generous tip of $500 and thought again, *What the hell, it's not my money. I know guys like Brent and Boomer are spending just as much if not more this week.*

He left the restaurant after he settled the bill and went back to the Bellagio Hotel where the Alsace NAMs were staying to see if any of his peers were gambling in the casino. Of course, he found Boomer at one of the tables playing craps, so Jackson decided to hang out for a while and try to learn the fast-paced game. After several rounds were played, he concluded that he had drunk way too much wine at dinner and found that it was difficult to keep up with the fast-paced action and to comprehend how to place bets on all the different numbers. After a couple more complimentary cocktails, he ended up going back to his room and fell asleep, and he was content in doing so since he had a round of golf scheduled at the TPC Canyons course for nine o'clock the next morning with two of his customers.

At two in the morning the telephone rang.

"Uh, hello?" asked Jackson. His head started to hurt. *I need to drink a big glass of water and take some Advil,* he thought.

"Big boy, it's me Boomer." The voice was slurred on the other end of the line.

It was not difficult to recognize Boomer's voice normally, let alone when he was obviously all tanked up. "Yeah, I know. What's up?"

"Jackie, I'm still down in the casino at one of the Pai Gao tables, and I ran into a little trouble."

"What do you mean, trouble?" Jackson asked.

"Can you bring me a thousand dollars?" Boomer asked.

"What?"

"I need you to bring me a thousand bucks right away," Boomer demanded.

"Boomer, I don't have a thousand dollars on me," Jackson replied. "I got maybe a couple of hundred dollars left."

"No, that's no good. I need a thousand bucks. Don't you have an ATM card?"

"Boomer, even if I had it, Lexi would kill me if I took that kind of money out of our checking account without talking to her first. You know, I haven't been at Alsace as long as guys like you to have the big bucks just lying around in my accounts. My money is tied up in mutual funds, Boomer."

"Can't you just call her up, Jackson?" Boomer asked.

"It's four o'clock in the morning back in Kansas City! Do you want me to die young?"

"OK, don't worry about it. I'll call somebody else." And the phone went dead.

What was that all about? Jackson wondered. He slept fitfully the rest of the night replaying the conversation with Boomer in his head over and over. *What could he possibly have gotten himself into this time?*

Early the next morning as he retrieved his golf clubs from the Bell Stand, Jackson saw Boomer walking across the lobby of the Bellagio.

"Hey Boomer!" Jackson yelled out.

"Hey Jackie! How are you doing this morning? Sorry about waking you up last night," Boomer looked like he was working off eight hours of sleep instead of the three hours that he actually got.

"What did you need a thousand dollars for?" Jackson asked.

"Oh, it was just a little misunderstanding with the guys that run the Pai Gao tables. Don't worry. I called up Jerry, and he was able to help me out."

"Jerry from National Healthcare? Jerry Kramer? That Jerry Kramer?"

"Yeah, Jerry. He helped me out. Hey, I gotta run. I'm meeting a couple of big shots from National to talk about a deal we got cooking for our new oncology drug. See you this afternoon!" He lumbered out through the revolving doors and into the back of a taxi as Jackson slowly shook his head.

After playing golf with his two VA customers, Jackson cleaned up and went over to the convention center. At the conclusion of the afternoon plenary sessions, the Alsace National Accounts department had made arrangements to host a wine and cheese party in one of the rooms just off the main convention center floor. It was by special invitation only and each National Account Manager and Regional Account Manager was allowed up to five customer invitations. Since he had already taken his key VA PBM and DoD Pharmacoeconomic Center customers out to dinner earlier in the week, Jackson elected to invite the Pharmacy Directors and staff from the department of Indian Health Services and department of the Federal Bureau of Prisons. These two markets were also under his responsibility, but they were less of a priority since the sales potential from the Indian reservation's medical clinics and the correctional facilities were small in contrast to the VA and Military markets.

The wine and cheese party proved to be a hit with over three hundred customers and spouses in attendance. The Account Managers attracted the most influential customers in the U.S. managed health care segment, which allowed for further interaction with Alsace senior management. Since Jackson's Indian Health and FBOP pharmacists only stayed about an hour, he was then able to work the room and talk with other managed care customers that had been invited by his peers, and at one point, he was even introduced to the infamous Jerry Kramer from National Healthcare. By the end of the event, Jackson had probably met ten of the most important Pharmacy Directors from large integrated healthcare systems and managed care organizations. Jackson felt good about himself and where he was with his career at Alsace, and he felt very much at home in the National Accounts department.

After all the ASHP events were concluded and the 15,000 pharmacists checked out of their hotels to go back home, the Alsace Account Managers were required to stay for two more days of business meetings and training scheduled at the Bellagio Hotel. The Vice President of Accounts Management, Jim Larson, and the Director of National Accounts, Rick Thompson, led the meetings where new business planning processes, customer account planning software systems, and contracting tools were presented. In addition to the ten National Account Managers, the forty Regional Account Managers and five Wholesaler Account Managers were also in attendance with their respective Regional Directors. A number of behind-the-scenes support personnel that represented departments such as contracts management, customer service, pricing, segment marketing, and information systems were also included at the meetings. Altogether, almost 100 Alsace personnel were in attendance that, ultimately, all reported to Jim Larson.

On the first morning of the Alsace business meetings, Larson introduced a motivational group called Afterburners whose purpose was to pump up the department personnel and to stress the theme of strategic planning and teamwork. The retired Air Force fighter pilots from the Afterburners group moderated several business planning and execution modules designed to improve the management and sales performance of the audience. Videotape was also shown to the group to underscore the drawbacks of focusing on the little things that can potentially make major account sales calls go awry. Larson had arranged ahead of time for the purchase of signed copies of the Afterburners' books that were then distributed to each participant at the conclusion of the session. The Alsace managers gave the Afterburners speakers a standing ovation as they exited the stage.

It's hard to beat the military guys when it comes to pumping up a crowd, Jackson thought.

Jim Larson was in his early forties, married with three children, and had been at Alsace since graduating from college. He had experienced a meteoric rise through the company ranks to get to a VP job before he was forty-five years old. Of course, he had Matt York for a mentor, which didn't hurt because at Alsace the boys all took care of and looked out for each other. Like a number of the other VPs, Larson had hundreds of thousands of Alsace stock options that he had accumulated over the years with the Company through hard work and a number of stock splits. Whenever he cashed in some of his numerous vested options, he invested the money very wisely with the help of a brother-in-law who worked as a Wall Street broker. He got in early on Apple, Microsoft, Amgen, and Cisco and earned exponential dollars in the stock market. Because York was his mentor, Larson was also a big believer in acknowledging his team and taking a personal interest in each of them. He always started off each meeting by recognizing employment anniversaries, birthdays, and promotions. Of course, with over a hundred personnel in the Accounts Management department, there was no way that Larson could possibly keep everybody's spouses or kids straight, but he tried. He carried a day planner that contained a roster of the employees, spouses, and the kids' names and ages. His secretary, Gina, updated the list each year, or sooner if there was a divorce. Several of his up-and-coming employees drew Larson's attention to detail where the list was not needed. Jackson was one of them.

At the morning break as they both headed off to the bathroom, Larson asked, "Jackson, how's the family?"

"Hi, Jim. They're great, thanks for asking."

"Does your son play any sports?" Larson inquired.

"He's just started basketball at his school, so he is excited. I'm with him at the YMCA every weekend working on ball-handling skills and shooting," Jackson said with pride.

"Well, give my best to Lexi."

"OK, I will, Jim. Thanks."

Since the entire Accounts Management division was present for the ASHP meeting, Tam was in attendance as well. Even though they had both been in Las Vegas for the ASHP convention and had spoken via their cell phones several times, the Alsace business meeting was the first time they actually got to spend any time together since they were both extremely busy with customer entertainment activities. They had planned to have dinner at the Commander's Palace restaurant the first night, but Jackson's flight out of Kansas City had weather delays due to a severe snow storm.

"Hi stranger!" Tam placed her hand on Jackson's forearm as the group broke for lunch. "Let's find some seats together at lunch."

"Sounds great! How did your customer dinners go?" Jackson asked as his hand moved freely across her lower back. They lingered a minute longer and waited for the crowd to clear.

Tam felt an eager affection coming from him, "They went well actually. I've got my Blue Cross plans of Florida and Georgia all set to go with the new contract language that we're getting trained on today. It should help our formulary access. How about yours?"

"You know, Tam, I had some of the best meetings ever with my customers. But I'm glad that it's over. I'm beat from all the late nights and big dinners. I haven't even had a chance to run while I've been here. I feel like I've gained ten pounds," his voice sounded tired.

"I hope you're not too tired to spend some time with me. I've missed seeing you since the last task force meeting in San Diego. I have to admit, Jackson, the weekly phone calls just don't do it for me anymore." Tam moved her fingers along his upper arm. "Hey, I hear there is going to be a great party tonight for the Account Management division. One of the other girls was telling me about it."

Jackson lowered his chin, his eyes blazed into hers, "First of all, don't worry about me. I'm never too tired to see you. So, where is this big party tonight?"

They shared a smile. "Well, you know Shelly Crawford right? She's the new Operations Manager who reports directly to Jim Larson."

"Yeah, I met her at the Wine and Cheese reception. Tall gal, with red hair? She's from one of the Chicago suburbs. Like Berwyn, I think. I told her that I was from around the Chicago area as well, and then she started telling me some crazy story about how she grew up there, and that they have alleys behind the houses in Berwyn. Then she said something about that if they get lots of snow in the winter, then it screws up getting out of the garages with your car because the City of Chicago doesn't plow right away or some damn story like that."

Impatiently Tam responded, "Yeah, whatever. Anyway, she was telling me that Larson has made arrangements for the division to have a private party at the ghostbar.

"What's the ghostbar?" Jackson asked.

"Get with it, Jackson," Tam laughed. She leaned lightly into him, tilting her face toward him, "The ghostbar is the hottest club in all of Vegas. It sits up on the fifty-fifth floor of The Palms hotel and has private elevator access that the bouncers guard like Fort Knox. I guess if you're not on the A List then you're not getting into the ghostbar because all the beautiful people are in there. It has these twelve-foot floor to ceiling windows and an outdoor patio deck that allows you to see these awesome 360-degree views of Vegas. And we get to go for a private party! Isn't that cool?"

Tam noticed that they were the only people left in the conference room. She reached out, lacing his fingers with her own. Jackson didn't pull back, but rather, let their hands linger intertwined for a long moment. He peered at her intently.

"Sounds great!" *Just another Alsace party story that I can't tell Lexi about,* he thought. She wasn't shy about expressing her feelings of disdain about all the extravagances at Alsace, especially now that he was in National Accounts. Jackson withdrew his hand slowly, "Looks like everybody's left. How about we go for a run?"

At six o'clock sharp the Account Management division met at the bus entrance of the Bellagio Hotel. Alsace had arranged for two buses to transport the employees to The Palms. It was just starting to get dark in Las Vegas, but it was an unseasonably pleasant 65 degrees even at this late afternoon hour because a warm front had moved up from Mexico and provided the warm temperatures. Jackson and Tam sat together on the bus in the back seat and chitchatted about their lives.

"So how are your wife and son?" Tam started as she moved her leg against his.

"They're good," Jackson said feeling uneasy with her being so physically close. Jackson sometimes wished that the timing had been different between him and Tam because he felt so comfortable with her. *I can tell her anything. She understands how important my work is to me, and she certainly isn't demanding of my time.*

"OK, so how are you and Lexi? She still not too jazzed about all your travel?"

"Not really, especially when she hears about all the dinners, golf, tickets to sports games, and these corporate parties. She just doesn't want to understand that to be successful in this industry there are a certain ways to conduct business in order to get the job done, especially at this level. But we have some great friends around us in KC, so she's never alone when I'm gone," Jackson explained.

"Ah Jackson, from what you've told me, it just sounds to me like she wants to see more of you. I can understand how she feels."

"Yeah, but even when I am home it's like she resents me for being there. You know that there are a lot of hours with these jobs, and I have to travel and be gone! My customers are spread out across the entire United States! You understand that, right?"

"Oh, believe me, I understand about the travel. I've had the same discussions with my husband, Mike. He works in the blacktop business, you know, sealing driveways and parking lots. His family owns the business, but he still just can't understand this whole drug industry and what I do. He also has this big entitlement attitude about prescription drug costs that prices should be next to nothing for all patients. He's such an idiot about some things," Tam laughed as she tossed her blonde hair back on her shoulders.

Jackson felt sheepish deep down about his personal situation, but he was happy to be able to spend some time with Tam. They could both tell that there were very strong feelings for each other just under the surface, waiting to emerge. As the bus took a corner a bit too sharply, Tam slid away from the window and into Jackson who had to grab hold of the armrest and Tam's leg to keep from being spilled into the aisle. While others on the bus expressed loud groans directed toward the driver, the two of them maintained contact with each other for longer than it should have taken once the bus was through the corner and had straightened out. After the incident, Tam slowly slid her hand toward him and found his hand. She felt a warm shiver race through her.

Jackson looked down and saw the sheer pink lace of Tam's bra that was peeking out of her blouse; he looked away quickly, pulled his hand away and started a new subject. "So what did you think about the Afterburners presentation? That Mad Dog guy was a great speaker, eh? I thought the stories about sortie runs and air-to-air combat over Iraq were awesome. I can't believe he had videotape of some of that stuff."

"Yeah, I definitely have some things that I plan to do differently with two of my regional HMO customers when I get back to Florida," Tam replied. She traced a path up his forearm with one finger. She leaned into him and whispered in his ear, "I want you to stay by me tonight at this party. No going off and smoking cigars with your buddies."

Her breath was warm and moist against his face, and it made Jackson's heart quicken. He turned his head and smiled in approval. His gazed slowly slid downward and lazily appraised her. "That shouldn't be too hard." *God, I can't believe that she wants to hang with me!* Jackson's ego soared as he sat up straight, which caused his chest to expand.

The bus pulled into up to The Palms Hotel front lobby entrance, and the Alsace group was greeted by members of the Alsace Travel department who carried signs bearing the name of the company. The group was then led to the elevator entrance for the ghostbar where the bouncers checked their nametags and admitted fifteen people at a time into the elevator. When they arrived at the ghostbar, the sound system pounded out some great tunes. The room was eclectic in design with blue hue lights around the perimeter and a ghostly-looking neon light on the ceiling. Jackson and Tam headed straight to the bar for cocktails. It was not your normal bar service where a few brands of beer and wine were available with your standard cheap hard stuff. Larson ordered that the entire liquor stock be available for pouring at the ghostbar, including the top shelf brands.

"What'll you have?" asked the bartender who was dressed in a pressed white long sleeve shirt and black slacks.

"I'll have a Grey Goose and tonic. Tam, I'm buying, what do you want?"

"Very funny, Jackson. You're buying! Ha! I'll have a Cosmopolitan Martini," Tam said as she curled an arm around his back. Jackson pulled away slightly and feigned reaching for their drinks.

After they received their drinks they went out on the patio to check out the view of the city lights. They also got to stand over a small three-foot square pane of acrylic glass that was embedded in the far corner of the patio deck. While standing atop the glass, one was able to peer downward to see the Skin Pool Lounge some fifty-five stories below. It was not for those who suffered from vertigo by any means.

They wandered around together talking and laughing with others in the division. As an icebreaker, Larson had arranged for everyone to be given a nametag with a celebrity's name written on it and affixed to his or her back. The objective of the activity was for each person to ask questions of others in the room in hopes of trying to guess their own celebrity name written on the sticker. Jackson's celebrity name was Willie Nelson, while Tam's celebrity name was Marilyn Monroe, and Boomer's was Tiny Tim. After the names were guessed correctly, they were permitted to wear the nametag on the front of their shirt or blouse. The icebreaker of questions and responses proved to be a hilarious event that added fuel to the exciting atmosphere already present in the ghostbar.

Dinner consisted of heavy hors d'oeurves, and the way that Jackson and Tam were pounding the free drinks, they had to eat a lot in order to slow down the effects of the alcohol. But the food didn't help them or any of the others in the room. Inhibitions slowly began to break down.

At precisely seven o'clock Jackson quietly excused himself to call home. With a two hour time difference between Las Vegas and Kansas City, he hadn't had a chance to talk with Lexi or Jake yet today, and with the way this party was going, he felt that it was now or never. He made sure that he had his Alsace nametag in his pocket so that he could be re-admitted to the ghostbar. After he exited the elevator, a bouncer directed him toward a bank of public telephones.

The phone rang several times and then flipped over into voicemail. Jackson hung up without leaving a message. *I wonder where they are? Surely they're home because it's getting late.* He dialed their number again. Just before it was to switch into voicemail again Lexi answered.

"Hello?" the voice was hurried on the other end.

"Hi, honey, it's me!" Jackson replied.

"Hi," came the distracted response.

"Lexi, what's the matter? Everything OK?"

"Jackson! No. Everything is not OK! What time is it?"

"It's seven o'clock here."

"And what time is it here at home, Jackson?"

Jackson realized that he had blown it again. "Ah, nine o'clock." It was 30 minutes past Jake's bedtime.

"How many times do I have to ask you to call me before I get Jake ready for bed? He misses you and gets upset when he doesn't get to talk to you before he goes to bed. I miss you too, Jackson." A pause, "You're just not connected at all to us anymore, are you?"

"Sorry Lexi, but the agenda ran late today, and they put us on a bus taking us to this dinner thing."

"Where are you? What's all that noise in the background?" Lexi demanded.

"I'm at The Palms Hotel. We have a dinner function upstairs in a private room that we're required to attend."

"So, once again you couldn't find time to call us when you were actually in your hotel room where it's quiet, and you could spend some quality time talking to me, right? You figured that you would just hurry up and get your call in from where ever the hell you are and check the box that you called in. Is that about right? Couldn't you call during a break or at lunch? Where's your cell phone?"

"It's back in my room. The battery was low so it's charging. Look, there wasn't any time during the breaks because I had meetings with other managers, and then again, no time between the meeting ending and having to get to the transportation lobby to catch the bus to come to the dinner." Jackson explained.

"What, you couldn't have taken a taxi from the Bellagio to The Palms? Isn't it just down the Strip?"

"I didn't think about that. They told us to catch the buses so I got on the bus!"

"So basically, you just did what you were told to do, huh?" Lexi asked.

"Well, yeah."

"So you'll do what Alsace asks you to do but not what I ask you to do. Is that about right? I mean, how many times have I asked you to please call home earlier so we can talk? But no, you do your own thing. Can't rearrange the almighty schedule of Jackson Ford. I feel like a single parent being married to you. And then you call now, it's late, and you want to talk to Jake and get him all worked up, and then I'd have to start all over again to get him calmed down and back into bed. You know he needs his sleep. And I need some quiet time just to talk with you. You're just so inconsiderate, Jackson!" Her voice was rising reflecting her frustration. "Just go back to your dinner, and tell everyone that you called home so they all think you're wonderful." She hung up.

Jackson redialed twice more, but Lexi didn't answer. Frustrated and angry with himself, he went back to the ghostbar and got another vodka and tonic for himself and a Cosmo for Tam.

"Your expression says that the conversation with the home front didn't go so well," Tam remarked as Jackson returned from the phones.

"You know, Tam, I'd rather not talk about it. Can we just change the subject and enjoy ourselves?"

She leaned in close to him and whispered, "I'd like to help you forget about it, Jackson." She gave him a knowing look as she dipped her chin and gazed directly into his eyes. Tam was feeling no pain from the liquor and quickly losing her inhibitions. She slipped an arm around his neck and started to pull his face close to hers.

"Hey slow down there, Party Girl. Let's go see what else there is around here to eat," Jackson said quickly as he pulled away and looked around to check out if anybody was watching them. He felt somewhat embarrassed by the aggressive behavior of Tam, but actually, he felt the butterflies that tickled his gut at the same time. "Tam, let's go see what else is on the buffet. Maybe they've got the desserts out."

Tam pulled Jackson in close again, "I'm looking right at my dessert."

Jackson blushed at that remark. He quickly maneuvered them both over to the dessert buffet where they helped themselves to some truffles, pastries, and whipped cream. Just then Shelly Crawford's voice could be heard on the sound system.

"Hi everybody. Can I have your attention, please?" She waited a minute for the crowd to settle down and become quiet. "To continue our fun tonight here in the ghostbar, we are going to have a karaoke contest. It will be a team competition so we need everyone to check the number on your celebrity nametag. You should see a number between one and ten which represents your team assignment." She then went on to assemble all the like numbers into separate groups throughout the room until all ten teams were together as a group. "Each group has three assignments: Number One—Come up with a team name and write it on the big scoreboard over by the bar. It can be the name of a band or a sports team or a name of your choosing. Number Two—Pick a song that your team would like to sing and give it to the DJ. Number Three—Pull out the items in the black plastic bag being placed in front of your team and get into costume. After each band performs, the other bands will rate them from one to ten on the scoreboard. The first place band with the highest overall score wins a cash prize of one hundred dollars each; the second place band wins fifty dollars each; and the third place band wins twenty-five dollars each."

"Band Number One, you have ten minutes to come up with a name, pick a song to sing, and take the stage in costume."

Jackson, Tam, Boomer and Gary Gant were all members of Band Number Seven. Gant was a National Account Manager located in southern California. He was assigned Kaiser Permanente, Scripps, and WellPoint health plans. Gant was married with a boy and a girl at home who were both in grade school, and he had come up through the ranks in the Finance and Marketing departments at Alsace. He was basically Larson's personal experiment; so to speak, to see if home office employees who had no pharmaceutical sales experience could be successful National Account Managers. So far Gant was proving successful. Larson called him G-Man, and it was quite obvious that Gant was the pet project in the division. G-Man was left handed, smoked Marlboros, and loved to hang out with the ladies. The rest of their team was from various departments at home office including Shelly.

Since the Afterburners presented to the Accounts Management division earlier that day, the group decided on Fly-Byes for a name. The song selected and turned in to the DJ was *Shake Your Booty* by KC & The Sunshine Band. Boomer was assigned the honors of opening the big black plastic bag and distributing the costume items. In it he found rolls of tin foil, bags of big round balloons, party hats, sunglasses, paper bags, a big bolt of cheesecloth, Mardi Gras masks, two hockey face masks, crepe paper, wigs, beards, and a full monkey costume. Boomer immediately blew up two balloons and stuck them under his sweater while putting a paper bag over his head that had holes cut out for his eyes and mouth. This earned him great laughs from the rest of the room and broke the ice for continued silliness as the rest of the room tore into their costume bags. G-Man laid claim to the monkey costume. Jackson suited up with some dread locks, a beard and dark sunglasses while Tam completed his ensemble by wrapping tin foil around his arms and chest. Tam and Shelly both put on psychedelic wigs and the Jason hockey masks. They later found two plastic guitars and Indian headdresses in the back dressing room. The rest of the Fly Byes team scrambled to get into the act with the remaining items. By the time they took the stage, they were dressed and ready for the competition. Tam and Shelly even had time to work out a few dance moves.

The first band opened with *YMCA*, the second band sang *We Are Family*, and the third band performed *I'm A Believer*. The crowd was extremely into it at this point and the generous scores reflected their excitement and blood alcohol levels. Of course, the bar remained open so that the inhibitions of the group could be lowered even further and, subsequently, the scores of the bands could be elevated. It was almost an hour after the Fly Byes were initially in costume before it was their turn to perform. Boomer had already gone through five balloons due to some pranksters that had popped his homemade boob-job. The crowd got louder and louder with each team's performance.

The Fly Byes entered the stage with G-Man leading the way in the monkey suit escorted on either arm by Tam and Shelly. This drew huge cheers from the audience since just before their performance the two women had gone into the Ladies Room, slipped out of their slacks, and fashioned mini-skirts out of the cheesecloth. The home office folks were next wrapped in togas from the cheesecloth and crepe paper while Jackson and Boomer brought up the rear walking out with their arms around each other like they were on a date. By far, the Fly Byes were the most creative in their use of the decorations if one were to judge by the applause received. *Shake Your Booty* was a huge hit garnering big scores by the team judges. The Fly Byes were probably put over the top in the rankings with the special dance moves exhibited by the monkey and his two leading ladies. Actually, several female members from the audience jumped up on stage to join the Fly Byes and got in on some of the dance action. Jackson and Boomer got pulled from the back of the stage and into the monkey three-some for the second half of the song much to the delight of the crowd. Boomer had given Jackson a Swisher Sweet cigar prior to coming on stage, and when Tam and Shelly grabbed the cigars out of their hands and began to smoke them during the final refrain, the crowd went totally nuts. When the song finally ended, Band Eight declined to come on stage, and Bands Nine and Ten each asked if they could request another karaoke song to perform. The DJ politely declined.

In the end, the Fly Byes had first place wrapped up and walked out of the ghostbar each with crisp new one hundred dollar bills in their hands. Of course, the wigs, balloons, mini-skirts and other props were all returned to the big plastic bags. Except for Boomer's boobs.

The night was still young according to Vegas time. Because it was just shy of eleven o'clock, with such wonderful weather, G-Man, Shelly, Tam, and Jackson all caught a taxi together outside The Palms. At Shelly's suggestion, the driver was instructed to proceed to the Stratosphere Hotel and Tower. Upon arrival at the Stratosphere, they took an express elevator 108 floors above the Strip where they found the X Scream roller coaster and the Big Shot thrill ride. After four rides on the roller coaster, they decided that they were sufficiently warmed up for the Big Shot. The Big Shot is a vertical thrill ride that shoots the rider 160 feet straight up in two point five seconds reaching a speed of forty-five MPH and a force of four G's. Upon reaching the top, the rider can peer down through the puke protector shield over 1,000 feet and see the Strip below. After strapping into the safety harnesses, G-Man was nearly ready to pee his pants but noticed that there was not a protective shield down there so he grimaced and pinched himself off during the ride. The foursome rode two more times before calling it quits in order to find G-Man a much-needed bathroom.

The group rode the express elevator back down to the Stratosphere lobby, and poured themselves into a taxi for the return trip to the Bellagio. Jackson sat on the passenger side of the back seat with Tam in the middle seat and Shelly on the driver's side while G-Man sat up front and shot the breeze with the cab driver. Tam's hand found its way onto Jackson's thigh in the close quarters of the back seat. By the time the taxi pulled into the Bellagio driveway, her hand had worked its way up to Jackson's front pants pocket, and that's where his hand tightened around her wrist to stop any more movement.

As Shelly and G-Man stepped out, Tam held Jackson in his seat and announced eagerly, "We're going to go out to breakfast at a place I know down the strip. We'll see you in the morning." Jackson waved from his spot in the back with a crooked grin. Shelly and G-Man simply looked at each other knowingly and smirked because they had seen this kind of thing countless times before at Alsace with other couples pairing off at company meetings.

As the taxi pulled away from the Bellagio, Tam informed the driver, "Just make a big loop up and down the Strip, and keep your eyes on the road in front of you."

A half hour later, Jackson paid the driver. He made sure to give him a generous tip for keeping his eyes front. *Tam is amazing. I think I'm in lust,* Jackson thought.

The next morning Jackson saw G-Man at the Account Management breakfast. They both looked rough, but awake, when one considers the night each of them had.

"Hey Gary, how're you doing today, bud? Did you get any sleep?"

"Well, I would've gotten another hour more except my wife called me at six o'clock this morning."

"Six? What was she calling you so early for? Are the kids, OK?"

"Well, it seems that I forgot to engage the keypad lock on my cell phone after I called home last night, and I must have butt-dialed her a few times while I was out. Apparently, she got one call before midnight. She said that there was a lot of screaming and what sounded like train noises. Then, as if that wasn't bad enough, I happened to be sitting in the small waiting area just off the casino smoking a cigarette and minding my own business. Two ladies of the evening happened to stroll past, and they were checking me out. Well, one thing leads to another and the three of us get to talking, you know, about what they do and stuff, and apparently, my wife got another phone call from my cell phone just about that time. To say the least, she didn't appreciate listening to me talk smack with two hookers at two in the morning. I'm probably going to be big time grounded when I get home."

Jackson knew a thing or two about that. He had already called a Teleflora company early that morning and ordered Lexi a dozen pink roses. Deep down he knew he had a lot of making up to do when he would arrive home later that night. The cab ride with Tam had started to work on his Catholic guilt.

CHAPTER 14
BROKEN TEE

Jackson enjoyed his National Account Manager position immensely. He took great pride in his work. It included the design of business plans and medical educational programs for the federal market. This enabled the Alsace hospital sales representatives to implement the activities in their local VA or Military medical centers. Jackson's plans and programs, in concert with his successful contract negotiations, provided Alsace hospital representatives the necessary tools to pull through product sales in this key market segment. Savvy hospital sales representatives who took full advantage of the market opportunity were able to put up big sales numbers within their respective districts, thus allowing them to earn huge bonus dollars. By flawlessly executing on Jackson's promotional plans, many of these same hospital representatives consistently made the various sales awards clubs that Alsace offered. These representatives, District Managers, and Region Sales Directors looked to Jackson for guidance and direction for their federal hospitals, especially with the implementation of the new regional design, under which the market segments were organized. There were hospital reps who snobbishly disregarded the VA and Military hospitals and only called on their ivory tower academic institutions. Their counterparts, including Jackson, embraced the federal hospitals and had excellent sales.

Jackson enjoyed calling on his VA and Military physician and pharmacy customers, and he found that some good friendships blossomed as a result of his work. Jackson also discovered that in the managed care arena, however, many contracts were developed and many deals were done through various entertainment venues. For example, he found that many of the Medical Directors, Hospital Administrators, Physicians, and Pharmacy Directors in the federal market loved to play golf, and Jackson quickly worked his way into an exclusive boys club of forty Big Pharma NAMs and federal customers who set up an annual trip to a premium golf resort to play their beloved sport for four straight days.

The outing was called the Broken Tee, and Bob Johnson and Colonel Frank Buck coordinated every detail of the event as if they were planning the invasion of Normandy. They carefully paired up the Big Pharma NAMs with a federal customer to accommodate the resort golf packages that were based on double occupancy hotel rooms and thirty-six holes of golf each day. The unspoken agreement was that the Big Pharma NAM would pay for the entire cost of the federal customer's resort package and then hide it in their respective company's expense reimbursement system. It worked beautifully, and the NAMs were more than happy to accommodate the junket so that they too could play golf."Jackson, this Michigan conference expense proposal seems a bit high," Rick Thompson said over the telephone.

"Rick, about twenty of my key customers are having an industry input forum to discuss a variety of issues pertinent to the federal market over the four day conference. I'm one of only twenty Big Pharma NAMs who has been selected to attend and provide input during the sessions. You know, Rick, this market is not very rich with funding of their own, so they've asked that the NAMs pick up the cost of the sleeping rooms for the customers since we'll be paired up with them as roommates. This is a very unique opportunity for building relationships with these important decision makers in my market," Jackson explained.

"You're going to have a roommate who just happens to be one of your customers?" Thompson asked in disbelief.

"Yes."

"Well, the way that this segment is performing against the planned sales goals, I guess that I'll approve it. Anything to keep the sales line trending upward is the right thing to do," Thompson said. "Just give me a call afterwards to let me know how it went."

In the end, the costs were not all that outrageous for the Big Pharma NAMs. Colonel Buck had negotiated a government rate with the resort for the rooms and golf so the room and green fees for two people ended up being about $1,500 for the four days. A drop in the bucket on the Travel and Entertainment expense budget line for the Big Pharma NAMs, and the face time with the customers was priceless.

The 144 holes of golf were amazing, yet challenging. Some of the older guys got blisters and sore backs early in the tournament play. With all the Icy Hot ointment being applied each morning, the practice tee area smelled like a high school wrestling team's locker room. The combination of Bloody Mary's and some non-steroidal anti-inflammatory tablets became the normal breakfast of champion golfers that kicked off the day. With Band-Aids applied to the blistered fingers, the boys came out each morning to play golf, gamble, drink beer, and smoke cigars!

The twenty Big Pharma NAMs formed a close friendship during and after the Broken Tee. They were all aware of the good thing that they had going, but yet they still worked for competing companies when it came to the federal market national formulary and contracting proposals. Setting those two business issues aside for one week out of the year, the NAMs chose instead to compete with each other by seeing who could bring the best golf giveaways from their respective companies for the Broken Tee participants.

"Jackson, you had better bring an extra duffle bag to the Broken Tee. You're going to get a whole bunch of goodies from your peers. Hey, make sure that you pick a good giveaway yourself from Alsace to bring for the guys," Steelballs told him about a week before the event.

Alsace had a huge storage room at headquarters that was filled with trinkets and product giveaway items for the National Account Managers to use with customers so the choice was difficult, but Jackson finally settled on golf balls. Just a few days prior to the trip, Jackson shipped two cases of LOMEC logo golf balls to the resort so that he could hand them out to the participants at the registration desk. He knew that it was forbidden to talk product or business during the golf rounds, but he certainly could get in some reminder advertising for his lead product to the physicians and pharmacists while they played with them. Of course, the way some of the guys sliced and hacked up the golf course, his LOMEC golf balls got blamed for every shot that hooked into the woods or skipped into a sand trap, or worse, the water. But then again, when a birdie putt was made, the LOMEC golf ball got credit along with the big stud that drained it in the jar.

Johnson and Buck had also set up various contests each day where some of the items were used as prizes: most skins, longest drive, closest to the hole, lowest gross score, and lowest net score were just some of the contests tracked on a large scoreboard set up in the resort bar each night.

Jackson brought home a golf club travel bag, an umbrella, two rain Jackets, one golf shirt, two golf towels, and a new putter all compliments of the other Big Pharma NAMs who had similar store rooms at their respective headquarters filled with giveaways. Most of the items had a competing drug name or Big Pharma company name on them but Jackson didn't mind. He loved the stuff. Lexi loathed all the drug company crap so Jackson had to store it in the garage.

Each night the Big Pharma NAMs picked up the tab for all the dinners. On most nights, several NAMs would simply split the bill so that it would not look too big on the weekly expenses and catch the eye of a company auditor. At one of these dinners, Jackson was in the process of splitting a bill with a guy he had just met who later become a close friend. His name was Rob Pickett or Pick for short. He was from a competing Big Pharma company, Schering Plough, and had been a National Account Manager for about the same length of time as Jackson. Jackson found out that Pick was married and had a young daughter in elementary school, and since Pick and his family lived in Tampa, he was able to play golf year-round. Pick was unique when it came to golf, he was right-handed at everything but played golf left-handed just like Phil Mickelson. Unlike Mickelson, he needed a lot of work on his game. Pick would shoot in the high eighties in the morning and then come right back after lunch and post a score of a hundred and five. Golf was his passion, but it frustrated him.

The first year Jackson played in the Broken Tee event, it was held in July at the Treetops Resort in Gaylord, Michigan. At the time,

Michigan ranked number three in the total number of golf courses in the state behind Florida and California. The resort used three champion golf course architects to design the four eighteen-hole courses located at the resort. With the beautiful summer weather that upstate Michigan typically experienced, all four courses were in fabulous condition for the Broken Tee group to attack. The players were paired differently for each round with handicap adjustments made according to skill level. On the days that Pickett shot the lights out, he came away with a lot of money from the skins pool because his handicap was a legitimate twenty-five. During the round that he and Jackson talked extensively about the federal market, their respective companies, and their families. Two best practices that Jackson picked up from Pickett occurred over an afternoon of playing the Rick Smith designed course named *Signature*. He did not know it at the time, but the two best practices would change his life.

"Rob, I really enjoy working in the federal segment, especially with the reorganization of the market into regions and a more centralized formulary system. What do you think?" Jackson asked his new friend while they were in the golf cart riding between holes on the *Signature* course.

"You know, Jackson, it was a lot like the wild west before where a company could just work the hell out of the 300 hospitals, get their product on the hospital formulary, and then sell like crazy. I agree that it's much easier to do with the current organizational design. What I really like is the contracting process and negotiating with old Steelballs at the VA PBM. Hey, you know where there is still somewhat of an open market within the military?" Pickett asked.

"Ah, no. Where?"

"In Europe and Asia at the U.S. military hospitals located on the big bases. In the European market, there are probably five or six base hospitals in Germany, three in Italy, two in Spain, and several in England. In Asia, there are three bases in South Korea, four in Japan, and one in the Philippines. Several of the NAMs here at Broken Tee have already submitted proposals to our respective companies for approval to travel to each one working like sales representatives and calling on the physicians and pharmacists promoting our products. There isn't a high control formulary system for the Military Theatre Command so the individual medical centers offer increased opportunity for the companies that are willing to send someone to work them," replied Pickett.

"What's the sales opportunity? I mean, what are the numbers of deployed active duty and their families and retirees in the overseas catchment areas?" Jackson asked.

"You know, a group of us have a proposal that's floated back and forth between companies with changes made to it depending on the therapeutic classes that your company competes in. It's a PowerPoint slide presentation. Why don't I just email you a copy of it? Give me your email address tonight when we get back to the resort."

"OK. Yeah, I'd be interested to see it. Has Schering approved you to travel to Europe and Asia?" Jackson asked.

"I'm scheduled to go to Europe for three weeks in late August, and then about two weeks in Asia in early December."

"Call me when you get back so I can get your assessment of the opportunity and potential sales impact," Jackson said.

"Why don't you come to Tampa in December for a couple of days? You can work the Tampa VA Medical Center and MacDill Air Force Base with your reps, and then I'll take you to play golf at the West Chase golf course so I can brief you on the trips. The course is right by the Tampa Airport Marriott."

"OK, deal. Thanks, Rob. Hey, it's our turn to tee off."

Jackson and Pickett both hit beautiful tee shots about 250 yards down the right side of the fairway. The two VA physicians were impressed with the shots and commented that they were probably going to have a hard time telling which LOMEC golf ball belonged to whom.

After getting back in the cart, Jackson asked Pickett, "Hey, what do you know about Dave from Merck setting up a team of Federal Account Managers reporting to a Director?"

"You know, I talked to him at breakfast, and it's an interesting proposal. Some of the other NAMs here are thinking about a similar move. With all these regions for the VA and DoD, it's a lot of work for just one National Account Manager to handle. I can see why Dave wants to deploy about five or six managers with each one responsible for six to eight federal regions all reporting to one Director. If some of these other Big Pharma companies do this, then you may want to seriously think about following suit from a competitive standpoint. I'm certain Schering would want to."

"Pick, are you going to be proactive with a proposal like that?" Jackson asked.

"Not until next year. I'm waiting until after I get back from Europe and Asia and demonstrate how much value there is from a sales perspective, and then propose that I need help with a team of Account Managers. I think that I'll use Merck as a model for what we should be doing from a competitive position. Schering's upper management are always trying to copy Merck any way that they can because they usually don't have an original idea of their own," Pickett replied.

"Hmmm...I think I better get a copy of your Europe and Asia proposal pronto, so Alsace doesn't get left behind. Then, I think I better have breakfast with the Merck guy to pick his brain on a federal team proposal. Looking ahead, that might be a way to keep Alsace competitive as well, but it could also be a way for me to move up within the Company," Jackson stated.

"Sounds good to me, my man! OK, a dollar for closest to the hole on this approach shot."

Pulling out a seven iron from his bag Jackson said, "OK. You're on, Nancy."

CHAPTER 15
WINTER SPORTS CLINIC

Although millions of dollars in grants are spent each year by Big Pharma companies to help grow prescription sales through managed care organizations, pharmacy benefits management companies, integrated health systems, wholesalers, and individual practitioners, there are also times when the big grant checks are allocated to non-profit foundations and organizations in an effort to be good corporate citizens and give back to the community. These organizations fully realize that Big Pharma is well positioned financially to make substantial contributions to their cause, but they just need to have the appropriate contact person to serve as their voice and to state their plea for money up the chain of command.

While he sat in attendance at the morning session of the sustaining members fourth quarter meeting of the Association of Military Surgeons of the United States or AMSUS in the Officer's Club at Andrews Air Force Base, Jackson heard one such plea from the National Commander of the Disabled American Veterans organization. While addressing the membership comprised mainly of National Account Managers from Big Pharma and Medical/Surgical companies from his wheelchair, the National Commander used a slide presentation to explain the DAV's mission and upcoming sponsorship opportunities.

"After wars end and peace treaties are negotiated, there are still other battles that are ongoing and never end. I'm referring to the battles of those disabled by war. These are brave men and women who have been injured in the line of duty, serving and protecting their country; they struggle each and every day to lead a new life outside the military as a civilian. New job skills must be learned and new professions sought, oftentimes accompanied by extensive medical care or just help with activities of daily living.

"To help disabled veterans learn to help themselves, the Disabled American Veterans organization, comprised of over one million disabled veterans, has come to the aid of these individuals, their families and survivors without any funding from Congress. Although Congress chartered the DAV in 1932, it remains to this day a non-profit organization relying solely on public and corporate donations as well as membership dues to operate at a regional and national level.

"One example of a critically important program is the DAV Transportation Network. Under this program, DAV volunteers drive disabled veterans to the VA Medical Centers for treatment and rehabilitation. These veterans are usually seeking care for service-connected disabilities or are financial hardship cases and have no other options for health care. The DAV has stepped in to fill a void after the cancellation of federal funds previously in place to provide our veterans with funding for transportation services. Under the DAV Transportation Network, volunteers donate their own time, car or van, and gas money to meet the transportation requests that come in from disabled veterans. Even though the DAV purchased a fleet of its own vans for this program, the Big Three automakers, namely Ford, donated additional vehicles to our program where the need was the greatest."

The audience was listening intently now after seeing images on the screen of many wheelchair-bound veterans stricken with spinal cord injuries or who had lost sight or limbs as a result of war injuries. Jackson's heart went out to these disabled veterans and families who clearly made substantial physical and emotional sacrifices for their service. He looked around the Officer's Club or OC conference room and saw his peers transfixed as well on the speaker and his message. Seated next to him was Rob Pickett who was taking notes on the information provided.

The National Commander continued, "Each year the DAV organization sponsors a week-long Winter Sports Clinic for our disabled veterans at the Crested Butte Mountain Resort in Colorado. The primary purpose of the clinic is to serve as a physical rehabilitation program for about 300 veterans who struggle to overcome their physical disabilities. For example, we outfit the disabled veterans in special ski sleds tethered to our volunteer instructors, we partner the blind skiers with an instructor who shouts out turning commands, and we conduct slalom course races for the amputees. Because many of the veterans believe that they can no longer lead physically active lives, we call the Winter Sports Clinic, 'Miracles on the Mountainside.' We know firsthand that lives are forever changed because of participation in the clinic. Although the disability stays with the veteran for the rest of his or her life, the psychological changes that are made on the mountain are amazing.

"This year we are seeking corporate sponsors and volunteers to join the Coke and Ford companies help fund the annual Winter Sports Clinic. You should have received an information packet at the registration desk today that includes sponsorship opportunities ranging anywhere from five thousand to fifty thousand dollars. With the various financial support levels, there are corresponding benefit packages for the sponsoring company. For example, with a ten thousand dollar sponsorship level, the corporate sponsor is provided with four lift tickets for the week, ten hours of complimentary private ski instruction, and discounted hotel rates and ski equipment rental rates. Of course, we also ask that the corporate sponsors volunteer at least one afternoon at the ski lifts providing assistance to the veterans helping them into and off from the lift chairs. If you have any specific questions or need further information, I will be available throughout the lunch break. You can also give me your corporate sponsorship pledge card today and then begin the grant check process when you return to your corporate offices."

When the presentation concluded, the National Commander gathered his notes and slides and wheeled himself toward the back of the Officer's Club. Touched deeply by the presentation, the audience rose and applauded him for several minutes. The National Commander knew by the length of the standing ovation that this year's event would have more than adequate funding to cover the costs of the Winter Sports Clinic. They might even be able to afford to bring in a big name entertainer like one of those major league baseball umpires or a NASCAR driver or even a retired professional athlete for the corporate sponsor's awards dinner that typically kicked off the week-long festivities. Those guys could tell great stories and make everyone feel good about their sponsorship dollars being spent on the DAV.

"This is an outstanding opportunity," Pickett said as he leaned into Jackson. "You've got to get Alsace to help sponsor this clinic. I'm going to submit a grant request to Schering for ten thousand dollars, which is the Gold sponsorship level. That'll get me the four lift tickets so I can bring my family. It's my daughter's spring break. I'll put her in snowboard school for a few days while my wife and I hit the slopes."

Lexi's not a skier, the shopping is lousy, and it would mean pulling Jake from school, Jackson thought.

"I'll probably consider the five thousand dollar Bronze sponsorship level because that's the grant of authority at which I don't need my manager's approval. I'm not going to be able to bring my family, however," he said to Pickett.

Jackson thought to himself, *The second lift ticket is going to go to waste...unless.* Jackson knew that Tam was a skier and that she usually took a trip with her girlfriends each year because her husband was not into any physical sports except fishing. He usually went to Canada for a week each summer.

On the drive back to Reagan National Airport to catch his flight for the return trip home, Jackson called her up. "Hi Tam!" He was always glad to talk with her, especially since they had gotten so close during their cab ride.

"Hi handsome! I was just thinking about you."

"I've been thinking a lot about you too, Tam. I was at an AMSUS meeting today in Washington DC, and we had a presentation by the National Commander from the Disabled American Veterans organization. It turns out that they host a week-long Winter Sports Clinic each March in Colorado attended by about 300 disabled veterans. They were seeking corporate sponsorship monies to help fund the program, and I'm going to contribute from my grant budget," explained Jackson.

"What does that have to do with us?" she asked.

"I'm getting to that. If I contribute at the five thousand dollar Bronze sponsorship level, then Alsace will receive two free lift tickets for the week and discounted ski rental rates. I'm wondering if you've made plans for your annual ski trip with your girlfriends. The DAV program is going to be held at Mount Crested Butte," he added.

"Are you thinking of asking me to come with you?" she asked.

"Yes, I am asking you right now. My wife won't want to go so I thought that maybe you might be interested."

"Jackson, I would love to!"

"What will you tell your husband?" he asked.

"Don't worry about me. You just worry about how you're going to explain a week of skiing to Lexi."

"I'll take her someplace warm over Jake's Spring Break to divert her attention from this junket."

"OK, then it's all settled. What are the dates? I've never been to Crested Butte. What airport do I use? And hey, I'm assuming that you'll let me bunk in your room, right? The Company is paying for your room since it's a business trip, aren't they? I'll make it worth your while," she said in a playful, teasing way.

"That was my thought, Tam. You are such a naughty girl!" he laughed.

They said good-bye after exchanging the necessary information to coordinate the trip. They decided that since Tam had thousands of frequent flyer award miles, that she would simply cash in some rewards points for a free airline ticket. Jackson would be able to submit the expenses for the hotel room, meals, and rental car because he would be on official Company business, and the DAV would provide a free week of ski lift tickets with the five thousand dollar Bronze level grant from Alsace. At the end of the telephone conversation, they figured that they only had to pay out of their own pockets the nominal rental fees for skis and boots that the resort charged.

I'll have to remember to request a suite with a hot tub, thought Jackson.

Jackson and Tam arrived the following March on a Friday afternoon in Crested Butte. Most of the other Big Pharma NAMs were not arriving for another day since the Sponsor's Awards Dinner was not until Saturday night. Because Pickett also lived in Tampa and would be traveling on Saturday with his family, there was a distinct possibility that Tam and the Pickett family would end up on the same flights. Jackson suggested to Tam that they come in a day early to avoid any of his Big Pharma peers spotting them together. He assumed he had a good chance of not being seen by his peers the rest of the week since the mountain resort was huge.

Jackson's flight landed an hour before Tam so he picked up the rental car and got directions to the resort. He then called Lexi and Jake. During the conversation, Lexi complained.

"I know I said this before, but couldn't you find someone else to take your place?"

"I'm the only National Account Manager for the federal market, and that means I'm the one that has to go to these events. The Company representatives have to volunteer certain hours to help with the disabled veterans."

"But you're missing Jake's game tomorrow! I still don't believe you had to leave on a Friday. What's her name, Jackson? I'm not stupid. We've been together too long for me not to think you've got something going. Who is she?"

"First of all, there's no one! Second, the clinic starts on Saturday morning with the sponsor's awards dinner that evening. I have to be here! Now, we've been through this already, OK? Put Jake on. I'd like to talk to him, please."

When Tam walked from the tarmac and into the small terminal, she and Jackson embraced and kissed like a couple of newlyweds. Jackson was proud of himself for suggesting that they come in a day early since the terminal was very small, and it would have been hard not to be noticed by the other Big Pharma NAMs. After they located Tam's luggage and loaded it in the trunk of the rental car, they drove up the mountain to the resort.

"Jackson, I could hardly contain myself this past week. I couldn't wait to see you!"

"Me too, Tam." Slipping his arm around her shoulder as she snuggled close he continued, "Thanks for coming. I'm really looking forward to spending time with you. So, how well do you ski?" he asked.

"My father used to take us to Colorado and Utah skiing every year since I was six years old, so I think I can handle whatever Intermediate or Advanced trails this place has to offer. How about you?"

"Wisconsin gets a lot of snow. No mountains, but there are ski resorts, if you can call them that. I grew up skiing at them. I think I'll be OK," he said.

"We'll just have to see now, won't we?" Tam placed her hand on Jackson's thigh. For the rest of the drive they talked about Alsace and particularly about how they would see each other again at the upcoming training session scheduled for Account Managers in Santa Monica in just two months.

Crested Butte was a former mining town until the 1960's when the mines closed and someone suggested putting ski lifts up on the mountain. Since then, it boomed into a great ski location with its deep powder, multiple lifts, and lack of overcrowded trails compared to some of the more popular Colorado resorts like Vail, Aspen, and Steamboat Springs. It wasn't as highbrow as Deer Valley in Salt Lake City, but Crested Butte stood out by offering skiing and snowboarding for purists in the sport. The resort developers cut over seventy trails and ten bowls in the mountainside that had an elevation of over 11,000 feet. The longest run was over two point five miles, and each year, new and improved grooming equipment was purchased so the crews could get the trails in pristine condition each night.

After they checked into the hotel, they loaded their bags on a luggage cart in order to transport it to their room. When they opened the door to their suite, they discovered a large fruit basket and bottle of white wine compliments of the DAV organizers. Since they had both only eaten airline food all day, they tore open the cellophane wrapping and started in on the fruit. Jackson went to retrieve a bucket of ice, and when he came back he opened the wine.

After pouring two glasses he proposed a toast, "To us, and the skiing!"

After taking a drink Tam gazed around the room, "I see that there is only one bed."

"Is that a problem?"

They spent the rest of the evening showing each other why it wasn't a problem.

Jackson and Tam woke up early on Saturday morning. They had a discussion about calling home during the week. Tam brought up the topic while they were lying beside each other.

"Jackson, I'm really attracted to you and want to see where this relationship goes, but like you, I'm married, and I lied to my husband about who I was going to be with this week. I have to call him once a day to check in."

Jackson's face had an expression of concern that matched Tam's. "I know that this is a little awkward for both of us. I didn't lie to Lexi but I didn't tell her the truth either about who I was going to be sleeping with this week," he grinned at Tam in an attempt to help break the tension. The concerned look melted off her face, and she smiled back at him.

Jackson continued, "I've got to call home every night as well and with the time change I should do it about five o'clock. Since there is no cell phone coverage up here on the mountain, we need to either use the room phone or the lobby pay phones."

"I should probably call between five and six o'clock as well. I would prefer to use the room phone."

"I should use the room phone too," said Jackson. *Lexi will get even more suspicious if I'm calling from the lobby every night.*

"OK, so we both use the room phone but the other person steps out and has a drink at the lobby bar, and then we switch places?"

Jackson agreed.

After they showered together and got dressed, the two went out to breakfast at the Avalanche Grill. It was a very casual bar and restaurant that opened each day at six in the morning. The only customers at that hour were the grooming crews just coming off the mountain after working all night and the lift operators and ski patrol who were preparing to go up the mountain to begin their shift. The crews were long gone by the time Jackson and Tam got there at eight o'clock. The mountain air and the altitude had made them both hungry.

To work off breakfast, they walked the long way back to the hotel through the village, which allowed them to window shop.

When they arrived back at the hotel, Tam took the elevator back to the suite while Jackson went to find the Winter Sports Clinic registration room. At the Clinic check in, he received his two lift tickets, the sponsor's awards dinner ticket, and the discount passes for equipment rental at a local ski shop. The DAV had also arranged all the corporate sponsor's giveaways that the NAMs had shipped to the hotel for distribution to the clinic participants. Jackson shipped a case of lip balm with SPF fifteen to the hotel. The tubes had an Alsace product logo that represented their antihistamine drug. He grabbed a couple of lip balm applicators, a bottle of sun screen, and two pair of sunglasses.

Just as he finished signing up for the one hour a day volunteer times for the chair lifts, the DAV National Commander wheeled himself into the room with a brown shoe box on his lap.

"Hello Commander! I'm Jackson Ford with Alsace Pharmaceuticals. This is my first time as a sponsor for the Winter Sports Clinic!"

"Hey, Jackson. It's good to finally meet you. Oh, I think you are really going to enjoy yourself this week. The snow is great and the weather forecast looks terrific. Do you ski?"

"Yes. I grew up skiing in Wisconsin but have never made it to the big hills of the Rockies, yet!"

"Great!" the National Commander was eyeing the wedding ring on Jackson's hand. "I see you're married. Did you bring your family?"

Jackson's face turned bright red as he lied, "No, I'm by myself on this trip."

Holding up the box from his lap, "Well here, I have some commemorative pins for this year's clinic. Why don't you take some home for your wife and kids? Have you got kids?" he asked.

"Just a son," came the reply.

"Here then, take three pins. One for you, one for your wife, and one for your son." He handed over the pins to Jackson. They were lapel pins or Jacket pins, like the kind sold at all the Hard Rock Café restaurants. The pins had an outline of the mountain and the snowflake design that was the same logo found on all the brochures associated with the Winter Sports Clinic.

"Thank you very much, sir. That's nice of you. I'll be sure they get them."

"Since you're alone, I'll make sure to save you a seat at my table tonight at the Sponsor's awards dinner. Most of the other corporate sponsors all brought family members so seating will be a little tight."

"OK, thanks again. I'll see you tonight!" Jackson said. He gathered up his giveaways and tickets and headed out of the room.

Jackson went back to the room to meet Tam and get ready for some skiing. She had laid out their snow pants, Jackets, and pullovers on the bed. After applying sunscreen to their faces they outfitted themselves in their ski apparel. Jackson took this opportunity to give one of the Winter Sports Clinic pins to Tam. Which he promptly pinned on her ski Jacket.

"Oh Jackson, I feel like I'm getting lavaliered like back at my college sorority." She drew his face to hers and kissed him. When she finished, Jackson put on his Jacket and his pin so that they would match.

They then applied the weekly ski lift stickers to the metal T bar and slid the ends into their Jacket zippers. The weekly tickets would allow them clear access to any of the ski lifts for the rest of the week.

As they left the hotel, they noticed that wooden ramps were being placed outside the front of the building and along sidewalks near several main intersections in the village. The resort area was not fully compliant with the state disability laws specific to wheelchair access so the workers were required to put in temporary ramps in order to accommodate the throng of disabled veterans that were expected.

Jackson and Tam held hands as they walked to the Mountain High Sporting Goods store. After presenting the discount card at the ski rental counter, a young guy with blonde dreadlocks took their measurements and proceeded to outfit them with the appropriate ski gear. They left within twenty minutes with top of the line Salomon skis, boots, and poles and were now officially ready to hit the slopes.

Tam had picked up a trail map the previous afternoon at the hotel so they reviewed it and planned which section of the mountain to ski first.

"Hey, Tam, would you mind if we stick to some of the beginner trails for the first hour just so we can get our ski legs under us?"

"What's the matter, Jackson?" she said teasing him. "Did I keep you up too late last night? A little wobbly are you?"

"No," came the reply. "I just haven't skied in about ten years so a bit of warm up would be nice is all."

"OK, Shirley. I mean Jackson! Let's head over to the Keystone Lift just past the ski school. There are some nice greens like Mineral Point and Houston that should warm you up."

"Thanks, Tam. I just need a little practice to get my balance before we start doing the blue runs."

After they snapped into their bindings, Tam leaned over and kissed him on the cheek. "Jackson, thank you again for inviting me. I really think we're going to have a great time together. And just remember, I am your only ski bunny this week!"

"I'm glad you came too." *She makes every outfit look great,* he admitted to himself.

They skied over to the Keystone Lift just a hundred yards away and took their place in line. After the getting their lift tickets scanned, they were next in line for the lift chairs. When it was their turn, they moved up to the Load Here board marked by a red stripe on the platform and sat back in perfect unison on the bench and raised their ski tips at the precise moment to clear the lift area. As the chair lifted above the loading area and headed up the mountain, Jackson pulled down the safety bar, and they began to look around at the mountain and resort area.

As they neared the top of the lift, they raised the safety bar together and prepared to unload. They slid their hands through the leather straps on the poles, and then started to inch forward up in the seat to position them for unloading. The key to unloading is to use the lift's momentum and propel oneself forward, and then ski down the short exit ramp. At the moment of truth when one's skis are supposed to be placed on the snow ramp to begin the exit process, Tam performed an expert move to exit the chair lift. However, as she was coming off the seat she turned half-way into Jackson, and as he started to raise himself out of the chair lift, Tam gave him a hard shove backwards sending him all the way back into the chair unable to exit. She laughed as she skied all the way down the snow ramp, and then she stopped and turned around to see Jackson still sitting in the chair lift.

With Tam's shove, Jackson was not able to recover in time to move himself forward, get his balance and ski tips up, and push off the chair to make it to the exit ramp in time. He could only watch in frustration and embarrassment as his lift chair swung around the corner ready to make the return trip down the mountain. Jackson's skis were dangling three feet off the ground when the operator finally got the lift to stop. At this point, Tam was bending over laughing hysterically. Other skiers who had exited before Tam were standing around and watching the event unfold, and upon seeing Tam laughing so hard, they too broke into cheers and shouts aimed in Jackson's direction. The applause was a bit muffled due to the heavy ski gloves being worn, but the effect was the same. Total embarrassment for Jackson.

"Dude, you're my first bull-whipper of the season, and the season's almost over!" said the shaggy looking lift operator as he ran out of the shack next to the lift. "Don't you know that you're supposed to get off on that ramp back there? You know, I just shoveled some fresh snow on it this morning to help unloading." He pointed a hand back toward the exit ramp covered with powder.

"I know, I know. Just help me down, man."

Jackson unsnapped his skis, slipped the poles off his hands, and passed them down to the young operator who asked, "My man, can you jump from there?"

"Yeah, I think I can." And he did. Tam stood below and waited for him.

"You!" Jackson exclaimed. He reached down, got a handful of snow, and threw it at her. She ducked which caused him to miss.

"Dude, if you're OK then I gotta restart the lift. We got a lot of skiers dangling in mid-air because of you," the operator quipped.

Tam reached down, picked up some snow and tossed it at Jackson hitting him in the back as he turned to avoid a facial hit. They laughed for another minute and began to ski away.

They skied the rest of the day without any more bullwhip incidents and returned to their suite to clean up and get Jackson ready for the Sponsor's dinner.

The sponsor's dinner was held in one of the banquet halls and lasted about three hours. The DAV brought in a major league baseball umpire to entertain the group for the evening followed by the awards ceremony. All of the corporate sponsors received a plaque indicating the level of sponsorship aligned to the financial donation level provided to the DAV. Jackson accepted his Bronze sponsorship plaque on behalf of Alsace Pharmaceuticals and had his picture taken with the National Commander.

Rob Pickett and his family were at the dinner. After the program Rob introduced his wife and daughter to Jackson.

"It's a pleasure to meet you, Rob's told me so much about you!" Jackson said to Rob's wife.

"Likewise. He's got a new golfing buddy with you. You didn't bring your family, huh?" she asked.

"No. Our spring break was two weeks ago so they weren't able to come because of school. We did the Disney thing in Orlando, however, and stayed at the Grand Floridian Hotel. We also found out that Jake doesn't like the big roller coasters, yet. Where are you guys staying, Rob?"

"I rented a condo on the other side of the village so we could keep the meal costs down. Schering is picking up my condo expense for the week which is actually comparable to the hotel suites, but we're on our own for the meals since we're not in the headquarters hotel."

Jackson thought that was good since Pick was the one Federal NAM from Big Pharma that he didn't especially want to run into with Tam, and if he was staying outside of the headquarters hotel on the other side of town, then the chances of that happening were pretty slim. "Well, I'm kinda tired with the time change and the altitude, so I think I'm going to head upstairs and relax. Maybe I'll see you on the slopes tomorrow!"

Rob replied, "I don't think so since we're taking advantage of the free ski lessons while our daughter is in snowboard school."

"Well, good night then."

When Jackson opened the door to the hotel suite he shouted, "Honey, I'm home!" He found that Tam was in her robe sitting in front of the fireplace, and that she had ordered a bottle of champagne from room service. Jackson lifted the bottle out of the ice bucket to refill her glass and fill a fresh glass for himself. Tam was very quiet.

"Tam, is everything OK?"

"Everything is OK now that you're here. Come sit by me and just give me a hug. I need you to hold me, Jackson."

Sitting beside her after placing his glass on the cocktail table he asked, "What's the matter?" He gave her a reassuring hug and noticed that she smelled like lavender.

"I called Mike while you were at the dinner, and we got in this huge argument. I've just come to the realization that we've grown apart because we're so different. I've just passed him by with my career, you know, and I don't think we're going to make it." Tears started to form in her eyes. "But you're here now, and that's all that matters. When I think about it, there is no comparison between you and Mike. You're going places with Alsace, and Mike isn't going anywhere. I need a partner who has a future, and that man is you. I love you, Jackson." She took his face in her hands and began to kiss him all over his cheeks and neck.

After a moment Jackson pulled back and looked into Tam's glistening eyes.

"Jackson, I'm in love with you, and I'm happy for the first time in a long time," she said smiling at him.

Jackson said nothing in reply. He didn't feel anything but lust for her. Clearly, Tam was in a completely different spot emotionally compared to Jackson, and he began to feel guilty about bringing her along for the week. Jackson cared about one thing only, and that was Alsace. They sat on the couch in silence and held each other while watching the fire until Jackson suggested that they go to bed. Neither one fell asleep for some time as they both thought about what transpired on the couch.

The next morning they awoke to a beautiful sunny Colorado day with a bright blue skies. It looked like it was going to be a gorgeous day at Mt. Crested Butte. After Jackson and Tam showered together and dressed, they found that they could not keep their hands off each other, nor their lips for that matter.

They ate breakfast again at the Avalanche Grill. After they retrieved their ski equipment from the hotel storage room, they were ready for another day on the trails. Jackson was scheduled to work his volunteer shift for an hour after lunch so they skied the bowls on the eastern side of the mountain. Lunch was at the Twister Grill located mid-way up the slope. After a bowl of chili and hot chocolate, they agreed to meet two hours later again at the grill to finish off the afternoon.

After kissing each other goodbye, Tam headed for the Twister Lift while Jackson skied his way over to the East River Lift for his shift. Upon his arrival he unsnapped his bindings and put his skis and poles to the side of the lift area and received some instructions from the volunteer who had just finished his shift.

"Position yourself near the entrance of the loading zone, and then you need to guide the Vets up to the red loading line. The operator will slow the lift chairs down and eventually stop them at the loading line so you can assist the guys onto the chairs."

"I think I can handle that. Ah, how do they get off at the top?"

"We've got volunteers up at the top of the lift so when they slow the chairs down again, they get help down the exit ramp. We don't want any bull-whippers up top!"

"No, we wouldn't want that to happen!" Jackson grinned.

For the next hour Jackson worked the ski lifts helping Veterans who were blind, paralyzed, had lost an arm or a leg or maybe even both. The courage displayed by the men and women to overcome such adversity touched Jackson's heart and made him feel good about these brave former soldiers and what they accomplished. He didn't exactly feel good about himself, however. He knew deep inside that he was shallow and callous.

Here these guys and gals have been sent off to war for their country, defending our freedoms, protecting our country, and making the world a safer place, and in the process they lost sight, hearing, arms and legs. What have I done that was even close? I've broken PDMA laws, lied to and cheated on Lexi, and been a lousy father.

He really felt low now.

When his shift was over he gave the loading instructions to the next volunteer, got on the lift, and then ascended up the mountain to the grill where he found Tam drinking a beer and one already on the bar for Jackson.

"Thanks for the beer," he said to Tam.

"So, how did it go?" she asked.

"These vets are my new heroes." He quickly changed the subject, "Let's look at the trail map and hit the slopes, I missed a whole hour of skiing. I was thinking that we should hit the Paradise Bowl until we have to go in."

"Sounds great, Jackson!"

They skied every day for six to eight hours, and they both agreed that the most challenging trail was the *Ruby Chief* run located just off the Paradise Lift. They skied it over and over again.

Once on the *Upper Treasury* trail, Jackson's skis slipped out from under him on some early morning ice which caused him to slide on his stomach before coming to a stop about fifty yards down the mountain. Both of his skis tore off and were heading down the slope rider-less toward the chair lift. Tam was behind him and witnessed the fall.

She came to a stop beside him and in a worried voice exclaimed, "Jackson! Are you OK?" She quickly unsnapped her bindings, threw down her poles, and knelt over him truly concerned for his safety because he lay motionless face down in the snow.

Jackson rolled over on his back and stared up into Tam's emerald green eyes while he faked a grimaced look, "You didn't get that on film by any chance did you?" he asked and then broke into a huge smile. Jackson grabbed her and held her in a bear hug embrace while they rolled together another five yards down the ski trail.

"Hey stop a minute!" Tam shouted. "If you just wanted to hug and kiss me, you didn't have to fall halfway down the mountain to do it. I don't want you breaking anything that I may want later," she said slyly. Then she kissed him deeply. After untangling themselves from each other, Tam strapped on her skis and swooshed away in search of Jackson's skis while he walked down the trail to meet her.

When they were too tired from the physical demands of skiing, they took a break from the slopes and rode snowmobiles, went on a sleigh ride, and even went on a dog sled ride where the two had to snuggle close with each other to stay warm. Tam was in love with Jackson. And while Jackson was physically attracted, he was not emotionally connected to Tam.

They had a long good-bye at the airport at the end of the week. Tam cried from the sheer joy of discovering her true feelings for Jackson.

When Jackson returned home to KC that night he found that Lexi had made a pot roast and vegetables. The aroma of filled their house. She greeted him with a hug and a kiss at the garage door. He could tell that her hair was newly cut by the long curls that framed her face. Not that he said anything, of course.

"Jackson, you looked tired. Didn't you get any sleep out there? No matter. You'll get a good night's sleep now that you're in your own bed."

Jackson was immediately uncomfortable and began to pull away from her embrace, "You know, between the time change, the altitude, and the volunteer hours at the lifts, I just didn't get much sleep actually. Hey, dinner smells great, honey! Where's Jake?"

"He's upstairs playing in his room. Come in the kitchen and talk to me, I've missed you, and I want to hear all about your trip? Let me pour you a glass of wine. Did you do any shopping, maybe bring me a present?"

"The stores were all sports gear so I didn't even think to get you anything because I knew you wouldn't like the stuff, but I did get Jake a pin for his collection. See!" He showed Lexi the pin that the National Commander had given him the first day.

"Jackson, I'm sorry that I've been so short with you. I just miss you because of your travel schedule, and it's coming out as anger." She came in close again and kissed his lips.

Jackson pulled away again. "Honey, excuse me a minute, OK? I need to plug in my cell phone and computer, and then I'm going to say hi to Jake. Yell up at us when dinner is ready." Jackson turned and left the room.

"Some homecoming," Lexi muttered in frustration.

CHAPTER 16
CONTRACT NEGOTIATIONS

The Vice President of the National Accounts division, Jim Larson, was a member of the Executive Oversight Committee or EOC for Alsace. Over the past week, he sat through what seemed like an endless number of forecasting presentations given by the Product Directors for each brand of medicine produced and sold by Alsace. The portfolio of products marketed by Alsace was broad; a fact that never ceased to amaze him. What his analytical mind noticed, however, was that there appeared to be a slowing in the sales growth rate in the managed care and pharmacy benefit management segments for which he was ultimately responsible. Because the overall growth trends appeared solid, the Product Directors glossed over the weakening performance of the managed care market.

Probably because these jackals don't understand our customers in the first place. Half of these Product Directors couldn't spell PBM or HMO before I got this job, Larson thought.

At the end of the meeting, Kevin Steer announced that the Alsace Regulatory department had submitted a New Drug Application file or NDA to the Food and Drug Administration for a new oncology drug for the treatment of breast cancer. Approval was anticipated within one year. The Product Director for the brand expected that this new novel therapy would receive an indication and label from the FDA that would allow Alsace to make the claim for better efficacy and safety than the current therapies on the market. Therefore, the drug would command a premium price. It would help boost overall

Company revenue and make up for two established drugs that Alsace expected to lose. The patent protection status would be lost at about the same time that the approval was expected for the new product. It was a well-known fact that Big Pharma companies depended on their clinical development pipeline for new drugs that could provide precious new revenues back into their coffers to keep the balance sheets healthy.

One of the older products that was to lose its patent was a cardiovascular medication for the treatment of high blood pressure or hypertension. It was in a category of drugs called calcium channel blockers, and it was truly an amazing story how the Alsace legal team, in concert with the R & D department, had kept a formulation of the product on the market for nearly twenty years while its competitors had all lost their patents after the normal seven to nine year period. The tactic employed by Alsace over the two decades all started because the medicine originally was indicated for a three times a day dosing regimen. Even with this extremely inconvenient dosing schedule, the drug was very popular with physicians because it was an entirely new class of agents that proved highly safe and effective. After being on the market for the first seven years and as the patent expiration date loomed for the three times a day drug, the Alsace scientists simply changed the drug's molecular structure slightly resulting in the dosing regimen being improved to two times a day.

The FDA approved the new two times a day medicine in short order because of the proven track record of efficacy and safety for the original three times a day molecule, resulting in a six-year patent extension. Of course, Alsace increased the cost of the new drug claiming that it deserved a premium price over the old formulation due to the increased patient convenience and compliance. The Alsace marketing strategy was to encourage managed care plans and physicians to change all of their existing patients over to the new twice a day formulation and, of course, expand the patient base even further. Then, as the twice a day medication's patent expiration approached, Alsace simply tweaked the molecule again to produce a sustained-release medicine that was dosed once a day that earned another six years of patent life and another price increase. With over $1 billion in annual sales, this single molecule fueled the Alsace R & D program with significant budget dollars for almost two decades.

But the end of the drug's life was inevitable, and that's when Kevin Steer took command of the product and negotiated a brilliant two-year legal and financial deal with the tiny generic company that won the first-to-file rights to manufacture a generic version of the once a day formulation. Steer met with the CEO of the generic company on his yacht, and while polishing off a bottle of twenty year old scotch, struck a bargain whereupon the generic company agreed to accept a one-time lump sum payment of two hundred million dollars from Alsace to keep their generic equivalent off the market and away from physicians and patients. The deal protected the life of the Alsace drug for an additional two years and, of course, the Alsace profit margins since the drug had already paid for itself over a decade ago. The obvious victims were patients who paid cash, particularly those over sixty-five years old and not covered under a prescription drug benefit, because they were denied access to a cheaper generic version of the blood pressure medication.

After the deal was inked, Steer told the Board of Directors, "Twenty percent of the profits on a one billion dollar drug given to the little generic outfit is nothing considering that we get to retain the other eighty percent. The deal gets even better if you think about it. If we didn't do it and the generic version was introduced into the market, then we would have lost eighty percent of the revenues in the first year just to generic substitution alone led by the damn managed care and pharmacy benefits management organizations. It would have taken the generic company almost four years to make the two hundred million dollars we paid them for two years of keeping their product off the market. I simply made him an offer he couldn't refuse!" Wall Street agreed with Steer's reasoning, as did the Board, since the value of the Alsace stock price continued to increase. But the terms of this particular deal were coming to an end, as would the stream of profit dollars flowing directly to the Alsace bottom line.

Since Steer was the last speaker on the agenda, the meeting would soon be over. Larson certainly did not want to take this opportunity to raise the flag about his division's slowing market share performance that he noticed on the graphs, so afterwards he went back to his office and called in his National Accounts Director, Rick Thompson.

"Rick, between you and me, I don't like some of the slowing in market share growth that I'm seeing with a couple of our products in this sector. I think that we should rework our contracting strategy and negotiate some better deals with our health plans and PBMs to get ahead of the curve. And I want to make damn sure that we have a solid contracting and pricing strategy in place well ahead of time for the new oncology drug launch coming up."

"I agree and will get right on it. You know, Jim, Boomer called me the other day to discuss the pending patent expiration for our calcium channel blocker, and he had an idea that he floated at the suggestion of National Healthcare. Apparently, Jerry Kramer at National suggested that we consider offering them a one-year deal for when the patent finally expires and a generic version is introduced on the market. He suggested that we incent them, through a contract, to keep our drug on their formulary as the preferred brand through a structured market share deal. Of course, National is looking for an even lower price and increased rebate dollars to maintain our market share. Their financial incentive is obvious. National would make about a hundred percent more in rebate dollars with us than they ever would with the generic substitute. Meanwhile, our overall dollar loss is significantly reduced due to the no substitution issue."

"I see. Interesting. Actually, that is a great idea and could easily be extended to other customers in order to maintain our market share and sales dollars while the Company islaunching the new oncology drug. This could make the department look good in the eyes of the EOC and the Board. You know, that Boomer can come up with some good ones despite being such a slob. If you recommend him for a Spot Stock award, I'll approve it. Maybe while you're at it, you should nominate old Jerry for a Spot Stock award since it was his idea! HA!

"Let's structure the deal," he continued, "and I'll get it approved by the EOC. OK, that leads me to the issue of training. How good do you think our Regional and National Account Managers are specific to their negotiating skills?"

"Jim, I'll be honest with you. They could use some work."

"That's what I thought. At the last conference I attended for health care executives, there was a presentation by a university professor from UCLA specific to contract negotiations training. Let me find my notes, make some phone calls to track this guy down, and see if he'll lead some training sessions for our account managers. You work with the Meeting Planning and Travel departments to coordinate a three day training meeting in May for the entire department."

"Yes sir," replied Thompson as he turned and left the office.

The Meeting Planning department selected the Loews Hotel in Santa Monica, California as the site for the Account Management training meeting. The property was located on the beach overlooking the Pacific Ocean just two hundred yards south of the Santa Monica pier famous for its roller coaster and Ferris wheel. All around the hotel were shops, art galleries, and restaurants that made it a perfect location where the Regional and National Account Managers could relax at night after a long day filled with negotiations training. The public beach on which the property was located offered a myriad of activities as well: bicycles, roller blades, and scooters could all be rented by the sun worshippers. Located just a short distance north of Venice, home to *Muscle Beach*, the Santa Monica beach area had its own share of fitness equipment available. The rings, parallel bars, chin up bars, and balance beam all proved to be challenging apparatus for the workout buffs to show off their machismo on the beach.

The Account Managers flew into LAX Airport and took cabs for the twenty-minute ride up Lincoln Avenue to Ocean Avenue and then to the hotel. The Company had set up a master billing system for the two hundred dollar a night rooms so the RAMs and NAMs simply needed to present their Corporate American Express cards at check-in to pay for any incidentals billed to their rooms.

Jackson arrived at the hotel just after noon. As he entered the lobby and walked to the reception desk he stared up at the four forty-five foot palm trees reaching up toward the ceiling. *Nice touch with the trees.*

"Hi, I'd like to check in please. The last name is Ford. Jackson Ford. I'm with Alsace Pharmaceuticals."

After tapping the keyboard for a moment and gazing at the computer monitor, the associate frowned, "I can check you in to your room, but I'm seeing that your room is still being serviced. It won't be available for another three hours. We can store your luggage while you have lunch in our restaurant or do some shopping nearby."

"Don't you have any other rooms available?" Jackson said with frustration. *I want to get some work done on my proposal over the next couple of hours so I'll be free when Tam gets in.*

"Unfortunately, we are completely sold out tonight. I could possibly place you in a smoking room with a queen bed or in one of our designated handicap rooms," the clerk said matter of factly.

Jackson thought for a moment. Being a non-smoker he hated rooms that reeked like cigarettes. However, he disliked the handicap rooms even more, especially the bathrooms. Although generally larger to accommodate wheelchairs, the mirrors were tilted downward so that he would practically have to get on his knees to shave. And worse yet, the showerheads were all so low, it was impossible to rinse the shampoo out of his hair.

"Come on! This is unacceptable! Do you know who I work for? Alsace Pharmaceuticals! We're one of the largest pharmaceutical companies in the world! We're bringing in over 100 managers and directors to this hotel, and you're telling me that you can't get me in my room for another three hours? That's unacceptable!" Jackson said raising his voice. "I want to speak to your supervisor," he demanded.

The young clerk was startled, "Yes, yes sir." She picked up the telephone receiver and pressed a button. "Could you come up here, please?"

Through the back door a well-groomed man wearing a black suit and dark blue shirt appeared wearing a nametag that said Quentin. "Is there a problem…" looking down at the computer screen, "Mr. Ford is it?" He looked up and smiled at Jackson. Quentin made Jackson feel uncomfortable.

"Yes, there is a problem. I've been traveling all morning and would like to get into my room, but your associate says that it's not been serviced yet and that the hotel is completely sold out. My only choices are a smoking room or a handicap room, both of which are unacceptable." Jackson said with exasperation.

"Hmmmm…I see. Well, yes the hotel is sold out this evening, but let me see what I can do." He tapped the keyboard for a minute and without looking up said, "It appears that we've had a last minute cancellation, and I can get you into a room immediately. It's an upgrade, however. One of our Junior Executive Suites located on the beach side of the hotel with a balcony. Would that be acceptable, Mr. Ford?"

"Well, of course it would. What about the extra room rate charge seeing how it is an upgrade? I would prefer that my Director not get the impression that I asked for the upgraded room."

"Oh, don't worry about it, Mr. Ford. I'll just tack it on the Alsace master bill, and it won't be affiliated with you. I'm sure that with over one hundred rooms that it won't even be noticed."

"Well, thank you very much."

"Do you need assistance with your luggage?"

"Yes, I do. Thank you."

The Front Desk Supervisor called for a bellman that placed Jackson's luggage on the luggage cart and led the way to the elevator. When they arrived at the room, the bellman carried the bags into the room while Jackson opened the doors to his balcony gazing out at the blue skies and ocean. *This is the life.*

"Will there be anything else, sir?" asked the bellman.

"No thank you," came the terse reply. Jackson pulled out a few singles out of his money clip and tried to give the guy a tip.

"Oh, I cannot accept that, sir. Your company is paying for all the gratuities and putting in on the master bill."

"OK. Thanks for the help with my bags." Jackson closed the door.

After he unpacked and hung up his clothes, Jackson went for a run on the beach. There was a bike path on the beach that stretched for miles in either direction where Jackson soon encountered other runners, bikers, walkers, and roller bladers during his three mile run. It was a gorgeous early summer day with temperatures in the high seventies pushed upward by an offshore breeze. After his run, he returned to his room and stretched out. He finished his workout with fifty pushups and fifty sit-ups.

He showered quickly and then sat down in front of his computer and began to work on his business proposal. It was already pre-approved by both Larson and Thompson so his written plan submission was just a formality. The proposal was a request for the approval of additional Travel and Entertainment or T & E expenses for a three-week business trip to Europe and a two-week business trip to Asia to work the U.S. military hospitals similar to what he discussed with Rick from Schering. With the significant number of active duty personnel, dependents of active duty, and retirees located on or around the military bases, the Alsace product sales were already good without any sales promotion, but Jackson was convinced he could make them even greater.

The opportunity, he saw, was to work the hospitals and position Alsace products as the preferred formulary agents in order to mirror the Federal markets back in the United States. Plus, from a strategic standpoint, the Pharmacy Chiefs and Medical Directors are generally stationed abroad for only three years before they rotate back to the U.S. where they assume roles of increased responsibility at one of the Lead Agent hospitals in the TRICARE Regions. Therefore, calls on these customers while they were stationed abroad were important to develop long-term business relationships. Jackson used these key points with Larson and Thompson, plus the fact that their main Big Pharma competitors were already sending NAMs overseas, to sell and gain approval for his proposal. Larson and Thompson both thought it was important to expand sales in all the managed care segments within the National Accounts division.

The proposal outlined the Federal market organizational design, demographics, strategic importance, sales growth, and sales opportunity along with the anticipated expenses for the trips. Jackson was requesting that an additional twenty thousand dollars be added to his T & E budget to cover the costs of both trips. When Jackson discussed the opportunity and costs with Larson and Thompson over lunch in the Alsace cafeteria, they both shrugged their shoulders and said, "Sounds reasonable. Write it up. We'll approve it and get you more money."

In order to fully concentrate on the task at hand, Jackson turned off his cell phone and unplugged his hotel telephone line. After he finished the document, he closed the program and opened his email database. He clicked on New Email, wrote a short note to Thompson, attached the file to the message, and clicked the Send button. After a few minutes the program was finished replicating, so Jackson logged off and powered down his computer. When the phones were all plugged back in and powered on, he noticed that the message light was blinking on the hotel phone.

Jackson dialed the hotel voicemail service and discovered that he had one unheard message. "Hello Stud! It's me! I've missed you, and I want to know if you're going to come over and see me before the cocktail reception and dinner. Call me back. I'm in room seven ten. I love you!" It was Tam who ended the call by blowing several kisses into the phone line before handing up.

Jackson's heart nearly burst with joy. He had missed her over the last two months since their ski trip to Crested Butte. He called her back immediately. "Hi Tam! When did you get in?"

"My plane landed about an hour ago. But with traffic I just got to my room." Then she asked in a sultry voice, "How about you?"

"I've been here since noon. I was able to go for a run and finish my Europe and Asia proposal for Thompson. I just sent it over email when you called. You said in your message that you wanted to know if I'm coming over." He paused for effect, "Well, I'm not. I don't go to rooms that are the standard guest room with a bed, a chair and a desk facing Ocean Avenue. I only go to Junior Executive Suites overlooking the ocean with a balcony. Therefore, if you want to see me, you'll have to come to my suite!"

"Don't tell me they put you in a suite! How did you luck out?" she asked.

"I've got connections with the Front Desk Supervisor," he laughed. "Come on over and see the view. We can 'catch up,' if you know what I mean. I'm in the Malibu Suite on the fourth floor."

"I'll be right there," Tam said with excitement in her voice.

Tam knocked at Jackson's door within five minutes of their phone call.

Jackson and Tam showed up fashionably late for the dinner, separated by fifteen minutes. Before going to the cocktail reception, however, Tam returned to her own room to fix her hair and makeup, which, thanks to Jackson, was a mess. They both realized they were playing with fire by seeing each other intimately at a company function, but after Crested Butte it was impossible to be apart for any length of time. Discretion would need to be a priority with all the eyes observing their every move.

She found Jackson ordering a Heineken at one of the three bars dotted around the banquet hall set up to serve complimentary cocktails, wine and beer to the hard working Alsace staff. Scott Evans was standing next to him. Several Marketing Directors were scheduled on the agenda first thing tomorrow to present product updates, and Evans was first on the list to address the Account Management division.

"Buy me a drink?" she asked Jackson.

"Hey Tam!" For Evans's benefit, Jackson added, "I've haven't seen you since the ASHP convention in Las Vegas. How have you been?" Jackson tilted his head slightly in the direction of Evans while maintaining eye contact with Tam.

Picking up on his cue Tam replied, "Oh, pretty good. I've been traveling a lot seeing my customers. Hi Scott, how's headquarters?"

Evans replied, "Busy. There's a lot of work to do at the home office as you can image. How's your husband? Still married?"

Tam turned bright red not knowing if Evans suspected anything between she and Jackson, "Yes, I'm still married, and my husband is just fine," she replied with a sharp tone.

Evans sensed he hit a nerve and quickly changed the subject. "So, what are the Account Managers supposed to be doing here again?" he asked with a trace of sarcasm.

"Larson has us scheduled for some Contracts Negotiation training with some consultant from the UCLA School of Business. Apparently, the company is looking to rework a lot of the existing contracts and prepare the managed care market for the new oncology product launch as well. Boomer told me that they're also looking at restructuring the calcium channel blocker deals for when the product finally goes off patent and the generic is actually introduced," Jackson replied.

Evans snorted in disgust, "What? A new deal structure on the calcium channel blocker? You know, a renegotiated contract basically means one thing: more discounts and higher rebates. You field sales people don't realize that I'm responsible for hitting a sales forecast based on net prices, after all the discounts and rebates are taken out of the sales numbers, and not like you guys who get paid the big bonus bucks off hitting a gross sales number. The only thing that an additional discount and rebate means for me is that I have to raise the sales line to make up for the lost revenue, which is nearly impossible on the calcium channel blocker product that's almost twenty years old!"

"You'll figure something out, Scott. You always seem to come out alright in whatever you do," said Jackson.

"Are you being sarcastic, Ford?" Evans challenged.

Jackson shook his head, "No, no, no. I just mean that your track record is pretty good for overcoming challenges and stuff. The word is that you find solutions to get the job done, that's all."

Evans backed down, "Well, that better be all you meant. I'm here for the next three days and already my schedule is filled with meetings at every breakfast, lunch, and break. All these Directors and NAMs want a piece of my time. It's hard to juggle it all, you know." Looking past both Jackson and Tam, "I see Larson over there so I better go remind him of our meeting first thing in the morning. No doubt, that's when he'll want to hit me up for those additional discount and rebate dollars you mentioned. Hey, Tam. Are you going to be around later tonight? Maybe we can go get a drink."

Tam glanced over at Jackson and then replied, "I don't think so Scott. I've got some paperwork to finish up later."

Evans shrugged and walked away in the direction of Larson.

"Maybe I shouldn't have said anything about what Boomer told me. I would have guessed that Evans would have known about any new deals coming up being a Product Director for the cardiovascular line. I need to learn to watch what I say around him," Jackson said.

"I just have to learn to avoid him. Was he coming on to me or what?" Tam asked.

"No, Scott's like that with every woman. He's just a real sleazebag."

"Do you think he suspects us? I can't look him straight in the eye when he talks to me when you're near me," Tam admitted.

"Well, let's just play it cool this week since he makes both of us uncomfortable, and he's obviously going to be here all week."

After dinner Jackson walked Tam back to her room. They were saying good-bye at her door when Tam leaned forward and gave Jackson a kiss that brushed quickly against his lips. As she pulled away, Evans happened to turn the corner after exiting the elevator on the way to his room.

"Hey, what are you two lovebirds doing? Is Jackson helping you with that paperwork there, Tam?" he stopped to ask.

Jackson and Tam both blushed having been caught with what could have been considered a simple kiss between friends.

"We were just saying goodnight, Scott. No big deal, we're friends. Goodnight, Tam," said Jackson as he turned to go back to the elevator and his room.

"See ya tomorrow," she replied.

As Jackson rounded the corner Evans stepped closer to Tam and asked, "So, you still got paperwork to finish or do you want to go with me and get something to drink?" His hand was now on her shoulder gently rubbing up and down.

"No, thank you," she managed to reply through stiff lips. She shrugged off his hand, turned around, and opened the door to her room. She slammed the door in his face.

As Evans turned to walk down the hallway to his room he heard Tam turn the deadbolt and slide the chain lock securely into place. He chuckled to himself; *Jackson's got a girlfriend.*

The next morning the Account managers found an agenda filled with product forecast presentations that would focus on the major accounts where Larson had initially noticed some slowing in the sales growth rates. These presentations set the stage for the negotiations training that would last for the next day and a half followed by an entire day of team breakouts focused on specific account contract strategy planning. Because the majority of the Alsace sales and subsequent profits passed through a managed care organization or pharmacy benefits management company, any slowing or decline in the growth rates of mega-products produced a reaction of concern from senior management, most notably, Kevin Steer.

"Do whatever it takes to get the trend lines back on track. We can't have even the slightest blip on our earnings record," Steer said to Larson the week before the meeting.

The negotiations training sessions were designed to improve the skills of the Account Managers specific to creating agreements with their managed care customers that would maximize market share for Alsace products. To accomplish this, the managed care companies would need to achieve low up-front acquisition prices and significant back-end rebates on Alsace products. These two factors were important for the Account Managers to fully understand because managed care makes money on both sides of the transaction. First, profit is made on the spread, which is the difference between acquisition price negotiated away from Alsace and selling price of the drug in retail pharmacy stores. The spread could range anywhere from one to fifteen percent depending on the type of product and its subsequent market share in the health plan. Second, profit is also made on the back-end rebates, which serve as a reward paid by Alsace for the health plan achieving a certain market share tier with the product. Historically, Alsace always paid the best up-front discounts and back-end rebates to the managed care organizations that exhibited the most control and influence over the formulary of drugs available to their employer group membership. The successful negotiation for a preferred formulary position was the ultimate goal of the Alsace Account Manager.

The UCLA Graduate School of Business professor that conducted the training sessions did an outstanding job over the day and a half session with the Account Managers. He led the group through a series of classroom theory modules that focused on the topics of escalation, framing negotiations, expanding the market pie, and integrative agreements. Time was also spent in breakout sessions where the Account Managers used actual business case studies to negotiate deals with and against their peers either individually or as a small team. The results, which were the mock deals that the Account Managers negotiated, were posted at the end of each session where it became obvious to everyone who were the best negotiators in the division. As it turned out, Jackson and Boomer each achieved the top results and received autographed copies of the Professor's new book entitled, *Rationale Negotiations*. No one expected Jackson to do so well since the Federal market was likened to more of a bidding system than an actual negotiations environment.

"It must have been all the practice I get negotiating with Lexi on a weekly basis," he told Tam.

For all their hard work over the past two days, Larson had Shelly Crawford work with the Meeting Planning department to plan a beach theme dinner party and reserve the private Santa Monica Beach Club to host the event. The Beach Club was located about a mile north of the Loews Hotel on the Pacific Coast Highway so buses were made available to transport the casually dressed group to the facility. The Account Managers were paraded through the lobby and allowed an opportunity to eye all the historic black and white photos of various

Hollywood stars. They were then escorted to the rear of the building and out to a grass courtyard that opened up to the beach. Here, they found a band that was playing beach music and a series of long tables decorated with seashells and miniature plastic palm trees to match the ones that lined the courtyard. Volleyball nets were set up in the sand with roller blades and bicycles available as well for the Account Managers to use on the nearby bike path that ran adjacent to the property.

I ran past this place this morning, Jackson thought as he looked around.

Jackson and Tam walked over to one of the bars set up in each corner of the courtyard. Shelly always made sure at any of these meetings that the Account Managers didn't have to walk too far to get a drink. They put themselves into a festive mood by ordering rum and Cokes. The music blared out of tall speakers set up on either side of the band and aimed out toward the ocean. Some people walking by on the bike path stopped and listened for a few minutes.

With drinks in hand, Jackson and Tam were visited by a number of servers who carried large silver trays filled with appetizers. Platters of sushi were brought out with small bowls of teriyaki sauce and wasabi. Tam used chopsticks while Jackson grabbed a fork off one of the tables. They helped themselves to crab cakes, swordfish, and fried calamari as they watched a group of people attempt to play sand volleyball.

Maybe some more rum would help a few of them with their serves, Jackson smirked.

After an acceptable time had passed, Shelly made an announcement about the dinner process. "OK, everybody! Can I have your attention please?" she asked. "We're having a lobster boil tonight. Does everybody like lobster?" she yelled.

The crowd let out a cheer in unison. Shelly continued as she pointed with her index finger, "You need to go over to the big silver tanks on my right. Once there, one of the cooks will help you select your lobster. You have the option of pulling your own out of the tank or letting one of the cooks do it for you! Don't worry, there are rubber bands around their claws so you won't get pinched." One of the cooks walked over and stood next to Shelly and held up a wriggling lobster in his hand. The crowd cheered again. "It takes about twenty minutes to boil them, and we've only got ten pots set up for boiling; so after you make your selection, have a seat at the table and the salads will be brought out while your lobster is cooking. OK, enjoy!"

When it was their turn, Jackson did the honors for Tam and reached into the icy cold water and pulled out a lobster for her. He held it up but quickly lost his grip, and the creature wriggled free and splashed back into the tank. They both threw their heads back and roared with laughter.

Evans stood in line at the next tank over and observed the two of them. His voice dripped with sarcasm, "Nice job, Ford. Do you want to come over and pull mine out too?"

"Shut up, Scott!" Tam shot back. Her eyes blazed with sudden anger.

Evans was stunned. Nobody ever talked to him like that.

Jackson plunged his arm in again to get another lobster for Tam, and he was successful the second time. He went back in again for his dinner and handed his entrée to the cook who smiled at both of them as he informed them that he would bring the lobsters out to their seats when they were done cooking.

The salad was chicken and artichoke with romaine lettuce served with warm loaves of freshly baked bread on wooden cutting boards. The serving staff delivered bottles of wine and sparkling water to the tables while the Account Managers started in on the salads and bread. As promised, the cooks brought the lobsters out precisely twenty minutes after they first went into the boiling water. The food was magnificent. Bowls of melted butter with garlic and lemon were placed all around the tables. The service staff tied plastic bibs behind the necks of the Alsace employees to help avoid any nasty food spills. Meanwhile, the band kept cranking out the tunes as the crowd watched the sun slowly sink into the Pacific Ocean. It was a perfect evening.

As darkness approached, Jackson and Tam went for a walk on the beach. Not on the cement bike path, but down by the water where they had to kick off their shoes and walk barefooted. With an offshore wind flow, the small waves gently lapped their bare feet as they slowly strolled in silence north, away from the Beach Club holding hands.

This water is freezing, Jackson thought.

Darkness slowly moved in from the direction of the Santa Monica Mountains and blanketed the beach, they stopped and turned to face each other. Jackson pulled her close with a firm grip on her back. Tam lifted her chin and opened her mouth to speak, "I love you, Jackson." She closed her eyes and kissed him.

Jackson pulled back, his lips puckered in annoyance. He was uncomfortable with Tam's feelings for him.

Tam blinked in bafflement, wondering if she did something wrong.

Jackson sensed the awkwardness of the moment and said in an apologetic tone, "Tam, why don't you come to Europe with me? You can take a week's vacation and meet me in Germany while I work the military hospitals. Then we could go to Paris for the weekend!" His hand massaged her shoulder in a circular motion as he tried to encourage the right answer.

She felt a warm glow rush through her and her lips parted in surprise, "Of course, yes! I'll come with you!" She leapt against Jackson and threw her arms around his neck and shoulders.

Jackson sealed his invitation with a kiss.

Just then a rogue wave washed in and splashed them. Their slacks were soaked up to their knees. Laughing aloud, they bounded up the beach and away from the water. Jackson decided that they should walk back to the hotel and avoid the scrutiny of the other Alsace Account Managers still partying at the Beach Club.

When they reached the Santa Monica Pier, they climbed the steps to ride the Ferris wheel and the roller coaster to help dry their clothes. Afterwards, they stopped at a booth on the pier and got matching henna tattoos of lobsters applied just below their navels.

I'm going to have to make sure that I've either have on a towel or bathrobe when I get out of the shower at home, or Lexi will skin me alive, Jackson thought with some apprehension.

As they neared the hotel, they decided that Tam would wait at a nearby hot dog stand while Jackson went into the hotel to return to his suite. They agreed that when he reached his room, he would stand out on the balcony and wave her up. She started inside when she saw his signal a few minutes later. What neither one of them noticed was that Evans had just turned up the sidewalk off the beach and walked toward the hotel. He saw Jackson waving his arm like a Chicago traffic cop.

What the hell is he up to? he wondered.

Evans stood behind a large palm tree as he watched Tam enter the lobby. He followed her into the hotel at a safe distance a she walked over to the elevator. He knew she was on the seventh floor; same as him, and by seeing Jackson wave to her that Jackson's suite was on the fourth floor. Evans hid behind a pillar in the lobby as the elevator doors opened for Tam. She entered and turned to press a button on the panel. Just as the doors had begun to close, Evans rushed in using his arms to push the elevator doors back open.

"Hey Tam! How are you doing tonight? Where's Jackson?" his eyes boldly raked over her.

"I don't know. I was hanging out with some friends at the pier," she lied as she crossed her arms to cover her breasts. Her pulse quickened in fear just from Evans' mere presence.

Evans leaned forward and noticed that the button for the fourth floor was illuminated. "You must have pressed the wrong button. You're on the seventh floor with me, remember? Or did you switch rooms?"

"Oh? My mistake. Thanks for catching that."

"Anytime. Hey, are you tired? Want to go back to the lobby bar with me for a little nightcap?" he asked as one corner of his mouth twisted upward.

Her voice was cold and exact, "No thanks, Scott. It's been a long day, and I'm going to bed."

The doors opened a moment later at the fourth floor. Evans reminded her, "Don't get out here. We're the next one. Hey, isn't Jackson on this floor?"

Tam knew she was being toyed with. "I don't know. He said they put him in a suite somewhere."

"Lucky bastard. That's kinda been the theme of his career though, you know. Just a guy with a lot of luck and no real skills."

"Jackson works just as hard, if not harder, as anyone else at this company. He's a very dedicated and talented Account Manager. His customers love him," she said with quiet firmness.

"How about you? Do you love him too?" Evans asked showing no sign of relenting.

"Don't be ridiculous. You know that I'm married," she ordered in a voice of authority.

The doors opened and Tam ran down the hall to her room to get away from Evans. She shook with anger and called Jackson immediately. He picked up on the first ring. "Jackson, I'm so mad. Evans cornered me about us in the elevator after he noticed that I pressed the button for the fourth floor. I couldn't get away from him fast enough."

"OK, calm down. He's not worth it. He's probably in his room by now. Just come over," Jackson said with impatience.

"OK, I'll be right there," she promised.

Tam left her room to return to the elevator. When it arrived she stepped in and rode it down to Jackson's floor. Evans had waited just down the hall from the elevator tucked into a room entrance out of sight. He knew Tam would go back out to be with Jackson. Her lame answers didn't fool him. When the elevator doors had closed, Evans sprinted down the hall to look at the floor lights above elevator to see where it would stop.

No surprise, right to the fourth floor.

Evans ran down the stairs two at a time to the fourth floor. He craned his neck to find her. He saw her.

On the ocean side of the hotel, of course.

She stopped in front of a suite and knocked. The door opened and Jackson appeared. As Tam walked past Jackson into the room, Evans could see that he was wearing a bathrobe.

Well, well, well. I can see that these two are going to have some fun tonight. He turned and walked back up the stairs with a spring in his step all the way to the seventh floor to think about what to do with the information.

CHAPTER 17
WORLD TRAVEL

Scattered throughout the continent of Europe are nearly two-dozen U.S. military bases that have historically served as a wall of defense against Communist aggression. An equal number of bases are also found in the Far East and Pacific Rim with a similar military objective. Typically, active duty military personnel are stationed abroad for three-year rotations before they return to a U.S. assignment, a fact especially true of Pharmacy Chiefs or Medical Directors that held a rank of Captain or Colonel and commanded in these foreign-based hospitals. Their rotation back to the U.S. usually meant a promotion and an increased pay grade. These chiefs and directors were especially important to Big Pharma companies whose intention was to build long-term relationships and influence within the military health care segment at home and abroad. Big Pharma federal segment NAMs never let a key player slip away to Europe or Asia for three years without somehow staying in contact with him or her.

"Lexi," Jackson announced in their bedroom one morning after he had finished a teleconference call, "I just got final approval from the EOC for my proposal to go to Europe and Asia."

She secretly wished that the Company would recognize the two trips for the boondoggles that they were, but apparently, her husband, the expert salesman, must have done a terrific job selling the benefits of the trips. Her heart sank when he revealed the approval.

"So, Jackson, that means that you're going to be gone out of the country for a total of five weeks, right?" she asked as she shook her head from side to side.

Jackson could see that she was not thrilled with the news, "That's right, honey, but the time will be split into three weeks and two weeks, and separated overall by at least two months. I control when I have to go."

"Jackson, why do you have to go to these foreign bases? Why can't the Company get a sales rep to go instead? Why not use the trip as a reward for somebody that is having an exceptional year? Alsace throws away so much money on just perks and other trips, why not one more? Why you? Why are you pushing this idea anyway?" She could feel the screams of frustration at the back of her throat.

Jackson's mouth was set in annoyance from all the questions, "Lexi, this is my proposal, and my way of setting myself apart from all the other NAMs in the department. If I'm successful on these trips and there is an increase in sales results, then I've really got a story to tell Senior Management when I propose the concept of my own team for this market with me as the Director! It's all part of the career progression plan that I've told you about."

Lexi's mind refused to register the significance of his words. "But at what cost? What about your family, Jackson? What about me? When are we ever going to spend any time together? What about the needs of your family?"

Jackson's eyes met hers disparagingly, "We spend time together now. We go out to lunch after Mass every Sunday, we go to Jake's games and school programs, and we go to dinner and a movie when we can find a baby sitter. I mean, what more do you want from me?"

Jackson was on the verge of deflecting the guilt and blame back onto Lexi when she cut him off. "Jackson, why don't you take me with you to some of these places you have to go? I mean, Jake is older now and my mom has offered to come out and stay with him if we ever wanted to go somewhere. You know, I could go with you on some of your trips to Washington DC or Chicago or San Diego. It's not like I would have to go with you on the appointments or anything."

"I hadn't really considered that," Jackson admitted.

Lexi continued, "I wasn't brought up to just sit in the house. I love being with Jake, and I'm thankful that we're able to have me stay home with him, but I love to travel. You know that! And I just really need to be with you, but you act like you don't want to be with me."

She gave him a leveled gaze, "Do you still want to be married, Jackson, or are you just settling for marriage because I make you look good? I feel like I'm always alone. Even when we're together I feel alone. You spend more time traveling with your damn golf clubs than with me!" *Jackson gets so much praise at work, and he desires it because he's very talented. I'm just looking for some attention from my husband.*

"Of course, honey, I want to be married. And no, I'm not staying married because it's better for my career. I love you!" His words were insincere.

Jackson's mind raced. *If Lexi came to Europe with me, it could solve a lot of my problems at home and probably earn me some major brownie points. But I already asked Tam to go! Dammit! Didn't think that one through very well did I? I can't let this thing spiral out of control and lose Lexi and Jake. They actually do make me look good to management. OK, think big picture. Corporate men with wives who stay at home progress much farther and faster than those who don't.*

Jackson took charge of the conversation, "You're right, Lexi. Jake is getting older, and we can get away more just the two of us. I'm sorry, honey. How about if you come with me to Germany for the first week, and then we'll spend a long weekend in Paris?"

Lexi's eyebrows rose, as did her spirits, "Hey, that's great! We'll go to the Louvre, Versailles, and Notre Dame. I remember a little café just off the Champs-Elysees, from when I went in high school and college. If it's still there we can have brunch on Sunday. They make the best pastries and coffee in Paris, and I've never been to Germany!" she exclaimed, clearly surprised that he had asked her. She rushed into his arms and kissed him tenderly. "Jackson, I miss you. I love you so much. This could be like a second honeymoon for us. OK, now I've got to call my mother and give her the dates. I'm glad that I kept my passport current." With a springy bounce, she was gone from the bedroom to get the telephone and her date book.

Alone in the bedroom, Jackson paced the room for the next few minutes and thought about what had just transpired. *What am I doing? What was that old country song? 'Trying to love two women is like a ball and chain.' Whatever. I certainly don't love Tam, and I do need Lexi. OK, I'll just call Tam and tell her that Lexi is putting her foot down, demanding to go to Europe with me. She's married, she'll understand. Then, I'll call the airline and change the award travel to Lexi's name. OK, I can make this work.*

The telephone conversation with Tam the next week was certainly not the cakewalk Jackson had anticipated. Jackson's voice was cold and exact as he explained the circumstances to her. Tam listened with bewilderment.

"Jackson! Are you sure that I can't go? Come on! You asked me first! A promise is a promise!" She was flushed with humiliation.

Jackson shook his head regretfully as he spoke into the phone, "Tam, Come on, you're married too! I would think that you'd understand."

In her heart she was afraid that he didn't share her feelings, she was suddenly filled with sadness. "I understand one thing, Jackson, and that is I love you. I want more than just a few days here and there with you." She swallowed the sob that rose in her throat.

Jackson felt guilty. *I don't love her but she makes me feel so good about my career,* he thought. *I have got to handle this delicately.* "Tam, I'm sorry that you can't go with me this year. Look, we've both got customers in Atlanta. How about if we coordinate our schedules for the last week in July so that we can see each other there instead?"

Tam felt utterly defeated. The rejection proved to her that she loved Jackson but the timing of their relationship couldn't be worse. She swallowed the despair in her voice and wiped the tears away, "OK, Jackson. I understand. I'm just so disappointed. Isn't there any way we can see each other before July?"

"As much as I want to, my travel schedule is pretty tight with two conventions coming up and some contracting meetings. It's the earliest I can do it."

She replied in a voice just above a whisper, "Alright. If that's the first chance we get. I do love you, Jackson."

"I'll call you later this week. Schedule some appointments in Atlanta. Let's stay at the Marriott Marquis so we can go to some restaurants at the Underground at night."

As Tam hung up the telephone, she was puzzled by the abrupt change in plans. *Jackson's never before caved in to Lexi's demands before.* She thought a moment longer. *I'll make sure that when he leaves Atlanta that he'll be completely satisfied, and he'll want me all the time. He'll leave that dumpy little wife of his after I'm through with him.* The tears gave way to a wicked smile.

Jackson called US Airways and changed the business class award ticket that had been originally ticketed under Tam's name to Lexi. The Alsace Travel Department had already booked his flight in business class so they were all set. They would fly on a Friday afternoon from Kansas City to Philadelphia in order to change planes for the flight to Frankfurt, Germany arriving on Saturday morning. Ten days later Lexi would depart from the Charles de Gaulle airport back to Philly and on to KC while Jackson would travel on to Italy, Spain and England.

The business class service on the flight from Philadelphia to Frankfurt was impeccable. Dinner was served about an hour into the flight while over the Atlantic Ocean. Jackson and Lexi both selected the steak entrée with red potatoes and steamed vegetables. Wine flowed freely during the course of the meal, and ice cream sundaes were the dessert. Lexi was content to sleep for the next few hours so Jackson requested an extra pillow and covered her with a blanket. She reached over and held his hand until she drifted off to sleep.

Several hours later as the plane neared French airspace, Jackson could see sunlight peeking up over the horizon. Lexi, as well as the fellow passengers in the business class cabin, had been asleep since the dinner trays were removed. It was at this crucial point where

Jackson violated the cardinal rule of travel from the United States to Europe. He should have slept for at least two hours to help offset the potential jet lag, but alas, he didn't.

About an hour prior to their scheduled landing in Frankfurt, the flight attendants gently woke up the passengers in the business class section with the exception of Jackson who never nodded off. The smell of fresh brewed coffee and croissants filled the cabin. For breakfast Jackson and Lexi had berries, orange juice and coffee. Jackson yawned the entire time.

"Tired Jackson? Didn't you get some sleep?" Lexi asked as she leaned over to give Jackson a kiss on the cheek.

He looked beat. Fatigue had settled in pockets under his eyes, and he needed a shave. "Yeah, I'm bushed," he sighed. "The coffee after dinner got me all wired up so I watched a couple of movies." He attempted a smile, "Hey, we're almost there."

Lexi was both excited and aggravated, "Jackson, you should have known better and gotten some sleep. You're going to be busy over the next ten days."

"I know," he replied as he stifled another yawn.

After a smooth landing the plane taxied to the terminal. Following the universal directional signs, Jackson and Lexi found the baggage area and claimed their luggage. They cleared customs and picked up a rental car. It was a BMW 325i with a five speed manual transmission. Lexi got directions to Heidelberg while Jackson loaded the trunk. His golf clubs had to be placed in the back seat of the car since the trunk was filled with luggage.

Lexi's lips thinned with irritation, "Why did you have to bring those damn things anyway?"

"I told you before we left that I have tee times scheduled with customers at all the bases that I'm visiting. Don't start in on me about my work schedule," came the response with an annoyed tone.

She halted, shocked. *This isn't starting off very well.*

Jackson maneuvered the car through the airport traffic and drove south on the Autobahn toward Heidelberg. They exited off the Autobahn within an hour and descended into the Neckar River valley finding the Marriott Hotel on Vangerowstrasse Street beside the river. At the front desk, a clerk immediately recognized the two as Americans.

Jackson spoke first as he approached her, "Guten Morgan!" he said trying to impress Lexi and the clerk. "Sprechen sie English?" Lexi rolled her eyes at the latter remark.

With her index finger and thumb held close together she replied, "A little." She picked up the telephone, pressed a number, and spoke rapid German to someone on the other end of the line. A moment later a smartly dressed woman in a black slacks and a Jacket wearing a name tag that Jackson assumed said manager appeared, "Good morning. May I help you?"

"Yes. My name is Jackson Ford, and I have a reservation." He pulled his American Express card out of his wallet and handed it over to the manager.

"May I have your passports, please?" he asked in a thick accent.

Jackson and Lexi handed over their passports. After the check-in process was complete, they headed off for their suite. It was a lovely, spacious room with European design and furniture. The king-size bed looked inviting so they crawled into bed for some much needed sleep. Because Jackson was a Platinum member of the Marriott Rewards program, there was a basket wrapped in cellophane on the cocktail table. It was filled with crackers, cheeses, a bottle of wine, bottled water, and some fruit. The ice bucket had been filled as well.

Lexi pointed at the basket excitedly, "Hey Jackson, did you order this for us?"

"No, it's just one of the many Marriott perks that they give me," he said without interest.

Before they laid down for a nap, Lexi took a fast shower and slipped into a fresh nightgown and then snuggled close to Jackson. Their plan was to get a short nap, wake up, and then go for a walk to help adjust to the time change. Lexi, of course, made the adjustment beautifully because of the rest she got on the airplane. But Jackson was exhausted having been up for nearly thirty hours straight.

Two hours later Jackson's watch alarm sounded. Jackson felt like he had just laid down, his eyes were glued shut. Jackson gathered Lexi into his arms. Her skin prickled pleasurably until she heard him snoring lightly drifting off into wisps of sleep.

"Oh no you don't!" she teased him. "We have to get up! Come on." She felt fully refreshed and excited about the week ahead. Her perky voice annoyed him.

"Just let me sleep another hour, and I promise I'll get up then," he mumbled as his head dug into the pillow.

"No. Come on now, get up," she was slid out from under the covers and stood by the side of the bed. Jackson didn't move which prompted Lexi to pull the covers off him.

Jackson grunted, "OK, OK. You win. I'm up." He turned to roll off the bed.

Lexi crossed the room into the bathroom to start the shower while Jackson dragged himself toward the sound of the falling water. *I'm so tired,* he thought.

As he entered the bathroom, Lexi pounced on him. Not in the mood for anything but a shower he responded with an edge in his voice, "Not now, Lexi. I'm beat and don't feel like doing anything except for taking a shower."

The rebuke stung. "OK, fine. You know, it's not every day we're in Europe together without having to worry about Jake walking in on us." She marched out of the bathroom. She closed the door behind her.

Jackson became glum-faced, shook his head, and lowered his boxers to the floor. The shower was hot and steaming, especially since the bathroom door was closed. As he shampooed his hair with his back to the showerhead, he heard the door open and the toilet flush within seconds. The shower water immediately shot up to a scalding temperature on the middle of his back.

"Ow! Lexi! What are you doing?" his voiced lashed out at her as his head appeared through an opening in the curtain.

Lexi lifted her head and met his eyes with cool defiance. She pushed it down again for another flush and more scalding water.

"Hey! Come on, please stop!"

With an abrupt step she was out of the room. This time she slammed the door behind her.

Jackson thought about stepping out of the shower to lock the door for a minute, but then decided that it was too much effort so he returned to his shower. With his back again into the flowing water, he lathered up a washcloth with soap that smelled of lavender. He had started in on his face and neck when the door reopened. Instinctively, he took a step forward and out of the direct spray of the showerhead. He never expected anything from over the top of the shower curtain. A bucket of ice water rained down on his head as Lexi squealed with laughter from above, "Are you awake now, big boy?"

Jackson's voice hardened, "If I wasn't before, I am now. Lexi, if you want attention from me this certainly isn't the way to get it. Will you please just let me finish my shower in peace? I'll be out shortly, and then we'll go for a walk, I promise." The door closed a third time without slamming.

Tam never pulls any of this. We've never even raised our voices with each other in all the years I've known her. Lexi is just too crazy and demanding, he thought. *Of course, Tam is not here right now? And remember, she's only the woman on the side while your wife is patiently waiting at home taking care of your son.*

By the time he finished drying off, the Catholic guilt was working overtime on him. Jackson walked out of the bathroom wearing just a towel and strode across the room to where Lexi sat on the couch thumbing through the latest issue of Town and Country magazine. "Honey, I'm sorry that I was so grumpy. I should have slept on the plane."

Lexi stole a glance at his face while she continued to page through the magazine. It was obvious that she was not reading it. Jackson sat down next to her, his thigh brushing her leg. She moved away slightly. His hand took her face and held it gently, "Come on, honey. I'm feeling much better after that unique European Shower. Let's go for that walk." He nuzzled her neck with his lips. Lexi moved her head to the side to allow him access.

After a minute she leaned her head back and gazed into his eyes, "Jackson, I love you so much. You've been so cold and distant for the past few years. You barely even touch me anymore or hold my hand! I don't know if it's the job or the travel or what…but I need you," her eyes implored him.

Jackson caressed her cheek. "It's the job, Lexi, nothing else." Then he added as an afterthought, "And I need you too." He wrapped his arms around her midriff and cradled her while he brushed a quick kiss across her forehead.

"I'm glad you came with me, Lexi," he said into the top of her head. "Come on, let's go for that walk. We'll start over, and I'll be better. I promise."

After a change of clothes, they made their way out of the hotel and onto a sidewalk that ran along the Neckar River. They walked holding hands south toward the Karl-Theodor Bridge and after about a mile could see the famous Heidelberg Castle high atop a hill where it sat overlooking the river valley and the city that was spared from the Allied bombs during World War II. Jackson and Lexi stopped at one of the many outdoor cafés located along the river and had a bratwurst and beer. It was delicious considering the fact that they had not eaten anything but airline food in the last twelve hours. Continuing their walk along the gently flowing river, they decided to turn into the main shopping square near the old university. The streets were cobblestone and flanked with buildings styled with Baroque architecture. They stopped to admire the 600-year-old Church of the Holy Ghost. They read a plaque on the wall and learned that inside lay the fifth teen-century tomb of the church's founder, King Ruprecht I, and his wife, Elisabeth.

They dined at the Bierstube restaurant that evening feasting on authentic German food where Jackson tried to impress Lexi by using more of his high school German phrases with the service staff. Their conversation was mainly about Alsace and Jackson's job. Throughout dinner there was nothing said about their marriage until dessert and coffee finally arrived.

Lexi sensed Jackson's uneasiness with the topic of their relationship, but she pressed him. "Jackson, we've got to talk about our marriage. We need to get it back on track. We've spent the last hour talking about nothing but Alsace."

His astonishment was genuine, "But Lexi, it's what I do for a living!"

"But it's just a job. It's only money!" She took his hand into her own. Her expression stilled and grew serious, "Look at me. I'm real. I'm your wife who's in love with you and has been since we met on Halloween at the 4th Quarter bar. But you keep pushing me away by choosing your job over me, by choosing to be gone over being home."

Jackson felt pangs of guilt over his behavior the last several years. With exactness, Lexi had uncovered the crux of the relationship problem. Alsace, his job, the travel, his desire for the next promotion, his want of money, and his want of power. All of these things had changed him significantly over the years. "You are so right," he said weakly as his eyes dropped to the table. "I've been an awful husband and father over the years."

He drew a deep breath. When he looked up, his face was full of strength and determination. His blue eyes were brimmed with tenderness and passion as he spoke with confidence. "That all ends tonight, Lexi. I am going to break out of this pattern. I know it's been hard on you these past years. Please forgive me, Lexi. I love you so much."

Their eyes met as their hands gripped each other's fingers tightly. Lexi beamed, confident that he would be different.

Jackson's mood seemed suddenly buoyant. His infectious grin set the tone for the rest of the evening when he asked, "How about some dessert, honey?"

Sleep came easy that night to both of them.

After they ate breakfast in the hotel restaurant on Sunday morning, they attended Mass at a local Catholic church just off the main square in town. Noticing a slow trickle of tourist traffic, they quickly made for the castle. Taking the trail marked Uberburgweg they climbed the hill, paid the entrance fee, and stepped into the magnificent castle courtyard with the same Baroque design.

At precisely eleven o'clock the sounds of bells could be heard drifting up the hill to the castle just as Jackson was about to take Lexi's picture in front of a rose garden. With purposeful strides they hurried over to the edge of the castle garden and leaned over the stone wall to gaze down at the town below. Above the orange-brown rooftops, at least a half-dozen church steeples towered and a symphony of bells rose from their belfries. The bells clanged loud and furious as if each was trying to outdo the other. Jackson and Lexi smiled at each other and wished that they had a tape recorder with them instead of the camera.

As the bells continued to reverberate off the wooden hillsides that surrounded them, they continued their tour of the castle built in the sixteenth century. With a cluster of ornate pilasters, columns and statues throughout the building, Jackson and Lexi were most struck by the sight of the two missing top levels of the castle. The tour guide explained that a lightning-induced fire destroyed most of the castle in 1764 that resulted in a massive reconstruction project. In one of the buildings they stopped to examine what was reported as the largest wooden wine barrel ever to have been constructed. Over 130 oak trees were used to build the 58,000-gallon wine barrel in 1751. Jackson got a picture of it while Lexi stood by the spout and smiled at him. They finished the tour down near the moat by passing through a beautifully detailed arch located at the entrance to the Gun Garden. Legend had it that Prince Elector Friedrich V had the arch located at the entrance to the garden built in a single night for his English princess, Elisabeth Stuart, thus the name, Elisabeth's Gate.

Jackson and Lexi made their way back into town via the Karl-Theodor Bridge. After some afternoon shopping back in the marketplace, Jackson and Lexi had dinner at the Hotel zum Ritter. The hotel was built in 1592 and proudly displayed Renaissance-era columns, curlicues, and carved figures. The special that evening was a five-course meal that consisted of two appetizers, pasta, salad, the main entrée and dessert. Both of them pushed away from the table with full stomachs and feeling a little tipsy from the two bottles of wine they drank.

As the bill for nearly $300 U.S. currency was presented, Lexi asked, "Jackson, I never did ask you, but how are we paying for my meals while we're over here? I just assumed we would repay your Corporate American Express account out of our savings account once we got back home."

"Rick Thompson asked if I was going to be taking you with me, and he basically gave me the approval to take you to nice restaurants while we're here and just write it down on my expenses that I took a customer out for a business entertainment meal."

Lexi couldn't believe what she was hearing, "You're kidding me right? He said that? Just cheat on your expenses?"

"Yeah, they do it all the time when wives go on trips like this. I guess it is their way of making up for all the long hours and time spent away from home."

Lexi did not feel comfortable with the reply but was too tipsy to protest, she lifted her wine glass and proposed a toast, "Thank you, Alsace Pharmaceuticals! I'm in Heidelberg and on my way to Paris in five days!"

Later that night back Jackson seemed distracted and distant. Disappointment filled Lexi's heart, but she wrote the episode off to his jet lag and hoped for another opportunity soon.

Jackson's work in Germany proved exciting. He got up early each morning to run on the river walkway, then showered and dressed quickly and was out the door. He visited customers at Heidelberg Army Hospital, Wurzburg Army Hospital, Ramstein Air Force Base Hospital, Landstuhl Army Medical Center, and Spangdalen Air Force Base. It was a busy week with an agenda focused on ensuring the proper positioning of Alsace medicines on the European Military Network's Preferred Drug List. His tactics included direct customer appointments, lunch presentations in the Officer's Club, in-service presentations to nurses, and tee times with key decision makers within the administrative staff. *The golf clubs came in handy again!*

He returned to the Marriott in the late afternoon, physically exhausted from the day. His mind raced as he thought of the sales he was generating, and how he could parlay the trip into a promotion to a Director's position once he got back home. *There is a lot of business to grow over here in the overseas military markets. I've got to show the value to the Alsace senior management as well as show the benefit of adding more headcount to this segment. We've got to keep up with the competition who are already adding more dedicated federal Account Managers. Merck, AstraZeneca, and GlaxoSmithKline already have teams in place!* He wrote notes in the car everyday outlining how he would structure his proposal for a dedicated team with Jackson Ford as the Director with an office at headquarters in San Diego.

Lexi slept in every morning. She was out in the late morning on the river sidewalk for her exercise routine followed by a leisurely shower. The market square was her daily hangout as she searched for gifts for their parents and Jake and also for a restaurant for dinner that night with Jackson. Although she would have preferred to be with Jackson all day, she conceded that he had to call on customers and was satisfied with the time by herself. When Jackson returned to the hotel in the late afternoon, Lexi would be all dressed up and ready to go out for dinner. She took the initiative to order appetizers and a bottle of wine through room service so that they would have a snack before leaving the hotel for the evening.

Heidelberg is lovely, but I can't wait to spend the weekend in Paris! she thought.

The week in Heidelberg flew by for both of them. On Thursday night they packed their bags and went to bed early to be rested for the long drive to Paris. They found beauty all around them during the eight-hour drive through western Germany, Luxemburg, Brussels and the Alsace Lorraine region of France. The sunflower fields and vineyards that stretched over the gently rolling hills were a delight to the eye as the BMW containing Jackson and Lexi motored through the countryside. They held hands in a warm clasp throughout the trip and listened to the unfamiliar sounds on the local radio stations understanding little of the language. Once in France, they drove past the expansive world headquarters of Alsace Pharmaceuticals. It looked both imposing and impressive.

At the Charles de Gaulle Airport, they dropped off the BMW at the car rental agency and took a taxi into Paris. Driving around the Arc de Triomphe, the Eiffel Tower stood proudly on their right, while ahead of them was the Louvre. The cab stopped in front of the Paris Marriott three blocks later on the Avenue des Champs-Elysees. Where Jackson's high school foreign language skills got them through Germany, Lexi's high school French classes paid off and earned them brownie points with the hotel staff. Lexi knew from past experience that if you at least tried to speak the language, then the Parisians cut you some slack and switched to English much sooner than if you did not even try to learn a few phrases of their beloved lingo. Jackson had absolutely no clue as to what he was going to do once he was in Italy and Spain.

I'll probably have to fake being a dumb American so that they'll pity me and speak English, Jackson thought.

After they unpacked for the long weekend Lexi remarked, "Jackson, we are in the city of lovers—Paris! Can you believe it? OK now, with the limited time that we have, we definitely need to plan our free time before we both leave on Monday. Because the gardens are magnificent in the morning and the temperatures will be cool, we'll start at Versailles and then back to Notre Dame in the afternoon. We'll visit the Arc de Triomphe just before dinner. On Sunday, I'd like to go to the Louvre for most of the day followed by the Eiffel Tower for dinner. That's about all we'll get to see because of the lack of time. Oh, I wish we had a week in Paris! We're going to miss a boat ride on the Seine and long walks through the Tuileries Gardens and the Opera House."

"There's always next year's trip, honey," Jackson replied with confidence.

The next morning after a hurried breakfast of croissants and coffee in the hotel restaurant, they hailed a cab and rode the thirteen kilometers out to the ornate palace of King Louis XIV, who was also known as the Sun King. They sauntered through the magnificent hallways and rooms filled with marble sculpture, gilded carvings, and crystal chandeliers. The Hearst Castle in San Simeon, California couldn't hold a candle to Versailles. Empires rose and fell, and a World War ended within its walls. Jackson couldn't believe that the grand castle had once fallen into disrepair after the French Revolution only to be restored to its grandiloquent stature through the donations of such notables as John D. Rockefeller and Jacqueline Kennedy Onassis. The history of the 270-foot long Hall of Mirrors was his favorite—Louis XIV entertained royalty here; Kaiser Wilhelm I was crowned the Emperor of Germany here; and World War I ended here with the signing of the Versailles Treaty. Lexi's favorite was the walk through the gardens to visit the Grand Trianon where Louis XIV kept his lovely mistress, Madame de Maintenon, as well as the Petit Trianon where Queen Marie Antoinette, the wife of Louis XVI, maintained a home away from home.

Jackson admitted to himself, *It's a real treat to be in Europe, and it makes it all the better to be here with the approval of Alsace and with the Company picking up the tab!*

After they dined on a late, light lunch in the garden café, Jackson and Lexi took a taxi back into the city to the Cathedrale de Notre-Dame located on the Ile de la Cite. After an unguided tour of the main building, they joined a small tour group to learn the rich history of the cathedral. Taking over 180 years to reach completion in 1345, only to be badly damaged during the French Revolution, and restored in the nineteenth century, Notre Dame had earned its status as the symbol of survival in Paris. The long 387-step climb to the top of the towers in the dark, cool narrow stairway made Lexi shiver with anxiety. Jackson's warm voice soothed her as his hands gently clutched her hand pulling her up to the top where they found the famous gargoyles and a spectacular view of the city. They took a picture of Quasimodo's bell in the south tower and thought about the fictional hunchback tolling it as he sang songs to his peasant girlfriend.

They walked back toward the hotel and stopped for dinner at an outdoor café just off the Champs-Elysees. It felt good to sit down after all the walking in the warm summer temperatures. Darkness descended on Paris and with it came a festive mood out on the street. Jackson and Lexi were pleased with themselves for having successfully achieved two out of their three tourist goals so far. The Arc de Triomphe would be their next stop after dinner. They ordered a plate of oysters and escargot for appetizers, which they washed down with a nice bottle of merlot. Dinner came and went, as did another bottle of wine.

Jackson has been so nice to me all day, and he's so handsome in the candlelight, Lexi thought.

After dinner, they walked the six blocks back to the hotel. Exhausted from the day's events, they fell into bed and slept soundly.

While in the shower the next morning, Lexi could not stop herself from thinking about their marriage. Jackson had been distant so long, and now he was being so attentive. Something was nagging at her. She thought, *I'll talk to him about it at home when he returns from London. I'm not going to let anything spoil our last day in Paris!*

Their visit to the world's greatest art museum was extraordinary. Le Louvre overwhelms the visitor in both size and contents so that it cannot be fully explored in one single day. Jackson and Lexi mapped out the must-see highlights: the Mona Lisa, the Venus de Milo, the paintings of Michelangelo, and the Greek sculptures. They filled the entire day strolling within the walls of the mammoth building. Finally, they emerged and headed for the Seine River for a short walk before hailing a taxi to carry them the rest of the way to the Eiffel Tower.

Created in two years by French engineer, Gustave Eiffel, for the World Exhibition of 1889, the Eiffel Tower is to Paris what the Statue of Liberty is to New York and Big Ben is to London. The nearly 7,000 tons of iron exalts the skyline of the city. Jackson and Lexi climbed the stairs to the second floor to access the glass elevator to the top of the tower. Once there, they leaned on the railings and looked over the vast spread of the city. The Champaign Bar nestled right into the

Tower's iron structure served chilled glasses filled with the delightful beverage. They felt as though they were toasting each other while on an airship tethered above Paris. They took it easy on the bubbly, however, because they had one more stop that evening at the colossal Arc de Triomphe. Located next to their hotel was Sephora's, a store famous for its line of perfume and makeup. Jackson bought Lexi a new perfume called, *The Good Life* by Davidoff, which she immediately applied. They had a wonderful day, but Lexi still felt uneasy about their marriage.

On Monday they took a cab together to the airport. Lexi missed little Jake, but thoroughly enjoyed her time with Jackson in Germany and Paris.

"I'm going to miss you terribly," Jackson told her as he kissed her goodbye.

"Jackson, I love you so much. I'm going to miss you too. This vacation has been good for us. I know we can get through anything if we work together."

"And play together. Work and play together," Jackson quipped with an irresistible grin.

Her smile found its way through her mask of uncertainty, "Yes, and play together."

"Honey, you have to go, and I have to check in yet. Give me one more kiss to get me through the next two weeks without you. Tell Jake that daddy says hello!"

They kissed, hugged, and said goodbye. Lexi would remember forever how her lips stayed warm from his last kiss. *I love him so much. Please, God, don't let him do anything stupid. I don't want to lose him. I just got him back.*

Jackson flew on an Alitalia flight from Paris to Venice. He felt like he was on top of the world. He and Lexi had actually had a good time together during their trip. *I do love Lexi. I guess that I forgot how fun she is. And beautiful. I just wish she would leave me alone about Alsace.*

Jackson's next two weeks of travel were definitely the hardest. He spent one day in Venice, a day in Naples, and two days in Sicily. The flights between cities nearly every day along with the language barrier made it tough. However, he did play golf with customers at the Bologna Golf Club in Monte San Peitro, Italy and at the golf course located on the Sigonella Naval Base in Sicily that made that particular portion of the trip half-way tolerable.

The best part of the week was to be his final destination in Cadiz, Spain at the Hotel Montecastillo Golf Resort for a long weekend of golf and relaxation. The flights to Cadiz proved troublesome, however. He had to fly from Sicily to Rome to Madrid all on Alitalia Airlines. Then switch to Iberia Airlines from Madrid to Jerez in the southwestern region of Spain located on the Mediterranean Sea. When he arrived at the airport in Jerez, he discovered in the baggage claim area that the damn Alitalia Airlines didn't put his luggage on the transfer plane in Rome. Nor, more importantly, his golf clubs didn't make the same flight that he was on, and they were not expected to arrive until the next morning.

If I have to, I can sleep nude, buy a new toothbrush, and maybe buy a T-shirt and shorts at a sporting goods store, but to be at this beautiful golf resort for a long weekend without my clubs is the ultimate torture!

He tried to explain his feelings and the special circumstances to the female baggage clerk who worked for Iberia Airlines, but he figured that most of his words were lost in the translation to Spanish. By luck, his luggage arrived by ten o'clock the next morning so he still got in thirty-six holes of golf that day.

The Rota Naval Hospital located on the Mediterranean was by far the hardest base to access for work the following Monday due to an enactment of Threat Condition Bravo. However, Jackson's up front planning to secure appointments via emails and faxes proved rewarded him with the access he desired to see the right people. It was a quick trip through the south of Spain, however, and then he was off to London for the final week of his European trip.

He arrived in London late at night and rented a car that proved to be his first mistake. After he climbed into the right side of the vehicle, he noticed that the stick shift was on his left while the foot pedals appeared to be the same as in American cars. Driving on the left side of the road, however, screwed him up. He hit more than a dozen curbs and continually forgot to get in the proper lane after turning corners. Fortunately, he did not run over any pedestrians or hit any other cars. Once he had the car parked safely in the Marriott parking garage across from the U.S. Embassy, he never drove it again the rest of the week. It was a waste of $500, but Jackson figured the price of a car accident would have been much higher for the company and him personally.

London's Tube or subway pleasantly surprised Jackson as being very efficient. It transported him wherever he needed to go within the city as well as to the outlying U.S. Naval Hospital and the Air Force Base Hospital that was shared with the Royal Air Force. Carrying his golf clubs through the subway terminal wasn't too big a problem except for having to heft it over the turn-style. It did feel odd to him to ride in the Tube to the private Royal Wimbledon Golf Club for a round of golf with the Chief Naval Medical Officer and a representative from the U.S. Embassy who was responsible for tee time on the members only golf course.

During their daily telephone conversations, Lexi and Jackson talked about how much they missed each other. Jackson was beat by the end of the week and looked forward to going home. They were closer than ever, and Lexi felt more comfortable with and trusting of Jackson than she had in years.

The fatigue Jackson experienced from the trip to Europe paled in comparison to the two-week trip to Asia that he did in November. Crossing the International Date Line halfway across the Pacific Ocean, on the way to work the military hospitals in South Korea, Japan, and the Philippines, nearly took out of him everything he had. Lucky for him though, he was able to finish up the return trip with a long weekend in Honolulu. He recovered by boogie boarding at

Waikiki beach and playing a round of golf at the Royal Kunia Golf Club. The two days that he worked at Tripler Army Medical Center, Pearl Harbor Naval Hospital, and Hickam Air Force Hospital were like a walk in the park compared to the U.S. military bases in the foreign countries where he had just visited. He was able to breeze through security much easier at the Hawaiian bases.

However, one thing that was not a walk in the park was the submission of his expense reports for the trips, especially with all the foreign currency conversions. It was a painstaking process. It took him a full day to perform the calculations for all his receipts and record the expenses for each trip. He thought he had everything straight, but at the end of the day, he wasn't so sure.

Expenses are like a nightmare for me just having to deal with regular U.S. dollars let alone foreign currencies.

The two trips firmly solidified Jackson's upward mobility potential. He demonstrated to the Alsace senior management his dedication to the company business and growing sales profits. The experience he gained by organizing and conducting the trips made Jackson invaluable to the Account Management division. Over the next month, he worked diligently constructing his proposal for a dedicated team of regionally deployed Account Managers who would report to a single Director, Jackson Ford.

YEARS 12-13

CHAPTER 18
SAN DIEGO

Jackson and Lexi had agreed during long talks in Europe that relocation to San Diego was an option for them only if Jackson was promoted to the Director level.

Lexi summed it up in one sentence; "I'll only consider a move to San Diego if you are going to be home more than you are now. Jake and I need you with us, not away traveling on business." She paused and then smiled up at him, "Oh, and a raise would be nice!"

"The only job that I'll move for, Lexi, is this proposal with me as a Director. At least our life will be stable if we do go to headquarters because we won't have to ever move again. I can finish my career right there in San Diego," Jackson replied. She agreed with his point, but was still skeptical of his commitment to changing his focus away from Alsace and to his family.

In the spring following his initial trips to the U.S. military bases in Europe and Asia, Jackson got his opportunity to form a team of his own dedicated to the Federal market. The Alsace Travel Department had booked him in coach for his flight to the Alsace San Diego headquarters, but as usual, he upgraded with one of the many upgrade coupons showered on him by US Airways. This was especially true after the international trips earned him a significant number of airline points.

Considering that Jackson had made similar flights to San Diego to the home office numerous times before with the Managed Care Training Task Force and the Total Hospital Call Task Force meetings, the flight was routine. The purpose of the business trip was to make a formal presentation to the Executive Oversight Committee in order to request an approval of his proposal to form a small team of six Federal

Account Managers reporting to a Director to cover the Federal market segment for Alsace. Upon arrival in San Diego, Jackson rented a car and drove out to the Alsace headquarters located in the Balboa Park area.

Jim Larson had already worked the back channels at Alsace to gain the pre-approvals needed for adding the additional headcount to the Account Management department. Basically, what Larson proposed to members of the EOC was that he would go on the float for the additional heads; meaning at any point in time during a calendar year there would be open territories, open District Sales Manager positions, open marketing positions, etc. that would take time to fill, but while they were open, would save the company money in terms of salary and benefits. Larson asked several EOC members to support the proposal and to approve the additional Account Managers on the premise that the open positions would neutralize any real headcount gains to form this new team.

Jackson's San Diego trip had two purposes. One, the EOC wanted to meet the newest rising star of the Alsace National Accounts division and give their stamp of approval on his proposal first hand. And second, Larson needed some time to talk to Jackson privately in his office. The EOC presentation by Jackson went beautifully. He answered their questions about the segment with appropriate facts and figures like a pro. With a resounding approval, the EOC promoted him to Director on the spot and welcomed him as the newest member of the EOC. Standard Operating Procedure at Alsace normally required that any open position was to be posted on the Human Resources website for ten days, but occasionally, the SOPs were ignored to do what was right for the business. The ever-present EOC member, Scott Evans, fumed as he watched Jackson get promoted without the standard interviewing process. To neutralize him, Larson met with him before the meeting and politely informed him to keep his mouth shut during Jackson's presentation and promotion process. Evans could only take solace in the knowledge that Larson would privately talk to Jackson later in his office about a certain piece of information that he was responsible for uncovering and turning over to Larson.

That jerk will get his, Evans seethed.

After a small celebration for Jackson in the Board Room by a select group of Account Management home office staff members, Larson asked Jackson to come to his office for a private meeting.

Probably wants to give me one of those Cohiba cigars he keeps stashed in his office humidor, Jackson thought.

Present in Larson's office when Jackson entered were two men that he had seen before at meetings, but had not yet been formally introduced to. All three men stood huddled in a corner away from the door, and they spoke in low voices. Jackson rapped his knuckles on the doorframe.

Larson turned toward the sound, "Jackson, come on in and close the door. I want you to meet a couple of people that you've probably seen around before at meetings." He turned to his right and placed his hand on the shoulder of a burly man with a shaved head and a goatee. He wore tinted wire-rimmed glasses, and his black eyes bored into Jackson. "This is Tommy Sommers, head of security for Alsace. You've probably seen him at a number of the national sales meetings."

Jackson stepped forward and shook Sommers' hand. It nearly smothered his own. "Hi Jackson. Good to meet you. Jim's told me lots of good things about you."

"Well, thank you, Tommy. It's good to meet you, too."

Turning next to his left Larson said, "Jackson, this is Herman Wedenbrook, a member of the Alsace Legal Department."

Wedenbrook was a rail-thin man who wore his hair in a ponytail neatly tucked into the back of his shirt collar. He was the one and only openly gay Alsace lawyer who had earned a reputation as a savvy negotiator called in when managed care contract negotiations reached an impasse. It was a well-known fact within the company that if contract talks got stalled, Wedenbrook would get the call to help break the stalemate. "Good afternoon, Jackson. It's a pleasure to meet you." His warm handshake was in total contrast to the Director of Security.

Jackson said hello while Larson asked everyone to sit down around the cocktail table in large leather chairs. "Jackson, congratulations on your promotion today. This job is a big step for your career. A Director position is one that will eventually lead to a Vice President job; and that's where you become an officer in the company. Quite honestly, you fit the profile beautifully by your start as a sales rep, then a sales manager, then a NAM, and now a Director. Plus, you've got a stable family life by being married with a son. Things are looking good for you long term, Jackson."

Jackson sat up a little straighter and shifted in his chair, "Thank you, Jim."

Larson continued, "Jackson, in a director level position here at home office, and particularly as a member of the EOC, you will be on the receiving end of some very sensitive, confidential information concerning our company, marketing strategies, and pipeline. In your previous positions, you weren't exposed to such privileged information making you relatively low on the competition's radar screen. But, moving into a home office position you'll have to be careful of your movements and conversations both inside and outside of the company. Quite frankly, I want to caution you about the possibility of being approached by the competition."

Nervously Jackson asked, "What do you mean approached by the competition?"

The lawyer who had been quiet up to now spoke up, "Jackson, in Big Pharma business is war. Many companies employ certain assets to not only protect their proprietary information, but also to investigate select employees that work the competition. The purpose is to uncover any character flaw or messy situation that can be used as leverage against the competition. For example, they might uncover a drinking or gambling problem, or a marital problem like a nasty divorce, or maybe that someone's kid is doing drugs at school. The information is then used against that individual to gain critical insider company information such as company financials or product strategies or pipeline drugs. These are all sensitive areas that Big Pharma companies have to protect, but that they critically need to find out relative to the competition. Inside information is crucial when a big company is looking to license a product or acquire a competitor or thwart a competitor's new product launch."

Larson chimed in, "Competitive information is important, Jackson, especially when a Big Pharma company is planning a hostile takeover or when a competitor's new product is in the final clinical development process that could jeopardize another company's profits and earnings records."

It was Sommers turn next to speak while Jackson's uneasiness mounted, "You know, Jackson, you've probably seen me at a number of our national sales meetings checking ID badges of the people entering our meeting halls and meal rooms. We do that to keep the competition out or, as I call it, keep the gators out. You may have noticed as well that after the audience is dismissed for a break or lunch, especially at the end of the day, that my team comes in and conducts a sweep of the room. They gather up confidential information left behind by the participants like binders, promotional pieces, PowerPoint slide presentations, and the like. Stuff the competition would love to get their hands on. Why do you think we require that your laptop computers be secured with cable locks to the desks in your hotel rooms? It's because when the hotel staff is servicing the room, there's no one to stop the competition from walking in and simply taking the computer while the maid is in the bathroom cleaning the toilet! The security of our assets and our proprietary information is a job that we take very seriously here at Alsace. And our assets also includes key people who have information up here." He tapped his forehead with his index finger.

Jackson spoke up weakly, "I'm just curious because this is all new to me, but how do we know the competition's tactics?"

Larson and Sommers looked to the lawyer who thought for a moment. Larson rolled his eyes but waited patiently for Wedenbrook's response. "Well Jackson, since you are now officially a member of the EOC, I guess you have the right to know." He leaned forward slightly and said in a voice barely above a whisper, "We know the competition's tactics because we employ the same ones."

Jackson's jaw dropped and his stomach turned over.

Wedenbrook continued, "Remember last year when BMT Biotech had the new lung cancer drug in Phase Three clinical trials, and it was being touted by all the analysts as the new breakthrough drug promising the company blockbuster status? It was the drug that was supposed to compete head-to-head with our new drug, Nesperia, which was also in Phase Three, but about six months behind in the development process."

Jackson nodded. He recalled that BMT Biotech was a small start-up company with very little assets or cash flow, but with what appeared to be this new breakthrough drug for lung cancer with survival rates that looked much better than any current therapy on the market. BMT was heavily dependent on venture capital funding that they were able to procure because of the new drug. Their stock price soared. Suddenly, however, a story broke about an increased number of deaths associated with the drug during the studies. The morning talk shows and financial news networks sensationalized the deaths, which caused the BMT stock price to drop precipitously. In fact, the stock price still trades about one-half the value of last year before the press release because the FDA ordered BMT to redesign and redo all of their Phase Three trials. Venture capital funding dried up overnight because the product would be least three more years away from commercialization. A lot of investors lost big bucks as a result of the unfortunate situation. Meanwhile, Nesperia moved forward in the development and FDA approval process. Wall Street analysts upgraded the rating on the company because of the future sales potential of the medicine that provided a nice boost to the Alsace stock price.

The lawyer continued, "The Wall Street Journal broke the story, Jackson. Do you care to guess from where it originated?"

Jackson shook his head from side to side and was afraid to hear the answer.

"We found a member of the BMT clinical development team who, shall we say, had incentive to talk to us because of a little habit that he did not want disclosed to his family or BMT. He liked to download dirty pictures of children off the Internet. He now works for us on the

Nesperia project, but only after he sold all his BMT stock just before the story broke and the stock price plunged. He made a killing." He let the news linger a minute before he continued, "Of course, we have him undergoing some intense psychotherapy, but he is a brilliant scientist."

Jackson's stomach dropped into his lap. Suddenly, he was sorry that he ate something at his little party because he felt ready to heave all over the cocktail table.

Larson could tell Jackson was uncomfortable with the information, "Jackson, this is big business, and we take it very seriously. You know, you've been a recipient of some of this behind the scenes activity."

"What do you mean?"

"Well, how many stock options do you have now?" Larson asked.

"After the last three-for-one split, I have over 50,000 options all with different strike prices."

"And over the course of your career with Alsace, you've probably cashed in a lot of options and, let's face it, Jackson, you're on your way to becoming very wealthy. The increase in our stock price is the way that we create value for the company and for ourselves. Some of the tactics employed might be untidy, but the result is the same, which is that Alsace delivers a consistent earnings growth from quarter to quarter. Additionally, you're going to benefit from the launch of Nesperia. You saw today that the EOC recognized the sales opportunity with all the lung cancer patients in the Federal market, and the need to capture that business with a dedicated team of account managers. Your team, Jackson, with you as the Director. And the good news is that we won't have any competition from BMT for awhile." He chuckled at the last remark.

"Well, thank you, Nesperia!" Jackson said quickly with a forced smile.

"No, thank Tommy Sommers here and his team for the work they've done. I'll let you in on a little secret. The BMT death data wasn't that bad. Hell, we had probably just as many patients die in the Nesperia study group. It's just that our university-based clinical investigators had more incentive, shall we say, when it came to submitting their data and doing the statistical analysis on Nesperia compared to the placebo group."

Jackson was floored.

"So Jackson, this position at home office means that you're in the big league now with access to sensitive information and big corporate decision-making processes. We're expecting you to be a team player. Can you handle it?" Larson asked.

"Yes, I can handle it," came the response. *This is a whole different league. They play hardball without gloves. Do I have I got the stomach for this?*

"So Jackson, the second purpose of this meeting is to let you know that we've only one minor concern with your promotion." Larson paused for effect. "It would appear that you have your own little zipper club going with Tam Martin."

Jackson's heart stopped for a moment, "Excuse me?"

Sommers stated matter of factly, "Another Director approached us after the negotiations training meeting in Santa Monica almost a year ago. He insinuated that you and Tam were having an affair."

"Evans!" Jackson seethed.

"I'm not going to confirm or deny that source, but since my security personnel are all former police detectives or private investigators, I had them do some checking," said Sommers.

"You had me investigated?" Jackson asked.

It was Larson's turn, "Jackson, as a Director, with great potential to move up to a VP position within a few years, you have to be very careful. A VP position means that you're an officer in the company and privy to a great deal of sensitive information. Promoting you into a Director position means we had to check into your background. It's standard operating procedure. We need to find this stuff before the competition does, as we spoke earlier, in order to protect the company. For example, don't you think we try to control Boomer? He's assigned the biggest single managed care account there is, and he's a walking time bomb of mischief! I'm sure that the competition would love to get at him."

Sommers leaned toward Jackson and said in a low voice, "Tam used her Corporate American Express credit card last March in a retail store in Crested Butte, Colorado."

"Weren't you in Crested Butte at the same time, Jackson?" asked Larson.

A sledgehammer hit Jackson's gut, "You know I was since you and Rick approved the trip to attend the DAV Winter Sports Clinic. Did Alsace have me followed?"

"No. We only do that with some of the R & D scientists traveling to Washington DC for meetings with the FDA about our pipeline. We have to ensure that they are not, oh shall we say, approached by the competition," came the response from Sommers as he leaned back into his chair. "They have a lot of knowledge, you know, about our proprietary products including the results of clinical trials, product efficacy and safety, and the discovery of new molecules. You understand. We don't feel it necessary to shadow a sales manager or NAM since they only have access to information that is already in the public domain. It's when you get to the Director level, particularly in home office, where we have to scrutinize our employees a bit more closely. We also know how many cell phone calls the two of you make to each other each week. You turn in your entire cell phone bill when you submit your expenses, you know. Oh, by the way, you're about two weeks behind again in submitting your latest expense report, Jackson."

Jackson felt like crap, and his knees shook from being so upset. "OK, so what are you suggesting? Tam means nothing to me compared with this opportunity, and I certainly do not want my wife to find out about her. It would wreck my marriage!"

"Smart boy, Jackson," replied Larson. "You need to talk to Tam because she can't work within the account management division any longer."

"What do you mean?" asked Jackson raising his eyebrows.

Larson moved closer to Jackson while turning to look first at both Wedenbrook and Sommers, "We've all seen her, Jackson. The gal is a knockout!"

Wedenbrook interrupted, "Well, she's not my cup to tea!"

Larson looked up at the ceiling and shook his head before he continued, "I have to admit that if I was getting some of that, I would have a real hard time stopping myself. How is she anyway? No, forget I asked that."

Jackson's neck was bright red and beads of sweat had formed on his forehead.

"Look, it's for your own good. You have to stop seeing her, and we're going to help you. With all the divisions here at Alsace there are lots of other opportunities for a bright, competent girl like Tam. We just need to keep you two kids apart so the competition doesn't have anything to use against you," Larson stated.

"Like I asked before, what are you suggesting?" Jackson repeated.

Larson leaned back, "The Company is prepared to offer her a couple of options. There are two openings in Tampa. One is a specialty sales rep and the other is a hospital sales rep."

The kiss of death for Tam's career, thought Jackson. "But they're both demotions from her current position."

"She'll get to keep her current salary and management level of stock option grants which are, as you know, substantially more than the grants we give to sales reps. That keeps her whole financially. She just won't be able to see you anymore. It's just too risky, Jackson, with your new position and your access to confidential information. You could be compromised by the competition if they discover Tam as your weak spot. You know, who's to say that your competition didn't see the two of you together in Crested Butte and maybe take a picture or two. That would be pretty devastating to Lexi now wouldn't it? We can only say that it's a good thing that we discovered this when we did so we can control it and protect you," Larson said.

"When are you going to tell her?" asked Jackson.

"We are not," replied Larson, "you are."

Jackson's eyebrows furrowed, "Me?"

"Yes, you. We have already gotten her transfer pre-approved by the two different Region Sales Directors in the southeast. She is such 'eye candy' that the two of them would love to have her in their areas.

And who knows? Maybe after things cool off between the two of you, she can work her way back up to a District Sales Manager again."

Jackson was glad he was sitting down. He just knew that if he was standing up that his knees would have buckled. It was bad enough that his stomach had flipped over and was in knots. "OK. I'll tell her, but I want to do it face-to-face and not over the phone."

Silence fell over the room for a minute as the men considered the offer.

"We can live with that," Wedenbrook finally said. "I would suggest that you take her to a nice quiet restaurant where she will be less apt to create a scene."

"OK, it's settled then," said Larson. "Jackson, welcome to the EOC! Now, you've got a busy schedule coming up. After you finish up the Tam thing, you need to start interviewing and hiring your new team of account managers. Then, you need to start looking for a house out here and get your family relocated! It's going to be great having you here at headquarters, Jackson!"

Later that afternoon, Jackson met with Dee Dee Wallace, from Human Resources, to review his new salary package and offer letter for the Director position. His new base salary would be $150,000 plus an annual target bonus of fifty thousand dollars equally allocated between management objectives, Federal market sales results, and national sales results. He couldn't believe that his bonus potential was going to be three times that of a sales representative! They were also going to give him an upgrade to the auto benefit; meaning, since he was fifty percent home office status and fifty percent field sales status, he could pick from a list of upgraded cars that included Volvos and BMWs. Ten thousand stock options were also being awarded to him just for accepting the new position. *Sweet!*

Dee Dee continued to pull forms out of her file folder during their discussion, "Next, I'll cover the relocation package with you. Because you're a Director now, you qualify for the premium relocation package."

"You know, when the company moved me from Indiana to Kansas City the package was just fine," Jackson stated.

"That was the standard manager relo package, Jackson. I'll think that you'll find this to be much more generous. First, we're offering you a twenty-five thousand dollar promotion bonus to help defray the costs of some of the initial new home furnishings like curtains, window shutters, paint, lighting, and so on. Second, Alsace will pay for two loan origination points and all the closing costs on your new home. Third, you need to list your Kansas City home on the market for sixty days on your own, but if it doesn't sell, then Alsace will buy it at the appraised price, and of course, pay all of your realtor commissions. Fourth, your moving costs, temporary storage for six months, and temporary housing for up to six months while your new house is being built will also be paid by Alsace. Fifth, you'll get three house hunting trips for you and your family. Sixth, to help offset the housing cost difference between Kansas City and San Diego, Alsace will buy down your interest rate for three years as follows: Year One—three interest points; Year Two—two interest points; and Year Three—one interest point. We call it the Three-Two-One interest rate buy-down program. By the fourth year, your salary should increase enough to cover the full cost of the higher mortgage payment. And lastly, to help you qualify for a high-housing cost mortgage differential here in San Diego as compared to KC, we will underwrite a second mortgage on your home for five years up to one hundred thousand dollars. All you pay is a monthly low interest rate, not the principal, for the five-year period. Then at the end of five years, most home office managers usually just cash in some stock options and pay off the hundred thousand loan. The result is that you've got instant equity in your home. And the way property values are increasing in southern California, your home is a going to be a great long-term investment, Jackson. Think of it as a forced diversification of your investment portfolio!"

He could not believe what he was hearing. *This package is a lot more than just plain old generous; it's out of this world generous! What a great opportunity. I was feeling a little apprehensive after my meeting with Larson, but not anymore. I can barely wait for the flight back home tonight to tell Lexi!*

The return flight to Kansas City got Jackson home after midnight. Lexi let him sleep in, and after she dropped off Jake at his school, she stopped by the local Starbucks to pick up an Iced Café Latte for herself, a Café Mocha for Jackson, and two blueberry scones. When Jackson heard the garage door open, he got up and met Lexi at the kitchen table to review his offer and relocation package with her.

Lexi was skeptical at first, "What's with all these relocation perks, Jackson? Not to slam you or anything, but you're just one guy! How many people each year get relocated to San Diego with all these same benefits? Think of the money that Alsace must spend!"

Jackson reassured her, "Lexi, this is a Fortune Fifty company. They make a lot of money, and they spend a lot of money. People and products are very important to Alsace. I just happen to be one of their key people now."

Lexi softened, "Jackson, I'm so proud of you and what you've accomplished with this company. You have provided for Jake and me, and for that, I love you. But I have to admit that I'm anxious about moving to California. You know Jake is settled in his school, we've got great friends, and a great social life through our church. We'd be starting all over again if we move."

"I understand how you feel, Lexi, but opportunities like this don't come along every day!"

Lexi took measure before starting again, "You're going to have to make some big changes, Jackson. We can't, I mean, I can't keep going on where you ignore Jake and me and put your work first. If that's the way it's going to be, then you can just go out there yourself and send us back your paycheck, because that's basically the way it is right now!"

Jackson thought, *Oh shit, this is not starting off very well. I can't go out there by myself without my family. What would the EOC think?* "No, please Lexi. I'll be different, I can change…I want to change. I need you and Jake with me. Come on, we'll find a good marriage counselor, a good church, a private school for Jake. I won't have to travel as much so we can be together and build a life. It won't be like now, I promise." The guilt of all the years of wanting to be away from his family and his affair with Tam hit Jackson like a ton of bricks.

Skeptical, but wanting to believe him, she replied, "We'll go on a house hunting trip, and I'll keep an open mind. But you have to show me real change, Jackson, and not empty promises."

"OK. I'll show you that I mean it. You know, I haven't been to confession in a while. I think I'll call Father Larry and schedule a private appointment with him for this week."

Lexi smiled, "I think that would be good for you." She walked around the table and hugged him. "I do love you, Jackson. I want you back in our lives again."

The private confession with Father Larry at St. Peter's church was very difficult for Jackson. He had a long time fear and anxiety complex with priests. It was beat into his head during parochial school and put together with his behavior from the last decade, it made him nervous for their meeting. But once he started in, the sins poured out like water through a broken dam. His last admission was about Tam, and this one caused the tears to start.

The priest listened in silence with sympathetic eyes and that encouraged Jackson to keep talking. "You know, Father, years ago Merck used to be called Merck Sharp & Dohme. There was a Merck guy in my old sales territory that joked that Merck Sharp & Dohme or MSD stood for Married, Separated & Divorced. It's like a badge of honor in Big Pharma companies to either have affairs or break up your marriage to get ahead." Jackson continued to relay other zipper club stories that happened all around him as he worked at Alsace. He cried as he declared his love for Lexie and Jake, and that he was sorry for his sin.

Father Larry sensed that Jackson's love for his family was true. They talked awhile longer and finally decided that Lexi should not be told about the affair. Rather, Jackson should end it immediately and not commit the sin of adultery ever again. The priest gave Jackson absolution as well as a new rosary, and then asked him to perform an Act of Contrition. He spent the next hour in the Adoration Chapel in deep reflection about his life over the last decade and how to end the affair with Tam.

He went home resolved to be a better man, "Lexi, I have been a complete and utter fool to have ignored you and Jake all these years, and to have put myself ahead of my family. For that, I am truly sorry, and I ask for your forgiveness. I'm glad I spent some time with Father Larry. He helped me put a lot of things in life back in perspective."

"I do forgive you, Jackson. We've got a second chance on life if you keep your family first. It's a living hell for all of us when you don't."

"I promised Father Larry that I would change, and now I'm promising you as well. I love you very much, Lexi. I'm sorry for being so selfish and insensitive for all these years." He wrapped his arms around her and kissed her passionately.

But before Jackson could move forward completely with his wife, he had to tend to one urgent matter as soon as possible, "Lexi, before our house hunting trip next weekend, I've got to fly to Atlanta for a customer meeting. You know I'm trying to keep a light schedule of customer appointments for the next two months because of our move, but I've had this dinner meeting scheduled for a while, and I hate to cancel it."

"I know you're going to be super busy finishing up your current job and starting your new one, plus trying to move us. Go ahead and do what you've got to do. I understand," she replied.

Tam agreed to meet Jackson at the Ritz Carlton hotel on Peachtree Street in Buckhead, Georgia, a wealthy suburb of Atlanta. When she had wanted to meet Jackson in his suite before dinner for a little fun as she put it, he quickly claimed that he had a teleconference with the home office. Disappointed, of course, she said that she understood and agreed to meet him in the lobby at seven o'clock.

"Where are you taking me to dinner tonight?" Tam asked with a low soft voice.

"I thought we'd stay here at the hotel and eat at The Dining Room downstairs."

Tam detected a distancing in his tone not ever before present. Shrugging it off to his upcoming teleconference call she spoke again in a silky voice, "I'm glad we're staying here so we can go upstairs to your suite for dessert and not have to wait for a valet to bring the car around at some off-site restaurant. Good choice."

Quickly he said, "I've gotta go, Tam. I'll meet you downstairs at seven."

Tam showered and shaved her long tanned legs and applied a fresh coat of polish on her nails. She had packed a low cut blouse, miniskirt and heels to wear. Before she left the room, she walked through a mist of the new perfume, *Envy* by Gucci that Jackson had purchased for her in London last August. Her small clutch carried only her room key and her bright red lipstick.

Jackson arrived first in the lobby a few minutes before seven o'clock. *Before last week's meeting with Larson and the boys, Tam and I would have met in my suite, and wouldn't have left unless absolutely necessary. Those were the days, my man. But not tonight, big boy, and not ever again if you ever want to make VP and keep your family.* Before coming down to the lobby, Jackson hit the mini-bar in his room for liquid courage consisting of two vodka tonics and one gin and tonic. The drinks helped calm his nerves initially, but when he saw Tam step out of the lobby elevator, he thought, *She is so hot.*

He slowly lifted the corners of his mouth as she approached. They embraced and kissed lightly. Not to mess up her lipstick, Tam quickly moved her lips to his ear and whispered, "Let's go back to your room right now, Jackson."

Remembering his promise to Father Larry, to God, to Lexi, and to himself, Jackson pulled back. *I should have had the other gin from my mini-bar,* he thought. "Let's go have some dinner, Tam. I haven't eaten all day."

Tam frowned, and with a sigh of disappointment said, "OK Jackson, if that's what you want to do, then let's go feed you!" She took his hand in hers as they walked to the restaurant.

After being escorted to their table, Jackson ordered two cocktails, a bottle of red wine, and two appetizers: the sautéed Hudson Valley foie gras and the seared baby scallops.

After their drinks arrived, Tam toasted Jackson's promotion, "I'm so proud of you, Jackson. They're going to love you at headquarters. I just know that you'll be a VP in no time!"

Jackson's voice was shakier that he would have liked, "We need to have a serious discussion about our future."

Tam's eyebrows flickered a little and a spark came into her eyes, *Could this finally mean that he's finally going to ask his wife for a divorce? Could my dreams be coming true?*

At that exact moment, the wine steward arrived and interrupted them. After Jackson had smelled, tasted, and approved the wine, two glasses were poured and allowed to sit for a few minutes to breathe.

Jackson had rehearsed what he would say next in his room several times before coming downstairs so he continued in a cool tone, "I can't see you anymore."

Nervously she ran her hand through her hair, "Don't you mean that you're just not going to be able to see me as much? Because you'll be in San Diego, right? But you'll still have to work with your southeast region account manager so we'll still see each other, maybe just not as much. Isn't that what you mean? So, we'll just have to put more effort into it. Come on, we can do this, Jackson!"

His words were cool and clear as ice water, "Tam, Larson knows about us. We have to stop seeing each other. As a Director in National Accounts, I can't be involved with you since we're both in the same department. He made it clear that we can't be involved even if you're outside the department."

She blurted, scarcely aware of her own voice, "What are you saying? I thought you were going to leave your wife for this job. I thought that we would have a chance to be together as a couple. I had a lot of hopes and dreams for us, Jackson. What happened?"

Jackson gathered his strength, "Tam, if I want to be a VP someday, I can't be having an affair with someone in the same department, nor can I be having an affair with someone that works at Alsace. We shouldn't have ever started this."

"So I can leave Alsace. I love you, and I want to be with you!" She paused a moment, "I'll leave my husband and move to San Diego. Jackson, we belong together!"

"We don't belong together. You're not coming to San Diego, and I'm not leaving Lexi." Jackson continued as if Tam had never spoke, "They want us to be separated. You have to leave the department. They've arranged for you to choose between a specialty rep position and a hospital rep position in Tampa so you don't have to relocate or anything. They don't trust us that we can break it off on our own and not still see each other at all the account management meetings."

Tam spoke in a suffocated whisper laced with anger; "They're demoting me because of our affair? And you're getting promoted? Is that about right?"

"Yes."

A cold dignity spread across her face as she realized what he was saying. "What else are they offering?"

"They said that your salary would stay the same as well as your management level stock option grants. They also said that after things cool off between us, that you could still be promoted again into sales management. The two Regional Directors both want you, Tam. They're trying to keep you whole financially while separating us." Jackson's eyes were flat and expressionless.

Tam cast her eyes downward, staring at her plate. She sat in unbelief at what she was hearing. After a minute of silence she lifted her head, and looked at him with a raw hurt in her eyes, "Jackson, I love you. I'm willing to leave my husband for you. You know we belong together, and how right we are for each other. Please Jackson, think about us. Don't all the nights together in Crested Butte, Santa Monica and here, in Atlanta, mean anything to you?

Jackson reached out and clutched her hand with both of his, "Tam, listen to me. I don't love you, and I never did. I love my wife and son, and I would never leave them. I can't. I have a responsibility to them. What we did was wrong. It was adultery, pure and simple. I care about you, Tam, I do. But I don't love you. It was made very clear to me by senior management at Alsace that I need to get my own house in order for this promotion and beyond. Continuing a relationship with you is bad business for me. Please, Tam, consider taking one of the rep positions that they're offering you. It's really for the best, Tam, it is." He held out his hands and offered an apology, "Tam, I'm sorry that it turned out this way. We should never have let this thing get so far out of hand."

She moved her hands up his forearms. In a choked voice filled with disbelief she said, "Jackson, I understand the position you're in, and that you have to do what's right for you. But, you know that I'm right for you. I was really hoping that we would have a chance to be together. I'm the one that supports your career, and I'm the one that understands your commitment to Alsace. Lexi doesn't! We deserve a chance to be together." She took a deep breath, withdrew her hands, and said matter of factly, "Listen to me. I'm going to leave Mike, resign from Alsace, move to San Diego with you, and then find another job. All you have to do is leave Lexi! I love you, and I know you love me! Go ahead and tell Larson that he'll have my resignation by the end of the week." She stared at Jackson but could see he was not moved, so she tried one more attempt, "Jackson, pay the bill, and let's go upstairs. I need you right now! Come on, Jackson. You know that we're right for each other."

Jackson drew a deep breath and said in a cold calculating voice, "Tam, listen to me. I don't love you. It's over. I'm not leaving my wife or blowing this chance for a Director position."

She pushed away from the table, stood up and walked to his side. She leaned down into him and paused for a moment. Her blouse dipped open and she whispered with a warm breath into his ear, "I've seen the picture of Lexi in your wallet, Jackson. I know I'm better looking than her. Now come upstairs, and I'll forget all about this silly conversation."

Jackson tore his eyes away from the temptation and looked back up to Tam's face. She could see the smoldering flame in his eyes, and she smirked at him. She kissed him, but Jackson's mouth did not become any softer as her lips lingered.

Jackson pulled back disgusted, "Tam, you are gorgeous, but I love my wife and my career."

Tam took her cue and turned to leave. "I'm not being pushed aside this easily, Jackson." She walked out of the restaurant toward the elevators with an air of confidence that Jackson would knock on her door before the night was over.

Jackson let out a long breath as he shook his head back and forth. He hit a few buttons on his cell phone and after a moment quietly said, "It's me, Jackson. Things didn't go so well. You were right though, Jim, we can't stay in the same department." He paused to listen to the voice at the other end of the line, and then he said, "She's a smart girl. She'll make the right decision by the end of the week." He listened again and then said, "Yeah, we're all coming out this weekend for a house hunting trip. OK, maybe I'll see you." He pressed a button to disconnect the call.

He signaled the waiter and asked for the check. After he signed for the bill, he grabbed the wine bottle and headed for his suite. His flight was scheduled to depart at Noon the next day. He called home and talked to Lexi for a long time. Before he hung up he said, "I love you more than anything else, and I can't wait to get home to see you."

Tam called Larson at the end of the week. In a terse voice she informed him, "You'll have my resignation first thing Monday morning."

"What are your plans?" he asked.

"Not that you really care, I'm sure. But I've decided to leave my husband and move to Washington DC. I have a friend that offered me a job with a major consulting company that specializes in Big Pharma legislative lobbying."

"Well, I'm sorry that things couldn't have turned out differently, Tam. Alsace is losing a valued employee." *And a damn good looking one, too!* he thought.

"Let's cut the small talk, Jim. I want a separation package from Alsace. I've talked to an employment law attorney, and he thinks that I've got a pretty good case. What are you willing to offer me?" she asked.

Larson knew that there was a possibility of this happening. He spoke to HR and Wedenbrook right after Jackson called to say that the discussion didn't go well earlier in the week. "Tam, I am authorized to grant you a very generous separation package. In addition to six months severance pay, you will still be eligible to receive your second quarter bonus payout, and be able to cash out all the stock options that you've accumulated over the years within sixty days of termination."

"Not just the vested stock options, right? Do you mean all the options? Vested and non-vested together, correct?"

"That's right, Tam. It's a very generous offer. If you give me your verbal approval, I'll have Dee Dee Wallace send the documents to you overnight."

"OK. I approve. Send the paperwork to my home address." She hung up the phone.

The Ford family flew out of Kansas City on a Friday morning just as a spring snowstorm ripped through the area. The tulips in front of their house were covered with about an inch of powder. Everything looked so beautiful blanketed in white as the plane lifted off and headed west. The weather in San Diego, however, was a stark contrast to the weather back east. It was sunny, of course, with clear blue skies and a temperature in the mid-seventies. Just another typical day in southern California. Jackson, Lexi and Jake walked off the plane and exited the terminal for the baggage claim area. Lexi procured a luggage cart while her boys grabbed the bags off the belt. They rented a car from National and drove the two miles to the Marriott Marina Hotel where their suite overlooked the marina. As they stood on the balcony, they watched the fighter jets practicing touchdowns and take offs at the Naval airstrip located just beyond the shipyard. Two Navy Destroyers could be seen moored in the dry dock area undergoing repairs.

Jackson had arranged for their local realtor to meet them an hour later in the hotel restaurant for lunch to review the relocation package, to listen to their housing and schooling needs, and to describe several potential new construction areas that would work within their budget. The spent the rest of the day and all of Saturday scouting out the new housing developments and driving past several private schools in the area. On Saturday night, they went out to the Gas Lamp District of San Diego for an early dinner. Afterwards, Jackson drove them north on the Pacific Coast Highway toward Laguna Beach to watch night fall over the ocean.

On Sunday morning, Jake wanted to go to the San Diego Zoo to see the pandas and koalas. After a few hours, they left the zoo and drove north to the La Jolla area where they visited the Sunny Jim Cave. They descended the steep steps of the cave where they found that it opened up to the Pacific Ocean. The surf crashed against the walls just a few feet from where they stood. La Jolla Cove was the next stop to watch the harbor seals play and sun themselves. Jake decided that it was actually better than the zoo since you could get up close to the seals in their natural habitat. Dinner that night was at the Crescent Café restaurant overlooking the ocean. As the sun began to set and the boogie boarders and surfers came to shore to call it a day, Lexi leaned over to Jackson during dessert and said with a smile, "I could live here!" Jackson's heart jumped for joy when he heard those words.

Jackson and Lexi bought a five-bedroom 2,800 square foot home with an in-ground pool in Rancho Santa Fe located just north of San Diego. The house took four months to build so the Fords took advantage of the temporary housing arrangements offered by Alsace and lived in a furnished three-bedroom townhouse over the summer. Since their house in Kansas City sold in only ten days, their furniture and effects were all stored in a vault, compliments of Alsace. The townhouse came with all the utilities paid and, of course, the rent was also paid as part of the relo package. Jackson and Lexi only paid for their food and phone bills so a nice tidy sum was socked away each month during their stay.

With extra cash in hand and a four month waiting period for their house to be finished, they spent their weekends like tourists and visited the beaches, Sea World, the Wild Animal Park, LEGOLAND, and Disneyland. Lexi bought Jackson and Jake matching black rash shirts to wear while boogie boarding in the ocean. The shirts were designed to reduce the skin irritation on one's chest that is usually associated with the sport. They fell in love with the sun and surf. Lexi had to be very careful with the sun and took extra precautions with her fair skin. Sunscreen with a high SPF number, a wide-brimmed hat, and an umbrella were always in the trunk of the car for their beach trips. In no time at all, they had settled into the southern California lifestyle.

CHAPTER 19
CEO

The Chief Executive Officer or CEO of Alsace Pharmaceuticals was a hard line businessman named Kevin Steer. He was a former U.S. Air Force Captain with a pharmacy degree and a MBA. Although middle aged, he still maintained his chiseled military look and approached every aspect of his life with purpose and discipline, particularly his exercise regime. He could be found every day at 5:30 PM in the Alsace Fitness Center working on his physique but also sizing up the minions who worked for him. Steer was a no-nonsense CEO who had worked his way up through the ranks of a competitive pharmaceutical company. He started by carrying a bag as it is known in the industry; meaning, he started his career as a sales representative.

Steer was heavily recruited by the Alsace Board of Directors at a time when the company was getting fat and sloppy and in need of discipline throughout the organization. Alsace negotiated a deal with Steer that required him to stay in the CEO position for fifteen years and if the company experienced twenty successive quarters of double digit earnings per share growth, then he would get a three year extension on his contract and a cool ten million dollar bonus. Plus, he would receive 500,000 shares of Alsace stock. Steer accepted the offer and moved from New Jersey to San Diego with his wife, Catherine.

Shortly after coming on board, Business Week magazine conducted an interview with Steer. The Alsace employees got their first impressions of him and discovered that the days of winging it were over. Historically, the U.S. division of Alsace conducted a lot of strategic planning through hallway or cafeteria conversations, the reps had little accountability for the number of doctor calls they made each day, the sales managers usually spent two days a week in their offices, and the marketing teams used a shotgun approach to promotional strategies. A management style of regimentation was going to be the new order throughout the organization to ensure profitability. In the end, it was a welcome change by the Alsace employees. Jackson and Lexi were awestruck by the man when they first met him on the awards trip cruise. Jackson thought that his over-confidence and blunt manner made him the be-all and end-all of corporate CEOs.

Over time, however, Lexi became less enamored with Steer. "I don't know if I can put my finger on it, Jackson. There's just something there that seems phony to me," she admitted once.

Although a disciplinarian by nature, Steer was a risk taker. His two children were grown and out of college starting families of their own, so the move to southern California was the cherry on top of the cake being offered by Alsace. Steer had several loves in his life up to this point, namely, Springsteen music, fast cars, and golf, but upon moving to San Diego he found he really liked sailing and California women. He immediately bought a yacht and docked it at the marina near the airport and across the harbor from the Naval Shipyard. He felt that it would be easy to fit in into his new surroundings.

It was rumored at Steer's previous company that a zipper club existed of which Steer was the president. In reality, the rumors were not that far off. The zipper club was a tight knit group of Directors and Vice Presidents who preyed on young female sales reps at national sales meetings or new product launch meetings, which essentially meant any company function where there was liquor available and live bands. Their aura of corporate power and good looks intoxicated the young ladies. The alcohol normally found in abundance at the corporate parties simply exacerbated the phenomenon since the women flocked to the executives, danced with them, and sadly, even slept with them in their suites. The parties were likened to a scene from a college frat party rather than a respectable Fortune Fifty company function. The drunkenness and infidelity seemed to be rather acceptable business practices.

An unfounded rumor was that an abortion was quietly arranged when one of the Directors got a frantic telephone call in the middle of the night from a distraught female rep from New Orleans. An actual true story, however, was about one of the Vice Presidents who, in his mid-forties, actually divorced his wife to marry one of the mid-twenties hospital sales reps that he met through the zipper club. "She is so beautiful," he would remark to his fellow club members. This raised the bar for the zipper club and nearly set off a rash of divorces until it was learned what the VP ended up paying his ex-wife in the divorce settlement. The boys concluded it was less expensive to just keep their wives.

The jokes whispered throughout the break rooms at Alsace that when Steer initially came on board as the CEO, the maternity benefits increased fifty percent for the secretarial pool. But Steer was not interested in the secretaries; rather, he had his eye on one of the Marketing Directors, Christi Marcum. A former clothing model in college, she had a brilliant marketing mind with her MBA from the University of Texas and fifteen years of marketing experience in Big Pharma. She was a tall single woman from Texas with jet-black hair, fair skin, and big brown eyes. She too, could be found in the Fitness Center after work participating in a step class. Steer did a double take when he first spied her exiting the women's locker room heading off to a class.

Their relationship started off all business at first by simply interacting at business meetings. Christi made the usual marketing presentations including promotional strategy, brand strategy, and sales forecasts to the Executive Oversight Committee or EOC on which Steer was an ad-hoc member. Her no-nonsense approach to product marketing coupled with her Texas drawl, infatuated Steer. At the first opportunity, Steer had Christi promoted to VP of Marketing whereupon she became a full-fledged member of the EOC. Their time together grew because of the promotion and slowly began to spill over into after-hours dinner meetings, mostly private social meetings.

Even with his busy CEO travel schedule, Steer specifically arranged to see more and more of Christi. Christi knew that Steer was her ticket up the corporate ladder while Steer simply thought, *She is just so beautiful*, in order to justify his actions. Soon, business trips together to Chicago, New York, and Paris in the company jet gave new meaning to the mile high club.

As all good things must eventually come to an end, so it came to be with Steer and Christi. Steer's wife, Catherine, grew increasingly suspicious of her husband's moods and behavior towards her.

"He is so distant," she would remark to her therapist. "None of my needs are being met."

While Steer was in the shower one morning, Catherine searched his wallet and found a new Bank of America Visa card that she hadn't seen before. Instead of confronting him, she quickly wrote down the account number. After he left for work, she called the customer service toll-free number and scrolled through the automated system to listen to the last ten purchases. Catherine was shocked by what she heard, and she went online to the access the card website and to review the account information. Since they both either used the dog's birthday or name for every PIN number they ever had, accessing the information was easy. She printed out copies of the last two statements. It was right there in black and white: on his last business trip to Chicago he bought a bracelet at Cartier, a watch at Tiffany's, and perfume at Sephora's for a total of $6,800. She knew damn well she didn't receive any gifts from him, and their anniversary wasn't for another six months!

That lecher, Catherine thought. *I've looked the other way, made excuses for him, and accepted his insincere apologies for too damn long! He's going to pay this time.*

Catherine then arranged for an appointment with the best divorce attorney in San Diego along with a private investigator. When all the evidence was assembled, Catherine pounced.

Her timing was perfect, and scorned women across the United States would have been proud. It was during the Alsace Board of Director's meeting with the EOC that Catherine chose to descend on her husband. The big black Lincoln Towncar drove slowly around the circle driveway and stopped in front of the main entrance to the

Alsace headquarters. Catherine was dressed in a Chanel suit and blouse with low heels. Her lawyer followed her into the building carrying two large black cases that the driver removed from the trunk of the Towncar.

As they approached the main reception desk, Catherine greeted the security guard seated behind the desk. He was wearing a headset and keeping an eye on several video monitors. "Good morning, Darnell, how are you today?"

"Good morning, Mrs. Steer. I'm doing just fine, thank you, and yourself?" he asked.

"I'm doing very well, thank you. Darnell, the gentleman accompanying me today is an old Air Force acquaintance of Mr. Steer's. He is in town visiting for the day. I know that there is a Board meeting right now, but Mr. Steer had asked me to stop by and interrupt him for just a minute so he could say hello to his friend. Would you be so kind as to allow us access upstairs for just a few minutes?"

Darnell suddenly became very nervous, "You're not listed in the logbook today, Mrs. Steer. I guess Mr. Steer forgot to have his administrative assistant call down. Our security procedures state that you need to have an appointment and an escort to go through the turnstiles. Mr. Sommers is very firm on me following procedures."

"I'll bet that my husband forgot to tell his assistant, Darnell. Come to think of it, he was in a rush to get out of the house this morning for this big Board of Directors meeting." she lied. "Don't trouble yourself by calling upstairs for an escort, I know the way by heart. Now if you would just be so kind to let us through the turnstile, I would appreciate it. And I'll tell Mr. Steer how helpful you were to me." Catherine stated. The last thing Steer would have wanted was for Catherine to show up during a Board meeting.

"Oh, well not a problem then, Mrs. Steer. Here, I'll use my badge. You know the way to the executive boardroom? You just turn right as you come off the elevator." Darnell said as he rose from the chair, removed his headset and walked around the reception desk to use his badge that activated the turnstile and allowed the access that Catherine wanted.

"Yes, Darnell, I know the way. Thank you, you've been extremely helpful." Catherine smiled at Darnell and nodded at her lawyer to proceed.

They stepped into an elevator and were whisked up to the executive suite level of the building. When the doors opened they walked with purpose down the hallway past offices and cubicles to the far corner of the building where the boardroom was located. Catherine pulled the door open for her lawyer whose hands still held the black cases. They then entered the conference room together.

The Board of Directors and members of the EOC sat around the large granite conference table. Steer stood in front of the projection screen that was filled with bar charts. His facial expression turned to disdain upon seeing his wife, "Catherine? What are you doing here? I'm in the middle of a meeting with the Board."

"This will just take a minute, dear," she replied. She turned and snapped her fingers in the direction of her lawyer.

The attorney lowered the cases to the floor, opened the tops, and began pulling out a stack of manila file folders. He handed half of the files to Catherine and gathered up the other half in his arms. The two then walked around opposite sides of the table stopping in front of each person seated at the table. Plop. Plop. Plop. Down went a manila file in front of each Board of Director and EOC member.

"Catherine, just what the hell are you doing?" demanded Steer.

"I'm just delivering your divorce papers and some pictures of you and your little girlfriend over there," she said matter of factly pointing in the direction of Christi.

Steer opened the file and a look of anger flashed across his face.

As the Board and EOC members opened the packets, their mouths hung open and their eyes stretched wide with amazement as they gazed at the pictures. "She had some pretty damning evidence in there," and "He's got a nice yacht," were the comments mutually agreed upon by several male Board members later that day in the private dining room.

As any well-mannered southern lady would have done, Christi picked up her complimentary file from Catherine and excused herself from the Board meeting. She rode the elevator down to the lobby, jogged to her car, and drove straight home to make some telephone calls of her own to find a good employment law attorney.

Their mission accomplished, Catherine and her attorney exited the boardroom and returned to the lobby and their Towncar.

Without missing beat, Steer closed the file and dropped it on the table. He addressed the room, "Well, you know boys, that's life," he chuckled. "Let's discuss the financial projections for next year. Please turn to page thirty in your prospectus." He advanced the slides forward.

Christi never returned to the Alsace campus. Rather, she demanded through her attorney that Steer pay her two million dollars and allow all of her unvested stock options to be considered eligible for exercising upon her resignation from the company. Two years of severance pay was also demanded.

Steer presented Christi's severance proposal to the Board in the same conference room a week later. They were angry with Steer to say the least. After a heated debate, they agreed to meet her demands on the severance pay and stock options if Steer agreed to pay her the two million bucks out of his own pocket. *It's only a year's salary, but with the amount I'll probably lose in the upcoming divorce settlement with Catherine, it's going to sting. I'm going to have to make good on the Company quarterly performance bonus contract with Alsace in order to recoup my losses here. I need that ten million dollar bonus just to keep up with my lifestyle after this little fiasco!* Steer thought

"We will hit our quarterly earnings number," Steer promised the Board.

What "Power Lunches" were to executives when they conducted business and cut deals, the Alsace Fitness Center had an equivalent power for improving one's status within the company. The Fitness Center was a state-of-the-art 30,000 square foot facility located on the Alsace campus. With the latest resistance training and cardiovascular equipment, it put any Bally's or Gold's Gym to shame. A group of qualified personal trainers led the Pilates, Yoga, Step, and Spin classes that were popular among the females, while another group of personal trainers were available to guide individual exercise regimes in the cardio and strength areas. After an invigorating workout, the Alsace employees could relax in the tanning center or work on their flexibility in the stretching area. A small basketball court, racquetball/squash courts, and a lap pool rounded out the facility amenities. To take advantage of the beautiful weather of San Diego, a half-mile jogging track was installed around the Alsace campus. There were no monthly membership dues for Alsace employees to use the Fitness Center, only a nominal monthly locker use fee that was like milk money for most of the employees.

If one had hopes to get exposure to the Executive Operating Committee and eventually get promoted within Alsace, your ass was in the Fitness Center either before or after work, preferably after work because that was when the EOC members generally congregated. It was a friendly atmosphere with back slaps and high fives generously distributed throughout the building. The lower level managers, however, kept a sharp lookout. Not so much for upper management members, but for Scott Evans who would pick on those who were below him in position and weaker than him on the bench press or bicep curls.

He would typically embarrass the people by shouting out, "Come on, ya baby! Is that all you can bench? Drop and give me twenty, you little weakling!"

Since Jackson was a Director with aspirations of getting promoted to the next level, he worked out after hours. Evans held back on any public comments about Jackson's fitness because he was Larson's pet, but did reserve a word or two occasionally when they were alone in the locker room. Jackson usually returned fire with a sharp comment of his own about Evans playing in softball leagues with his buddies. After he ran two miles around the campus track, Jackson would hit the weight room for some upper body strength work and sit-ups. Lexi tolerated the additional time away from home since he did not travel as much anymore. After only minor discussion, they ended up with a compromise where Jackson would only work out three nights a week at the Fitness Center. With the move to San Diego, Lexi tried very hard to support Jackson's career, especially when he reciprocated with their home life.

The only exception to the time-of-day workout rule for the regular Alsace employees was the VP of Human Resources, Dennis Fredericks. He ran two miles around campus every day precisely at one o'clock in the afternoon. No one else at Alsace could have gotten away with such a blatant violation of workout hours except for the head of Human Resources. A long-time Alsace employee who benefited from seven stocks splits over a ten-year period, Fredericks owned over 500,000 shares of stock that had been invested wisely over the years. He was a millionaire many times over to the point where he finally had to set up the Fredericks Family Foundation in order to take advantage of the substantial tax breaks afforded by the IRS in order to care for the generations of Fredericks' that would certainly follow him.

Rick Thompson was one Director who desperately wanted to get promoted to VP. Because he had made a number of bad investment choices over the last ten years with his stock option proceeds, he could not afford for things to go badly if anything should ever happen to the company or if he should fall out of favor with Larson and Steer. His investment choices in strip malls and high-risk venture capital schemes burned through over three million dollars without any significant return on investment. *Better to have just flushed the money down the toilet for what it was worth now,* he often thought. His bitterness about his personal financial situation bore itself out in a foul temper and vulgar language toward individuals who reported to him and messed up.

This guy could peel paint off the walls, Jackson thought once after he had been on the receiving end of a Thompson tirade for being late in submitting his expenses one month.

The VP level brought so many more additional financial perks and power than his lowly Director's position. *It's a real opportunity to influence the direction and performance of a Fortune Fifty company,* Thompson thought. He was a middle-aged, plump and balding man who used extensive amounts of Rogaine to try and grow hair back on the crown of this head where typical male-pattern hair loss would strike. He was fighting a losing battle, however, as each year the bald spot grew slightly larger, and, unfortunately for him, he was starting to experience some of the long-term usage side effects. Erectile dysfunction.

Thompson would typically leave the Fitness Center and arrive home by eight o'clock where his dinner could be found in the warm oven, wrapped in tin foil. His wife and boys were usually found in other rooms of the house doing homework or getting ready for bed. *Even the dog doesn't greet me at the door anymore,* thought Thompson. His wife barely spoke to him and his sons loathed him. He was a victim of corporate greed. He had tried to reach his personal career goals even though it trashed his family life along the way. Thompson became even angrier as he continued to see his peers get promotions to the VP level. His thirst for power could not be quenched.

Since he was at least fifty pounds overweight, Thompson worked out diligently at the Fitness Center. He noticed that a number of members of the EOC weren't as round at the middle like he was so he hit the Stairmaster with a vengeance. Nothing he did seemed to help him lose the weight because Thompson just couldn't give up the six Mountain Dews a day and the never-ending snack foods available throughout the break rooms and meeting rooms. And his day consisted of nothing but endless meetings. Marketing, Contracting, Promotions, Customer Service, Medical Affairs, and Legal. The National Accounts department that Thompson managed worked with all the various support divisions within Alsace. The biggest health care plans in the United States were very demanding of resources from Alsace, and it was Thompson's job to ensure that the resources were delivered.

Thompson was known as the-buck-stops-here guy who had ultimate control and approval over every contract negotiated and executed by the Account Managers on behalf of Alsace. Hundreds of millions of product sales dollars as well as hundreds of thousands of dollars of rebate and discount dollars were all under his area of responsibility.

After the Board of Director's fiasco encounter with his wife, Steer met privately with Thompson in his office on the top floor of the Power Pod. The Power Pod was the common name for the executive suites where the company officers had their private offices, and it was in Steer's office that new direction was given.

"Rick, you can image that I'm under a tremendous amount of pressure to hit our quarterly earnings goals, right?" asked Steer.

"Yes, Kevin. We're all acutely aware of the quarterly goals and performance measures," replied Thompson.

"Well, the division that offers Alsace, and me, the greatest opportunity to achieve these goals is National Accounts," stated Steer.

"Yes sir, I know," said Thompson.

"Rick, I need and expect you to work closely with Finance on a monthly basis to monitor our ex-factory sales. If, at the end of a given quarter, we are trending short of the goal, then I need you to call in some favors from your corporate buyers to push product out of the factory to the wholesalers and pharmacy chains. I personally don't care what terms you have to offer them, just get the product out the door so it shows up on the sales side of the company books. I made a commitment to the Board of Directors that Alsace would not miss an earnings report, and I intend to keep that commitment," said Steer matter of factly.

"I understand. We have some wholesalers, national pharmacy chains, and integrated health systems that can buy whenever we need them to, for the right price and terms. I'll make sure that we have tight management of their inventories," Thompson responded.

"Good, Rick. I appreciate your help in being a team player, and I won't forget it. You know, I've seen you around the Fitness Center lately. Have you lost weight?" asked Steer as he guided Thompson toward the door.

"Maybe a little," replied Thompson now feeling uncomfortable. "I really like how I feel after a good workout. My energy levels have really taken off…"

"OK, that's great. I have another meeting to attend, Rick," said Steer cutting him off. "Don't let me down, I'm counting on you."

With that, Steer led him to the door. "Say hello to your family for me!" exclaimed Steer with virtually no sincerity.

"Yes sir, I will," replied Thompson as the door closed in his face.

CHAPTER 20

SOFT SALES

Several major business events occurred simultaneously. The changes significantly affected the financial condition of Alsace Pharmaceuticals. Had only one of these events occurred in a given year or had they been strung out over an extended period of time, the company would have been able to manage the financial impact with a reasonable and measured response. But that's not what happened. The market place changes sent waves of trepidation throughout the organization because the overall net profit growth and shareholder return were threatened.

The first event to impact Alsace was the reduction in reimbursement payments that the federal government's Medicare program would make for the use of a red blood cell stimulating product, REMPRO. Alsace had the corner on the market since they acquired REMPRO from a small biotech company years ago and, due to the high risks and complexities involved in the discovery and manufacturing process of the product, had no competition in the therapeutic class. Annual sales were nearly two billion dollars, but the new reimbursement policy would mean a significant reduction in the overall sales line of the medicine.

Patients with End Stage Renal Disease or ESRD suffer from compromised kidney function, and in order to manage the hematocrit levels of these patients, nephrologists used REMPRO exclusively as an adjunct therapy to the weekly hemodialysis treatments, or blood filtering process, that ESRD patients must undergo once the kidneys fail. Hematocrit levels indicate the proportion of the blood that consists of packed red blood cells and are expressed as a percentage. As carriers of oxygen, red blood cells are essential to the proper functioning of the body. The normal range for hematocrit levels in adults can be anywhere from thirty-eight to fifty-four percent, and at these levels patients look and feel great. The higher the hematocrit level, the better the patient can function. Patients with compromised kidney function have hematocrit levels under thirty-three percent, and at these levels, daily life activities become severely compromised.

For example, a walk up a flight of stairs would require a patient to stop and rest. ESRD patients are extremely sick and oftentimes have a life expectancy of less than five years.

The federal government agency known as the Centers for Medicare and Medicaid Services or CMS, is the national health insurance program for more than 500,000 patients afflicted with ESRD. Once a patient loses kidney function, no other managed care insurance coverage is provided because the ESRD patients are then automatically enrolled with CMS as the sole insurance provider for their expensive patient health care services. Because of the overall high costs to manage these difficult patients, CMS designated a separate line item for REMPRO in the federal government budget, but the organization did so without any foresight relative to the development of drug utilization guidelines or price controls. CMS simply requested annual funding increases allocated to the REMPRO budget.

As the REMPRO federal budget line escalated to over two billion dollars a year, Congress became outraged. Since it was long believed that Big Pharma took advantage of the CMS at any opportunity, certain members of Congress felt that this was just another blatant example of a company, specifically Alsace, benefiting from the federal government assuming all the financial responsibility for the high drug costs of these very sick patients. A congressional oversight committee ordered CMS to conduct an extensive fiscal evaluation that included a yearlong study to determine how nephrologists treated patients with ESRD and, more importantly, how nephrologists billed for dialysis services, how they used REMPRO, and how they profited from it. The oversight committee members and CMS were appalled by the findings, and as a result, promptly lowered the reimbursement rates for REMPRO and designated fixed hematocrit ranges that qualified for reimbursement from CMS. Under the new guidelines, nephrologists were only able to treat patients with REMPRO that had hematocrit levels below thirty-six percent and who were maintained within a hematocrit range of thirty-three to thirty-six percent. The new policy would effectively eliminate a majority of their patient visits. In addition, the guidelines stated that the rate of reimbursement for REMPRO would be substantially reduced. Even though dialysis patients had improved quality of life and the ability to function better in daily activities, CMS would not reimburse for REMPRO were it to be used with patients whose hematocrit levels were greater than thirty-six percent.

The second negative market event involved a new blockbuster cholesterol-lowering agent scheduled for introduction to the market by Pfizer. It was learned that in one of the clinical development pivotal trials for Pfizer's new drug, that the product showed dramatic reductions in total and LDL cholesterol and also increased HDL cholesterol. Clearly, it was a superior product compared to the Alsace medicine, MEGACHOL, which was the leader in the fifteen billion dollar market. The Alsace security team, led by Tom Sommers, got an advanced copy of a Pfizer manuscript that depicted the study results from one of the university-based cardiology investigators for the new product. The product truly had the potential to knock MEGACHOL out of its market leadership position and could cost Alsace billions of dollars in long-term sales.

The third competitive market event would come from a pending AIDS product launch from Roche Laboratories. Alsace security had discovered that the FDA had put the new product on a fast track for approval so that it would be on the market within six months. Typically, AIDS patients receive a variety of protease inhibitors each day, known as a drug cocktail, for the treatment of the HIV virus. Alsace had one of the three cocktail drugs, NORVIRAN, which was the cornerstone of the lifesaving therapy for AIDS patients. However, through well-documented head-to-head clinical studies, the new Roche product was shown to be superior to NORVIRAN because of improved safety and efficacy, and it had the potential to erase most of the $500 million a year in sales. Fortunately, Alsace had just launched a new combination drug, KALMATRON, which actually contained all three of the AIDS cocktail therapies in one sustained release capsule taken once daily. But sales of KALMATRON lagged projections because managed care plans were slow to add the product to drug formularies since the price of KALMATRON was about fifteen percent higher than the acquisition costs of the three cocktail products sold separately. It was feared that because Roche had a history of aggressive pricing tactics with new product launches, that

KALMATRON would probably never get on any formularies, and most likely, the new Roche product would replace NORVIRAN!

Steer called for an emergency session of the EOC early one morning in the Board Room to discuss the three market events. Since Jackson was now a member of the EOC, he sat between Jim Larson and Rick Thompson. Jackson knew that he was about to observe something quite unique to Alsace simply through his attendance at the EOC meeting. In his tenure, the company had never before been in the crisis mode that it now faced. He felt a rush of adrenaline just being in the same conference room filled with powerful executives whose collective knowledge included hundreds of years of pharmaceutical marketing experience. *Meetings like this are why I came into headquarters. You just can't get this kind of exposure to the inner workings of a company and the decision making processes out in the field,* he thought as he watched Steer stand up to address the room.

"Good morning ladies and gentlemen. We are facing some tough times with the market changes that are before us. I've only had summary briefings on each of these events, but from what I gather, each of them individually does not bode well for the organization, and collectively, they represent a colossal storm. We told the Wall Street analysts that we would have consistent quarterly performance over the next two years, and quite frankly, at this juncture I am worried about our ability to deliver on that promise. I want to take each of these situations one at a time. I don't care if we're here all day and night, or all week for that matter, because I want solutions. First item, how the does this CMS ruling affect REMPRO sales?" Steer asked the marketing team.

As a Senior Product Director responsible for several therapeutic teams, one of which was the dialysis market, Scott Evans chose to address the issue, "Kevin, there are two major changes here with the CMS policy change. First, the nephrologists buy REMPRO from Alsace at significant discounts off the catalog cost, or about seven dollars per thousand units, but they are allowed to bill CMS for reimbursement of REMPRO at a rate about equal to the average wholesale price, which is about eleven dollars per thousand units. Their profit margin on REMPRO is nearly fifty-seven percent between their acquisition cost and the CMS reimbursement rate. Now, since most nephrologists manage about fifty dialysis patients a month, and they administer about forty-thousand units of REMPRO per patient a month, they make about a hundred grand a year in profit just off the utilization and reimbursement of REMPRO. By CMS cutting the actual payment or reimbursement rate to nine dollars per thousand units of REMPRO, the nephrologists' profit gets cut in half as well."

"I don't care about the nephrologists, Scott," replied Steer. "What's it mean to Alsace?"

"Well, to that point, the second major change is that CMS is limiting the ESRD patient hematocrit treatment range to only the thirty-three to thirty-six percent levels for which they will reimburse the nephrologists for REMPRO. Therefore, the number of ESRD patients that nephrologists can even treat with the drug is significantly reduced. This is the part of the ruling where we get hurt. You have to remember that before these new guidelines that restrict the upper level of hematocrit treatment to thirty-six percent, the physicians routinely raised the hematocrit levels way above that by using REMPRO and billing CMS for reimbursement. The nephrologists basically used REMPRO as a pure income mechanism. So the main problem here for us is that nephrologists will not buy as much REMPRO since the majority of patients that they can manage, treat, and bill for is significantly reduced by the new CMS ruling."

Steer asked in disbelief, "So what's the downside for product sales with these new CMS guidelines and reduction in the total number of patients treated?"

Evans looked around at the table to his marketing department peers before he gave the bad news, "We estimate that nearly thirty percent of REMPRO use was for treating patients above the thirty-six percent hematocrit levels range. If CMS will not pay for anything above thirty-six percent, then we take it in the shorts to the tune of a thirty percent sales forecast reduction. In surveying nephrologists this week, we found that the overwhelming majority of them will simply not buy and use REMPRO for patients who are over the thirty-six percent hematocrit level if CMS won't reimburse for it. They are not going to be out money just to make the ESRD patient feel a little better when they walk out of the house to get their newspaper in the morning. You know, CMS has been after us for years to lower our prices because we're the sole supplier of REMPRO, which, of course we won't do and don't have to do. Since CMS couldn't force us to discount REMPRO, they took the tactic of reducing the reimbursement rate and the hematocrit treatment range thereby directly hitting our bottom line and sending us a clear message of 'you play ball with us, or we'll bury you.' We forecast that sales of REMPRO will decrease fifty percent over the next year which equates to about a six-hundred million dollar loss."

Steer asked, "Can we make it up for it with other products?"

"No," came the terse reply from Evans.

Steer swore silently under his breath. After a moment, he took a deep breath and let out a low whistle while his head shook from side to side. "OK, I want solutions. We have six hundred million dollar shortfall to make up, plus the fact that we've had this product growing at twenty percent rate every year. Wall Street isn't going to like this."

Evans seized the moment to step in with some ideas that came from a special task force he assembled the day before. The group worked until midnight. "I pulled together some people last night and came up with three proposals. I have a slide presentation that I would like to show the group. Can I have five minutes to set it up?"

Steer agreed and gave the EOC a ten-minute break to help themselves to the array of food found on the tables in the back of the Board Room. Food service was standard at all meetings attended by more than five Alsace employees in any of the hundred conference rooms located on the headquarters campus. Cookies, sweet rolls, bagels, fruit, juices, sodas, bottled water, and coffee had been brought in before the meeting by the Alsace cafeteria catering staff. What no one wanted to acknowledge was that the treats actually ran about two million dollars a year. After the break, Steer called the meeting to order and turned the floor over to Evans.

Evans began to speak as he advanced his slides, "Let me go on the record by saying that our Washington DC lobbyists totally dropped the ball on this one, and some heads need to roll." He paused for effect, "On the surface, the new CMS ruling appears to cut a tremendous amount of profit from the nephrologists and Alsace. But, after close review of the policy there appears to be opportunity in three areas. First, there is a clause that permits the nephrologists to submit medical justification to the CMS fiscal intermediary or provider at the individual state level to treat ESRD patients who they deem will benefit medically to be maintained above the thirty-six percent hematocrit level. The fiscal intermediaries are required by law, which is the new CMS policy, to have a process in place for physicians to apply for medical justification allowing treatment and reimbursement as an exception. Now, we have Account Managers deployed at the state government level who work specifically with these fiscal intermediaries. Let's simply turn these folks loose with whatever resources they need in order to find out the medical justification process for each of the fifty states. Once we have that information in place, I propose the second phase of the response."

Before he could continue Steer interrupted him, "So the CMS ruling has a section addressing some kind of medical justification exception for treating and reimbursing REMPRO above the thirty-six percent hematocrit level? You better be sure about this Scott because I don't want us to waste any time going down a path that doesn't even exist."

Evans had anticipated the question. He snapped his fingers at one of the REMPRO marketing directors who stood up and began to pass out a single piece of paper to the EOC members. Evans bent over his computer to open a document that appeared on the screen a moment later. It was the same text from the document that was being passed out in the Board Room. "The document in front of you, and what you see on the screen behind me, is the section of the CMS ruling that describes the medical justification clause. It was buried deep in the policy, I'm sure by design, so that it would be very difficult to find, and probably just as difficult to implement." He paused to let the group read over the clause.

Steer remarked, "Great job, Scott. It appears valid, and it looks like we've got something to go on here. There's an awful lot of dialysis centers in the U.S., how do you propose that we get the word out about this medical justification clause and fiscal intermediary process?"

"We currently have a group of about fifty Dialysis Clinical Specialists, comprised mainly of former dialysis center nurses who have been in place for several years at Alsace. Their main job responsibilities now are to conduct patient and staff education programs on kidney diseases, mostly value added service nonsense. The beauty is that they already walk-the-walk with the dialysis center staff because of their former nursing experience, but more importantly, they can play on the sympathies of the individual nephrologists who are set to lose a substantial amount of personal income from the new reimbursement ruling. I suggest that we hire another fifty staff members to shore up our presence in the dialysis center community while the Medicare Account Managers are working the back channels with each fiscal intermediary to determine the exact medical justification process for each state. The two, that being the hiring process and medical justification process, should come together about the same time for us to roll out my next proposal."

"Sounds good so far," said Steer. "What's the rest of it?"

Evans knew that this could be a huge coup for his career if he pulled off his overall proposal, so he continued, "We do two more things. First, we specifically ask the Dialysis Clinical Specialists to work with the dialysis center staff to identify all the ESRD patients that fall below the thirty-three percent hematocrit level and who are not being treated to the new CMS goal of thirty-three to thirty-six percent. We estimate that about twenty percent of all the ESRD patients are being treated with inadequate levels of REMPRO where physicians are just not using high enough doses of the product to get them to goal. Second, I am proposing that we quickly develop a database management software package through our Information Technology department to help address this problem of patients who are under treated with REMPRO. The Dialysis Clinical Specialists will ask the nephrologists for specific chart information such as hematocrit levels and REMPRO doses on each ESRD patient, which, in turn, they will maintain in our database. Of course, we'll put in the database all kinds of superfluous crap like outcomes data just to make it look like it's on the up and up. It could be called the *Hematocrit Optimization Program* or something; we haven't gotten that far yet. No matter, in the end, we simply want our Dialysis Clinical Specialists to manage the hematocrit levels and REMPRO doses for all the ESRD patients on a monthly basis."

Jackson perked up at this last statement, *What is he suggesting? That we have access to patient charts and information?*

Evans continued, "If a patient is falling below the thirty-three percent level, then the instruction to the nephrologist will be to get the hematocrit level into the CMS recommended range by using higher doses of REMPRO. If a patient is being maintained within the thirty-three to thirty-six percent range, then our people will push the nephrologist to use the medical justification process designated by that state's fiscal intermediary to push the hematocrit levels higher and seek reimbursement for REMPRO as outlined by the CMS exception policy. If we approach the nephrology community in a partnership concept, I believe that we can actually expand the number of patients being treated above the thirty-six percent goal level and increase the overall sales of REMPRO."

Heads nodded at the conclusion of the proposal. Steer asked the group, "Other ideas?" People looked around and kept nodding. There were no other ideas that could top this. It was big, and it was bold.

Evans knew he had succeeded. Since the momentum was in his favor, he quickly added his last piece of the overall proposal. "I would like for Alsace to provide some financial incentive to the dialysis centers that actually get on board with us. Let's face it; we've got a lot more to lose as a company than the individual nephrologists do. I propose that we incent the dialysis centers with contracts or service agreements that force them to provide the patient information we need to pull this off. Let's pay them a fee for every patient enrolled in the Hematocrit Optimization Program and offer additional discounts on REMPRO purchases depending on the percentage of their ESRD patients who are maintained either within or above the CMS guidelines. If a large percentage of their patients fall below the thirty-three percent threshold, then we cut off the existing discounts they are already receiving until they get their act together. This would cut their profit margins even further providing more incentive to get on board with Alsace and REMPRO. It basically guarantees that a nephrologist will play by our rules if they want the kind of profits from REMPRO that they were enjoying before this new CMS ruling."

"Outstanding!" exclaimed Steer. "I like a program with some teeth in it, and one that provides incentives to physicians for performance. It would be remarkable if we could expand the sales line for REMPRO given this ruling. CMS won't know what hit them. I approve all elements of the proposal. I'll talk to Finance to make sure we've got adequate funding for the fifty additional Dialysis Clinical Specialists. Good work, Scott."

Applause erupted inside the Board Room as Evans returned to his seat.

"OK, let's take a short break and come back with the cholesterol market," said Steer.

As the break concluded and Jackson returned to his seat, Larson turned to him and said, "What do you think so far, Jackson? This is pretty important stuff that you're seeing here, isn't it?"

"It sure is, Jim. You really get first hand exposure and can see that business is really like doing battle against other companies, or in the case with REMPRO, doing battle with CMS," replied Jackson. He then lowered his voice and leaned into Larson, "Jim, is it OK that our Dialysis Clinical Specialists have access to patient charts? I mean, that's confidential information isn't it?"

"Jackson, you just said yourself, 'business is war.' Sometimes a company has to do whatever it takes to stay on top and win. Besides, it's still up to the nephrologists to grant our people access to the patient charts. But with their motivation of personal income from the reimbursement of REMPRO, I don't think that there will be any significant issues with access. You just wait. We've got a couple of really tricky issues coming up for discussion."

After the break, Steer pulled the participants back into focus. "I had my secretary order in lunch for us and to refresh the food service break area. Please help yourself throughout the day at the back of the room. Devon, would you please come up and brief us on the next issue?"

Devon Smith was the Product Director for MEGACHOL. He was a former running back who had played for the San Diego State University football team and who from his physique, looked like he could still take the ball and crash through a defensive tackle to get a first down. Devon was a bright guy who had earned his MBA from

Pepperdine University in Malibu, and who had successfully managed the MEGACHOL marketing team for the past two years. He was also the only black male in the entire Board Room. He began, "The cholesterol market is valued at fifteen billion dollars a year with a twenty percent annual growth rate. With MEGACHOL in the market leadership position, and as the flagship product for Alsace, we simply cannot allow for a disruption in the sales trend line by a competitive product. We must protect the core business of MEGACHOL at any cost."

Evans took the opportunity to chime in, "If we know the product is coming, and its major attributes from the manuscript that the security team received, why not design some countermeasures that will simply squish it like a bug? Just kill the product before it gets to market and as it gets launched."

Smith replied, "An interesting concept, obviously, but I believe that there is room in the market for another product entrant, which would be the fifth cholesterol-lowering drug. I don't recommend that we crush Pfizer's product altogether because the promotional voice from their sales force around the identification and treatment of cholesterol can help fuel the growth of the overall market that can actually boost MEGACHOL sales. We did see from the clinical study results that Pfizer's product has a slightly higher incidence of elevated liver transaminase levels compared to MEGACHOL, which for a number of patients who do not totally give up alcohol while on therapy can run into some problems. We plan to differentiate the product from MEGACHOL on the safety profile asking physicians to reserve Pfizer's drug as a medicine of last resort when all other choices have failed. Are there any questions from the group?"

Steer's head rocked back. "That's it? That's the response from my MEGACHOL marketing team? We're going to just have our sales force discuss with doctors the fact that if a patient drinks beer while on Pfizer's product, there might be a slight chance of elevated liver transaminase levels compared to MEGACHOL, and to reserve the product for difficult to treat patients? Am I hearing this right? Please tell me you've got more than this!"

"No, we don't. Pfizer's product is pretty solid, Kevin."

Steer's jaw set and his lips formed a thin line. He paused for a moment before turning away from Smith and toward the rest of the EOC members, "Devon, stay up here and take notes. OK, the floor is open for suggestions."

Larson spoke up quickly, "I've heard of a few things that other companies have done in similar situations. Let me throw a few things out to the group. First, Devon, what's our refill rate on MEGACHOL prescriptions after a patient has been on the product for at least six months?"

"It's low. About forty-five percent after six months of initial therapy," Smith replied.

"So, Devon, it's safe to say that patients go on MEGACHOL therapy, but after six months they feel fine and fifty-five percent of the patients stop taking the drug. So we are constantly seeking new patient starts to fuel the overall growth of the product, right?"

"Yes."

"OK, what we can do is work with the biggest retail pharmacy chains and the pharmacy benefits management mail order programs to initiate a compliance or refill program specifically for MEGACHOL. There are programs already in place with most of the biggest companies where we can set up a service contract that would pay them to call or send letters to patients reminding them to refill their prescription every month. I've heard from some of my peers at other companies that the refill rates in similar therapeutic classes is very high," Larson stated.

"What's the cost of something like that?" asked Steer.

"We'd have to negotiate the cost, Kevin, but refill reminder programs usually have initial costs of about ten bucks per patient to set up and then the price comes down to maybe two dollars a month. Or we can set up a service agreement that simply pays for a certain number of calls per month," Larson replied.

Smith took the opportunity to jump in and perhaps salvage some of his self worth, "Kevin, our cost of goods is approximately six percent on MEGACHOL so another one percent cost added onto the product, particularly if we get a higher compliance rate from the patients who are currently dropping off from therapy after six months will more than make up for the overall program costs."

It was Larson's turn again, "Devon, I just want you to know that these programs aren't cheap on the front side. We're going to have to pay substantial grant monies to the pharmacy chains and PBMs ensuring that they sign up for the program. The up front costs could be several million dollars that we'll be paying out in grants to these organizations. Have you got that kind of money in the MEGACHOL brand budget?"

"Yes, I do. You know, a concern that I have is around Medicaid best price calculations with this kind of program. If we pay substantial fees through these service agreements, then are the funds added into the pricing discounts and rebates that we currently offer to the organization and that we subsequently use to calculate best price for the state Medicaid programs?" Smith asked.

Rick Thompson replied, "No. Service contracts fall into what we call safe harbor. They are outside of the normal discount and rebate parameters for calculating best price. Programs like this are very favorable to Big Pharma companies. I personally like it and think we should do it."

"OK, so this is one idea, which I approve by the way. Jim, get your team on this right away. What else do we have? Pfizer's no pussycat, you know. They're going to come after MEGACHOL in a big way." Steer's voice boomed across the conference room.

The room was silent for a minute. Larson spoke up again, "Kevin, I think we need to look at restructuring our contracts with the HMOs and PBMs. We could set up tiered market share contracts that guarantee us the lion's share of the business within each of the health plans. Considering that we are the market leader and that the health plans are already earning significant discounts and rebates already on MEGACHOL, I think that they would be hesitant to make a move with Pfizer's product against us. They would have too much to lose from the way they make money off us already."

"What are our contract terms currently?" asked Steer.

Thompson addressed Steer's question; "The most common contract terms right now ask the health plans to increase their utilization of MEGACHOL over the prior year in exchange for additional discounts. We don't even bundle any of our other products to MEGACHOL. The product stands on its own as a straight MEGACHOL contract. We may have to look at adding some other products to it with certain plans because you have to figure that Pfizer will do the same."

"A bird in the hand is worth two in the bush," said Steer. "If we anticipate what Pfizer will do contractually but beat them to the punch with bundled product contracts and market share terms for MEGACHOL, they will have a hard time gaining a foothold against us. We can let them get into the market in the lower margin sectors like state Medicaid hospitals and maybe the VA market."

Jackson's hand shot up, "Kevin, just to let you know, the federal market that includes the VA and DoD are off limits for Pfizer's new drug."

"What do you mean?" asked Steer with furrowed eyebrows.

"I've already locked up a national contract for MEGACHOL for the federal segment for the cholesterol class. It's a three-year deal where MEGACHOL is the preferred product on the national formulary. Pfizer won't be able to get any utilization except through a prior authorization process where patients fail MEGACHOL."

"Good work, Jackson. OK, so if I'm the CEO of Pfizer, and I want market share, where am I going to get it?" Steer asked the group.

It was Smith who answered, "They basically have Medicare eligible seniors who pay cash for their prescriptions and maybe some PHS hospitals. We can lock down the rest of the market through these service agreements and tiered market share contracts that bundle our other products. I'll make sure that we take and run with these initiatives." Smith was trying to get off the hot seat at this point.

Steer wrapped up the morning session, "OK everyone, thanks for your input and ideas so far. I see that lunch is being catered into the back of the room so let's eat and resume our discussion in an hour."

No applause was heard this time for Smith as he returned to his seat and the rest of the EOC stood up to get in the buffet line. Smith sat in his chair and finished writing some notes on the ideas discussed.

Steer took the opportunity to chastise him once more in private, "Devon, let this be a lesson to you. Don't ever show up at an EOC meeting again without a backup plan. You saw what Evans did just before you, right? He's vice president material. You need to model yourself after him, OK?"

Smith pressed his lips together and nodded, "OK, Kevin. Sorry I let you down."

"There are some great ideas that came up here. Don't let me down again. Go out of here today and execute flawlessly on the initiatives. Come on, let's go have some lunch." Steer smiled at Smith and patted his shoulder.

After the lunch break Steer again brought the meeting to order. "OK, let's address the last item. Nate, what about this new Roche drug coming out in soon?"

Nate Cannata, a new product director for the infectious disease therapeutic class strode to the front of the Board Room to address the question and the group, "It looks like a very good product, sir. During the head to head studies with NORVIRAN, the Roche product demonstrated a faster onset of action, lower re-infection rates, and a better side effect profile. Roche also applied for a lower dosing schedule than NORVIRAN in order to try and improve patient compliance and convenience. Lastly, we know that Roche historically likes to gain market share very rapidly with new product launches. We anticipate that they will buy market share through aggressive discounting to try and convert the NORVIRAN business to their product."

"Solutions?" asked Steer. "Wait! I first want to know where KALMATRON is in all this? Why does KALMATRON continue to lag behind our sales projections? How come physicians aren't switching from NORVIRAN to KALMATRON? Hell, we gave the market a combination product that eliminated the need for cocktail therapy; and it has once a day dosing! What gives here?" Steer had suddenly become inflamed over the issue.

Cannata tapped his fingers nervously on the conference table, as he was well aware of the bad news that he was about to deliver, "Well sir, the managed care organizations are blocking the use of KALMATRON."

"How is that exactly? And stop calling me sir!"

"The HMOs and PBMs are using the prior authorization process on KALMATRON through the use of hard edits at the pharmacy terminals," Cannata responded.

"What's a hard edit?" Steer asked.

Larson took over since this was his area of expertise, "A hard edit is the part of the pharmacy claims process by which the pharmacist types in the name of the drug, patient identification information, and health plan information. He then waits about thirty seconds for the response from the pharmacy benefits management companies who process the claim based on formulary or benefit design status for that drug and employer group. Now in most cases, commonly used drugs are approved by the PBM so that the pharmacist can dispense the prescription and collect the appropriate co-pay from the patient. But in a hard edit scenario involving specialty drugs like KALMATRON, the health plan and PBM do not want the drug dispensed to its membership due to its higher costs compared to other therapies on the market, like the cocktail therapy of which NORVIRAN is a part of. They mostly set up the prior authorization process to make the physician and patient jump through all kinds of hoops to get KALMATRON."

Cannata picked up the conversation next, "Kevin, it boils down to cost minimization. The current three cocktail therapies cost a total of a hundred dollars per month with NORVIRAN making up about half of that amount. Although KALMATRON combines the three cocktails into one capsule taken once a day, it costs a hundred and fifteen dollars per month. Managed care organizations simply do not want to increase their drug costs by fifteen percent in return for a perceived improvement in patient convenience and compliance. We've shown the health economics data depicting the reduction in missed doses and hospitalizations, therefore, reducing the overall health care costs to the plan, but they're just not buying it, especially pharmacy directors. They just don't care if an AIDs patient has to take multiple pills several times a day. They've got this damn silo mentality around only being concerned with holding down drug costs in their department."

"What do the HMOs care? Don't they just pass along the drug costs to the employer groups, who then, in turn, pass along the costs to their employees?" asked Steer.

"Not in this class, Kevin." Larson replied. "Most health plans are what is called at-risk for injectables, vaccines, and AIDs drugs. Meaning, they contract with the employers for a set amount of money on a per member per year basis for each of these categories. Once the per-member per-year contracted drug budget is spent, the health plan absorbs the cost of any dollars over the original contracted amount. So a voluntary shift by the health plan from the multiple dosed cocktail therapy to once a day KALMATRON, which has a fifteen percent higher cost base, is just something that the health plans are going to be very reluctant to approve. That's why we see all the prior authorizations and hard edits being applied to KALMATRON."

Steer asked, "What options do we have, if any?"

"A price increase," quipped Thompson.

The room fell silent for a moment. Price increases in normal times were something that took months to get approved with all the steps that had to be followed, particularly on the legal side. There was an extensive analysis that included sales projection models, promotional planning, wholesaler stocking, and manufacturing runs just to name a few. Then there was the complicated investor notification process where the analysts wanted to know the expectation from such an action. Price increases were like pulling teeth unless you had ample time to kill waiting for an approval.

Steer's jaw was set. He knew the complicated process because ultimately the approvals needed his authorization. "Tell me more, Rick."

"We have about a six month window before the Roche product comes to market, right? And we also know that once it's on the market, that it is highly likely that it will bump NORVIRAN out of most managed care treatment protocols resulting in a huge hit to our sales and market share. It will also most likely freeze KALMATRON in a prior authorization status indefinitely. We need a bold pricing move that will force the health plans to shift their business to KALMATRON before the Roche product launches."

Thompson let his words sink in. Heads began to nod up and down as he continued. "I'm suggesting a four hundred percent price increase on NORVIRAN which would make the overall therapy costs for the HIV cocktails about fifty percent higher than the cost of our single agent, KALMATRON. Now, we also know that Roche will be paying royalties on their product to the little biotech company that they bought it from, meaning, they will not be able to deep discount their product at launch to come in under the old price of NORVIRAN before this pricing action. In addition, didn't they have to implement some extra safety studies for the FDA?"

"Yes, they did," replied Cannata. "I can confirm that Roche probably spent another two hundred million dollars on the extra safety studies, so you're right, Rick, there are some extra developmental costs built in to the pricing model for their product. Also, with Roche's new hypertension drug being voluntarily withdrawn from the market for safety reasons, the company is counting on the increased revenue with the HIV drug to make up for the losses. That, obviously, comes at the expense of NORVIRAN sales."

From the back of the room Wedenbrook crossed his legs and raised his right index finger straight up toward the ceiling. He had been absent during the morning session but had come in late in the lunch hour. He still had his plate in front of him.

"Yes, what is it, Herman? I didn't see you back there." Steer said with impatience brimming in his voice.

"Well," started Wedenbrook, "Isn't this four hundred percent price increase against the law?"

"You know, Herman," said Steer crisply; "I'd like to suggest to you that you excuse yourself from this meeting." It wasn't a suggestion. It was a demand.

Wedenbrook's mouth dropped. He had never in his career with Alsace been asked to leave a meeting, particularly one where the problems and solutions were so sensitive in nature, and where there may be legal issues to address. "Are you sure, Kevin, that you don't want me here?"

"Yes, I'm sure. I'm going to need just the sales and marketing team here for this part of the meeting. We're not at a point where we need a legal opinion," said Steer.

Wedenbrook was shocked. But he uncrossed his legs, stood up, and proceeded to walk out of the conference room. He stopped as he passed the food service table to pick up a chocolate chip cookie and a napkin before he exited through the Board Room doors.

Jackson thought, *Something big is about to happen.*

"OK," Steer began as the door closed behind Wedenbrook, "We can speak frankly again. Rick, what was it you were starting to say about a price increase for NORVIRAN?"

Thompson went on to lead a discussion for the next several hours specific to a four hundred percent pricing increase for NORVIRAN. If done correctly, it would force the HMOs and PBMs to shift the HIV market from the established gold standard cocktail therapies solely to KALMATRON. The topic of the legalities specific to the pricing action never came up again after Wedenbrook had left the room.

There's something funny with this pricing initiative. Otherwise, Wedenbrook wouldn't have raised the issue, Jackson thought, *and Steer wouldn't have asked him to leave the Board Room.*

It was late in the afternoon and Steer wanted to address several additional topics since the EOC was assembled. "I've noticed that the sales of NEUTROPHIL seem to have flattened over the last several quarters. I've given the brand team ample time to correct this problem but the ideas that they've implemented don't seem to be working. I'd like to bring up the Product Director for the oncology product so that we can have a full discussion. Let's take a ten-minute break so everyone can call home and let your families know that we'll be here for several more hours. I'll have my secretary order in dinner for us."

Steer reconvened the EOC after the short break and brought up Carl Phillips to the front of the room. Phillips was a former point guard on the Indiana University basketball team that won a national championship. After graduation, he stayed at IU to earn his MBA and was hired right out of graduate school as a sales representative for Alsace. He worked in the field for less than two years before being promoted into the marketing department where he worked his way up through the ranks over a ten-year period to become a Product Director for NEUTROPHIL. Phillips was also known as *The Referral Guy*. He got this nickname because he took full advantage of the employee referral program at Alsace. To hold down the costs of using head hunters or recruiters to find qualified candidates for open sales and management positions, the Human Resources department offered up to ten thousand dollars per referral for any newly hired Alsace employee who stayed with the company for at least one year. Phillips usually made fifty thousand dollars a year through his referrals that became full time Alsace employees.

The CEO began, "Carl, I know that I didn't ask you to prepare anything for this meeting but since the EOC membership is all here, and we've had some great marketing ideas come out of the previous discussions, I'd like to take this opportunity and proactively discuss other ways to boost the flat sales performance for NEUTROPHIL. Why don't you begin by giving the group a brief medical overview on the use of this product?"

"Thanks, Kevin." Phillips replied. "When cancer patients are injected through an intravenous tube over several hours with powerful chemicals designed to kill cancer cells, the drugs can also take a toll on normal cells, the immune system, and special body functions. One component of the immune system that can be affected by chemotherapy treatment is the release of white blood cells from the bone marrow to areas in the body where inflammation or bacterial infections are present. The white blood cells basically surround the bacterial cells through a process called phagocytosis and eat them up. The formation of pus at the site of a boil or abscess is essentially the end result of the phagocytosis process. If this important primary defense system is compromised with either low white blood cell counts or irregular cell formation, then the patient can die. That is why cancer patients must take every precaution to prevent the common cold or an upper respiratory infection while undergoing chemotherapy treatment. Oftentimes, the physicians will ask the patient to wear a mask covering their mouth and nose whenever they come in contact with other people as it can help sustain their life by preventing infection."

He continued, "NEUTROPHIL is our product that boosts white blood cell counts during the chemotherapy treatment process. The drug literally keeps cancer patients alive by being an integral component of the immune system. Oncologists administer the product by injecting the patient while in the physician's office, typically starting on the day that follows the administration of chemotherapy, and the injections are supposed to be administered for the next ten days in a row for every one of the four to five chemotherapy cycles that is provided to the patient."

Evans asked, "So it sounds like a fairly routine regimen, right? The HMOs and Medicare all reimburse for NEUTROPHIL. Why the flat sales?"

"There are several elements," Phillips responded, "but it boils down to two main components. One, the HMOs require that the physicians follow a medical justification process similar to what we heard earlier today for REMPRO for any NEUTROPHIL injections greater than five. Most of the big health plans all feel that more than five injections is a waste of money because of a lack of outcomes data depicting a reduction in emergency room visits or hospitalizations. We currently have some clinical studies in place to evaluate those types of outcomes, but the studies could take another twelve months to complete and get published. The other component is physician laziness. Although the medical justification process is not really cumbersome, most physicians simply do not treat past five injections up to our FDA approved prescribing information of ten days due to the hassles from the HMOs and Medicare. The health plans will approve the extra injections, it's just that physicians don't bother to get the patients back to the office for the shots and then bill appropriately for them."

"Wait a minute, Carl," replied Evans, "physicians buy NEUTROPHIL directly from us, right?"

"Yes."

"Like with REMPRO, do we offer anything to them that would financially incent them to change their behavior?" asked Larson.

"We really haven't had to because there isn't any competition to NEUTROPHIL," Phillips said.

"Well, I can think of a few things just off the top of my head that we can do to incent the physicians to expand the number of treatment days," Thompson said.

"Like what, Rick?" asked Steer. "Don't hold back. Let's put everything on the table. Also, Wedenbrook isn't in here so don't be shy."

"OK, we've got a group of Health Science Liaisons already deployed to the biggest cancer centers around the country right now. They've got a similar role to our Dialysis Clinical Specialists doing in-service programs, patient education, and product education. Again, it's a value-added role whose ultimate goal is customer service," Thompson began.

Evans saw where he was going and jumped in, "Hey! Rick's right. They are a great resource that is really under-utilized. Why don't we have the IT department design a database that tracks the white blood cell counts of chemotherapy and radiation therapy cancer patients and also tracks the number of NEUTROPHIL doses. If the white blood cell counts are not high enough, the HSLs simply promote additional doses of NEUTROPHIL specific to that patient."

Jackson raised his hand, "But doesn't that mean the HSLs will be reviewing patient charts right there in the physician office?"

"Yes, Jackson, it does," Steer replied curtly. The implication was clear, and it caused Jackson to shrink down into his chair. "Let's keep going with this topic. I think we've identified a core problem as to the flattening of sales and a very viable solution to get patients more days of NEUTROPHIL injections."

Larson leaned over into Jackson and whispered, "Jackson, careful what you say and ask. You saw what happened to Wedenbrook."

"OK," came the response. Jackson happened to see Evans out of the corner of his eye. Evans smirked at Jackson's blunder.

"We still need to address the issue of the medical justification process," Phillips reminded the group.

"Most physicians will overcome their complacency around additional paperwork if we demonstrate the value to them of actually doing it," Thompson stated.

"What do you mean?" asked Steer.

"Have the IT department create a software program that we put on the HSLs laptop computers that depicts the profit made by the physician for the additional doses of NEUTROPHIL. It's basically the spread or the amount they make between what they buy NEUTROPHIL from Alsace and what they bill and get reimbursed for the product from the health plan or CMS. Then, show the physicians what the additional paperwork for a medical justification is really all about. Hell, I'll bet that most of these oncologists have never even actually seen the forms before," suggested Thompson.

Larson took a turn next, "I would suggest that we sweeten the pie some. If we aren't discounting NEUTROPHIL to the oncologists already, then provide some minimal price concessions where the oncologist can make another five percent or so. I'm a big believer that you gain partners in any initiative if you give a little bit up front. Think about it, if we pick up another three or four days of therapy per patient it's a pretty hefty increase in overall product sales for NEUTROPHIL."

"Something that we're considering for REMPRO since it is shipped directly as well to physicians is setting up the nephrologists with their own credit card issued by Alsace through our local bank here in San Diego that handles all our financials," Evans said.

"A credit card, Scott?" asked Steer.

"Yeah, we've been in discussions with our bank around issuing credit cards to our big nephrology customers to streamline the purchasing and billing process for REMPRO. These accounts would have huge lines of credit on them, and get this, we can link them to airline or hotel points so the doctor can earn free plane tickets or hotel stays. It's really a sweet deal that I think will get us a lot of customer loyalty."

Steer chuckled, "The things they'll think of next. I like it. Let's look into that for both REMPRO and NEUTROPHIL. And let's get IT to develop that software program for NEUTROPHIL as well because I agree with Rick's assessment that if these oncologists know what kind of profit that they can make by providing additional injections of NEUTROPHIL to a patient's overall therapy, and if they can get reimbursed through the medical justification process, then we're doing them a big favor. Carl, I want some of these ideas flushed within two weeks. We can't go on forever with sales of NEUTROPHIL flat lined."

"You got it. Thanks for the suggestions, everyone," Phillips remarked.

"I see that our dinner is here," Steer remarked. "Let's take a break and resume the meeting with a discussion on some cost-cutting initiatives that can help ensure even greater profitability."

Jackson got home at ten o'clock that evening. He was extremely disturbed by what he had witnessed that day during the EOC meeting.

He and Lexi stayed up until midnight as Jackson recapped the day's events and discussions. She had grave concerns, too.

"What are you going to do, Jackson?" Lexi asked.

"I really don't know that there is anything that I can do. Before I moved inside to this position, I was always so isolated in my own job and market segments that stuff like this didn't ever affect me. I mean, I'm hearing stuff like access to patient charts, promoting the profit spread to physicians, setting up credit card accounts, and that four hundred percent pricing action! I know that this isn't right!"

"Jackson, you've got to seriously look at other opportunities and get out of Alsace."

"But what about all the perks, Lexi? We've got a lot in stock options, I've got a Director-level position, we've got a huge home in southern California, and I don't think too many other companies can even come close to my salary and bonus! I'm kinda stuck, and, besides, I love my job!" Jackson was clearly irritated with the topic.

"OK, calm down, Jackson. I didn't mean that you've got to do something else tomorrow. I'm just saying that this company has no moral compass or values at all. They showed their true colors today that when their backs are against the wall, they go to the dark side for answers to their problems. They are all about growing sales and the almighty Alsace stock price. They don't care about their people, Jackson, because if they did, they would realize that its real people that have to go out and implement their illegal programs. These are real people with families that are going to be asked to promote the spread, and read patient charts, and manage medicine dosage levels; all to grow sales for the company. I don't have the answer for you, but I do know that the stuff you described is not good, and I'm just saying that you really ought to look at other opportunities."

"OK, you bring up some good points. I haven't had to look for another job in over a decade. I don't even know where to begin. Let me think about it, alright?"

They said goodnight, then tossed and turned all night because of the ominous cloud that hung over them.

YEAR 14

CHAPTER 21
DIRTY BOMB

The Federal Bureau of Investigation had recently received a number of threats to homeland security of a biological and radiological nature. Ever since 9-11, the United States was forced to form a number of federal, state and local task forces to address real and anticipated attacks. The Homeland Security Act tasked the Department of Homeland Security to develop procedures throughout the country ensuring basic preparedness and responses to national emergencies. One important initiative was the establishment of the Strategic National Stockpile or SNS that consisted of warehouses filled with pharmaceuticals and medical supplies managed jointly by the Homeland Security and Health and Human Services departments. The SNS program worked with a number of government and non-government partners to ensure the nation's public health in response to national disasters so that medicines could be inventoried, staged, and dispensed efficiently. The Food and Drug Administration, the Centers for Disease Control, the Federal Emergency Management Agency, and the National Nuclear Security Administration were all key government agencies assigned to the special SNS task force.

Antibiotics, chemical antidotes, antitoxins, life-support medications, IV drugs, and medical supplies were all items included in the SNS. Organized for an immediate and flexible response, the goal of the program was to provide caches of pharmaceuticals, antidotes, and medical supplies within a twelve-hour timeframe anywhere in the country in the early hours following a terrorist event. Follow up supplies were to be shipped from vendor managed inventories within twenty-four hours. The medical vulnerability of the U.S. civilian population was the most significant factor that determined the composition of the pharmaceutical stockpile.

Jackson's first exposure to the SNS initiative came through an email he received from the Alsace Customer Service Director. It read: *Jackson, since you have responsibility for the federal market, I thought it best that you be the Alsace point person for this important initiative.*

What the heck could this be? he wondered.

As he read the email attachment, his eyes grew wide while his stomach sank into his chair. He was being summoned to Washington DC for a meeting at the Armed Forces Radiobiology Research Institute located at the National Naval Medical Center in Bethesda. An Air Force officer, Colonel Robert Adams, had requested that a representative from Alsace attend a meeting to discuss the therapeutic utilization of REMPRO and NEUTROPHIL following the detonation of a dirty bomb device, and the stockpiling of the two products within the SNS initiative. Jackson was nervous about the concept, but after getting the appropriate briefings and approvals from Jim Larson and Herman Wedenbrook, he had the Alsace travel department book his flight arrangements back east for the Dirty Bomb Task Force meeting scheduled in two weeks.

Larson had some parting words of advice for Jackson before he left, "Don't you be calling Tam while you're in DC. She lives out there now, you know, working for some big lobbying firm. Don't tempt fate, OK?"

Jackson assured him that those days were over. "My family and career are the most important things in my life now, Jim."

It was a late afternoon in November when Jackson's plane touched down at the Reagan National Airport in Washington DC. Through his first-class seat window, Jackson saw that dusk was starting to cast a shadow over all the familiar national landmarks as the 757 cruised over the Potomac River toward its scheduled runway.

Looks like the repair work is nearly complete on the Pentagon, he thought.

He always got a great feeling of pride whenever he visited the nation's capitol. In all his trips for customer meetings, he had been very fortunate to be able to visit all the major monuments and museums in the DC area. The most memorable trip was when he had flown Lexi and Jake out from Kansas City using airline points for a long weekend following a summer AMSUS meeting and golf tournament. They stayed at the JW Marriott, also on reward points, and had a suite with a balcony that faced the Washington Monument. Through one of the Alsace lobbyists' extensive congressional contacts, Jackson was able to get tickets for a private White House tour and a theatre production at the Kennedy Center that Lexi thoroughly enjoyed. Jake's favorite thing was the four hour guided bike tour around the Mall to visit the different monuments and Arlington Cemetery.

I remember when Jake held a salute during the changing of the guard at the Tomb of the Unknown Soldier, Jackson thought. *This city does bring out my sense of patriotism and duty.*

He rented a car for the short drive to Pennsylvania Avenue and Fourteenth Street to check into the JW Marriott once again. When he arrived in his room, he called home, retrieved his email messages, ordered room service, and then went to bed early in hopes of getting a good night's rest with the three hour time change. *It always feels weird going to bed at 7:30 PM Pacific Time!* After a run around the Mall the next morning, he showered and dressed, checked out of the hotel and drove north on Wisconsin Avenue toward Bethesda and the National Naval Medical Center. The security level was Threat Condition Bravo so it took a few extra minutes to verify his identification and meeting appointment in order to gain clearances to the conference center located on the university portion of the medical campus.

Jackson arrived at the conference room about twenty minutes early where he was introduced to Colonel Adams and the other members of the task force who, he discovered, represented a number of different federal agencies.

"Colonel Adams, am I the only representative from Big Pharma?" Jackson asked.

"Yes, you are. This meeting is strictly to discuss the two Alsace products specific to the needs of the Strategic National Stockpile

Program. This committee is the Medical Preparedness and Response Sub-Group, and we will be making a recommendation concerning a vendor-managed inventory program for the manufacture and supply of your products to the SNS program. By the way, welcome aboard! You are now officially a member of the Homeland Security Working Group."

"Can you tell me what exactly the Armed Forces Radiobiology Research Institute does?" Jackson asked.

Colonel Adams gave Jackson a leveled gaze and said, "Please call us AFRII, the other way is simply a mouthful, even to those of us who work here! Our purpose is to study the clinical effects of exposure to biologic, radiation, and chemical weapons on military personnel, and it's not only the effects of exposure to the agent, but also the available medical treatment options. We have physicians from all branches of the military working here on research projects. You're here because our researchers are very familiar with your products and their treatment application to conventional war and terrorist devices."

Jackson felt somewhat apprehensive after he heard the explanation. *This is some serious stuff!*

"Why don't you have a seat, Jackson? I've got a phone call to make before the meeting begins."

Steven Dayne, an agent from the FDA, sat next to Jackson during the entire meeting. He was a pleasant man in his mid-fifties of medium build who preferred to wear his horn-rimmed reading glasses perched atop his shaved head. Agent Dayne asked Jackson to complete several background information documents prior to the start of the meeting, "It's just routine paperwork for the Task Force."

Jackson complied with the request that asked for his contact information, previous positions at Alsace including cities worked, home addresses, and specific job responsibilities. He got the distinct impression that Agent Dayne was more of a police detective than a representative of the FDA.

I guess that I don't really know what it is that these FDA guys do, Jackson thought. *I always thought that they hid in closets with tape recorders in a doctor's office trying to catch pharmaceutical reps making off-label claims about their products or that they rummage through trash cans after a rep leaves the office trying to get their hands on company promotional pieces.*

Colonel Adams, who was in full military dress, began the meeting by introducing an agent from the FBI who reviewed some of the recent terror threats that his organization had received. The dirty bomb threat, in particular, was most concerning to the agency, and hence, the premise for the meeting.

"Jackson, how much do you know about a dirty bomb?" Adams asked after the presentation.

"Please assume that I know nothing," came Jackson's reply.

"Very well. The formal name for a dirty bomb is Radiological Dispersal Device or RDD. It basically combines a conventional explosive, like dynamite, with powerful radioactive material. Now the dynamite part is the component that would have more of an immediate lethal application, but it's the radioactive material that concerns this group due to the exposure variables and contamination of up to several city blocks with such a weapon."

"We're not talking about Weapons of Mass Destruction are we?" Jackson inquired.

"No. They are two different things. Think of the bombs that were detonated over Japan at the end of WWII as WMDs. What we're talking about is a device that's hidden in a busy train station or airport or museum, and then is detonated by a remote control mechanism. Again, the dynamite component would cause immediate death to the surrounding people, but the long-term effects to people exposed to the radiation in the blast area would pose significant health care concerns and actions. As you probably know from your training in the oncology market, cancer patients that receive treatments of either chemotherapy or radiation therapy always experience bone marrow destruction that results in reduced red and white blood cell production, which ultimately can lead to uncontrolled bleeding or infection. These patients typically die from infection caused by something as simple as a common cold due their compromised immune system, right?"

"That's correct," said Jackson.

"Well, patients who are accidentally exposed to high doses of radiation from a dirty bomb would experience the same type of problems with bone marrow destruction, leaving them vulnerable to infections and possible death as well. Again, as we know from oncology radiation treatments, their bone marrows do not recover in time to produce enough levels of red and white blood cells. So, there would be an immediate death toll from the conventional explosive component of a dirty bomb, and there would also be a death toll longer-term that would mount from exposure to the radiation component of the device. This second part is what we can control through the use of the Alsace products, REMPRO and NEUTROPHIL," Colonel Adams explained.

"What do you require from my company?" asked Jackson.

"First, to your knowledge has Alsace ever conducted clinical studies with these two products in a patient population that has been exposed to high doses of radiation like we're discussing?" Adams asked.

"I don't believe so, but let me ask and get back to you."

"Second, the treatment estimates for the SNS Program depict that patients would require a full course of therapy of your NEUTROPHIL product, or eleven days of treatment. Our models indicate that we need to be prepared to treat approximately one hundred thousand patients."

Jackson took out a calculator and touched some buttons. When finished he thought for a moment and then looked up, "Colonel Adams, that's over a million doses of the NEUTROPHIL!"

"Yes, it is. And we would also require four hundred thousand vials of your REMPRO 10,000 unit-of-use dose in order to serve the same hundred thousand patients. We estimate the treatment dose for radiation exposure to be four vials of the ten thousand unit dosage strength over the course of the first month following the incident," Adams stated.

"Can you give me just a minute, please?" Jackson did some calculations from the figures Colonel Adams had just provided. "OK, at wholesale acquisition cost, which is our retail list price, you want to buy two-hundred and fifty million dollars of NEUTROPHIL and forty million dollars of REMPRO. Is that right?"

"The total number of vials in your calculations for each drug are correct, but your costs are not correct," replied Agent Dayne who had peered at Jackson's notepad while he performed the calculations.

Jackson opened his portfolio binder and checked his most recent price sheet for Alsace products, "No, I have the prices right here with me. The list price calculations are correct."

"Jackson," replied Colonel Adams with a smile, "remember where you are. You're sitting in a conference room located on federal government property. We're not going to pay list price for your drugs! Since you're the Director for the federal markets at Alsace, I'm assuming that you've also got a Federal Supply Schedule price sheet with you."

Jackson flipped over a few pages and replied, "Yeah, I've got an FSS price sheet right here."

Adams grinned and said, "Good! Now look at those prices. The prices that you see there are where we generally begin negotiations, and then it's in a downward direction that we move. Considering the quantity of your products that we're going to purchase for the SNS Program, we expect a considerable discount. These would be much deeper price concessions than you negotiated with your buddy, Bob Johnson, over at the VA PBM. It would take the VA ten years to do the volume that we're taking about here."

Thinking back to my negotiations training in Santa Monica, these guys have at least provided me with a few key pieces of information. Quantities and starting prices. What I don't know is their rock bottom price, Jackson thought. "I'd like to ask a few more questions if I might. Where does the SNS budget come from, and what other kinds of products and quantities are you also considering for the initiative?"

I need to determine what the total budget that they have just for my two products if that's possible.

"Jackson, don't worry about trying to negotiate with us because there isn't going to be any negotiation. You're simply going to go back to Alsace and inform your Board of Directors that the SNS Program needs NEUTROPHIL and REMPRO in the significant quantities that we discussed, and that the federal government will offer a fair price that's approximately twenty percent over Alsace's cost to manufacture and store them," Adams explained. "And know this, we're not going to pay twenty percent above the costs of goods sold, which is the price that Big Pharma uses after including the costs of marketing, advertising, and paying a sales force. No, we will pay twenty percent above the cost to produce and store the products."

"Uh, OK. You just mentioned storage. First, the quantities of NEUTROPHIL and REMPRO that you need would have to have a special production run. Then, the drugs would have to be shrink-wrapped and placed on pallets and loaded onto a semi-trailer. A refrigerated semi-trailer. Then they would have to be shipped to wherever your warehouses are located. Remember that these products have to be refrigerated. Do you have a refrigerated storage facility that can hold this much product?" Jackson asked.

"No, we don't. But Alsace has storage space," replied Agent Dayne.

"I don't know that we do. I mean, I met with our people in the manufacturing plant and at our storage facility before I flew out here. There just isn't any excess storage capacity over and above what we maintain for the commercial use of our products here in the U.S. market."

Agent Dayne maintained eye contact with Jackson while he responded, "Jackson, at the FDA we know a whole lot more about the Alsace facilities and operations than you do because we are the government agency that regulates the pharmaceutical industry. Because Alsace is located on a fault line in San Diego, the company has to file with the FDA their contingency plans in case of a natural disaster, such as an earthquake. We know that if the Alsace production and storage facility received extensive quake damage, then the company would simply pack up their refrigerated products, like NEUTROPHIL and REMPRO, and drive them over to the next county where there just happens to be, a huge Budweiser brewery facility. Your semi-trailers would be sitting in a refrigerated beer warehouse until your own production and storage facilities were back on line. Since we don't need your products within the first twelve hours of a dirty bomb detonation, we're proposing that Alsace simply park the refrigerated semi-trailer at the Budweiser plant."

Jackson nearly fell over. *These guys have got it all figured out! We could have done this over the telephone or by videoconference. So why the hell did they bring me all the way out here for this meeting? There's got to be something else they want.*

The rest of the Task Force participants laughed and slapped each other on the back. Several of them suggested that they volunteer to go and pick up the NEUTROPHIL and REMPRO if the products needed to be staged somewhere in response to a disaster. "We can grab a few six packs of Bud before we drive the truck off the lot! All in the line of duty, sir, for Homeland Security!"

The meeting had a much lighter tone after the beer warehouse comments. Jackson was informed that he would be assigned as a member of the Tactical Advisory Response Unit or TARA, and that he was the point person for Alsace for the NEUTROPHIL and REMPRO vendor-managed inventory system. As a member of TARA, he was given a special beeper with text messaging features and instructed to keep it with him at all times until further notified. Agent Dayne gave him a laminated list of telephone numbers and email addresses for the group, and he also received the drug quantity orders and government contracts from Colonel Adams before he left the conference room. He was told to present the information to the Alsace senior management staff and coordinate the special production run for both products and appropriate storage.

"Terrorists never take a day off, Jackson," Adams stated, "You have to be available to us twenty-four hours a day, seven days a week. Especially throughout the upcoming holiday season when the country is most vulnerable. Make sure you know how to get in touch with the appropriate managers in your company to access the medicines while in storage at the brewery for possible shipment anywhere in the U.S. within a twenty-four hour period."

As he walked out of the conference room, Agent Dayne pulled Jackson aside and said, "Thanks for coming today, Jackson. We'll be in touch."

Jackson was deeply troubled by the meeting. It seemed that the stockpile initiative stuff was legitimate. But he couldn't help think that there was another hidden agenda. When he arrived back in San Diego he went immediately home to discuss the events with Lexi who shared his concerns.

"I don't like this at all, Jackson. Why you? Why do you have to take on this responsibility? Surely there is someone else at Alsace that can do this!" Lexi exclaimed.

"I'm going to go in to the office tomorrow and see if I can dump this off on someone else. I just don't feel comfortable with this whole setup."

Just then his new beeper chirped. They both jumped at the sound. Jackson checked the number and pulled out his laminated contact sheet. It was Agent Dayne. *What is happening?* he thought.

Jackson dialed Dayne's number on his cell phone, "It's me, Jackson Ford."

"I was just checking in with you to make sure the beeper was working. Everything OK, Jackson?"

"Everything's just fine. I plan to talk to my superiors tomorrow about the information from the meeting today."

"OK, Jackson. Well, I'm available anytime that you want to talk to someone. This program is a big responsibility, but from what I could tell from meeting you today, you seem like a stand-up guy that will do the right thing when asked," said Agent Dayne.

"Yes, I will. Is there anything else, Agent Dayne?"

"No, I just wanted to check in with you. Is your family doing well? Lexi and Jake?"

A sinking feeling hit Jackson's gut at the mention of his family's names, "Aside from you scaring my wife and me just now, they're doing just fine. Agent Dayne, if there's nothing else, I need to go. It's been a long day."

"OK, goodbye Jackson. I'll talk to you soon." The line went dead. Jackson stared in disbelief at the cell phone in his hands.

"What's going on, Jackson?" asked Lexi.

"I'm not sure, honey. But that Agent Dayne from the FDA is starting to creep me out. He's a member of the Task Force, but a call like that just to check on the beeper seems out of place and character for him. Why would the FDA guy call me to test the beeper? Why wouldn't someone like Colonel Adams who would actually have to mobilize pharmaceutical products in response to an emergency call me? Something's not right but I just can't seem to put my finger on it."

"Maybe you should talk to Larson," Lexi said.

"Yeah, he's the first person that I plan on seeing tomorrow."

The next morning Jackson spoke at length with Larson and Wedenbrook about the Dirty Bomb Task Force meeting and his appointment. He expressed concern about his role and how uncomfortable it made him and his family. "The FDA guy beeped me at home last night just to check and see if the beeper was functioning properly!"

Larson perked up immediately with concern in his voice, "There's an FDA agent on the Task Force?"

"Yeah, it's standard procedure according to Colonel Adams. Since the Task Force is recommending the use our products outside of the FDA approved indications, exposure to high doses of radiation from an improvised nuclear device, the FDA has to approve the expanded use of NEUTROPHIL and REMPRO by physicians in accordance with the Homeland Security policies. So Agent Dayne is a member of the Task Force," Jackson replied.

"Sounds reasonable," said the lawyer.

"I guess it is," Larson said with a skeptical look on his face.

"Jim, is there any way at all that I can get out of this responsibility?" Jackson asked.

"I don't see how, Jackson," Larson began. "After all, you're the guy they wanted. You're the most experienced guy at Alsace when it comes to the federal market, you went to the meeting, you've got the beeper and contact list…you have to do it. Let's review your notes and the contracts so we can get you prepared for the presentation to the Board of Directors."

Reluctantly, Jackson accepted the burden of being the Alsace point of contact for TARA. The Board approved the government's proposal and ordered the special manufacturing production of the additional product quantities. It ended up as a thirty million dollar order instead of the nearly three hundred million dollar order at list prices, but the Company accepted terms and payments as outlined in the contract. Jackson was given another Spot Stock Award for 5,000 shares for bringing in the order and for serving as the point person for the Task Force. He barely cracked a smile when Larson stopped by his office to give him the stock option certificates.

The Thanksgiving and Christmas holidays came and went with the Fords making their annual trips back to the cold weather of Wisconsin to visit their families. Jackson's beeper went off several times between Thanksgiving and New Year's Day, which scared the daylights out of both him and Lexi. Each time it was the same person paging Jackson. Agent Dayne. And each time he did nothing more than make small talk and wish Jackson and his family holiday cheer.

However, after New Year's Day the rhetoric changed. Agent Dayne became more and more interested in Jackson's role in the Company. "So Jackson, it sounds like you've got a pretty big job there at Alsace.

My guess is that you've probably got lots of responsibility as well. You manage Account Managers, and you've probably got a fancy office with a secretary who brings you coffee. What kind of meetings do you go to, Jackson? Probably the kind where the vice presidents and CEO attend, right?"

Uncomfortable with the probing questions but not wanting to be rude, Jackson replied, "I'm a member of the EOC, Executive Oversight Committee, which is comprised of all the Product Directors, Marketing Directors, National Account Directors, and the VPs for the different divisions within Alsace. Kevin Steer, our CEO, usually chairs the meetings."

"So that's where all the big important decisions are made about strategic planning, product promotions, contracting, and marketing programs, right?"

"Pretty much, yeah," came the reply. Jackson was really uncomfortable about the direction of the conversation and knew that he better stop talking. "Agent Dayne, I've got a meeting to run to, so, ah, I need to go."

"Oh, one more thing, Jackson. Please call me Steve. We've got another meeting of the Dirty Bomb Task Force in two weeks that you need to attend. We're trying to finalize the off-label use of your products for the treatment of radiation exposure, and we think that we've got the final recommendation ready for presentation to the group. Since the topic is strictly the treatment guidelines, the meeting will be at the FDA office in Rockville, Maryland. I'll send you an email with the address and directions."

"OK, I'll watch for it, Steve. I gotta go."

It was late when the tall, lanky man arrived at his home in Alexandria, Virginia to eat the dinner left for him in the oven by his wife. The kids had eaten much earlier. His lobbyist job in Washington DC for Alsace typically involved long days filled with meetings with members of Congress and their aides. It was unusual that he did not have a dinner meeting scheduled for tonight, but as a result; he was looking forward to a good home-cooked meal, even if it was by himself. As in sat down at the kitchen table, the private telephone line rang in the office that he maintained at the house. The youngest of his three kids yelled to him over the sound of the television, "Dad, you're office phone is ringing!"

He pushed his chair back from the table and hurried into his office lifting the receiver after the fourth ring. As he raised the receiver he glanced at the number on his Caller ID and said in a deadpan voice, "It's late so this better be important, Tommy."

"Oh, it's important alright. I just got a call from one of our District Managers in Indiana. Apparently, some FDA agents have been snooping around a couple of physician offices looking for old copies of Sample Request Forms from when one of our Directors was a sales rep there. The way that we found out is because the office staff complained to the rep and manager," said Sommers.

"Who is it?" the lobbyist asked.

"Jackson Ford. He's a Director in the federal market."

"So what do you want me to do?"

"I did some checking here and found out that Jackson's a member of some Homeland Security Task Force. He attended a meeting in the Washington DC area and has made some calls into the FDA between Thanksgiving and Christmas," Sommers replied.

"How do you know that?"

"Since he has a company-issued cell phone, I checked his call records. I don't like the fact that the FDA is doing background checks on one of our employees."

"I know of some people that are on some of these Homeland Security Task Forces, from what I understand, the background checks are standard procedure by not only the FDA but also the FBI. Do you know what specific sub-group Ford is involved with?"

Sommers replied in a gruff voice, "It has something to do with the national pharmaceutical stockpile initiative. We've got two products that the government wants included in the stockpile in case there's a terror attack using a dirty bomb. Look, that doesn't matter. I want you to check with your contacts at the FDA. If you hear about even the slightest hint of an investigation involving Alsace, then I want to know about it. And if you hear that Ford's name is associated with it, then I really want to know about it. I'm going to have him followed on his next trip."

"OK, I'll let you know what I find out." He replaced the receiver and returned to the kitchen to enjoy his now cold dinner.

CHAPTER 22
INSIDER

The Alsace Travel Department once again booked Jackson's flight from San Diego to Washington DC, and with his airline points he upgraded to first class seating for the nearly six-hour flight. Because of the time change from the west coast to the east coast, it took all day to travel to the nation's capital from southern California. He checked into the JW Marriott and got his usual suite overlooking Freedom Plaza with a view of the Washington Monument from the Pennsylvania Avenue side of the hotel. After his morning workout, he drove to Rockville, Maryland for his ten o'clock meeting at the Food and Drug Administration building on Fishers Lane with the members of the Dirty Bomb Task Force. Agent Dayne had apparently supplied the front desk personnel with Jackson's name and appointment information ahead of time so he was able to easily clear the security procedures that included an x-ray screening and a manual body pat down. Afterwards, one of the security officers called Dayne's office to inform him of his guest's arrival.

Dayne met Jackson with a firm handshake in the lobby, "Good morning, Jackson! How was the trip from San Diego? I'll bet it's much warmer in southern California than here!" The beginning of a smile tipped the corners of his mouth. He carried a black briefcase in his left hand.

It was a brisk, cold day in Washington DC with twenty mile per hour winds whipping off the Atlantic Ocean. When he left San Diego, it was a pleasant sixty-five degrees with plenty of sunshine. "The trip was good, Steve. Thanks for asking. Your weather here is awful! I guess my blood is really starting to thin living in sunny San Diego," Jackson replied.

Dayne led Jackson toward the elevator banks and then to a small empty conference room on the fifth floor. In the middle of the conference table was a console with a number of switches and dials. Jackson looked around the room and saw several video cameras that hung suspended from the ceiling in the corners. Somewhat anxious, Jackson remarked, "Is this room going to be big enough for all the Task Force members? The conference room that Colonel Adams had at AFRII building was three times this big." When Dayne didn't respond immediately Jackson continued, "Hey, I'm a little early, I know, but where is everybody? Did they all get deployed overseas or something?" He grinned an uneasy smile.

Dayne closed the door and sat down. He then motioned for Jackson to take a seat across the table from him. His mouth was tight and his face grim, and with a resigned voice he said, "Jackson, you're the only participant today for this meeting because we need to have a serious conversation about your work activities at Alsace."

In a shaky voice Jackson replied, "What do you mean my work activities at Alsace? And why would I be the only person here?"

Dayne reached over to the middle of the table and flipped two switches on the console. Jackson looked up and saw that two of the video cameras now had red lights illuminated above the lens. "What did you just do?" he asked.

"I turned on the video cameras and voice recording system. It's for your own benefit and protection, Jackson," Dayne said matter-of-factly.

"Agent Dayne, I am very uncomfortable with this situation. I demand that you explain to me what's going on here." Jackson said with a cool authority.

Dayne lifted his briefcase onto table and opened it. He pulled out two manila file folders and slid one across to Jackson. "Go ahead, open it."

Jackson opened the file. He saw copies of Alsace Sample Request Forms dated over ten years ago from his some of his old doctor offices back in his Indiana sales territory. There was also a list of names of some of his VA and military pharmacy customers. Jackson shook his head. In a voice that was smooth, but insistent he asked, "What is all this? Where did you get copies of these SRFs?"

"I got them from a couple of offices in your old sales territory, Jackson. Remember when you were selling and how the SRFs carbon forms were in triplicate, and how you had to leave a copy with the office?"

"Yes, I remember."

"Well, I think now a days Alsace gives their sales reps little hand-held computers to record sample deliveries and physician signatures. But back then the offices had to maintain their copies of the SRFs for several years. Well, several of your offices had boxes of these forms in storage that they never discarded. So a couple of us from the FDA found the offices, located the storage boxes, and sorted through all the old SRFs until we found what we were looking for. Of course, the office staff was very cooperative. A few even said that they remembered you buying them some nice dinners at several of the local restaurants. It was apparent to me that you were very well liked, Jackson."

Jackson let out a heavy sigh. He pointed to the file on the table, "What's all this for?"

"Jackson, the Prescription Drug Marketing Act is a piece of federal legislation that was passed over ten years ago permitting the FDA to regulate pharmaceutical companies and their sampling policies and activities." He picked up his manila file and held it up in his right hand, "This file is the beginning of a federal investigation by this agency into you and your activities specific to PDMA violations." He placed the file back on the table and continued, "While conducting the Dirty Bomb Task Force background checks on you, I discovered that a few physician offices in Gary, Indiana had come under investigation by this office some years ago for selling samples of certain medications. One of those medications was a hypertension drug from Alsace, and you were the Alsace sales representative at the time the diversion activities occurred. A lot of samples of your blood pressure drug were being sold as prescriptions, Jackson. I'm wondering what knowledge you might have had of the illegal activities that took place in that office, and, specifically, what role you had in supplying the samples. We elected at that time to not scrutinize you or Alsace because the real culprits were the staff in the offices. They don't sell samples anymore in case you're interested."

"I just left samples with the offices like I was requested to do by the physicians! I didn't do anything wrong."

"Maybe so, but we'll check it out and be the judge of that. Also, as you can see from some of the copies of the Sample Request Forms in the file, some of the physician signatures don't match up from visit to visit. The signatures are different. How do you explain that? Didn't you witness the physician signature on each of your calls? It's another PDMA policy violation, you know."

"Sometimes the office staff wouldn't let sales reps in the back to actually see the doctor signing the form for samples! Come on, I wasn't the only sales rep in the whole industry who didn't have access to the doctor to watch him actually sign the form!"

Dayne sat still with folded hands on the tabletop and stared at Jackson with a raised eyebrow.

Jackson was floored, and the color drained from his face. His hands shook as he picked up the single sheet of paper with the list of the federal pharmacists where he saw at the top of the list the names of Bob Johnson and Colonel Buck. "What's with this list of federal pharmacy names?"

"Oh that! Well, just as there are PDMA laws that regulate the pharmaceutical companies specific to sampling and promotional activities, there are also laws that serve to guide the actions of federal government employees. Specifically, there is a policy that states that no federal government employee can accept a gift from a vendor, meaning you, valued at over fifty dollars per year. Included in the category called gifts are examples like golf clubs, golf course green fees, expensive dinners, hotel rooms like at the Broken Tee, sporting event tickets like the World Series or The Masters, bottles of wine, etc. I don't believe that I need to go on, Jackson, because I think that you get the point."

"But I didn't do anything different than any other company! Why are you coming after me?" Jackson shouted.

In an even voice Dayne replied, "Jackson, remember at the first AMSUS Sustaining Members meeting you attended? When you initially paid the Alsace company membership dues, you also completed another form." He pulled out another piece of paper from the file. "Do you see this? This is the agreement that you signed on behalf of Alsace stating that you would not engage in the gift-giving activities with federal government employees that I just described. You blatantly violated government policy!"

"But so does every other company!"

"But we're not talking about every other company, Jackson. We're talking about just you now, aren't we?"

Jackson felt sick to his stomach. "So now what?"

"Well, like I said earlier. This file is just the result of a preliminary investigation. Since I'm the lead agent for the investigation, it's up to me to recommend to my superiors the appropriate follow up action by the FDA. In other words, do I recommend that we investigate your alleged activities any further, which means the deployment of additional agents, or not? I'm wondering what we'll find when we start looking at the number of Alsace products that just so happen to populate the VA and DoD National Formulary and how the pricing practices, or more importantly, what influences were used to gain that formulary status for your products. Meaning, we'd be conducting a thorough investigation, including interviews and affidavits, to research the steps leading up to and including the various formulary decision-making points. Hey Jackson, don't your in-laws have a summer home on some little lake in Wisconsin just down from Bob Johnson's place?"

Jackson's mouth fell open. *How is this happening? Is there anything that these guys don't know?*

"You're in a lot of trouble here, Jackson. Not only will you be investigated, but your customers will as well. The downside for your federal customers is that they can lose their jobs over this because they accepted gifts from you in excess of the policy guidelines." He picked up the piece of paper from the file and waved it in the air. "Like I said before, this is only the short list of names. Once we start digging, who knows how many names we'll end up with?"

"So what am I looking at?" Jackson asked weakly.

"Oh, you're definitely looking at disbarment from the pharmaceutical industry plus significant fines. Prison is also a possibility. That probably means that you'll have to give up the big fancy house in the gated community and your son's private school."

Jackson seethed. "You're going to wreck my life!"

"You did it to yourself, Jackson."

"I just did what is common practice at Alsace and at every other Big Pharma company! Don't you understand that?"

Dayne replied, "Oh I understand perfectly. Alsace is a very bad company. They don't follow the PDMA rules. And neither do any of the other Big Pharma companies."

"Do you have to go after the VA and DoD guys? Come on, they're really just innocent by-standers here."

"I appreciate your loyalty to your customers, Jackson, I really do. But you are responsible for putting these guys in a situation where federal guideline violations occurred. The FDA doesn't make a habit of backing off in an investigation."

Jackson's body felt as if he were in a complete body cast. He hung his head, his chin touching his chest. His folded his arms across his chest to stop his hands from shaking.

Dayne let the weight of the evidence sink in for a minute before continuing in a low voice, "Maybe I can help you out, Jackson."

Jackson's chin lifted, and he quirked his eyebrow questioningly. "How?"

"Maybe if you help me, then I'll help you."

With his jaw clenched and eyes slightly narrowed, Jackson asked, "How? It seems like you've got all the evidence you need to nail my customers and me. Why would I help you out?"

Dayne sat forward and looked at Jackson intently for a moment before speaking, "You're not who we want, Jackson. And quite honestly, we don't want the federal pharmacists and physicians either. I'm a federal government employee so I have some empathy there." He paused for effect, "We want Alsace because we know that they have a history of implementing shady promotional practices that violate PDMA law, but they're so good at covering their corporate tracks. It makes it very difficult to put a case together against them on any one particular violation. But you're inside the company, Jackson. You can help us put together a case. Tell me again, what's that fancy committee you're a member of?"

"The EOC. Executive Oversight Committee," replied Jackson.

"Right, the EOC. That's the one where the big-time decisions are made. Decisions that affect your product marketing and promotional strategies. Decisions on pricing and contracting actions. Decisions on patient confidentiality and Medicare billing. The FDA can't get inside Alsace or, for that matter, any of the Big Pharma companies, Jackson. The only evidence we ever come by is when one company tattles on another company by sending us some promotional piece or clinical study reprint being used in the field that some rep left in a doctor's office. That's nothing. We know that Big Pharma companies compete against each other, but they all hate the FDA and would rather go out of business than help us. So the big stuff, the stuff that the FDA needs in order to correct the corrupt corporate behavior that is widespread in this industry, we just can't get. Until now. Until you came along. We want to make Alsace an example to the rest of the industry, and you're going to help us. And for your help, I'm willing to offer you immunity from any prosecution of your PDMA violations, gift-giving activities, and from any charges brought by the evidence that you supply to the FDA."

Dayne's statement was like a sledgehammer to his gut. Jackson slumped in his chair as he fully realized what exactly it was that the FDA agent wanted him to do. *He wants me to rat out the whole industry.* "I think I'm going to be sick. Can I use your bathroom, please?" he asked in a voice barely above a whisper.

Dayne quickly escorted Jackson to the restroom and waited outside the door for him. Through the wall he could hear Jackson empty the contents of his stomach and then flush the toilet. He felt bad for the guy, but he had a job to do. *These Pharma companies have been living the high life for too long! I hope our boy here has the stomach for what he's about to do.*

When he walked out of the bathroom, Jackson's face was ashen. Water spots covered his tie and shirt. "Thanks, I feel better."

"You don't look so good, Jackson. You want something to eat or drink? You're going to be here for a while yet."

"Yeah, maybe a muffin and some juice would help." Bile rose up in the back of his throat, and Jackson tried to clear it by coughing.

Dayne looked at his watch, "It's lunchtime here so let's go down to the cafeteria."

After he had gotten something to eat, Jackson felt much better and the color returned to his face. Throughout lunch a number of people came up to their table to say hello to Dayne. Jackson's head was spinning, and he found it hard to focus. It was all he could do just to get his blueberry muffin down. Afterwards, they returned to the conference room where Dayne turned on the cameras and microphones.

"Jackson, we need to have a discussion about how we move forward from here and how we're going to communicate with each other."

"OK," Jackson replied numbly.

"Let's first have you describe some of the activities in which Alsace is involved, and then I'll tell you if the FDA is interested and what kind of evidence we would need from you."

Jackson started slowly, "Recently, there was a big EOC meeting held because of some market events that could significantly impact the short-term financial condition of the company."

"What events?" asked Dayne.

"CMS recently came out with a new policy specific to the reimbursement of REMPRO to nephrologists. It's going to cut the revenue flow in half for the nephrologists who are treating kidney failure patients. Alsace intends to deploy a staff of dialysis education managers to pull patient charts in the dialysis centers to identify where nephrologists need to use increased doses of our product to get patients to goal. They will also help the physicians submit medical justification forms to allow for treating patients with REMPRO to increase hematocrit levels above what CMS allows."

"How are these Alsace clinical managers supposed to keep all the dialysis patients straight?"

"Alsace has either designed or is designing a database that the dialysis managers will use in the clinics to track patient hematocrit levels and REMPRO doses. They're also looking to do the same in the oncology market with our NEUTROPHIL product," Jackson said.

"So we've got some serious patient confidentiality violations with this program?" Dayne asked.

"Yeah, but that's not the half of it. They're planning to provide additional financial incentives to get patients above the CMS thresholds."

Dayne mulled that statement over for a moment, "I don't know that I can do anything with that part. But let me think about it some more. What else have you got?"

"I just mentioned NEUTROPHIL. They're also going to use the clinical managers to promote the spread to oncologists."

Dayne was puzzled, "What do you mean promote the spread?"

"They plan on developing several promotional aids or detail pieces that depict the difference in acquisition costs and CMS reimbursement payments for NEUTROPHIL. The difference is called the spread. It's the profit that the oncologist makes from CMS for Medicare patients, and it can be substantial."

"I've heard about this from another agent. I'm going to have you come back here for a follow up interview after you provide some hard copy evidence of this allegation," Dayne said.

"The last I heard it was going to be a few weeks before the new promotional pieces were ready for distribution to the clinical managers."

"We're going to need a copy. This area could be significant if CMS is involved. Anything else?"

Jackson thought for a minute, "Alsace is going to raise the price of NORVIRAN by four hundred percent in order to get the HIV cocktail therapy market to switch over to our once-a-day combination drug, KALMATRON."

"When?"

"They're doing it already. They plan to make the cocktail therapy cost prohibitive so that the HMOs and PBMs will force the patients to KALMATRON before Roche's new drug comes out."

"OK, this is big. I need some kind of internal memo or emails from you showing a deliberate attempt to manipulate the market through a pricing action. Do you think you can do that?" asked Dayne.

Jackson felt numb. "Yes, I'm sure I can get something. I have access to a Lotus Notes database where all the minutes of the EOC meetings are stored. I'm sure there is some documentation in it. I'll need some time to look into it quietly so I don't raise any suspicions."

"What about in the past with some of the new drug launches that Alsace has had? How do they get their drugs so widely accepted on the HMO and PBM formularies? How did you do so well in the VA?"

"Agent Dayne, we agreed that you would not go after the VA and DoD guys so I'm not commenting on that market. In the commercial markets, the Company uses a variety of financial methods to gain access to patients covered by the big health plans and employer groups. They set up very lucrative service agreements for a number of therapeutic classes, but the monies and contracts are not counted in the state Medicaid best price calculations. So I don't think that you can go after anything there because it's in what's known as safe harbor," Jackson replied.

"I may not be able to right now, but with our contacts in Congress there may be something we can do in the future. I'll take whatever you can get me around their service agreements as well. OK, this is a good start. I'm sure that there will be more areas to explore in the future," Dayne remarked.

"How does this work? Do I get a get of out jail free card or something? How do I know that I've got immunity from this and the file from this morning?" Jackson asked.

"I'll have document for you when you come back in about two months with some hard copy evidence," Dayne said.

"A couple of months? How about a couple of weeks?"

"No Jackson, we're still a part of the federal government with all its bureaucracy and red tape. It's going to take me at least two months to set up this investigation because we're going to have to involve several departments here at the FDA as well as someone from CMS. The Attorney General's office will be responsible for drafting your request for immunity. The next time you come out we'll need to set up an interview for you with a few people. You met a couple of them today in the cafeteria. I want you to go home now and talk to your wife. You need to tell her everything, but most of all you need to tell her to keep this quiet. She can't say a word. Not even to her closest girlfriends because it could get back to Alsace."

"Should I start looking for another job?"

"Jackson, I need you to stay at Alsace until this whole thing is over. You can't even think about leaving or putting your resume out on the Web for recruiters to access. And you can relax about Alsace finding out about what you're doing or about having to come to this building. You were originally scheduled to meet here today for the Dirty Bomb Task Force, remember? So you're covered. Just stay put and don't do anything stupid."

Jackson was nauseous the entire flight back to San Diego. He couldn't even open his laptop computer for the trip home. He kept replaying the day over and over in his mind. *What am I going to tell Lexi? We just got our lives and our marriage back together, and now this!* He arrived home close to midnight and went straight to bed.

Jackson called in sick the next morning feigning the stomach flu. After he dropped Jake at school, he returned home to see Lexi. "Honey, we need to talk." His face was drawn and filled with worry.

"Jackson, what's the matter? You look terrible. Is your stomach any better?" Lexi asked.

They talked for two hours. The weight of the situation was overbearing. They hugged and cried, and then hugged and cried some more.

"Jackson, I'm really proud of you. You're doing the right thing. I've seen big changes in you since we've moved to San Diego. You're a better husband and father, Jackson. We'll get through this together. Cooperate with Agent Dayne, do what he tells you, and when it's all over, we'll leave Alsace and start fresh somewhere else."

"I love you. Thanks for sticking with me and believing in me all those years when I was a being so selfish and putting Alsace first. You were right all along. In the end, it's just you, Jake, and me. And that's what's most important in life." His eyes were moist and his voice choked, "The more I got and the more successful I was, the more I just wasn't satisfied. I just lost sight of what makes a man who he really is, and that's his family. Don't get me wrong. The money has been great, and the perks have been unbelievable. But it's like anything else, if you can't look yourself in the mirror, then what good is it?"

Lexi was crying as she hugged him, "That's right, Jackson. It's us and how we care for each other and look out for one another. None of that other stuff matters. I'm so glad you're back with us."

The private line rang at the house in Alexandria. "Hello, Tommy. What can I do for you?"

"Jackson Ford was at the FDA offices in Rockville today. Have you been able to find out anything yet from your contacts?" asked Sommers with an urgent tone.

"No, I haven't. I'll keep trying. Be patient, these things take time. It's a delicate situation," the lobbyist replied.

"For what you're being paid, we expect results," shot back Sommers just before he slammed the phone down.

CHAPTER 23
ARREST

Two months later it was a beautiful sunny Saturday with temperatures in the low seventies; a rarity for late March in Washington DC. The weather had brought out all the weekend warriors who, up until now, had either been cooped up all winter in their homes or at their local health clubs getting in their workouts. She was on roller blades heading up Pennsylvania Avenue toward the Capitol when she cut over at Twelfth Street in the direction of the Smithsonian Museum. A mass of bronze-gold hair stuck out from under her helmet, and her long, lithe legs worked the skates in perfect rhythm. She had lived in Washington DC for almost two years working for a lobbying firm. She saw a familiar face running on the gravel path that snaked its way along the Mall, and she stopped. The young female runner was just out of college, a Senator's daughter, and one of her newest contacts at the FDA who got the job because of her father's position.

"Hey Bridget!" the skater called out.

"Oh, hi Tam! How are you today? You're getting some exercise I see," remarked Bridget.

"Yes, I am. It's such a pretty day. How's work?" Tam asked. "You know, we've got a meeting next week on Thursday morning."

"Hey, that reminds me. I'm actually glad I ran into you, it saved me a phone call. I'm going to have to reschedule our appointment. My division chief has pulled me in on a special project investigating some pharmaceutical company from San Diego. Alsace, I think is the name."

Tam's lips parted and her eyes widened. "I used to work for Alsace. What's going on?"

"I really don't know the specifics, but there's an interview panel set up that they want me to be a member of. I think that I might have met the guy once before in the cafeteria. Tall, good-looking, blonde hair. I remember that much. I think I heard that he works in their federal division or something."

Jackson, Tam thought immediately. "This guy got a name? Maybe I know him."

"I think it's Jackson something or another. Like I said, I've only met him briefly once before in the cafeteria. He didn't look too good that day. I won't actually get any real face time with him until next Thursday when I help with this interview panel. Do you know him?" Bridget asked.

"If it's who I think it is, then I know him very well, actually."

"Do you want me to say hello from you?"

"No, I don't think so," Tam said cautiously.

"Well anyway, that's why I have to reschedule our meeting. I probably shouldn't have said anything, but seeing how you don't work for Alsace anymore, I guess it's OK. It's my understanding that he's giving us some information about their promotional and pricing practices in exchange for immunity." Bridget glanced at her watch, "I've got to get going. I'm running late for a lunch date with my boyfriend. It was good seeing you again, Tam. Call me to reschedule our appointment!"

Tam stood on the sidewalk as she watched Bridget jog away from her down the gravel path. *Could it really be Jackson? What's he doing working with the FDA on an investigation? Immunity? What is going on?*

Tam agonized over the conversation for the rest of the week. Unable to stand it any longer, she finally called him on the following Friday afternoon.

His cell phone rang as he walked to the Alsace cafeteria from his office with a couple of his Account Managers who were at headquarters for a training meeting with plans to stay over the weekend for some deep-sea fishing, "Hello, this is Jackson Ford."

Her feelings for him rushed back at the sound of his voice. "Jackson, it's me," she said.

He recognized her voice immediately, "Just a minute, please." He covered the mouthpiece of his cell phone and turned to his Account Managers, "Hey guys, I've got to take this call. I'll meet you in the cafeteria in a few minutes." After they walked ahead he ducked into an empty conference room and spoke into the mouthpiece, "Tam?"

"Hi, Jackson."

Slightly irritated he said, "Why are you calling me?"

His tone stung. "Were you at the FDA yesterday morning?" she asked.

A long pause during which time his stomach dropped, "How do you know about that?"

"In my job at the lobbying firm I work with a number of people at the FDA and in Congress concerning the pharmaceutical industry's promotional practices and legislative efforts to control the industry. I ran into one of my new contacts last weekend, and she told me that she had to cancel an appointment with me for yesterday morning in order to interview you. And she also mentioned something about immunity. What's going on, Jackson?"

"Tam, I can't talk about it. It's complicated."

"Does Alsace know what you're doing?"

"No. Tam, I really don't feel comfortable discussing this with you."

She lowered her voice, "Jackson, be careful. Alsace can be ruthless."

"I will. Tam, I really oughta go. Thanks for the heads-up."

"OK. Goodbye Jackson. Take care of yourself." As she hung up, a tear formed in the corner of her eye.

Jackson didn't go to the cafeteria right away, rather, he punched a familiar number into his cell phone. When the call was answered he spoke quickly, "It's me. I can't help you anymore."

Agent Dayne let out a sigh before he answered, "Calm down, Jackson. What's the matter?"

"What's the matter? You're asking me what's the matter? Do you mean aside from the fact that I'm supplying you with confidential emails, memos, contracting information, and promotional pieces? Are you asking me 'what's the matter' besides all that?" Jackson's voice was loud as he spoke into the phone.

In a measured voice Dayne replied, "Jackson, tell me what the hell is going on."

Jackson took a deep breath, "I just got a phone call from an old friend of mine who's a lobbyist in DC. She was told by someone in your office that I was involved in a meeting yesterday at the FDA. Apparently, this person was a member of yesterday's interview panel."

"So what? You're a member of the Dirty Bomb Task Force! We had a meeting here in Rockville!"

Jackson lowered his voice, "The term immunity was mentioned." He continued sarcastically, "It's quite obvious, Agent Dayne, that one of your people can't keep their mouth shut!"

The Senator's daughter, I'll bet. That spoiled little brat! "Jackson, don't worry about it. I'll take care of it."

"No, I'm taking care of it. I'm done. You've got enough to launch a full-scale investigation. You don't need me anymore!"

"Jackson, I'm good on the NORVIRAN pricing piece and the patient confidentiality violations, but I still need some additional evidence on the Medicare pricing spread with NEUTROPHIL. I need a copy of the sales piece or the computer program that the reps are going to use for NEUTROPHIL so I can stop the promotional activities," Dayne said firmly. "So I need you to stay engaged here for a little while longer. Jackson, you're doing something important!"

"It certainly doesn't feel that way when I get a phone call like the one I just got!" Jackson was still angry.

"You know it's wrong for Alsace to promote the spread to physicians, Jackson, just to make a certain profit margin. Come on, just one more piece of evidence. Then you can be done."

Deep down he knew Dayne was right, "OK, Steve. Sorry I lost it there for a minute. This has been pretty stressful for Lexi and me. Look, if you know who blabbed, then tell them to keep quiet. If this old acquaintance can find out what's going on, then so can Alsace. My family and I just can't handle any more additional stress right now." He ended the call and continued his walk to the cafeteria to search for his two Account Managers.

Jackson passed a small private dining room with tinted glass windows as he entered the cafeteria. Inside the room were Sommers, Larson, Wedenbrook and Steer.

"There he goes," Sommers said as Jackson walked past the window. The other men all looked up at the same time from their lunches. "I don't trust him."

"We don't know that he's done anything wrong or that he's cooperating with an FDA investigation," said Wedenbrook in Jackson's defense.

"But we don't know that he hasn't either." It was Steer. "What's our Washington contact say?" he asked of Sommers.

"Nothing specific. All he says is that the name Alsace keeps buzzing around the investigational department. The only thing we do know is that Ford is on this Dirty Bomb Task Force, and that he's working closely with some agent by the name of Steven Dayne to develop treatment guidelines and stockpiling specifications for REMPRO and NEUTROPHIL in the event of a terrorist attack," stated Sommers.

"But there are also other members of this Task Force, right? It can't be just the FDA guy and Jackson that develop these guidelines!" exclaimed Wedenbrook.

"Well, of course there are other members from the various Homeland Security divisions that are on the Dirty Bomb Task Force. What we do know for sure is that this Agent Dayne from the FDA is assigned as well, but we just don't know his specific role at the FDA. He's got a very non-descript job."

"What else have you found out about Jackson, Tommy?" asked Larson.

"He's made a number of cell phone calls to a Colonel Adams and this Agent Dayne over the past several months. However, he's never received any calls from either of those two. I've searched his emails, and he's sent and received some that look pretty straightforward.

They're all related to this Task Force business. But his secretary told me that he's recently mailed some things to Agent Dayne directly."

Steer perked up, "What things? What was mailed to the FDA?"

"She said that the packages and envelopes were always sealed before he brought them to her, so she couldn't say what exactly was in them," Sommers replied. "That's what makes me nervous about him. She said that he would normally just give her papers or presentations or whatever for her to put into mailing envelopes that would go out to his team or his customers. But the stuff going to the FDA is always sealed up ahead of time. I don't like it."

Steer chimed in, "I'm with Tommy. Something doesn't smell right. What are our options here?"

Sommers began, "If he's already given the FDA confidential information, then we're screwed. We can't get it back, and we'll just have to weather the storm. I say that we get rid of him, quickly."

Wedenbrook interrupted him, "Hold it! We don't know what he's done exactly, if anything!"

Steer flashed a look of anger across his face, "Herman, don't make me ask you to leave the room again! We can't take the chance of the FDA investigating us. Think what will happen to the stock price! The analysts won't be too thrilled about a Fortune 500 company having FDA agents crawling all over their headquarters!"

"I'm just saying that if Jackson brought a wrongful termination suit against us, that would not be good," Wedenbrook explained.

"We can settle a suit like that out of court, Herman, and keep it quiet. We can't keep an investigation or fines or penalties from the FDA quiet!" Steer exclaimed.

It was Larson's turn, "I like Jackson a lot. I brought him into the department and promoted him to headquarters. But he can be replaced. If he did give something to the FDA and we bring him in and question him, he'll just deny it. Then we'll have alerted him that we suspect him, and eventually he'll leave the company. If he didn't do anything and we question him, then he won't trust us, and he'll be angry about it and eventually, he'll leave the company. Either way, he's outta of here."

"All valid points, Jim," said Sommers. "Still, the problem is that the FDA is doing something, and somebody from Alsace is supplying them with information. That's the only reason why they open an investigation into a company. The stuff they get from competitors isn't worth their time and effort. It's the insider information that they can't get, but that they need in order to make a move on a company. Again, somebody at Alsace has got to be helping them."

"What do you suggest?" asked Steer.

"I say we send a message," replied Sommers.

"What do you mean?" asked Wedenbrook.

"Herman, you may want to go get some dessert and come back in about ten minutes," said Sommers as he gave Wedenbrook a serious look and nodded toward the door.

Wedenbrook looked to Steer for help but could see that the CEO agreed with Sommers. "Why don't you go get some dessert, Herm?"

After the door had closed behind Wedenbrook, Sommers outlined his plan, "Jackson is notoriously late on his expense reports. He submits them late, and the forms are generally filled out incorrectly. He is constantly getting expense reports kicked back from the auditors with either math errors, missing receipts, incorrect electronic checking deposit amounts, or incorrect electronic payments to his American Express account. You name it, the guy has struggled with his expenses ever since he started as a sales rep for us! I can remember his former trainer and District Manager, Kurt Braden, used to make fun of him over it!"

"I can attest to that. Jackson is terrible with his expenses. And I'll bet you that he doesn't have a clue how much money is in his expense checking account that he keeps for business. I've seen the checkbook register that he keeps on his desk; he'll sometimes go for weeks without recording any checks, deposits, withdrawals or debits! I know his wife doesn't help him with it. The guy is a real a train-wreck in this one area!"

"What are you suggesting, Tommy?" asked Steer directly.

"Although I can't prove it right now, my gut tells me that Ford is giving the FDA confidential information. I say we have to send a message and get rid of him. If it's not him, well then, too bad. We got the wrong guy, but we send a message to whoever it is. If it is Ford, then we did the right thing and protected the company."

"Be specific," demanded Steer.

"I'd like to arrange for a few deposits to be made directly into his business expense checking account. More than likely he won't even realize that the money was deposited. Then I'll turn the information over to the San Diego County Sheriff's Department so that they can conduct an investigation."

"Do it," said Steer coolly. "I want Jackson Ford out of the company so we can then concentrate on stopping anything that he may have started at the FDA."

Four weeks later the EOC met in the Board Room to review the quarterly financial results. Steer was being prepped by the Finance Department for a presentation that he was scheduled to make to the Wall Street analysts at the end of the month. Jackson was seated in his usual spot between Larson and Thompson in the middle of the conference table when Sommers escorted two Sheriff's deputies into the room.

Sommers stretched out his arm, pointed at Jackson with his right index finger and said, "He's right there."

The room fell silent as all heads turned to look at Jackson.

One of the deputies stepped forward and asked, "Are you Jackson Ford?"

Jackson was shocked. His eyes opened wide, "Yes, I am. Are my wife and son OK?"

"As far as we know, Mr. Ford. Would you stand up, please, and place your hands behind your back?" asked the deputy.

"What's this all about?" Jackson asked as he stood up and turned his back to the deputy.

The deputy pulled out a set of handcuffs from the back of his utility belt and began to place them on Jackson's wrists. "Mr. Ford, you're under arrest for grand theft, which is a felony offense. We have evidence that proves you used the Alsace expense reimbursement system to make unauthorized deposits of company funds in excess of ten thousand dollars into your personal checking account over a ten day period."

While the second deputy began to read the Miranda Rights, Jackson yelled, "What are you talking about? There must be some kind of mistake! I've done no such thing! Jim! Tell these guys that there must be some kind of mistake!"

Larson spoke in a calm voice, "Jackson, I've seen the evidence. You made a number of deposits where you didn't have legitimate business expense documentation. I'm sorry, but I can't help you. The Alsace Value that states 'Adhere to Ethical Business Practices' was clearly violated."

The deputies escorted Jackson toward the conference room doors with Sommers two steps behind them.

Scott Evans, who was seated in the back of the room, stood up quickly and held one of the doors open. "Tough break, Jackson," he said with a grin.

About an hour later, Jackson called Lexi from the interview room at the Sheriff's Department, "Lexi, I was arrested at work. I'm at the San Diego County Jail."

"What are you doing there? Are you OK?" she asked.

"Yeah, I'm OK. I'm being charged with grand theft. The deputies said that I stole money from the company through the expense reimbursement system. I don't know what they're talking about!" he said angrily.

"What do you mean you stole money? What money?" Lexi asked in disbelief.

"I can't explain it right now, honey. I've got to make arrangements to get outta here. Look, I need you to make three phone calls for me. The first should be to Agent Dayne, and you can find his number on my desk. The second call should be to any bail bondsman that you can find in the yellow pages. Lastly, call the lawyer who helped us when we closed on the house. Ask him for a referral to a good criminal defense attorney."

"Wait, let me write this down," she said. "I can't believe this is happening!" A moment later she said, "OK, what else do you need me to do?"

"You need to call one of the other moms and arrange for Jake to stay with them after he gets out of school and until we can come by and pick him up. Then I need you to drive down here and pick me up after I make bail. I don't know how long this is going to take so plan on being here awhile."

"Where is your car? Do we need to go pick it up?" Lexi asked.

"No. Alsace fired me before they had me escorted out of the building. First though, they paraded me through the hallways, in handcuffs, back to my office from the Board Room. Once there, they made me tell them where my company car keys were and the password to my computer. They then took my Corporate American Express card out my wallet and cut it up, and then they took my cell phone off my belt. Finally, they walked me downstairs and put me in the back of the squad car. Of course, the deputies just had to turn on the siren as they pulled out of the parking lot. Oh yeah, they stuck my separation papers in my back pants pocket just before I got escorted out of my office. I didn't even get a chance to ask what happened! It's like Alsace just called up the cops to have me hauled away!"

"Jackson, do you think that they know about Agent Dayne?"

"Maybe. I don't know. I can't think right now! Let me get out of here first, and then I'll talk to him and try to figure this out."

"OK. Let me make these phone calls, and then I'll be down in about an hour," Lexi said.

She met Jackson at the exit door to the holding cells after the bondsman posted the ten thousand dollar bail that released him. Lexi hugged him and held his hand as they walked out of the Sheriff's Department and out to her car. Jackson's body shook visibly as Lexi drove toward their home.

"I never got Steve Dayne on the phone, Jackson. I only left him a message."

"Let me try." Jackson picked up Lexi's cell phone and dialed Dayne's direct telephone number. He answered after the second ring,

"Steve, it's me Jackson. I just got arrested by the San Diego County Sheriff's Department and fired from Alsace both in the same day! You've got to help me!"

"What are you talking about? Arrested! On what charge?" Dayne asked.

"Two Sheriff's deputies came into the middle of an EOC meeting today and arrested me for grand theft. I'm being accused of stealing ten thousand bucks from the company through our expense reimbursement system and having direct deposits made into my business expense checking account; which I never did! Then, as I was being escorted from the building, in handcuffs by the way, the Alsace Security Manager handed me my termination papers. I just posted bail and have got an arraignment hearing in court set for next week! Do you know anything about what's going on?"

"I haven't got a clue, Jackson. This is local police stuff, and it has nothing to do with the FDA."

"Come on, Steve! You've got to get me out of this. It's all a big mistake! Something's not right here!"

Lexi elbowed Jackson in the ribs and said in a low voice, "Immunity."

"Hey! I've got immunity! I've got an immunity agreement from the FDA!" Jackson exclaimed.

"Unfortunately, we don't have any jurisdiction or influence over a county police matter in San Diego, Jackson. Your immunity agreement only protects you from federal prosecution specific to any PDMA violations involving your activities at Alsace. I just don't see how I can help you."

"But they fired me, Steve. What am I going to do now?"

Dayne thought for a moment, "I would suggest that you find a really good defense lawyer and fight the charges. You'll have some explaining to do, however, if you've got ten thousand dollars in recent deposits sitting in your checking account. As far as your employment goes, I've seen the FBI's report on your financial portfolio when they ran background checks for the Task Force. Jackson, you're sitting on over two million dollars in investments. I should be so lucky. Just get through this grand theft charge thing, and start looking for another job. You'll get re-employed."

"But can't the FDA stop this county legal process? Don't you need me to testify or something?" Jackson asked.

"No. We videotaped your interviews, remember? And we've got the evidence that you sent to us so, we're good to go with the charges and penalty phase of the case. The investigative portion is over thanks to your help."

"So what happens to Alsace?"

"First, I'm going to recommend that KALMATRON be withdrawn from the market for one year as a penalty for the four hundred percent price increase on NORVIRAN. Second, I'll recommend a two hundred million dollar fine for the NEUTROPHIL promoting the spread activities. Third, I'll recommend that Alsace discontinue the promotional practices specific to the patient privacy violations. These are very stringent penalties, Jackson. We've never been able to go to this length before. You should feel good that we accomplished what we sought out to do, and that is to punish Alsace and send a message to the rest of Big Pharma to clean up their act."

Jackson's voice was filled with frustration, "Well, I'm glad the FDA got what they wanted because I feel terrible now. It's obvious that Alsace got wise to something, and then set me up to get rid of me. I don't know how else ten thousand dollars could have been deposited into my account!" He paused a moment and said quietly, "Alright Steve, I've got to find a good lawyer right away and start making plans to take care of my family through this mess."

Dayne spoke in a voice that attempted to instill confidence, "Let me just say this, Jackson. You did the right thing. In the end, you proved that you were a standup guy, and you should be proud of that. I'm proud of you." He paused for a moment and then continued, "I want you to remember something. Sometimes all it takes is one guy to make a difference. The case against Alsace is solid, but it's only the tip of the iceberg for this whole industry. If I have my way, big changes are going to result from this first case. You helped us an awful lot, Jackson. Look, I know that you have to go. I'll check in with you periodically. Give my best to the family and good luck."

"Thanks, I think I'm going to need it." He disconnected the call.

"The FDA can't help us can they?" Lexi asked.

"No. My immunity only applies to any PDMA violations. He told me how they're going to nail Alsace. The fines and penalties are pretty harsh. They have to withdraw a product for a year. That'll really hurt the stock price," he said.

"What happens to all our vested stock options that we haven't cashed out yet?"

"When an employee leaves the company, they've got sixty days to cash out their vested options. We better do it right away before the price tanks because we're going to be starting over once this legal thing is done."

Lexi reached over and held his hand, "We'll get through this, Jackson. We'll find a good lawyer and just deal with whatever happens. We're a family, and families stick together," she reassured him. "Besides, it's not like we're broke!"

"You're right, Lexi." To ease the tension Jackson broke into a wide grin, "I guess this is one way to get out of Alsace!" He leaned over and kissed her cheek.

A smile swept across Lexi's face, "This situation is not exactly what I had in mind." She paused and looked over at him, "We'll get through this. You're a smart guy. Other opportunities will come along."

YEAR 15

CHAPTER 24
THE RECRUITER

He was with his family at the dinner table when the telephone rang. He excused himself and answered it after the third ring.

"The Marcus residence," he said.

"Good evening, my name is Larry Hooper of the Hooper Staffing Agency. I'm a headhunter. I'm wondering if Tim Marcus is available."

"Yes, this is Tim Marcus."

"Tim, I pulled your resume down off one of the Internet job boards. Is this a good time to talk?" he asked.

"I was just finishing dinner with my family actually, but yes this would be a good time."

"Tim, I've been retained by Alsace Pharmaceuticals to source candidates for a specialty sales force expansion for KALMATRON, it's a combination product for HIV patients that's been off the market for the past year but is going to be reintroduced by Alsace."

"Why was it off the market for a year?" Marcus asked.

"I've been told by my contacts at Alsace that the FDA wanted the Company to conduct some additional safety studies, which have been completed," stated Hooper.

"So why is Alsace expanding their specialty sales force if the product was on the market at one time and then removed for twelve months? Don't they already have a sales team to sell KALMATRON?"

"They do, but they need more sales representatives. Apparently, Roche Labs is coming out with a competitive product in the cocktail therapy arena at the same time. I understand that Alsace had a stroke of luck with the Roche product getting held up at the FDA for a year longer than anticipated. So the two companies will be launching their respective medicines at the same time. Alsace believes that by adding more sales reps to the specialty group that they can get KALMATRON to outperform Roche's product."

"Sounds reasonable."

"If you're interested in this opportunity, then I'd like to give you some background information on Alsace. Would that be acceptable?" asked the recruiter.

"Yes, it would. Tell me more about Alsace."

EPILOGUE

The organization known as PhRMA, the Pharmaceutical Research and Manufacturers of America, represents United States research-based pharmaceutical and biotechnology companies. PhRMA is also a powerful organization whose corporate affiliates spend tens of millions of dollars a year on political lobbying efforts in order to influence favorable legislation and pricing laws.

Recently, due to increased public scrutiny related to questionable promotional practices, the PhRMA Executive Committee created a new code that serves as a guide for interactions with health care professionals by the more than one million employees of the U.S. pharmaceutical industry. The premise of the new guidelines is to ensure that the promotional practices by industry representatives follows the highest ethical standards and adheres to all applicable legal requirements.

However, the adoption of the new PhRMA guidelines by the member organizations is strictly voluntary.

Lightning Source UK Ltd.
Milton Keynes UK
UKOW02f2037210416

272687UK00001B/48/P